A PROPHECY OF FLOWERS AND LIGHTNING

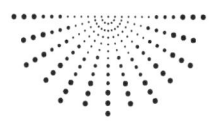

MICHEAL FERGUSON

Copyright© 2023 by Michael "Kwezi" Ferguson. All rights reserved.

No part of this publication may be reproduced, distributed, or transmitted in any form or by any means, including copying and pasting, photocopying, recording or other electronic or mechanical methods, without the prior written permission of the publisher, except in the case of brief quotations and embodied in in critical reviews and certain other non-commercial uses permitted by copyright law. For permission requests, write to the publisher addressed "Attention: Michael "Kwezi" Ferguson at michaeljohnferguson13@gmail.com

Front cover: Miblart

Map: Vicki Venter

Back cover and spine: Ane Bobbert

Story editor: Ryan Ferguson

Copy editor: Isabelle Fouquereaux

Disclaimer

This is a work of fiction. Names, characters, businesses, places, events, locales and incidents are either the product of the author's imagination or used in a fictitious manner. Any resemblance to actual persons, living or dead, or actual events is purely coincidental. I seriously had to put this bit in 'cause a guy actually threatened to sue me once.

ALSO BY MICHAEL FERGUSON

Ephemera: Short Fictions and Anomalies
The Acrimonious: Paranormal Fictions

For my mothers,
Laetitia and Annalie.
There is so much of both of you in this book.

PROLOGUE

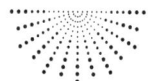

WICKED IMMORTAL CHILDREN

"A child conceived by magic will forever be touched by it," the witch wheezed. Her voice was like burnt wood being crumbled to ash.

It was stuffy inside the hut. The air, thick with incense smoke, caught in the back of Rebekah's throat like a fishhook … or was it just her nerves?

The bones of a thousand dead things dangled from the ceiling. Skulls glared down at her in judgement with empty eyes. Why had she decided to come here?

"You live in the shadow of your predecessor," the witch wheezed from under her tattered, grey hood. Her voice was strained and raspy, like something inside her had been stretched tighter than it should go. "It looms over you like a great storm over the plains."

"What do you know of my shadows?" Rebekah asked, trying not to cough.

"My goddess tells me everything I need to know," said the witch, raising an arthritic finger and pointing at a dark idol on her altar.

The idol stood tall and proud, surrounded by candles and

offerings of incense, dead flowers, honey-soaked bread, and dusty bones. Lucigia was not one of the deities widely worshipped in Naphtali, and her workings were as much a mystery to Rebekah as the crone that sat before her. The goddess belonged to far-flung lands and ancient times. She was a deity of witchcraft, shadows, and prophecy—things humble farmers had little interest in.

"It's true," Rebekah said. She tried to speak over the shame rising in her heart, yet her voice still sounded small and insignificant. "I am my husband's second wife. The first died giving birth to his twelfth son, and I have been unable to give him even one."

"Remember, my dear," the witch hissed, "in Naphtali there is no such thing as a barren woman, only a dead one."

Rebekah did not need reminding. By the laws of their people, if a husband saw fit, he could have his wife stoned to death if she bore him no children. She'd seen it once. She was a small child when it happened, but the memory still haunted her dreams, these days more so than ever. She didn't want to end up like that poor woman, her body beaten to a bloody pulp by a storm of rocks and angry screams.

"Why else do you think I would come to this place?" asked Rebekah, glaring at the witch through the smoke-polluted air.

"You have nothing to fear," said the witch, unphased by Rebekah's disgust. "A child shall inhabit your womb soon. But know the child will never truly belong to you. He will be a child of the gods."

"*He?*" Rebekah asked in a gasp. "I will conceive a son?"

"You will conceive a legend," the witch replied.

"Tell me more," Rebekah said. "I don't understand. What do the gods have to do with my son?"

"Come closer, child." The witch beckoned as she leaned over and reached up for her hood with skeletal hands that ended in sharp, yellow fingernails. "Look into my eyes and you will see all you need to know."

The grey hood fell back to reveal eight dark eyes as slick as oil all gaping directly at Rebekah.

She gasped. She would have fallen backwards, but she was locked in the terrible gaze that froze her body in place.

Mesmerised and unable to blink, Rebekah's mind fell into the darkness of the witch's spider eyes.

The thirteenth son of the House of Canaan shall be a child of Astaroth, the witch's voice croaked from all around Rebekah. It was thunderous. She threw her palms over her aching ears, but it did not help to dim the voice; it was coming from inside Rebekah's own head.

THE SOUL with two bodies will make itself whole again.

The son of prophecy and the son of flowers will be tangled like the roots of an ancient tree.

A legendary love will bloom only to be brought to ruin.

Their fate is tied to the fate of everything the sun touches.

The blood of the crown will commit a fault so great the gods themselves will cower.

The forgotten god will return, and his lightning will tear the skies.

His ravenous darkness will lay waste to the land.

Their love will be their victory and their demise.

THE VEIL of darkness surrounding Rebekah gave way to the dim candlelight of the witch's smog-filled hut.

"How can all of that come to be?" Rebekah asked, her chest heaving and out of breath. Her head was spinning and her stomach was gurgling.

"My goddess does not lie," said the witch, throwing her hood back over her eyes.

"And if I refuse this god?" Rebekah asked. "This Astaroth?"

Rebekah knew the gods well enough, but Astaroth, the god of prophecy, like his sister Lucigia, was not widely worshipped in the farmlands.

"The gods are not easily refused," the witch wheezed, "But if you do, then you doom us all. Your son will one day save the world."

Rebekah's chest and throat grew tight and hot tears streamed down her face. "All I wanted was a child," she whimpered.

"And a child you shall have," said the witch, "but you will also have a hero. It is the will of the Fates. Their Great Web has been spun for millennia. It is the only true unstoppable force in the universe. Any attempt to avoid it will only bring more suffering upon you, and it will make no difference to the outcome."

Rebekah wiped at the tears streaming down her face. She knew the crone was right. Rebekah's mother had taught her all the stories of their people. She told her of the heroes and monsters that lived and died by the will of the gods, the Fates and their Great Cosmic Web.

To defy the Fates only begot tragedy, and their will cannot be changed. If the old stories had taught Rebekah anything, it was that what the Fates have planned would come to pass one way or another. The Great Web was immovable, invariable, and indestructible.

"When?" asked Rebekah coldly. She was a farmer's wife with a simple request. She had no interest in being a plaything of the gods. And yet here she was, a helpless insect at the whim of a group of wicked, immortal children.

"Astaroth will inhabit the body of your husband the next

time he enters you," said the witch. "You will then be impregnated. Your son will not be of the blood of the gods, but he will be touched by them. He will be imbued with their magic."

Rebekah's tears were relentless. "I don't think I can do this. The gods—" her voice broke into a whisper, "they're cruel. My son's life will be plagued. They bring ruin to all the human lives they touch with their meddling."

"Ruin they may bring," said the witch, "but also greatness."

"A legend my son may be, witch," said Rebekah, choking on her own sobs, "but not all legends are looked upon with admiration."

"I am but a vessel. I am sorry you didn't get the answers you were looking for, but a bitter truth is always better than a sweet falsehood. The gods have decided to grant you a child, and in doing so your life is spared."

"But his life will be cursed, and he is destined to die. Could the gods make more cruel a joke?"

"Are we not all born to die?" asked the witch. "Only the gods are eternal."

Rebekah said nothing. The tears streaked long and hot over her face.

"A final word of caution," the witch continued. "The child is never to know about this prophecy. Those who know their fate are often driven to madness trying to avoid it and drag those they love into madness with them."

"I understand," said Rebekah through her tears.

Rebekah got to her feet. As she turned to leave the hut, she thought of the stoned woman she'd seen in the street all those years ago. Life was suffering no matter the path she walked. She was destined to die or to birth a child destined to die.

She made the journey home under the light of the full moon while choking on her tears.

1
THE THIRTEENTH SON OF CANAAN

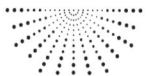

*C*adence's brothers tried to murder him only a few hours after his birth ... or so they'd told him. They'd had many good reasons. The first being that Cadence was the thirteenth son, and thirteen was a very unlucky number. In the farmlands of Naphtali, the people were as superstitious as the earth was fertile.

Farmers who rely on the grace of the gods for their crops to grow and their herds to thrive avoid tempting fate at all costs. They were at all times just one terrible plague away from total annihilation. The gods were lovers of mortal suffering, and nothing made mortals suffer more than a plague. Offending a god or goddess, even by mistake, could bring ruin upon a household, or worse, the entire region of Naphtali.

The second reason for Cadence's brothers' attempted infanticide was that their baby half-brother was strange. In Naphtali, the only thing worse than being unlucky was being strange.

Cadence didn't cry when he was born. He came into the world so silently that the midwife thought he was stillborn.

Were it not for his mother insisting she could see the slight rise and fall of Cadence's tiny pink chest, he'd immediately have been sent back to the gods with fire and smoke.

"I've been birthing babes for almost forty years," rattled the old midwife as she shook her head, making the loose flesh under her chin wobble, "and *that* is not normal. It is a bad omen!"

The story of his birth was just one in a compendium of terrible tales his twelve brothers enjoyed tormenting Cadence with. Each story served as a bitter reminder that he was not like his father's other sons and never would be.

"You came into the world peacefully," his mother said when Cadence asked about his birth. "Nonsense falls from the mouths of your brothers as easily as wine from a cracked amphora. They wouldn't know a bad omen if it bit them on their backsides."

Her words were of little comfort to him. It was not just in behaviour that Cadence was different from his family, but also in appearance. He was dark of hair with green eyes that looked back at him from polished copper mirrors and pools of water. His brothers all had hair the colour of dust and the same dark brown eyes as their father.

"Green eyes," his father would often grumble at Rebekah. "Where did those green eyes come from?"

It was a fair question, no matter how harshly it was asked. Rebekah's eyes, just like all the other people of Naphtali, were in the different shades and hues of the earth. Cadence's family had eyes like soil after the first thunder storm in spring. When Cadence thought about it, he could not think of a single person in their village or even in Naphtali that he'd ever met with eyes the same colour as his.

Every time Canaan interrogated Rebekah, she remained calm. She would simply look up from her loom and say,

"Calm yourself, husband. His green eyes, along with the rest of him, are a gift from the gods."

As far back as he could remember, Cadence envied his mother's ability to remain unshaken by his father, or anything else for that matter. There was a quiet strength to her that Cadence admired and had also unfortunately not inherited from her. He was a jumpy child, startled by anything bigger than a field mouse or louder than a clap.

Despite his mother's words, Cadence never felt like a gift of any kind. Gifts were precious things that people cherished. No one in the village cherished him.

He was five years old when the dreams and visions started.

They were small predictions at first. He was able to find things that were thought to be lost. He knew if it was going to rain or if one of the sheep had given birth during the night.

Once his father had misplaced his favourite sickle. Canaan searched for the tool for days and had even gone as far as accusing some of the farmhands of stealing it. Cadence closed his eyes and thought hard about the sickle with its half-moon blade and hard leather handle. The harder and longer he thought about it, the clearer it showed up in his mind's eye.

It had fallen behind the workbench in the barn. Cadence ran to retrieve it in the hopes that, at the very least, his father would stop accusing the farm hands of thievery. There was also a small part of him that hoped his father would even be pleased. That part of him had turned out to be as wrong as it was small.

"You hid the damn thing from me, you foul little demon!" Canaan screamed at him while snatching the sickle from Cadence's hands.

Cadence stood for a moment frozen in shock before, all at once, his insides melted with fear. He ran from his father as hot tears and mucus streaked down his face.

Cadence's predictions were also a source of great discomfort for Canaan.

"Don't be a fool," he would bark at Cadence. "The rains are not due for another two weeks! I have been farming these lands my whole life and my father before me and his father before him. *I* am the one who knows when the rains will come!"

The only thing that would upset his father more than the predictions themselves was when they would come to pass.

Canaan would fly into a rage, kicking over bags of grain and smashing pots of honey before storming away. The house of Canaan was held in high esteem among the farming villages of Naphtali. His father's line was a long one filled with good and honourable men who served their Emperor, the Luciferian Empire, and the people of Naphtali. They grew food from the land to feed the ever-expanding Empire. The Emperor's hunger for power was matched only by the hunger of his armies. Having a peculiar son who made people uncomfortable brought shame to his father's proud house.

Canaan's rages would always leave Cadence in tears.

"You need to be still, my child," his mother would warn as she comforted him. "It would be better if you held your tongue. Our people don't like to know what the future holds."

It was obvious advice that Cadence understood and tried with everything inside of him to follow, but it was no use. He had no control over when the visions would come, and he could not contain them. Something inside his heart would whisper to his mind. That whisper would then travel from his mind to his mouth where it would escape and enrage or estrange whoever was around him.

"Why don't they want to know what is going to happen, mother?" he would ask as his tears poured onto her dress, turning the fabric darker where they fell.

"Prophecy and premonition are tools of the gods," she said. "Some believe that when the magic of the gods mixes with the affairs of mortals, disaster always follows."

"Is what they believe true?" Cadence sobbed. "Will I bring disaster?"

"I don't concern myself with the beliefs of others," said Rebekah as she cradled him. "What I know to be true is far more important."

"And what is that?" asked Cadence, wiping his tears away with his forearm.

"I believe," she said, holding him close, "that anyone as brilliant as you can only bring wonder wherever you go."

Once again, his mother's words were of little comfort when Cadence's own brothers wanted nothing to do with him. All twelve of them were far older than Cadence, with a five-year age gap between him and Nazareth, the youngest from their father's previous marriage.

When he was six, Rebekah had tried to coach Cadence into impressing his brothers and father by helping him write all their names into a poem.

My Brothers' Hands Work the Land

My brothers' hands work the land
With brows that are sweating and skin that is tanned.
Sinai and Gilead sow the earth;
Zeboim and Admah help the sheep give birth;
Sidon and Sodom plough the endless fields;
Elam and Hebron harvest the crops that they yield;

Jordan and Mizrah chop wood for fires;
Ekron and Nazareth sort grain for buyers.
Thirteen sons from large to small;
Father Canaan watches over us all

CADENCE PRACTICED the poem for weeks, but when he was finally ready to recite it to his brothers and father, he was not met with admiration.

"Stay by the hem of your mother's dress where you belong," snarled Sinai, pushing Cadence aside.

"And keep our names out of your cursed mouth, lest you bring the wrath of the gods upon all of us," said Gilead.

Sinai and Gilead were the eldest of Canaan's sons and made no secret of the fact that they hated Cadence the most.

Cadence didn't blame them. He understood, even then, that his brothers' disdain for him was caused at least partly by fear of their father. They didn't want any of Canaan's rage towards Cadence spilling over onto them. It was better and safer for everyone to avoid Cadence altogether.

AS CADENCE GREW OLDER, his visions became larger in scale and more accurate. By the time he was ten, word had spread of his visions, and it wasn't long before the whole village was aware. Cadence was an outcast, and, by default, so was Rebekah.

He would hear the whispers from the other farmers' wives. As gossips often do, the women made little effort to hide what they were gossiping about.

"That's the one," a woman once hissed behind her hand to a friend as Cadence and his mother passed them by. "The one touched by darkness."

"Let us make ourselves scarce," the other woman hissed

back, "before he curses us with an unfortunate prophecy. If he sees it, then it *will* come true and our fates are sealed!"

They shuffled away from Cadence and Rebekah, raising their hands to their foreheads and making horns of their pinkie and index fingers. Cadence knew the hand sign well—it was the one people in Naphtali made to ward off evil.

There were days when the hate was strong but Cadence's spirit was stronger. However, there were also days when his heart could not bear it and he would be reduced to a tearful, quivering heap. When the time came for him to be schooled in letters and arithmetic with the other boys his age, Cadence considered it a fate worse than death. He lay awake the night before, his pillow damp with tears and his chest filled with bubbling dread.

He'd imagined being separated from his mother and forced into closed quarters with his peers would be terrible, but in reality it was so much worse. None of the other boys would sit next to him. When the teacher wasn't looking, they would pelt him with pebbles that stung like wasps and left red welts against the back of his neck.

"Freak!" he would hear, like the crack of a whip from a faceless voice.

"Demon!" cackled another.

"Accursed swine!" spat one more.

When they grew bored of taunting him, calling him names, shoving him, or pulling on his hair, the other boys treated him as if he didn't exist. He had become invisible to them—a ghost.

The first few weeks were a tear-stained blur, but after that, Cadence decided it was better to be a ghost. At least as a ghost he was left alone. The problem was that the longer he was treated like a ghost, the more he began to feel like one. Slowly he began to feel like nothing at all. To be a ghost, one would have to live first. At a point, he felt less than real, as if he'd never been a person to begin with.

He grew to ignore the other children as much as they ignored him. As much as he hated the idea of school, he could not help but grow a love for learning. He could make sense of letters and numbers better than he could of any person. Letters and numbers, however, could not offer him a kind word, a warm embrace, or what he wanted most of all —acceptance.

No matter how empty he felt, Cadence knew that he could seek shelter with his mother. She would fill him up again as he sat with her at her loom. She would tell him the stories of heroes, the gods who fathered them, and the monsters they would slay.

She told him of Hermia, the goddess of spring and flowers. Hermia was powerful and beautiful but vain. Eons ago, her vanity led her to claim that her beauty outshone even that of her aunt Lerato, the goddess of love and desire. Enraged by the claim, Lerato challenged Hermia to a beauty contest.

In truth, both goddesses were both of immeasurable beauty. Their dark skin was as rich and glistening as fertile earth. They shone with the golden inner light of immortality and held themselves with graceful strength. The supple curves of their elegant forms were unchallenged by any other goddess or mortal.

"State your terms," Hermia said, closing her eyes and smirking at Lerato with an arrogant confidence.

"Very well," Lerato said with a sneaky grin. "Whoever can make the most mortal men take their own lives out of desire for them before the sun sets is truly the most beautiful of us two."

Hermia was not a creature of desire, but a lover of all

living things within the realm of nature. She was a giver of life, not a taker of it. The very thought of death repulsed her, and she could not bring herself to ever be associated with it.

"I—," Hermia stammered as her confidence melted away like snow in spring, "I cannot be the cause of death and suffering."

"Those are my terms," Lerato said as her luscious, dark pink lips curled into a cruel smile.

"I cannot," Hermia said as her shoulders sagged under the weight of defeat.

"Then you know nothing of true beauty," said Lerato, who was older and wiser than her niece, "for love, death, desire, and suffering are all equal in the beauty they hold."

And so the goddess of spring and flowers lost miserably, her ego damaged beyond repair for eternity. Ashamed, Hermia fled into hiding for six long months. In Hermia's absence, the gods and goddesses of winter, summer, and autumn sprung into creation and with them the seasons they ruled over.

Cadence would listen to the tales with bated breath, for his mother's mouth could weave them with words as elegantly as her hands could weave fabric from thread.

She told him of the three Fates: Mormo, Melantha, and Mirabai—spider goddesses who wove the Great Web of space and time. Into their web they wove the destiny of every man, woman, child, god, and goddess that had ever existed and would ever exist.

She told him of the Inkanyamba, a nomadic warrior race of terrible giants who prayed for the ability to see the future. When Astaroth, the god of prophecy and son of the three Fates, appeared to them, he came to strike a deal.

"I will give you and all your descendants the ability to see the future," the pale god said. "But in exchange I want the right eye of every member of your tribe now and forever into the future."

The Inkanyamba carefully considered the god's offer and finally chose to accept. The temptation of being able to see into the future and secure their victories in battle was too great for them to ignore.

The dark night around their camp filled with the sounds of agonised screams. One by one, the Inkanyamba lined up in front of a fire and put their right eyes out with a smouldering iron poker.

When they awoke the next morning, Astaroth had made good on his promise. The Inkanyamba could indeed see the future, but the god had tricked them. The only futures they could see were the exact time and nature of their own deaths.

Horrified, the Inkanyamba abandoned their camp and fled deep into the mountain ranges of Memunaptra. There they live to this day as shepherds who will devour any unfortunate mortal that enters.

"Am I an Inkanyamba?" Cadence asked his mother.

"What a question!" Rebekah exclaimed with mock shock. "Do you have green scaly skin?"

"No!" Cadence laughed as he crossed his forearms and rubbed his palms over his smooth upper arms.

"Do you have one eye or two?" Rebekah asked as she gently pinched his nose and gave it a wiggle.

"Two!" Cadence screamed with laughter.

"Then you cannot be an Inkanyamba!"

"But I can tell the future sometimes," he said, the laughter dying away.

"That is the point of all our stories," said Rebekah, pulling Cadence closer and into a tight embrace. "To teach us things. What you have is a gift; what the Inkanyamba have is a curse. I told you their story to teach you the difference."

When no stories came to mind, Rebekah would sing to him. Once he'd learned all her songs, he would join her, and the two would sing together as her hands wove tapestries, linens, and wool for clothing.

Uninvited and unwanted by his brothers to help with their chores, Cadence learnt the women's work from his mother by helping her instead.

At her feet, he learned the domestic arts of weaving, sewing, cleaning, and cooking. She taught him how to prepare fragrant and delicious meals. Together they would make roast lamb, chicken, and wild boar, ostrich ragout, and fried veal. Sides would be made up of lentils with coriander, soft boiled eggs in pine nut sauce, and spreads of grapes, figs, and oranges with cheeses.

Cadence's favourite things to make with his mother were the desserts. They baked everything from nut tarts to banana bread and sweet biscuits, but his favourite thing to make with her were honey cakes. He loved the way their sweet smell filled the kitchen as they baked in the oven. The aroma seemed to saturate every part of the house; it settled on the surfaces and pulled into the walls and ceilings. Cadence liked to close his eyes and breathe the smell in slowly and deeply. He'd let the aroma fill him up from the inside like a jar of milk until he overflowed. It was the smell of love itself. He knew the house didn't have a soul, but if it did, it would have been the smell of his mother's honey cakes.

Together they would also clean the guardian statues that were scatted throughout the house and its surroundings for protection and abundance. Cadence and his mother would spend hours scrubbing and dusting and wiping until the polished marble likenesses of the gods they worshipped sparkled in the sunlight.

THERE WAS HOLLIS, the god of farming and abundance of the earth. He was a joyful god that brought good tidings, fair weather, and bountiful crops. The only thing wider than his smile was his belly. His stomach protruded outward and strained against the fabric of his tunic like a bag swollen with grain. Hollis was the most popular and most widely worshipped god in Naphtali, but the Canaan homestead also hosted guardian statues of Aneris, goddess of fertility, childbirth, and the home; Lethe, the god of health and healing; and Zamora, goddess of fruit, fruit trees, and fruitful abundance. Cadence and Rebekah would prepare offering bowls of sweet meats, flowers, fruit, and incense to be laid at the feet of the guardian statues and burned. The saccharine smoke would twirl in thick grey ribbons over the statues and into the heavens where it would find the god the offerings were intended for and remind them of the family's piety.

Cadence enjoyed the work with his mother. It gave him a sense of purpose, but Canaan could never know about it. If Canaan ever discovered that, on top of predicting the future, his youngest son was also performing tasks meant for women, Cadence would certainly be stoned alongside his mother. Cadence and Rebekah hid from Canaan well enough during the long days when he was out tending to the fields and animals.

Were it not for Cadence inheriting his father's sharp nose and strong jaw, more questions would have been raised, and his mother would probably have suffered for it. In Naphtali, the only thing that came easy to women was death. Cadence saw it all the time. They died in childbirth, at the wrath of their husbands, and from diseases. It was rare for a woman of Naphtali to pass into the Underworld from old age while working at their looms or peacefully in their sleep.

When Cadence was not at his mother's side or at school, he spent his time exploring the lands of Naphtali. He would walk through the seemingly endless fields of corn and wheat, discovering their different moods as one season gave way to another.

He would spend the summers wandering through the emerald temples of corn stalks that reached up towards the heavens as if praising the gods. When spring arrived, he took long walks through the vast fruit orchards where the aroma of orange and peach blossoms danced in the air. When autumn came, just before the harvest, Cadence would disappear into the golden fields of wheat. The ripe crops would sway in and out of the corners of his vision as he watched rainless and solitary clouds slowly drift through the forget-me-not sky. When winter came, bringing the snow and ice with it, Cadence would venture to the frozen rivers and lakes. There he would stand perfectly still and watch the clouds of his breath leap from his mouth and gallop into the frosty air. He would close his eyes and let the death-like silence of the sleeping land envelop him.

Cadence explored until all the secrets of his father's lands and beyond revealed themselves to him. Summer, autumn, winter, and spring passed over and over again in an ever-changing cycle. Season after changing season, one thing remained constant—Cadence would watch them come and go alone.

2
UNINVITED GUESTS OF HONOUR

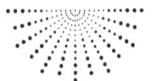

By his sixteenth year, Cadence was an expert in reading his father's moods. He could tell exactly how his father was feeling or how he was going to react to something just by the angle of a raised bushy eyebrow, the twitch of a jaw muscle, or the way the corners of his mouth pulled.

Decades of farming had turned Canaan into a behemoth, and combined with his terrible temper, he was a force to be reckoned with. Sixteen years of experience had made Cadence not only an expert on his father but also an expert at avoiding him. He'd taught himself to melt away into the shadows when he was around Canaan. When no shadows were at his disposal, Cadence chose to remain as silent as possible and out of Canaan's line of sight.

At meal times, Cadence was sure to keep his gaze down at his plate and not participate in conversation. When his father was present, Cadence would find himself terrified that anything that came from his mouth would send Canaan into a rage. The family shared most meals together, making them the most challenging times for Cadence to avoid his father.

Canaan would sit at the head of the table with Rebekah to his right. Sinai, being the eldest, would sit to his left. The rest of the brothers would filter down the table in birth order.

As adept as Cadence was at avoiding his father's wrath, there were times when even his best tactics would fail him. When Canaan was in a particularly foul mood or had indulged in too much wine, nothing and no one in Hathuldria would escape the scope of his scrutiny.

"Why do you sit like that, boy?" Canaan barked. His face twisted in a grotesque form of disgust reserved only for the lowliest of creatures that dared to offend him. The shadows cast by the lamps and candles only served to make him appear even more menacing.

His father didn't have to call him by name for Cadence to know he was being addressed. Canaan's criticisms were hurled like spears and always found their mark. Cadence did not answer but instead just looked at his father from the opposite end of the table.

"Sit up straight!" Canaan boomed as his massive fists slammed into the table, causing the clay plates and goblets to rattle. The candle flames danced around their wicks. "It is bad enough that you are a cursed outcast of a boy. Do you have to sit there like a quivering and withered wheat stem?"

A withered wheat stem was an accurate description of Cadence's body. The tender and plump flesh of childhood had been stretched out of him three summers before. He stood tall, awkward, and gangly, like a vine that could not decide which direction it wanted to grow in.

Cadence's entire body began to tremble as the fourteen sets of brown eyes belonging to his family members turned on him. Each set held a different emotion. His brothers' eyes —some glinted with annoyance or distain, others with disgust, and one or two with fear. His mother's eyes flashed pity and regret, but it was his father's gaze that made Cadence tremble the worst. His eyes held more than just anger—they burned with a hatred so intense Cadence broke out in a sweat.

"Look at me when I am talking to you!" Canaan boomed, smashing his tightly clenched fists into the table a second time.

Cadence fought hard against his shaking limbs to adjust his posture. Slowly he straightened his back, but no matter how hard he tried he could not hold his head up or meet his father's eyes for longer than a brief moment at a time. Looking at his father's face was like staring into the mouth of Obsidian's Underworld itself. Demons with sharp talons and long fangs waited at the entrance ready to pull Cadence down into the darkness.

"For the love of the gods!" Canaan bashed his fists into the table once more, this time causing a water goblet to topple over, its contents drenching the platter of bread and cheese. "You cannot even sit properly! Sharing a meal with you ruins my appetite! Get—"

Canaan's outburst was interrupted by a sharp knock on the door. Canaan pushed himself away from the table without taking his ferocious gaze off Cadence until he reached the entrance of the family home.

"What is it?" he barked as he swung the door open.

On the other side stood a messenger boy, not much older than Cadence. He was draped in a crimson tunic and wore a bronze breast plate that bore a single lotus blossom. The breast plate moved up and down at a rapid pace, keeping time with the boy's breathing, his brown hair turned a shade darker by sweat and dust.

"News from the city of Luciferian, my lord!" His voice was pitchy with excitement and exhaustion as he held out a sealed scroll for Canaan to take.

Canaan grabbed the scroll from the messenger, broke the

wax seal, and unrolled it. His dark eyes scanned over the words printed on the parchment.

"What is it?" asked Rebekah as she got up from the table and stood behind Canaan.

"The Emperor," said Canaan as if someone had just died. "He and his family will be joining us for the Harvest Festival at the end of the summer."

"A great honour," said Rebekah. "The Emperor has not graced us with a visit in years. Not since you and I were wed."

Canaan let go of the scroll, letting it snap back into a roll, before closing the door in the messenger boy's face. "A great honour," he grumbled, "and a great amount more work to do in a short space of time. It is best that we begin preparations as soon as possible."

Excitement spread through Naphtali like a whirlwind. News of the Emperor's Harvest Festival visit had the farming capital abuzz with preparation. As the leader of the community, Canaan was at the helm of plans involving the celebration and the royal visit. He made sure all tasks were being executed to perfection. Woe betide the poor soul who was even a minute late or had any excuse for not having done something the way Canaan had wanted it.

Gigantic marquee tents and pavilions were erected, fine crockery and cutlery was hauled out of storage, and decorations were being made in hoards.

More so now than ever, Cadence made sure to stay out of Canaan's way. Fortunately for Cadence, his father had been so busy he was often unable to make it to the family table for meals, and when the whole family did dine together, Canaan was too weary or distracted to notice or criticise his youngest son's many shortcomings.

A week before the Harvest Festival feast and the arrival of the Emperor, Cadence and his family were sitting down to dinner once again. This time Canaan was present and had brought with him a tension that filled the air like smoke.

The meal was a simple one of cheese, olives, and bread. Everyone had been so busy with the preparations for the festival on top of the harvest itself, so there was no time to prepare anything more elaborate.

Cadence was staring down at his plate in silence when Canaan cleared his throat and addressed him.

"Cadence," he said in his deep and gruff voice. He said the name like it was a curse word. Cadence tried to stop himself from shaking when he was addressed once again. "I am told you have a talent for singing and that you are familiar with all our songs. Is this true?"

Cadence had to fight the urge to check behind him and make sure his father wasn't addressing another Cadence. "Yes, father," he said, shocked by how small his voice sounded. "Mother has taught me all the songs."

"You will perform at the Harvest Festival feast for the Emperor and his family next week," Canaan said. "Be prepared, and do not disappoint me." His words were sharp and concise when he gave instruction, never saying more than he needed to.

"Yes, father," said Cadence, trying his best to stop the quivering that was breaking out over his body.

"And none of your ... *antics*," Canaan added referring to Cadence's visions. "The time has come for you to stop bringing the good name of this family to shame. Do you understand me?"

Cadence didn't speak, just nodded.

"This is wonderful news," said Rebekah. "We shall start

preparations first thing in the morning. You should think about which song you would like to perform. Perhaps *Oh How Golden is the Wheat* or even *The Reaping Song*. Both would be equally appropriate for the occasion."

Hebron smirked, "Or perhaps he should just squeal like a starved pig. No matter what he chooses to do it will be a disaster. It always is with him."

"Hebron is right," said Jordan, turning to face Cadence with a scowl. "You weren't even father's first choice."

"Father's first choice was Magdalena," said Mizrah. He spoke through his nose in a whiny tone that sounded like a bull passing gas. "But she has taken ill and will not have time to prepare. Father is very concerned you will do something to dishonour him. You probably will."

Cadence fought the tears pushing themselves up from the growing tightness in his throat. He would not cry in front of them. That is what they wanted, and he would not give it to them.

CADENCE AND REBEKAH spent the next week before the festival preparing for his performance. He practiced his song while she worked at her loom weaving a special ceremonial tunic for him. She had chosen the best wool and dyed it a rich yellow with turmeric. They'd decided to work outside and make the most of the summer's final days before the autumn chill got a strong grip on the air.

Cadence finished singing the song for what felt like the thousandth time and fell still.

"Very good," said Rebekah with a wide smile, not looking up from her busy hands. "I think you are ready. You will make Naphtali and your father proud."

Cadence let out a deep sigh. His mind was far from lyrics, melodies, and his father's pride.

"What if I have a vision in front of the Emperor?" he asked his mother. "Worse still, what if I foresee something terrible? Father will kill me."

Perhaps he wants me to fail, Cadence thought. *Perhaps he wants to give me the opportunity to dishonour him and the family so badly that he will finally have an excuse to kill me. It is a trap, and I am a fool for walking into it.*

Cadence knew that no matter how badly Canaan wanted to kill him, it was forbidden. It was a cosmic law even the gods themselves were bound to. The killing of a family member was seen as the most disgusting crime any mortal or god could commit against nature. The consequences of slaying one's own blood could be a terrible plague, a curse of madness, or being transformed into some kind of monster. Cadence was convinced that the great and ancient law was the only thing that kept Canaan from murdering him.

The stories his mother had told him were filled with ill-fated heroes who killed their own kin, sometimes on purpose out of rage or jealousy, and other times by some cruel twist in The Great Web—by accident. No matter the circumstances, the outcome of familicide was never pleasant and always tragic. Yes, Cadence knew that Canaan could not kill him, but banishment was a close second to murder. Cadence never doubted that punishment was ever far from his father's anger- and hate-infested mind.

Over the years, his brothers often tried to frighten Cadence with banishment. Their barbs echoed through his brain like footsteps in an abandoned hall.

"Father should have you shipped off to Dis where you can toil away with the rest of the criminals, undesirables, and abominations," Gilead had once said when he was out of Rebekah's earshot.

"If I were father, I would have done it years ago," Sinai sneered in agreement. "A small, inescapable island surrounded by monster-infested waters sounds like the perfect place for a wretch like Cadence."

"I hear they make the prisoners there mine the iron for the Emperor's airships and weapons," Admah chimed in. "And there is nothing to eat but the rats they catch for themselves."

"Father told me it is a lawless place," said Elam. "But Admah is wrong, there are no rats in Dis, so the prisoners eat each other! A weakling like Cadence wouldn't last ten seconds before becoming a murderer's dinner or a rapist's lunch!"

"Stop fretting," Rebekah said, bringing Cadence's mind back to the present and away from thoughts of the penal colony of the Empire.

"Easier said than done," Cadence croaked back at her.

"You will be fine," Rebekah comforted him as she continued to work at her loom. "You will dazzle everyone in attendance with your beautiful voice, and all will be well."

She sounded confident. Overly confident. There was no telling when and how one of Cadence's episodes would befall him.

"What is it like?" he asked, "for the people around me when it happens? When I have a premonition?"

His mother's hands froze in their place on the loom, and she did not look at him. She was still for a moment before answering. "It's frightening," she said. "But frightening to different people for different reasons."

"How do you mean?"

"When it happens, you look as if your mind leaves your body behind, and you speak with a voice that does not belong to you. You speak with the voice of ..." Rebekah stopped herself.

"The voice of what, mother?" Cadence pressed.

"The voice of someone much older than you," she said, finally looking at him. "People are unsettled by children who sound older than their years. Most men and women aren't as wise as they pretend to be and feel threatened when children are worldlier than them. The people of Naphtali are grateful for the grace of the gods, but they harbour what they would consider a healthy amount of fear for them."

"Are *you* frightened of me when it happens?" he asked, equal parts of him wanting and not wanting to know.

"I am never frightened of you my darling," she replied. "But sometimes I am frightened *for* you."

"Let's keep practicing," Cadence said, changing the subject.

3
SUNG OFFERINGS

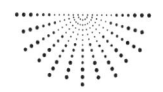

"This royal visit is costing a fortune in time," Canaan complained to Gilead.

Cadence and the rest of his family were busy preparing for the arrival of the royals. As head of the community, Canaan and his immediate family were to remain close to the proceedings. Canaan's household would be on display for everyone to see, and Canaan would have them appear no less than perfect. The pressure tied Cadence's stomach into knots.

The family had spent most of the early afternoon bathing, shaving, plucking, and brushing themselves to a shine. They had all dressed in their finest tunics for the affair. Belts and armbands of leather and polished copper were wrapped around their waists and wrists. Their sandals, freshly oiled, gave off the scent of oranges and beeswax.

"It will be worth it in the end, father," Gilead replied as he adjusted his belt, "Naphtali will stay in the Emperor's favour."

"Naphtali is always in the Emperor's favour," barked Canaan. "Hungry soldiers don't win wars, and starving citizens revolt. The royals should be the ones trying to stay in *our* favour."

Gilead fell silent. Every member of Canaan's household knew it was a bad idea to stoke the flames of one of his rants.

Cadence looked down at his new tunic, crafted by his mother's talented hands and dyed the yellow of autumn leaves. The wool did not make him itch in the way the other children would complain about when their mothers made them new clothes. He wore no belt around his waist but instead a thin string of braided leather ending in two tassels that dangled just under his hip. A headband made of the same leather braid had been tied around his head.

He looked around at his family as they gathered to leave. His father and brothers looked the most handsome, strong, and presentable Cadence had ever seen them. But Rebekah outshone them all. Her light blue linen peplos fell over her like it had been cut directly out of the sky. A long string of fresh water pearls hung from her neck, complementing her soft skin with their iridescent shine. She wore her hair up, showing off her neck, and had chosen to adorn it with ribbon the same colour as her peplos.

"You look beautiful, mother," said Cadence, admiring her.

"Finally the boy says something I can agree with," said Canaan before Rebekah could reply. "Line up all of you, let me look upon my family."

The boys stood like soldiers at attention, looking ahead in silence. Canaan's dark eyes slithered like a serpent over each of his sons, looking for an imperfection to prey on. Cadence did not have to be looking to know the relief on each of his brothers' faces as Canaan passed over them and moved on to the next.

Being the youngest, Cadence always had to wait the longest to be judged, and he knew, no matter what, that he would always be the one found wanting. His stomach writhed like an octopus had just taken up residence inside of him. He did all he could to prevent his limbs from shaking.

When the time finally came for Cadence to be inspected, the weight of Canaan's gaze fell on his shoulders like a load of firewood.

Canaan loomed over Cadence. He lifted his arms as if to pull Cadence into an embrace, but Cadence knew better than to expect affection from his father. Canaan locked his hands around Cadence's upper arms and squeezed so hard Cadence thought he would crumble away. He gritted his teeth as his face twisted and pulled at the pain burning through his arms. He began to lose sensation in his fingers.

Tightening his grip, Canaan leaned in to Cadence's ear and said, "Bring shame upon me tonight and I will end you with my bare hands. My damnation by the gods will be worth being rid of you."

Canaan unclenched his grip, stood up to his full height, and walked away without another word. The rest of the family followed—Rebekah first and then the sons from oldest to youngest.

Sensation slowly began to return to Cadence's arms. His father's grip had left behind an ache that ran all the way into his bones. He walked as slowly as possible behind his family, desperately fighting back the tears trying to escape from his eyes.

THEY ARRIVED by way of a great airship. The golden beast moved through the air as if it was no heavier than a dandelion seed. Cadence watched the ichor glitter through the immense balloon that reminded him of a gigantic wineskin. Rigged to the bottom of the balloon was a gondola easily the size of five standard homes in Naphtali.

People from all across the region had shown up in droves to welcome the Emperor and his family. The crowd gathered like a great red storm, clothed in crimson and waving bright red flags, the colour of the great house of Titan, adorned with the lotus flower sigil. They cheered and chanted for the arrival of their magnanimous ruler. For many of them, the airship would be the most incredible thing they'd ever witnessed.

Canaan waited to the side of the landing platform with Rebekah, Sinai, and Gilead to welcome the royal family to Naphtali. Gifts of wildflowers, jars of Naphtali's finest preserved fruit and honey, amphorae of sweet wine, and bundles of expertly woven linens and wools had all been laid on the platform—an offering to show how grateful the people of the farmlands were for the royal visit.

Cadence had chosen to watch from the camouflage of the crowd. His face would melt into the thousands of others; he liked it better that way. Becoming invisible had started as a survival instinct but had become second nature to Cadence even when his father was not around.

"Look at the light of the ichor flowing through the ship!" said a boy standing in front of Cadence to a friend standing next to him. He pointed at the landing airship and jumped up and down.

"I've heard the obelisks and pyramids in Luciferian glow with it!" the friend replied, just as excited.

"My father told me the capstones of the pyramids glow *and* levitate!" the first boy shouted back, as if he was trying to outdo his friend with his knowledge of the capital.

Every child in Naphtali grew up hearing tales of the glittering city of Luciferian, but very few ever got to see it. Farm folk were born and bred to be out in the open, working on the land in the fresh air. Many were of the strong opinion that large crowded cities full of lights, noise, and the magic of the gods would surely kill them.

"Their airships are powered by ichor," his mother had told Cadence when she shared stories with him, "the energy source of the gods reserved for the royal, the rich, and the famous."

In her stories, the favourites of the gods lived privileged lives while the rest were born to toil in the sun and dirt, growing food and fighting in wars. Ichor did not flow through the Empire in an even distribution. The airship was the closest Cadence had ever been to seeing the precious substance in action. It ran through the ship like glowing blood. It was like sunlight, golden and warm but deadly if not worked with correctly.

Cadence's mother had also told him the story of where the ichor, the royal family, and the great city of Luciferian had come from. As he watched the great ship come in for its grand landing, he remembered her words.

The God Who Fell from Heaven

A VERY LONG TIME AGO, the sky lord Mithras, god of lightning, and his younger brother Lucifer, the god of light, ruled as equals in the heavens. Together they created everything the eye can see and even that which it cannot. Lucifer loved humans and wanted them to have the best lives possible. He wanted to give them everything. But Mithras was more cautious. He knew the dangers of overindulgence. If Lucifer gave too much, the humans would grow arrogant and maybe one day even revolt against the gods.

Lucifer and Mithras got into a titanic battle over the future of humankind. The battle resulted in a great storm that swept through Hathuldria. The poets and scholars recorded that, for seven days and seven nights, the sky looked like it was going to tear itself apart. The wind howled, gold lightning crackled, and thunder boomed, but no rain ever came. This great battle went on for six days, but on the seventh day, Lucifer lost. He was wounded in the way only one god can wound another and was cast from the heavens by his older brother.

Lucifer fell from heaven at a meteoric speed. He had been badly beaten and knew that he would never be able to return to the realm of the gods ever again. In that moment, he decided to gift humanity with something precious. Where his body struck the ground, a fountain of pure ichor erupted from the earth. Around the fountain sprung the city of Luciferian, so named after the god who fell from the heavens, giving his immortal life to create it. As the city grew, the ichor from the fountain flowed through it and brought it to life.

The other gods mourned the loss of Lucifer and wanted to honour their fallen brother by making Luciferian the greatest city the world would ever see. And so they bestowed gifts upon the city.

Amaranth, the blacksmith of the gods, and Fragma, the god of war, imbued the city's walls, towering obelisks, and ornate pyramids with magic, making them indestructible. They gifted the city with powerful and mysterious divine defences that would come to life if ever Luciferian was threatened.

Obelisk, god of the Underworld, blessed the city with precious metals and stones that could be forged into the finest jewellery or the strongest armour. Eris, god of wealth, opulence, and pleasure, granted Luciferian a golden fortune.

Hermia, the goddess of spring and flowers, and Zamora, the goddess of fruit, fruit trees, and fruitful abundance, created plants and flowers with magical properties that could only grow inside the city walls. Hermia also blessed Luciferian with celestium, the soil of the gods. Lush gardens bloomed inside the city at her whim and covered the courtyards and rooftops.

Harmonia, the goddess of good fortune, and Hollis graced the city with luck and ensured that it would always be filled with art, music, and great thinkers.

When the gods were done bestowing their gifts, from the fountain where Lucifer fell, a giant lotus bloomed, and from inside of it the first Emperor, Nestis, was born. Four petals fell from the lotus and transformed into the Emperor's wife, Emris, and their three sons Rhadamanthus, Tartarus, and Letus. The Emperor was the god Lucifer reincarnated, and his line have ruled the Empire of Luciferian ever since. To this day, the sigil of the Titan family is a flowering lotus blossom—a symbol of self-regeneration and rebirth.

For the crime of killing a family member, an act against the laws of nature, Mithras was banished from the realm of the gods. Exiled, he wandered out of the hearts and minds of mortals and gods alike, never to be seen or heard from again. His fear of the mortals overthrowing the gods had been his ultimate undoing.

"Do you think Mithras will ever come back for revenge?" Cadence had asked when his mother was done with the tale. "Do you think he is still afraid humans will revolt against the gods?"

"Such serious questions for someone so young," she responded before planting a kiss on his forehead. "I worry more of the fact that my son is revolting against his bed time. Now close your eyes and go to sleep. We have a big day tomorrow. I need your help to dye the wool for our new winter tunics and coats."

THE MASSIVE AIRSHIP landed gracefully for a thing of its immense size. Golden and brilliant, it looked completely out of place in the surrounding earthy tones of vast fields sprinkled with modest clay brick farm houses and thatch-roofed dining halls. Cadence had heard the airships of Luciferian described to him before, but seeing one for the first time was a sight to behold. The crowd cheered with an excitement that crackled through the air like lightning.

The descendants of the first Emperor were about to stand before the people of Naphtali. The doors of the gondola moved like the opening jaws of a gigantic, legendary monster.

Everything about the royals was ornate, beautiful, and excessive. Their clothing draped luxuriously from their shoulders in regal weaves of intricate patterns adorned with gemstones that glittered in the light, a far cry from the plain tunics worn by the humble farming families of Naphtali.

To Cadence, the most striking thing about the royal family was not their clothing or their lavish mode of transportation but the way they carried themselves. They moved with the same ease and grace as a summer breeze dancing between leaves. They were gods made corporeal. The crowd erupted into a roar of applause and waved the crimson flags so rapidly they became a blurry ocean of red.

Arsinoe, Empress of Luciferian, was the first to leave the doors of the ship. Her skin reminded Cadence of hammered bronze—dark, rich, and shining. It was said she was a great, great granddaughter of the goddess Hermia. She looked like someone who had the blood of the gods in her veins. Her robes of white and gold glittered down her slender form as if fresh cream had been poured over her. Her long, tight curls of thick ebony had been scooped up inside a sparkling crown and tumbled all the way down her back. She was the most radiant being Cadence had ever seen. Her face was a dark diamond, with cheekbones like spearheads and amber eyes that shone in the late afternoon sunlight.

"There she is," croaked a grumpy looking old woman to Cadence's right before spitting into the dirt. "The Viper of the Empire herself!"

"Mother!" reprimanded the old woman's daughter. "You can't talk about the royal family like that!"

"Why not?" the crone shot back. "It's the truth! She is a witch who brews poisons for her husband to use on his enemies!"

"Hush, mother!" the daughter reprimanded.

"I think she's pretty!" said a little girl from her seat on her father's shoulders, her eyes wide with wonder.

"Don't be fooled by her appearance," said the old woman. "Her beauty is not real; it is merely a glamour. At night her skin peels off to reveal her true form—a serpent she-demon with scales and fangs! She is a witch from Aroastria. She had a child with the Emperor many years ago, but she ate the little girl in exchange for her dark powers. As punishment, the gods cursed her with infertility and transformed her into a monster."

The little girl gasped in response.

"Stop it, mother! You are scaring her!"

"Did you know," said the old woman, ignoring her daughter, "the queen wears her hair like that to hide her demon horns?"

"Mother, that's enough!" the daughter snapped. "If you can't be nice then you need to go back to the house."

The woman's reprimands were drowned out of Cadence's ears by the swelling roar of the crowd.

Arsinoe was followed by the crowned prince of Luciferian, His Royal Highness Prince Arlo. He was rumoured to be the son of a goddess, and, seeing him, Cadence could believe it. He was beautiful, like something a master artist might paint on a temple wall. Cadence had never seen a sapphire, but the prince's eyes were how he always imagined them to look. His golden hair glowed in the light of the late afternoon sun like freshly harvested honey. His skin lacked the deep olive tan of the field workers and farmers of Naphtali; instead, it held a vibrant, sun-kissed tone—warm, smooth, and rich as rose petals. He looked to be of about the same age as Cadence—sixteen, perhaps seventeen—but the prince was taller.

His features were handsome and well-defined. His whole body bloomed with the lean muscle of youth—toned and strong but not yet engorged and battle-hardened like those of older men. If Cadence concentrated hard enough, he could see the features of the man the prince would one day look like.

Cadence's gaze fell to the wide mouth of the young prince. His full pink lips were closed in an expression of regal neutrality, neither a smile nor a frown, but was pleasant to look upon. Cadence found himself wondering what the prince looked like when he smiled.

The spell Cadence had been ensnared by was broken when the final member of the royal family emerged from the doors of the airship. Abydos, Emperor of Luciferian, a monolith of a man in stature and reputation. He stood at least a head taller than Canaan and looked as if he'd been carved out of rock. His heavy brow served to make the already stoic expression on his face look even more intimidating. Cadence could not tell what the man was thinking or feeling, a quality he assumed was shared by most royals.

"That is the Emperor," said a man to Cadence's left, speaking to his small son who was propped up on the man's shoulders. "No Emperor in our history has ever conquered as much land and resources as he."

"It's true," said the boy's mother, "in the space of a few decades, he has taken Luciferian from a powerful kingdom to the most colossal empire in the known world. He is mighty."

"Mighty," the toddler repeated from his father's shoulders as he gazed on in awe.

Abydos was feared as much as he was respected. Rumour had it that when he wanted to obtain Arsinoe as his bride, he presented her father with a thousand severed heads, taken from a barbarian army. A shiver skittered through Cadence's spine as he recalled the story.

The three royal family members stood on the landing platform and waved at the crowd.

In the shadows behind the royals, Cadence saw small, skittish movements. They were difficult to make out at first as they were hunched over, forcing themselves to be smaller than they really were. *Slaves*, Cadence thought to himself. *They have brought their slaves with them.* He felt almost foolish for not expecting this, but the idea of slaves could not have been more foreign to a farmer's son.

The people of Naphtali were not accustomed to such luxuries as free labour. In Naphtali, all labour was free. If they didn't work, they didn't eat. No one in the Empire would eat. He imagined that in the great cities like Luciferian and Amun-Ra, slavery was as commonplace as air. It was said that slaves were generally taken from lands conquered by the Empire—savages and barbarians in need of order, culture, and education.

Something deep inside of Cadence began to whisper to him. It was not the same as when he had a premonition; this was more subtle. The royal family did not visit Naphtali for every Harvest Festival. This was the first time in many years. Something special was going to be announced. Looking upon the royals, he knew that this feeling was true, but what was to be announced was still a mystery to him. As the whispers grew louder and more defined, they told Cadence not to expect something special, but terrible instead.

THE ROYALS WERE RECEIVED at Naphtali's great dining hall, which had just weeks before undergone much needed restoration. The timber frames of the hall had been inspected, cleaned, and polished along with its wattle walls. The thatched roofing, turned a dead grey colour from years of exposure to the sun, had been combed out and replaced with fresh thatch the colour of dried wheat.

The gardens around the hall had been clipped, trimmed, and pruned to perfection and boasted evergreen shrubs and cypress trees that stood tall as stone columns. More crimson flags bearing the lotus blossom sigil and oil lamps had been hung to illuminate the pathways leading from the gardens and into the Great Hall.

The royal family, led by their own group of officials and courtiers, were the first to fill the courtyards and gardens surrounding the great hall. A representative from each family in Naphtali had been invited to the festivities. Most were the heads of their households, the fathers and husbands, joined by their wives or eldest sons. Canaan's was the only family with every member in attendance. The rest of Naphtali would be holding their own harvest celebrations in halls across the farming capital.

The massive oak doors of the Great Hall opened to an extravagant banquet. Canaan had ensured no expense or effort had been spared. The walls and pillars of the hall had been festooned from top to bottom with wildflowers native to Naphtali. Lamps and candles provided warm and welcoming light, while a band filled the air with music from their lyres, flutes, drums, and cymbals. The banquet table ran the length of the room and back around again in the shape of a giant horseshoe and had been filled with the finest food the farming capital had to offer. The rich aromas of roast boar, lamb, chicken, and beef twisted together in the air, making Cadence's stomach lurch with hunger. Trough-loads of cheese, nuts, berries, figs, oranges, and grapes had also been laid across the tables.

"I've never seen so much food in my life!" Mizrah said, his jaw falling open as he and the rest of Canaan's family followed the royals to their seats.

"Close your mouth," Rebekah scolded him in a sharp whisper, "before your father sees you walking around like a surprised fish."

The royals were to be seated at the head of the table with Canaan to the Emperor's left and his family following their usual order behind him. This left Cadence far enough away to go unnoticed while still providing him with a good enough view of the Emperor, the Empress, and the young prince.

Once again, Cadence was drawn to the boy. They could not have been more different. Arlo was graceful but relaxed in his seat next to his father. Cadence was seated thirteen people away from his father and felt like a deer being pursued by a pack of ravenous wolves. The young prince had an effortless beauty to him, not just in the way he looked but in his presence. The prince was surrounded by a group of other royal youths Cadence did not recognise. They must have been the sons of some of the courtiers. They all seemed to bask in the presence of the prince.

Being around him must be like laying in sunshine, Cadence thought, as a heat developed in his chest and spread up his neck and into his face. Arlo was the kind of son even Canaan could be proud of.

Seated closest to Arlo was a girl of striking beauty. Long deep red locks of hair leapt from the top of her head like flames that burned down her back. In contrast to her fiery hair, her pale porcelain skin seemed to glow. She watched the prince with grey eyes that sparkled as she laughed almost too hard at something Arlo had said.

A princess of Amun-Ra, Cadence thought to himself. He'd heard tales of the people from the lands of endless rain with milk in their skin and fire in their hair. She touched the prince incessantly, gently strumming her dainty fingertips over his forearm as she spoke to him, or lightly pushing at his shoulder with a laugh that was more performative than sincere. Her grey eyes never left Arlo's face, and Cadence quickly found himself annoyed by the sight of her.

THE EMPEROR ROSE to his feet and the hall fell into immediate silence. He raised his hands and graced his audience with a slight smile.

"People of Naphtali," he said, speaking in a voice that was deep but not as booming as Cadence had expected. Every eye in the hall was on him, as was every ear. The Emperor had no need to project his voice. He could have whispered and everyone present would still have heard every word.

"My family and I thank you for the most hospitable welcome. More importantly, the Empire thanks you for your service!" Abydos clapped his hands and the hall erupted in thunderous applause.

"Not only has the work of your hands fed every man, woman, and child in the Empire, but also every soldier. The harvest is a time not only to reap the fruits of your labour but also to rest and reflect on how your work has helped make Luciferian the greatest empire the world has ever seen!"

More applause tore through the air before dying down again, and the Emperor continued.

"The gods smile upon you tonight!" he said, raising his wine goblet. "Luciferian, the great city of light, will continue to lead the Empire into glory and power! That is why we celebrate in Naphtali tonight; it is and forever will be the breadbasket of the Empire!"

All present raised their glasses to the Emperor, drank, and applauded. Abydos then set his goblet down on the table before looking up, and the hall fell silent once more.

"The Empire relies on Naphtali now more than it ever has before. Our might and the might of our gods reaches from corner to corner of the known world, but the time has come for more lofty ambitions. As we speak, the force of the Empire spreads itself to the farthest reaches of our world—The Scorched-Over Lands!"

This time the Emperor's words were not met with applause but instead a wave of gasps followed by a tide of whispers.

"Has he gone mad?" the man sitting to Cadence's right hissed to his companion. "Everyone knows The Scorched-Over Lands are home to the dark gods and their followers. Only a handful of outsiders ever to have set foot there have been heard from again."

"And those that have returned came back plagued by madness and disease," the companion replied. "I've heard the people there eat their own children and that the gods there turn their followers into monstrous abominations unlike any that walk the earth or the world beneath it."

Cadence was by no means worldly, but even he'd heard horrific tales of what lay beyond the Empire's borders to the east. The Scorched-Over Lands were rumoured to be worse than even the darkest pits of the Underworld. The people of Naphtali were so terrified by them that to even speak of The Scorched-Over Lands was considered bad luck.

Abydos smiled as if he knew this was exactly the reaction his words were going to receive. He raised his hands and the hall fell silent once more.

"I understand your hesitance," said the Emperor. "But I assure you, the power of the Empire and the favour of the gods will protect you from invaders and barbarians as they have always done. The Scorched-Over Lands hold a vast amount of resources, and our armies are powerful enough to take them. Sew your crops and breed your animals; the Empire is counting on you now more than ever before. Victory and glory will be ours!"

Slow and hesitant applause rang through the hall that eventually swelled, but it felt hollow.

"What are we to do?" the man sitting next to Cadence asked his companion. "To disagree with the Emperor would surely bring a swift death."

Cadence felt all too familiar with the man's sentiment, but the man Cadence could never disagree with was far closer to home than the Emperor.

"Now," Abydos said, raising his goblet once more, "I am told that special entertainment has been arranged to officially open the Harvest Festival. A son of Lord Canaan is to perform a song for us."

Cadence begged his legs to lift him from his seat, but it was like begging a statue to come to life. His mouth tasted like he'd just swallowed dirt as a cold sweat broke out under his tunic. His gaze flew to where his father was seated next to the Emperor. It had only been a few moments, but already Cadence could see the rage building up behind his father's eyes. His words from earlier that day echoed through Cadence's head.

Bring shame upon me tonight and I will end you with my bare hands.

Whether it was by the grace of the gods or the fury of his father, Cadence's legs finally became unstuck. He rose to his feet and made his way over to where the musicians stood waiting for him. His body felt less and less like his own with every step he took. His throat grew tight as if an invisible noose had been fastened around his neck.

Cadence looked around the hall to find every eye locked upon him. The noose grew tighter. Just as he began to pray for the earth to open up so Obsidian's Underworld may swallow him whole, his eyes fell upon the young prince. Arlo looked upon Cadence with a slight smile. It was warm and full of excited anticipation. His blue eyes glittered in the candlelight, and the invisible noose around Cadence's neck dropped away. Cadence found he was able to breathe easily once more, and his muscles turned from stone back to flesh.

As the music started up behind him, Cadence kept his focus on Arlo, allowing the rest of the hall to fade away. Using the prince's bright blue eyes as an anchor to keep him tethered to the calm feeling, he took a deep breath, waited for the right note, and began to sing.

MARLOW LAY by the willow tree dreaming of his bride to be.

Upon one summer morning fair, she came to him with auburn hair.

Call on me when the day is long.
Call on me to be strong.

Call on me when life isn't fair.
Call on me and your load I will bear.
Though their love grew true and strong, for the world she was not long.
The Fates had other plans for her, and from her sleep she would not stir.
Call on me when the day is long.
Call on me to be strong.
Call on me when life isn't fair.
Call on me and your load I will bear.
Marlow wept by the willow tree mourning all that would not be.
In flames and smoke that rose up high, Odette was given to the sky.
Remember lovers everywhere, Odette and her auburn hair.
Short and long run the threads of Fate
Confess your love before it's too late.
Call on me when the day is long.
Call on me to be strong.
Call on me when life isn't fair.
Call on me and I will be there.

As the last note left Cadence's lips, a terrifying and all too familiar sensation rippled through his body. It started as a chill and built to a shiver. His heart began to whisper and his vision was whisked away from the safe harbour of the prince's eyes to a scene dark and terrible.

Everything that could burn was on fire. Screams filled the air like a plague of locusts ravaging a crop. It took a moment for Cadence to realise where he was, and when he did, he fell to his knees. Naphtali was under siege. From where he stood, as far as his eyes could see, the farming capital was burning. Great pillars of smoke bellowed up towards the cloudless sky from every home, field, barn, and stable. The smell of burning crops filled the air like a bitter poison while ash rained down on the land.

The men, women, and children of Naphtali ran like terrified sheep as dark shadows chased them down and slayed them. The shadows moved so quickly there was no way they could be human.

A woman fell at Cadence's feet screaming, tears, mucus, and blood running down her swollen face. She had been badly beaten, and almost all her clothes had been torn from her body. She could not see Cadence, but even if she could have, something much more terrifying held all of her attention.

One of the shadows had come to a full stop and loomed over the woman with its sword raised. The weapon was unlike any Cadence had ever seen before. The blade was pitch black, oily, and worked into a sickle-like formation.

The creature wielding the sword may have been a man once but was now something not of the world of the living. Under the black rags and fractured armour he was dressed in, his skin was grey and lifeless. Cadence looked closer and saw the man's eyes were two sticky, glistening pits. The demon growled at the screeching woman to reveal a blackened mouth filled with broken teeth filed to a spear's edge. Open wounds in the creature's flesh writhed with the squirming of maggots, beetles, and flies.

The monster brought the sword down on the woman, cleaving her face in half and bringing her screams to an abrupt end.

CADENCE'S VISION was blurred once again as his mind's eye floated away from the carnage. When his eyes were able to focus, he found himself looking up at the thatched ceiling of the Great Hall. The screaming in his hears had given way to soft murmurs and chatter all around him. His mother's face was the first he recognised. She was on her knees next to him, his head rested in her lap.

"Cadence!" she gasped. "Thank the gods you are alright!"

Cadence turned his head away from his mother, his heart still racing from the horror he'd witnessed in his vision. He saw his father speaking with the Emperor and sat bolt upright, almost head-butting his mother.

Dread, cold and unforgiving, locked his insides in an icy grip. Hot tears found their way into his eyes as his muscles stiffened in panic.

"Gods," he whispered through his throat as it grew tighter. "What have I done?"

He jumped to his feet but was unsteady. For a moment he almost fell again but found his balance.

"A bit too much excitement for the boy," he heard Canaan chuckle nervously to the Emperor.

Cadence didn't wait to meet his father's gaze. He ran. He ran from his mother's calls. He ran past the guests down the length of the Great Hall. He ran into the oak doors, pushing them open with all the force he could muster. The crisp night air embraced him, cooling his skin as he sprinted down the steps onto the gravel pathway and into the darkness. He stopped only when he reached a short stone wall at the boundary of one of the courtyards. He leaned against the wall with the full weight of his body as he caught his breath through his tears.

He wanted to scream at all the gods, for he did not know which one had cursed him. He wanted to rip his heart from his chest and squeeze it until it stopped beating. He wanted to tear at the flesh on his face until he struck the bone underneath with his fingernails.

He tried to calm himself but his chest shuddered with every breath he took.

The harvest moon was full and cast a bright light on the courtyard. He looked upon the rows of Cyprus trees, their branches too small and flexible to successfully hang himself from. There was a yew grove not far from him that would do nicely. He had but to fetch some rope from one of the barns.

4
EMBERFLIES AND BIRTHMARKS

*C*adence leaned over the wall with his back to the Great Hall. Over the chirping of the crickets, he could still hear the sounds of the festivities in the distance continuing despite the devastating interruption he'd caused.

The tears had stopped but his breathing was still shaky, and his face was still hot with embarrassment and dread. The dread weighed the heaviest on his heart. Dread for what his father would do to him over something Cadence wanted desperately to control but could not. Dread for the future of his home.

Naphtali will be burned to the ground, he thought to himself, *and I will probably not live to see another sunrise.*

He looked up at the stars, trying to calm himself further. He was as good as dead. Canaan was the kind of man who always made good on his promises or, in this instance, his threats. Canaan had kept his composure in the Great Hall for the sake of the Emperor and not wanting to be shamed any further. Later, when he was in the walls of his own house, he would unleash a rage over Cadence that would see him beaten to death. Anxiety writhed through Cadence like an enraged serpent that was about to tear its way out of his body.

"You sang really well tonight," a warm and friendly voice said from behind Cadence. "If I didn't know any better, I would have thought I was in the presence of a siren."

Cadence spun around to find prince Arlo standing before him. Shock threw everything else Cadence had been feeling and thinking from his body.

The prince looked even more radiant up close. His skin seemed to glow with the light of the gods. He had abandoned his formal regalia for a more simple and stripped down crimson tunic absent of the gold belt and leather straps. He still looked out of place among the common shrubbery and wildflowers of Naphtali. Even without all the finery he was still something precious that belonged in a palace.

Cadence stood awestruck for a moment as his brain scrambled for something to say.

"His Royal Highness humours me," Cadence eventually managed, keeping his gaze low. "I was a disaster. I apologise."

"I like to look at them too," said the prince, ignoring Cadence's words and lifting his head up towards the stars, "and please, call me Arlo." The prince's voice carried all the depth and warmth of a fireplace on a frigid night.

Cadence didn't look at the stars; he looked instead at the boy's neck. It was slender and beautiful, just like the rest of him. The royal youth was so attractive it hurt to look at him, in almost the same way that it hurt to stare into the sun. Cadence found himself having to fight the urge to reach out and press his fingertips against the skin of the prince's upper arms. He wanted to make sure Arlo was real and not some beautiful vision his mind had conjured up.

A sudden sadness came over Cadence; when Cadence looked at Arlo, he saw everything he wasn't but wanted so desperately to be—attractive and well liked. Cadence remembered seeing how the other royal youths had flocked around him like excited sheep around a feeding trough. He wondered what that felt like to be adored instead of shunned.

The heat in Cadence's face and neck that he'd experienced in the Great Hall made a sudden and unwelcome return.

His father wouldn't be so ashamed of him if he was like Arlo with his golden waves of hair and athletic build. Perhaps his brothers would also not hate him as much if he were more like the prince. But he was no prince, not even close. He was a lowly, underdeveloped, gangly farm boy everyone was afraid of because he could predict the moment they were going to die or when disaster would strike. He was sad and pathetic. But most of all he was alone. A spark of ugly, green jealousy crackled to life inside Cadence's heart, but before he could fan it into a flame, the prince turned to him.

"I wanted to give you this," he said before producing a single yellow lily and holding it out. The pearly petals held an iridescent quality to them that refracted in the moonlight. "My stepmother taught me that they mean gratitude and joy. The way you sang tonight reminded me of them."

The sweet fragrance coming from the flower flowed over Cadence. His heart was warmed once more, but this time by a far friendlier feeling than jealousy.

"Thank you," Cadence said, taking the lily by the stem, and for a brief moment his fingertips touched the prince's and Cadence's heart missed a beat.

Does he have this effect on everyone? Cadence wondered to himself. *Or am I going mad?*

"I hope I won't have to wait until the next Harvest Festival to hear you sing again," said the prince.

Before Cadence could respond, a high-pitched whine rang through the stone corridor of the courtyard.

"Prince Arlo!" the voice rang out. "Where have you disappeared to now? You promised that you would dance with me!"

"I made no such promise," said the prince under his breath. His face turned to an expression of slight annoyance.

"She seems to think otherwise," said Cadence.

"Angelica has a habit of being told one thing and hearing another," the prince replied.

Cadence thought back to the girl with the milky skin and fiery hair. He remembered how she clung to Arlo the way a hawk clings to a field mouse with its talons.

"Who is she?" asked Cadence.

"A princess of Amun-Ra and my betrothed," Arlo said flatly as his lips fell into a slight frown.

Cadence had been half right about the girl, but he could not understand Arlo's lack of feeling towards her.

"She is very beautiful," uttered Cadence.

"Prince Arlo!" The sweet, high voice rang out again, getting closer.

Arlo cringed at the sound. "She can do nothing peacefully."

"You must be missed at the celebration," Cadence changed the subject, feeling uncomfortable with the discussion of the princess. He really wanted to talk about something that would return the smile to Arlo's face.

Instead, Arlo frowned dismissively and shook his head. "I don't really like parties. I don't see the point of them. My father throws them all the time back home. It's just a bunch of people drinking too much and getting louder and more obnoxious as the evening progresses. It's worse if they partake in bliss."

Cadence didn't know what bliss was or how to partake in

it. He didn't ask for fear of sounding like an ignorant country peasant, even though that is exactly what he was.

"You don't have to go back if you don't want to," said Cadence. "You're a prince after all; surely that means you get to do what you like."

Arlo smiled. It was bright and wide, and Cadence didn't have to wonder about what it looked like anymore.

"That isn't exactly how being a prince works," he said through his brilliant, white teeth, "but you make a fair point. If we don't go back to the party, then where shall we go?"

"We?" gasped Cadence, sounding more shocked than he meant to. "What do you mean *we*?"

"You know these lands," said Arlo, his hands falling open at his side. "Take me somewhere."

Cadence considered the prince's request for a moment. Was denying the direct request of a royal considered treason? If it were, was the punishment death? What if he accepted and they were found? He would be accused of kidnapping the prince and probably be put to death. He looked at Arlo, his deep blue eyes shining in the lamplight with flecks of gold. They were a god's eyes.

He looked at the excited grin on the prince's beautiful, soft face. It was a face of kindness twisted into excitement by potential mischief.

"The emberflies," said Cadence as an idea bloomed in his head.

"The what?" asked the prince.

"The emberflies by the river," said Cadence, tucking the stem of the lily securely into his headband. "It's not far from here. I could take you to see them. It's almost the end of their mating season."

"Lead the way," said Arlo, his easy smile breaking out into a radiant grin.

A PROPHECY OF FLOWERS AND LIGHTNING

PRINCE AND PAUPER ALIKE, excited youths do not walk anywhere. They run. Cadence bolted from the courtyard and Arlo followed. The chilled autumn evening air whipped at their tunics and burnt against their cheeks and noses as the dying grass crunched under their swooping feet. They were a blur of yellow and crimson under the full bright moon, streaking across the barren harvested fields. The two reached a boundary marked by thickets caught in the twilight of turning from green to a bright display of oranges, reds, and yellows.

Cadence skidded to a stop at the boundary and leaned on a tree to catch his breath. Arlo stopped next to him, not a drop of sweat on his brow and breathing as easily as if he had been on a stroll. Cadence said nothing of it and instead closed his eyes.

"Listen," he said. "Can you hear the river?"

"I can," said Arlo. "It's just on the other side of those trees and bushes."

"There is a pathway," said Cadence, having caught his breath. "Follow me."

Guided by the light of moonbeams, the two ventured into the thickets and onto a thin, foot-worn pathway. The pathway grew wider until it opened up into a clearing at the edge of the Vassago River. The cool water gurgled and sparkled in the moonlight.

"It's beautiful out here," said Arlo, looking around in wonder.

"The Vassago flows all the way from the Andras mountain range to the Charybdian Sea," Cadence said, reciting a fact that he'd once overheard his brothers discussing. "Are there no rivers in Luciferian?"

"There is the Rhiannon, but she is not as striking as this." The prince's eyes were wide as he watched the water tumble and fall into the path the river had cut for itself over centuries. "The City of Light is very different from anywhere else in the world."

"I've never been," said Cadence, feeling abashed, but he couldn't help but be honest with the boy. "I've never set foot outside of Naphtali."

"You should come to Luciferian," Arlo said, his eyes wide with excitement. "It would be an honour to have you perform at the palace. Then I could see you again."

Cadence's cheeks flushed, but before he could come up with a response, something shimmered in the corner of his vision.

"Over there," he said, pointing to a cluster of bushes on the other side of the river. Between the waxy green leaves, pinpricks of glowing orange and yellow light began to float into the air. "We're just in time."

Arlo's eyes widened and a smile broke over his face, "Do you think they will come closer?"

"Those are the males," Cadence replied, "they will have to cross to this side of the river to find the females. If we are still enough, some may even land on us."

A moment later, as Cadence said, thousands of the little lights emerged from the bushes and started floating over the river towards the boys. Some of the lights passed them overhead and for a moment blended in with the night sky and looked like stars, while others began to land on their heads, arms, and shoulders.

The prince held his hand closer to his face and smiled as he closely inspected an emberfly crawling between his fingers. The glow of the emberflies illuminated the prince's soft and perfectly smooth skin. Cadence watched as the lights from the insects reflected in Arlo's bright blue eyes.

"My stepmother taught me that the emberflies came into existence when the first sparks of molten metal flew from Amaranth's forge," said Arlo, "and that they are—"

"His messengers," Cadence said, finishing the prince's sentence.

Arlo smiled at Cadence, and for a moment he thought some of the emberflies had somehow managed to find a way into his stomach. Cadence didn't allow himself to enjoy the feeling before pushing it away.

"That's a very unique birthmark," said Arlo, pointing at Cadence's right shoulder blade.

Cadence's tunic had slipped down, exposing the flesh where his birthmark, the shape of a large crescent moon three shades darker than the rest of his skin, had been branded. An emberfly rested just above the birthmark, drawing the prince's attention to it.

He immediately pulled his tunic up to cover the birthmark. The emberfly took off from his shoulder and flew off into the darkness to find a mate.

"Don't cover it up," said Arlo, taking a step closer. He raised his hand and gently pushed Cadence's tunic back down again. He traced the curve of the birthmark with his thumb, his touch sending a vibration of warmth through Cadence's body. "Beautiful," he whispered in awe.

"I don't think it's a good idea for you to be around me," said Cadence as he stepped away from Arlo. The emberflies that had been resting on his arms and head abandoned him.

The prince's smile faded into a look of sad disappointment. "Why not?"

"The other people in the village and pretty much the rest of Naphtali say I'm bad luck. If anyone knew I was alone with the prince of Luciferian, I would be stoned to death."

A look of concern wound itself over the prince's face. At first Cadence thought the concern was for himself, but Arlo then proved otherwise.

"Why would they call you bad luck?" he asked, stepping

closer to Cadence and not further away in the way Cadence had expected he would.

"I am cursed by the gods," Cadence said, not meeting Arlo's gaze. "And that birthmark is proof; everyone says so."

The moon was a symbol of darkness and mystery to the people of Naphtali. The fact that Cadence bore it as a symbol from birth only added another layer of peculiarity to his already feared reputation.

"You don't look cursed to me," Arlo said.

His voice was kind and gentle, and it made Cadence want to step closer to him. Arlo asked no questions. He was not curious about the nature of Cadence's curse or how it affected him. He just stood in place looking at Cadence with an open and warm expression.

Cadence said nothing. The flow of the river and the fluttering of the emberflies' wings were suddenly deafening. No one had ever reacted to him this way before. Most in the farming capital already knew about him and his visions. There was the rare occasion when Cadence did meet someone who was unaware of his curse and things felt blissfully normal. But Cadence knew the feeling would not last long. As soon as that person discovered Cadence was touched by the gods, they quickly made themselves scarce.

The boys were still for what felt like a lifetime to Cadence until Arlo finally broke the silence.

"My stepmother says the gods do not play well with mortals, but we all fall into The Great Web of the Fates. A curse to some may be a blessing to others."

Cadence wanted to scoff but stopped himself. "If the people of Naphtali have made anything abundantly clear, it is that I am no blessing," he said instead.

The prince then lifted his arm and took Cadence by the shoulder. Brushing against the birthmark once more. His touch was warm and Cadence found himself dizzy.

"Don't allow the ignorance of others to remove you from a path that has yet to reveal itself to you," said Arlo.

He spoke with the wisdom of someone much older, a trait Cadence had learned a long time ago was not welcome in children. Not the children of Naphtali anyway.

"And besides," the prince continued, "if you are cursed then so am I."

Arlo turned his side to face Cadence and shrugged his own tunic from his right shoulder. The crimson fabric fell to reveal the prince's torso. Arlo's body was an ocean of lean muscle that undulated beneath a current of smooth skin made golden by the sun.

Cadence's eyes ran over the prince's bare upper body and he felt his pulse grow rapid. Looking turned quickly to admiration and then possibly even ... desire. Cadence did not have time to dwell on his feelings as his gaze fell to the prince's side. There was a crescent moon birthmark identical to Cadence's.

Cadence stepped closer as his eyes widened. Instinctively, he reached out and gently brushed over the prince's birthmark with his fingertips. The skin on Arlo's side broke out into a prickle of gooseflesh.

"How is this possible?" Cadence whispered, not taking his eyes off his birthmark's twin.

"The gods work in mysterious ways," said Arlo.

Cadence looked up to meet the prince's ocean eyes. A smile played across Arlo's lips and somehow also made it to Cadence's. The youths stood, frozen for a brief moment before Cadence's senses returned to him. He pulled his hand away from the birthmark. Arlo slowly pulled his tunic back over his body, but his smile had not faded.

Cadence didn't want their time together to end, but he was already in enough trouble as it was without being accused of kidnapping the prince. He felt drawn to the boy like the tide to the shore, but they couldn't stay away any longer.

If the night didn't end with Canaan's hands clenched around Cadence's neck over what had transpired earlier, it would be nothing short of a miracle. Cadence's mind wondered back to the terrible vision. An overwhelming feeling enveloped him that the vision was somehow connected to the Emperor's planned invasion of the Scorched-Over Lands. A knot of anxiety began to tighten between his shoulders and pull on the back of his neck.

"What are you thinking?" Arlo asked, tilting his head a little to the side as he adjusted his tunic.

"I wanted to ask you something," Cadence replied.

The prince raised his eyebrows. "Ask me anything you wish."

"After I finished the song and before I collapsed, did I say anything?"

Arlo thought for a moment and his brows furrowed as if seriously contemplating the answer.

"Well," he finally said, "I saw your lips moving, but no one could hear you."

"Why?" Cadence asked, thinking out loud and not expecting an answer.

"The applause was so loud it would have been impossible to hear you even if you had been screaming."

A wave of relief broke over Cadence, and the knot that had tightened in between his shoulders loosened. If that were the case perhaps his father would not be as angry.

"Thank you," said Cadence with a sigh.

"You're welcome," said the prince, once again not asking any questions or probing Cadence for details. "Thank you too, for showing me the river and the emberflies."

The boys turned at the same time making their way back

to the courtyard at a much slower pace than when they had left it.

The memory of the vision returned to Cadence, and an icy grip clenched around his heart. A struggle began to take place inside him. If he revealed himself to the prince, there was no telling what he would be risking, but the memory of the vision was so sharp in his mind. If there was a chance he could change the course of the devastation to come, should he not try no matter the cost?

"I need to ask something of you," said Cadence. "Something important."

"If it is within my power to grant it then it shall be yours," Arlo replied.

"You must tell your father that he cannot invade The Scorched-Over Lands. If he does, it will bring ruin to Naphtali and possibly even the entire Empire."

"Is that what happened after you finished your song? You saw something? Are you blessed with the gift of prophecy?"

"I've never heard it described as a gift before, but yes. I see things, and what I see always comes to pass."

"If it always comes to pass, then why are you trying to stop it?" Arlo asked with a furrowed brow.

It was a fair question but not one that Cadence had an answer to. "Naphtali is my home. I do not wish to see it burned away."

A sombre look came over the prince's face. "I will try to explain to my father. There are many in Luciferian who claim to have the gift of foresight but few really do. It is a rare gift. If he caught wind of a true oracle, he would want to use them as a weapon of war."

There was that word again. *Gift*. Cadence battled to understand how a word and its meaning could feel so far removed from one another in his mind. There was no judgement or disgust on the prince's face but instead a serious concern.

"My father ..." the prince continued but then hesitated, struggling to find the words he was looking for. "He isn't very good at listening and strongly dislikes being told what to do. Nothing short of an act of the gods could stop him from invading The Scorched-Over Lands. Once he gets an idea in his head, there is no stopping him, especially when it comes to expanding the Empire."

A thousand questions flew through Cadence's mind like a swarm of bees, but instead of asking them he said, "Thank you for offering to try. It means a great deal to me."

They walked on in a comfortable silence, another thing Cadence was unaccustomed to. As they approached the wall where they had met earlier, the calls of Arlo's betrothed came into earshot.

"Prince Arlo!" the faceless voice of Angelica screeched out to the night sky.

Arlo started to chuckle and Cadence couldn't help but follow. The boy's joy was contagious.

"I better go before she gives herself a nosebleed," said the prince, smiling at Cadence.

He turned to leave before bolting up the gravel pathway but then stopped. He turned and waved at Cadence. "It was nice to meet you," he called before turning and darting into the darkness back to the Great Hall.

Cadence stood silent and alone once more. But he didn't feel as alone. Had he possibly made a friend? He pulled the lily from his headband and looked down at it and then back at the spot where he'd watched the prince's golden hair glimmer into the shadows. Perhaps he had.

5

THE WRATH OF CANAAN

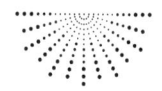

Cadence strongly considered running away. Traveling would be easy for him as there wasn't much he could think of that he would want to take with him. He could weave anywhere he could find a loom and make food anywhere he could source ingredients. It would not take much to make him happy.

All he really needed were his best tunics, one of which he was wearing and the other was safely tucked inside the chest in the room he shared with five of his twelve brothers. Hebron, Jordan, Mizrah, Ekron, and Nazareth had yet to be married and so still lived in the same house as Canaan, Rebekah, and Cadence.

Canaan had a hard time marrying his sons off. As handsome as the twelve of them were, few women were willing to marry into the family, and Cadence got the blame.

"No self-respecting woman would want to marry into a cursed line," Hebron had once complained.

Cadence had listened from the shadows as Hebron bemoaned their father.

"Any woman with half a mind would steer clear of us for

fear of the children she bears suffering Cadence's affliction," Mizrah agreed.

"That cursed gnat is a plague upon our entire family!" Ekron chimed in. "How are we ever to find wives if most women in the region are too afraid to even look at us?"

"We will die old, alone, and childless thanks to that cursed imp of a half-brother!" Nazareth added.

Unsurprisingly, Canaan did not defend Cadence. Fearing the teeth of his father's response would bite too deeply into the flesh of his heart, Cadence tiptoed away and out of earshot.

Their inability to find wives was just another reason on an ever-growing list for Cadence's brothers to hate him. No one ever considered potential brides were put off by the fact that Canaan's sons may have inherited his volcanic temper and frenetic moods. Cadence was not the only member of his family with a reputation. Canaan's tempestuous nature was legendary among the people of Naphtali. This, coupled with Cadence's peculiarity, also made the fathers of those potential brides think twice before marrying their precious daughters off to a son of Canaan.

Cadence's thoughts turned back to running away. Perhaps he would make his way to Luciferian where his new friend, Prince Arlo, would welcome him and have him sing for the royal court. Every night would be an extravagant party and people would applaud him instead of changing direction when passing him in the street. The prince had not painted much of a picture of the capital; he had just called it different. For Cadence, anywhere would be better than staying in Naphtali.

But what of his mother? His heart ached at the thought of leaving her behind. Could he abandon the only person who had ever truly loved him? His whole life long she'd been his only source of solace and protection from a world that hated him. Protecting him had cost her a great deal.

Perhaps she too would be better off without me, Cadence pondered with a heavy heart.

In the end, Cadence found his feet leading him down the same familiar path that took him home. He held hope that Canaan's wrath would not be too great. Considering no one had actually heard what had come out of Cadence's mouth, perhaps he would only suffer a beating instead of an execution.

CANAAN'S FARMHOUSE stood at the top of a hill that overlooked his precious fields and heads of cattle and sheep. If any lamps were burning inside, Cadence could not see them. The windows were all dark, and the only sounds being made were those that belonged to the night—a gentle breeze embracing tree branches in a dance to the song of the crickets.

Cadence, used to moving quietly and going unseen, snuck into the house through one of the open windows. The window led into the kitchen. Once inside, he removed his sandals to avoid the soles smacking against the tiled floor. He crept across the kitchen towards the room he shared with his brothers. To get there he would have to pass his parents' bedroom.

In the hallway, a dim light came from their doorway accompanied by hushed and frantic whispers. Cadence stepped closer and listened while being sure to stay well out of sight.

"He cannot help it, Canaan," his mother hissed. "His premonitions are the will of the gods. And he sang so beautifully. Can you not just be proud of him?"

"Proud?" Canaan spoke loudly; he did not know how to

whisper. There were no such thing as half measures with him. Rebekah had to hush him and he lowered his voice. "The boy was an utter disgrace. How could I possibly be proud of that? Not only did he embarrass me, but the gods alone know what came out of his mouth!"

"No one heard anything," said Rebekah.

"There is no telling what could have happened," Canaan growled. "Had the Emperor overheard him and was offended, all of us could have been put to death. Letting the boy sing tonight was a mistake. *He* is a mistake."

"No," said Rebekah, her voice bitter and tired. "Cadence is a blessing. The only mistake made was on my part for choosing to have him with you!"

The strike came quickly, with the speed and precision of a serpent's bite. The sound of the back of his father's hand landing on his mother's cheek was unmistakeable for anything else. Cadence had heard the sound too many times before.

Rebekah did not gasp or cry, but Cadence did hear her spit something from her mouth that hit the floor with a splat.

"He is no son of mine and you know it," spat Canaan. "No son of mine could be so pathetic. So cursed."

"I know far more than I care to," said Rebekah. "It is a burden you will never be able to fathom, and I know for certain he is without a doubt *your* son. Just because he is not like you in every way possible does not make him cursed. You are blind to anything other than your own reflection! You never wanted sons, only mirrors."

Canaan struck again, and this time Rebekah stumbled into something. Cadence didn't know if it was the bed, a chair, or the chest they kept at the foot of the bed. The clatter rang out around his ears and tears found their way to his eyes. He wanted to storm into the room. He needed to see if his mother was alright. He wanted to beat his father into a bloody pulp. He wanted to make sure his father would never say another hateful word or raise his hand to her again.

But he did none of those things. He was frozen in place by fear. By weakness. By everything his father hated him for being and for what he wasn't able to be.

The sounds of movement came from the room. The fight was over, Canaan's fist having had the final word, and they were getting into bed.

Cadence let go of the breath he was holding in. At least he knew his mother was alive even if she was worse for wear. The lamp was extinguished and the light pouring through the doorway died.

Ashamed at being unable to protect his mother, Cadence made his way to the spot where he slept. He climbed on to his horsehair mattress; it was on the far end of the large room as far away from his brothers as the walls would allow.

SLEEP DID NOT COME easy to him. His mind ran wild with his mother's words. What had she meant when she'd said she knew more than she cared to? He tossed and turned wondering about the secrets she was keeping.

His thoughts wandered between that of his mother to darker ones of his father. The pit of his stomach burned with resentment. He hated Canaan as much as Canaan hated him. The sound of Canaan's hand striking his mother's face still rang like bells in his ears. Cadence knew the terrible sound was coming from inside his head, but he pulled his pillow over his ears anyway in a futile attempt to block it out. It only seemed to make it louder.

If Cadence was normal then none of this would be happening. If he was more like his brothers then Canaan wouldn't hate him as much and his mother wouldn't suffer because her son was peculiar and cursed. In that moment,

Cadence began to hate himself just as much, if not more, than his father did.

HE WOKE UP SCREAMING. His body was sticky and cold with sweat and his heart clobbered inside his chest. When his eyes flew open, his family was standing over him. Their grim faces stared down at him, glowing in the soft blue light of the dawn creeping through the window.

His eyes darted around desperately searching for his mother's face. When he finally found it, he saw that she was sobbing.

Before he could ask what was wrong, his father grabbed him by his shoulders and began to shake him violently from side to side.

"What in the name of the gods is the matter with you?" Canaan screamed. "This has gotten out of hand!"

Cadence could not respond. Not just because he did not know the answer, but also because Canaan was shaking him so hard he feared if he spoke he may bite his tongue off. He struggled against his father's grip, but Cadence was no match for Canaan's raging strength.

The faces of his family turned into a blur as his father continued to flail him around. Canaan's massive fingers clamped over Cadence's shoulders like the jaws of a jackal.

When Canaan was done shaking Cadence, he held the boy by the neck of his tunic and began to slap him.

"If I have to beat this curse out of you then by the gods that is what I am going to do!"

Each blow landed hard and struck like the crack of a whip. Pain seared through Cadence's body like a wildfire. His face and neck ached, his shoulders stung, and his head throbbed.

"Stop this!" Rebekah shrieked through her tears. "You are going to kill him! Canaan, please!"

Canaan ignored his wife and continued to slap Cadence's face from side to side. Canaan's hot and stale breath broke over Cadence in heaves accompanied by acrid spittle that landed on Cadence's face.

"You scream about the unspeakable as if to sew panic and dread into existence!" Canaan yelled. "You are no son of mine! You are a demon sent from the depths of the Underworld to torment us!"

The edges of Cadence's vision began to grow dark when he realised he'd been holding his breath. He gasped as his father threw him to the ground. His head and back struck the stone floor and a flash of white broke over his sight. His face and body clenched up in agony. A warm and metallic taste found its way across his tongue.

Cadence opened his stinging eyes to the sight of his father towering over him. Canaan was out of breath; his barrelled chest heaved up and down, but his brown eyes still smouldered with rage.

"Get out of my sight!" he bellowed.

Cadence scrambled to his feet as quickly as his aching body would allow and stumbled towards the door of the room.

"Do not," Canaan's voice boomed from behind Cadence, "set foot in this house until you have purged this wretched curse from your mind, body, and soul! Be gone!"

Pain shot through Cadence's body with every step he took. He managed to carry himself to the door that led out of the house and did not slow his pace until he was at the bottom of the hill. Only then did he allow himself to cry. The tears came in streams that mixed with the blood trickling from his nose. His feet led him without instruction further and further away from the farmhouse. When he wiped the cloudy tears from his eyes, he found himself at the yew grove he'd contemplated hanging himself from the night before.

The grove was small but thick, overgrown and ancient. He knew it well as one of his favourite places to hide from the world. The twisted trunks wound around each other while the branches and leaves reached up to the sky and folded around themselves, providing perfect concealment. Cadence climbed into the grove and vanished from the sight of the world. Nothing grew on the shade-drowned ground inside the grove. When Cadence collapsed, he sent clouds of red dust into the air that then slowly settled on his legs and bare feet.

This was the worst his curse had ever been. He was well aware that he sometimes had visions while he slept and then spoke them out loud. Normally they would be incoherent mumbles, or so his mother had told him. The visions he had while dreaming had never been severe enough to pluck him screaming from his sleep. What had he seen? What had he said? It must have been more of the destruction of Naphtali.

He tried to remember the dream, but it only made his head throb harder. There had been more fire and more screaming.

Canaan was easy to anger, but whatever had left Cadence's mouth must have really been horrific to have sent his father into a rage like that first thing in the morning.

Morning sunlight dappled by the yew leaves broke over the inside of the grove. Cadence wanted to despair but his aching body would not allow it. He wanted to think of what he would do next, but he could not keep his thoughts ordered enough to do that either. He reached behind his head and gently touched the spot where it had struck the floor. It was tender and stung when his fingertips grazed it.

His swimming head gave way to dizziness before nausea clapped through his stomach and he was sick on the ground.

He wiped his mouth with the back of his hand and shuffled away from the spot of dirt he'd turned into stinking mud. He sat with his back against the trunk of one of the yews as the branches and leaves began to melt away in front of him before giving way to darkness.

6

A BETRAYAL OF BROTHERS

Cadence woke to find he'd been gagged, blindfolded, and bound. Ropes dug into his hands, arms, legs, and feet. Someone had thrown him over their shoulder. He couldn't see anything, but he could hear the crunch of dirt and gravel under several pairs of feet as he bobbed up and down.

His head still pounded and his body ached with a stiff swelling that pulled on every one of his muscles.

"How did you know where to find him?" a voice whispered. Cadence immediately recognised it as Admah's. He'd slung Cadence over his broad shoulder.

Cold fear and confusion tore through Cadence like a sudden and violent lightning storm.

"I followed him after he ran from the house," a voice that belonged to Hebron replied.

Even if Cadence could break free from his bonds, he would be no match for the brute strength of his older brothers. They were all grown men with muscles forged by years of farm labour.

"We need to get off the road," a third voiced hissed. This

one was Elam. "If we are seen, father will have our hides for sandals!"

"If you were quiet, then we would stand less of a chance of being seen!" Zaboim snapped. "We will be off the road soon enough. I've arranged for them to meet us not too far from here."

The darkness of the blindfold left Cadence with no idea where they were or how far his brothers had brought him from the yew grove. The chilled air against his skin told him that it was night. He strained his hearing for the familiar sounds of crickets or the breeze through leaves, but all he could hear was the thumping and crunching of several pairs of feet against a dusty road.

"I don't think father would be upset. He would probably thank us," said a smaller, much younger voice. Ekron.

"Father is always upset and wouldn't thank us for putting him out if he was on fire," said Nazareth.

"He'd probably find a way to blame one of us for setting him on fire in the first place," Ekron laughed.

"I wouldn't mind setting *him* on fire," Hebron chortled.

"Shut up, you idiots!" Zaboim spat. "We're here."

Admah came to a sudden stop and tossed Cadence to the ground. His body hit the dirt with a hollow thud, knocking the breath from his lungs. He groaned before the push of a foot sent him rolling into a ditch on the side of the road. His fall was broken by dead brambles that left scratches on his arms and legs and small sharp rocks that dug into his back.

"For the gods' sake!" scolded Zaboim. "Be more careful! They won't take him if he has any broken bones!"

The blindfold was yanked from Cadence's face. He looked up at his brothers from the bottom of the ditch. In the moonlight, they were nothing but silhouettes, but he knew them by their voices.

"Do you know when they will be here to collect?" Admah asked. His voice was unsteady with anxiety.

"Soon," Zaboim replied. His tone was deep and harsh. He sounded like father when he was upset. "But we have one last thing to do before they get here." He shook a glass bottle and the fluid inside sloshed around.

"Is that really necessary?" asked Admah.

"Of course it is, you idiot," Zaboim barked. He was more than a chip off Canaan's block; they were cut from the same awful stone. "You don't want anyone recognising him, do you? If anyone finds out about this, they'll ask questions I don't want to answer."

"I wish Sinai was here," Nazareth whined.

"Well, he isn't," barked Zaboim before he pointed down at Cadence with the bottle of fluid. "Sinai is home with his wife and children. If we are ever to have wives and children of our own, then we need to rid ourselves of this accursed creature!"

"Be careful with that!" Admah snapped. "I don't want any of it getting on me."

"I know what I'm doing," said Zaboim as he popped the cork off the bottle and poured the liquid into the ditch.

The darkness hindered his aim but he still managed to hit Cadence on the left side of his face.

There was a cold splash followed by a tingling sensation that ran over Cadence's face, neck, chest, and left arm. The tingling turned to a searing burn. He screamed through the gag but only a muffled moan escaped.

His eyes closed tightly as he writhed in the dirt like a worm. He choked on the smoke rising from his sizzling flesh and burning tunic. The only thing more overwhelming than the pain was the smell. A miasma of noxious bitterness and burning flesh clouded the air around him as he continued to scream. As he struggled, the ropes that bound his hands and feet cut into his wrists and ankles.

The burning continued, like his flesh was being run through by pokers freshly plucked from the fire of the Underworld. It was agony in its purest and most absolute form, made so much worse by the fact that it was carried out by his own flesh and blood.

Tears streamed from his face as his muffled screams turned to stifled shrieks under the gag that filled his mouth. His screeches tore at the inside of his throat like a jackal at the carcass of a ewe.

"Roll him over," Zaboim barked.

Cadence felt the soles of three sandals push into his side, and he turned onto his stomach. He tried to keep his burning face away from the dirt, but another pair of feet pressed hard against the back of his head. Sharp gravel pierced into his melting flesh.

"Stop squirming!" Zaboim spat as he straddled Cadence and tore the back of his tunic open.

The crushing weight of his older brother on top of him sent the air rushing from Cadence's lungs.

Cadence heard the pop of a knife being unsheathed. A sharp sting ran across his right shoulder blade over his birthmark followed by another and then another. The cuts ran deep. Blood gushed from them, soaking the front of Cadence's tunic and pooling under his stomach.

"The Akra?" asked Admah, leaning over Zaboim. "What do you expect slave traders to do with him if he is branded as cursed?"

Zaboim, done with his carving, grunted to his feet, and Cadence took a deep and quick breath. Every inch of his body was on fire. Tears streamed from his eyes and stung the wounds on his face.

"I don't care what they do with him," Zaboim said as he

wiped the blood from his knife with a shredded piece of Cadence's tunic. "Wherever he goes, people need to know he is cursed so they may avoid the suffering he brings. You heard him this morning, screaming in his sleep about how father, Rebekah, and all of us are going to be slaughtered by demons clothed in shadow. He was shrieking about how all of Naphtali will be reduced to ash. I will no longer share a roof with an abomination such as he! If we do not get rid of him now, his terrible curses will come for us all!"

"Did you have to cut so deep?" asked Nazareth, a slight hint of concern in his voice that could also have just been nervousness. "There is so much blood. I think I can see bone!"

Zaboim didn't answer and instead made a hacking noise in the back of his throat. He spat, hitting Cadence in the back of the head.

"We cannot risk him being identified," Hebron said, "and that abomination of a birthmark would have given him away."

"And we need there to be a lot of blood," Zaboim eventually snarled as he got back on his knees and started ripping shreds from Cadence's blood-soaked tunic. He held a handful of the yellow and red tatters up to the rest of the brothers. "We'll leave these on the outskirts of the farm. When anyone goes looking for him, this is all they'll find, and it will be assumed that he ran away and was eaten by a pack of dragon jackals."

"*If* anyone goes looking for him," Ekron sneered.

"Look," said Nazareth. "Lights on the horizon."

"Is that them?" Admah asked.

"It must be," Zaboim replied, sheathing his knife. "No horse travels that fast. It must be a scuttle."

His brothers continued to talk among themselves, but their voices began to warp and muffle in Cadence's ears. His body shuddered in pain under the squeeze of the ropes as whatever Zaboim had poured on him continued to burn away at his flesh. His mouth was so dry around the wad of filthy fabric that had been stuffed into it. He'd screamed his throat raw behind the gag and could now only manage rasping wheezes.

Cadence lay there quivering as the earth underneath him turned to mud with his blood, sweat, tears, and melting flesh. Bright lights blurred in his vision as the muffled sounds of mechanical whirring and crunching grew closer. He tried to lift his head to get a better view, but instead the world around him disappeared.

※

His screaming skin ripped him back into consciousness—that and the liquid being doused over his whole body. He shuddered and tried to get away, but he was still bound.

"Hold still, you miserable filth!" a cruel and sharp female voice spat as more liquid spilled over his body. But this time it did not burn. "We are trying to help you!"

Cadence had been stripped naked. That much he knew. His eyes had swollen shut and his face, neck, chest, and arm were still aflame. The gag had been taken from his mouth, but now all that escaped was a low moan.

"Hhhhmmmm," he croaked. His throat burned. With the gag removed, his mouth filled with the taste of blood. He could feel the hard, cold dirt at his back. It must have still been night. He would have felt the warmth of the sun otherwise, and the cicadas would have been singing instead of the crickets.

"Be still, you little maggot," another more masculine voice said. "Petra, get him on the scuttle before we are seen or heard!"

"We can't move him yet!" the female voice snarled back. "I don't want him to bring any acid in with him! It could get on the others. We need to finish rinsing him off first. Go get another bucket of water."

"Why would they do this to him?" the man asked.

"These farm people have their reasons," the woman responded. "It happens more often than people know. They live like animals out here. I can't wait to get back to civilisation."

Cadence heard the man shuffle away. When he returned, more water was thrown over him. The burning on his face slowly subsided but was replaced with the sting of swollen and blistered skin. Under normal circumstances, the cold water and the cool night air would make him shiver, but his skin was radiating and nothing about what had happened so far that night was normal. Nothing would ever be normal again.

The world went dark around him once more. When he awoke, it was because his body was rocking back and forth with the swaying of the scuttle. He opened his eyes and saw nothing but blurs and smudges. The ropes that had bound his hands and feet had been replaced by heavy metal shackles attached to what felt like long chains. His ears ached with the sound of grinding metal and the constant roar of a straining engine.

He'd only ever heard stories about the people-moving machines that ran off a cheap by-product of ichor called chum. The scuttles had insect-like legs that could manoeuvre across multiple kinds of terrains. They were a far cry from the glamourous airships but were far cheaper to run and maintain.

"Why don't we use scuttles to farm with?" Cadence remembered once asking his father on a day he'd caught Canaan in a rare good mood.

"They pollute the soil and the air," Canaan had grumbled back at him. "Chum kills any plant it comes into contact with, and the fumes the scuttles give off are foul and poisonous."

There was an unpleasant and unfamiliar smell in the air. It was thick and dirty and stung in the back of Cadence's raw throat. Cadence found himself hoping his father was right and that whatever he was breathing would indeed kill him.

His head was heavy on his neck, and not just because of the swelling. He lifted his right hand—to lift his left would've hurt too much—and touched his face. His head had been wrapped up in soft fabric, softer than even his mother's best quality woven tunics, the ones that she only used the best wool for.

"We can only hope that we got to you in time," said the blur of the woman who had earlier been addressed as Petra. "The ichor bandages will heal you quickly, but there will be scarring. It's a great pity. Ugly slaves never sell for as much as the pretty ones."

Slave. The word fell upon him like a boulder. Cadence wanted to cry but he did not have the energy, and he was afraid the salt of his tears would burn in his wounds. Could he even still cry? How much of his face had the acid eaten away?

"Drink this," Petra commanded as she thrusted a wooden ladle into Cadence's focus. "It will make you feel better."

Cadence leaned forward until he felt the ladle touch his lips. Petra tilted it, and a cold, bitter liquid filled his mouth. He fought the instinct to spit the liquid out and swallowed instead. It burned all the way into his stomach.

"He'd better make the money for the healing equipment back," Petra continued, addressing the man. "We don't need another waste. Healing potions and ichor bandages don't come cheap."

"He was free, my love," said the man. "We are looking at pure profit no matter how much we get for him."

Free. Another boulder fell on Cadence, crushing his heart. His brothers hadn't sold him into slavery; they had given him away. His mother's words echoed through his aching head: *A gift from the gods.* He was no gift from the gods; he was a gift for these slave traders. Easy money for them and an easy way for Cadence's brothers to be rid of him.

Cadence didn't have anything inside of him to give to sorrow or heartache or rage. There would be time for that later. If he survived. If he even wanted to survive.

7
THE PRIEST IN PURPLE

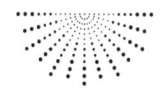

Cadence found himself unstuck from time. From the cargo hold inside the dark, roaring metal casing of the scuttle, there was no telling when night gave way to daylight or how many hours had passed. He drifted in and out of consciousness between visits from Petra. She would clean and dress his wounds with fresh ichor bandages and feed him more of the bitter healing potion. As terrible as it tasted, he gulped it down greedily. It was the only relief from the sweltering heat inside the cargo hold and radiating from his own burning body.

Petra's touch was rough and uncaring. It reminded Cadence of how his father and brothers would handle sheep when the time came for them to be sheared. Thoughts of his family caused his heart to sink and his stomach to churn.

He thought of his mother, and his chest wanted to burst open. Certainly by now she would think him dead. Perhaps she had even started mourning. Ripped from time and trapped in his mind, Cadence only had his thoughts for company and was tortured by them.

This is all just a terrible nightmare, Cadence prayed. *Soon I shall wake up in the yew grove and this will be over.*

But the nightmare did not end; it just went on and on.

The only constant was the swaying movement of the scuttle as its metal legs creeped and crawled over the terrain. There was also the occasional low roar of the engine that would rip Cadence back to consciousness.

His vision had not yet cleared, but his hearing still worked well. Through the thick, sticky bandages around his head, he listened to the moans and cries of the other captives. Sometimes they wailed for their families as they rattled their chains, and other times they lay still and begged to be killed.

He hadn't noticed when he'd become accustomed to the smell of the scuttle, but he realised that it no longer bothered him. He did notice when another smell reached his nostrils. It was so strong it woke him. The smell of human waste.

"I told you to use the bucket!" Petra shrieked before the crack of a whip split the air inside the cargo hold. The blow landed on flesh with a wet pop followed by a sharp scream.

Cadence flinched at the sound, and his burned flesh pulled painfully under his bandages.

As time passed, he began to slip into unconsciousness less and less and started to regain some of his strength. It still hurt to move, but when he needed to he could lift himself from the cot in his small section of the cargo hold.

His vision had also begun to clear. When he adjusted the bandages away from his eyes and was able to look around properly for the first time, he noticed that the cargo hold was poorly lit with low-burning lamps attached to the walls. There were several other captives—five men and three women of different ages. They did not look like they were native to the Luciferian Empire. They wore their hair in a fashion foreign to Cadence and they spoke in a tongue he couldn't understand. The scraps and tatters left of the clothing that still clung to their filthy bodies bore patterns and designs he'd never seen before. They all lay in their own cots across the hold.

They were not dead but they looked like ghosts, as if they were practicing for when they would haunt the scuttle for eternity. It seemed to Cadence that their wide, almond-shaped eyes held no light behind them. Their emaciated faces, made even more sullen by the dim light, held no emotion, not even despair.

Looking at them made Cadence think of the lost souls that wandered the Underworld in the stories his mother would tell him.

There was far less screaming and moaning than when Cadence first arrived. He didn't know if they had gone quiet out of fear of Petra's whip or if they had just given up and died.

Surely this is a fate worse than death, Cadence thought. He'd much rather be lost in the realm of Obsidian than be a prisoner on a seemingly endless journey trapped inside a rocking and grinding metal beast. Unlike the others, he still held room in his heart for despair.

As endless as the torturous journey seemed, Cadence knew it could not really last forever. Their captors travelled with a purpose. At some point he and the others would be offloaded and sold like livestock to the highest bidder. Cadence knew that the journey would indeed end, but as he looked around, he couldn't help but wonder how many of his fellow passengers would live long enough to walk off the scuttle.

He tried to determine what direction the scuttle was traveling in, but it was an exercise in the most frustrating futility. Without a view of the stars, even the little he knew of navigation was useless. Instead, Cadence tried to remember all the places in the Empire his mother had taught him about and the ones he had overheard in conversations.

There was Amun-Ra, which was an easy one to recall. A city second only to Luciferian with its famous hanging gardens that stretched so far up it was said the gods could pick flowers from the very top. Then there was the great port city of Aroastria. It was home to a great lighthouse gifted by the god Solaris that could either guide ships safely into the city's harbours or decimate them with powerful blasts of fire. It was a place shrouded in mystery and magic. The only place he was certain they were not destined for was the island of Dis. No profit could be made from convicted criminals. At this thought, a glimmer of gratitude found its way into Cadence's heart. However terrible their destination, *nowhere* would be worse than Dis.

The island of criminal cannibals aside, it didn't matter where Cadence was being taken. He would be treated like less than an animal no matter where he was dropped off and sold. Panic rose in his chest as he remembered stories his brothers would tell him of the slaves from far-off territories taken by the might of the Empire.

"I heard if they are sold to any of the noble houses their tongues are cut out with hot knives," Gilead had once said.

The reaction of the boys around him, including Cadence, had been one of utter horror.

"Why would they do that?" Mizrah had asked, eyes wide with terror and disgust.

"So they can't share any secrets they might overhear," Gilead replied. "And that is nothing compared to what will happen to you if one of the ichor alchemists gets hold of you."

"What happens then?" Mizrah asked with a quiver in his little voice.

"They parade as priests, men who worship the gods, but

they are in fact dark sorcerers. They experiment on slaves with black magic," Gilead said. "Sometimes they even turn people into monsters."

Cadence pushed the memory out of his mind. His body felt stronger but his spirit was frail, and his tongue had suddenly gone bone dry inside his mouth.

THE SCUTTLE SHUDDERED before coming to a complete stop, pulling Cadence from his restless sleep. Before he could sit up in his cot, gears at the back end of the cargo hold began to twist and grind. With a metallic screech, a crack of hot white light appeared. The crack grew larger and larger until light poured into the brig and Cadence had to shield his eyes with his good arm.

"Up!" screeched Petra before delivering a sharp kick to Cadence's side.

Cadence fumbled to his feet, trying to get hold of his bearings. The screaming pain in his face, neck, back, chest, and arm had subsided, but his wounds were still raw under the bandages. He manoeuvred the bandages away from his eyes. His vision was still blurry but clear enough to make out what was in front of him. He was pushed forward and almost lost his balance as he made his way forward into the blinding light.

The light was then broken by a gigantic silhouette that cast a long shadow over the line of prisoners. As the shape came closer, Cadence saw that it was some kind of guard. The man was dressed in black armour with golden detailing. As he came closer, Cadence's eyes immediately started darting over the guard's onyx breast plate for any kind of symbol or marking that would give away any information about how far he was from home. Cadence's heart sank; the gold details in the armour were only decorative filigree and offered no useful information.

The guard stopped when he saw Cadence and leaned in closer. The black helm he wore only showed parts of his broad face, but Cadence could see enough to know that the man was angry.

"What the fuck happened to this one?" His voice was gruff with the wear and tear of a lifetime of yelling commands.

"There was a small accident," said Petra. Her tone shifted when she addressed the guard as if she was trying to win his favour. Gone was the harsh, whip-brandishing woman, and in her place stood a sweet old lady, complacent and polite. "But he is still good. We dressed his wounds with the best remedies."

The guard grunted back at her dismissively. "Get him and the rest of your shipment to the processing tents. There are clients who want first pick of this batch before the main auction."

Cadence heard Petra gasp with excitement. "The palace?" she asked quickly, her voice dripping with greed.

Cadence did not catch the man's response before he and the other captives were unshackled and steered off the scuttle in a series of bumps and shoves. He didn't get far before he stumbled and fell to the ground. His knees and palms burned from being scuffed on the rough and foreign soil. Wherever he was, the sun was searing down hard around him. The air was thick with heat, sweat, and the stench of human filth.

"Let me help you," he heard a female voice say before he felt the touch of two small, cool hands on his upper back and arm.

Cadence didn't answer the girl, but he did allow her to help him to his feet and stood beside her. He recognised her from the brig. She'd been in a cot towards the back and had not moved much, not while Cadence was awake anyway. She was older than Cadence, perhaps eighteen or nineteen. She looked exhausted, starved, and filthy. Her dress was in tatters, but underneath it all, her exquisite beauty shone right through. Under the bright sunlight, Cadence gawked at her in awe. She did not look like any of the women or girls in Naphtali. Her skin was the colour of a ripe plum, just as dark but twice as rich. Her coarse black hair floated on top of her head and around her face like a dark storm cloud ready to burst. Her body was long and supple, her cheekbones high and sharp, and her lips thick and full. The most striking thing to Cadence about her were her eyes. They were as golden as a wheat field at sunset, but they held a sadness and fear that he recognised too well. A lump formed in his throat.

"Try not to show them weakness," she said with a warmth in her voice Cadence was unable to understand how she could muster. She spoke with an accent that was new to Cadence's ears. The words rolled slowly but smoothly from her lips.

"Thank you," he said before both his hands flew over his mouth and then moved to his throat. The words had come from his lips but the voice was not his own. The sound that came from his mouth sounded like broken pottery being swept up from a stone floor.

"I didn't think you would make it," she said. "If you were strong enough to survive those wounds, then you are strong enough to survive anything."

Cadence didn't respond and instead fought back tears. He didn't feel strong … he felt broken. His lips quivered. He didn't want to hear what his voice had become again, but he needed to speak. He needed to tell someone what had happened to him.

"I don't belong here," he croaked, and a fresh hatred for

himself began to brew at the sound of this new voice. It was an ugly sound. A noise that made him want to tear into his throat and rip it out.

"None of us do," said the girl as her face hardened. "But the might of the Empire has other plans for us."

"How are you so calm?" he asked.

"I am not calm," she said coldly. "A storm has been raging inside of me since my village was burned to the ground and I was taken. But I am not going to give them the satisfaction of knowing that."

She jerked her head towards the guards leading the procession of new slaves towards a large tent the colour of dust. As they approached the entrance of the tent, the female slaves were separated from the male.

Just before they were broken away from each other she leaned closer to Cadence and whispered, "Always remember, they may have our bodies, but our minds and our souls will always be ours and ours alone. Guard them closely and they will protect you in return."

She was then whisked away from Cadence's sight as he entered the tent. It had been divided with a tarp down the middle, one side for the women and girls and the other for the men and boys. More guards in black armour kept a watchful eye as Cadence was shuffled forward before several sets of hands shot out towards him. The faces that belonged to the hands were a blur of scowls and frowns as they went to work poking and prodding Cadence from every direction.

The bandages around his head and body were unravelled too quickly and stung as they were peeled away from his raw skin. His sandals and what was left of his tunic were stripped from his body. The lump in his throat returned as he watched the ruined garment disappear from his sight. It was the last thing his mother made for him, and now it was lost to him forever. The hands continued with their work.

Cadence was doused with buckets of cold water that left him shivering before being lathered with a waxy substance that smelled strongly of cinnamon and ash. Rough cloths were then used to wipe him down; the raw scars on his arm and chest burned as the cloths were rubbed over them.

As the hands worked, he looked down at his arm for the first time without the bandages and cringed. The ichor bandages had healed him but Petra had been right. The acid had left angry pink scars all the way down his chest, arm, and even his hand. His flesh had been melted, twisted, and reset into something grotesque. It reminded him of the monsters in his mother's stories, beasts that terrorised cities and villages and were eventually slain by the sword of a great hero. Is that what he'd been turned into, a monster to be slain?

His stomach twisted at the sight of himself and the thought of what his face must have looked like. He was not brave enough to lift his head and search the tent for a mirror. Once again, cold water was thrown over him before he was dried with more prickling cloths that scratched and irritated his skin. He was then rubbed down with a sweet-smelling oil before being dressed in a plain grey tunic with a rope belt. The fabric of the tunic was a far cry from the soft woven wools and linens of his mother's loom. The garment made him itch and smelled of dust.

NOW CLEAN AND PRESENTABLE, Cadence and the rest of the slaves that had arrived on Petra's scuttle were herded out through the other side of the tent. A small wooden stage awaited them in a private but sparse courtyard. Once again, the sun beat down on him, causing the oils on his skin to glisten. At the edge of the stage, Petra, accompanied by a strange-looking man, stood waiting.

The man was short, and his fat body was wrapped in an intricate purple robe. His bald head looked like a great grey egg and was being shielded from the sun by a large parasol held aloft by a slave man who was following him around. The yellow tassels on the points of the parasol swung back and forth as the man turned to face the slaves. His pudgy face was heavily caked in pale makeup that was melting off in places as he perspired. The centre of his forehead had been adorned with a circle that held a single dot in the middle, making it look like he had a third eye. His thin lips had been painted with a colour that matched his robes. Thick dark lines had been drawn over his bottom and top eyelids, making his small, dark brown eyes look completely black. From the pudgy rolls of his ashen neck hung a long silver chain. Attached to the chain, a smooth silver vial swung back and forth across the man's distended belly like a pendulum as he moved around.

The fabric of his ornate robes ruffled as he moved through the line-up of slaves, carefully eyeing each one before moving to the next. Petra followed him while saying nothing, a completely different person from the screaming mad woman on the scuttle who would dish out lashes and force feed Cadence healing potion. The man stopped dead as he came face-to-face with Cadence.

His dark eyes widened and his stained mouth broke into a smile. The smile revealed a mouthful of jagged, yellowing teeth that reminded Cadence of rotting corn.

"What a beautiful specimen," said the grey man. "A little worse for wear, but beautiful nonetheless. What happened to him?"

"I am not sure, Father Gemini," said Petra. "He came to us with the burns, and we treated them as best we could."

"Bring him to my tent," Gemini commanded with a flourish of his chunky hand, not taking his eyes off Cadence.

He spoke through his nose in the pitch of a hinge that desperately needed oiling. "I wish to examine him privately."

Cadence was herded down the steps of the stage by another black-armoured guard and followed by the grey man Petra had called Father Gemini. When he reached the other end of the courtyard, the flap of another tent was opened and Cadence stepped inside.

The inside of the tent was ornately decorated with vibrant rugs and large, soft pillows to lounge upon. Ribbons of blue incense curled through the air, filling it with a spicy aroma that stung Cadence's nostrils.

In the far corner of the tent stood a large box shape draped in thick burlap cloth. Beneath the cloth, something shuddered and snarled.

The fat, grey man followed closely behind Cadence. The guards were excused with another wave of the man's hand. Cadence and the strange-looking man were then alone. The man walked slowly to the burlap-covered box, his purple robes trailing behind him like wisps of cloud. He raised his arm. Short, stubby fingers ending in overgrown and filthy fingernails pulled the burlap away to uncover an iron cage. Inside, two of the most hideously deformed creatures Cadence had ever seen snarled at him and rattled the cage.

They had the look of something that had been human once but had long since been violated, corrupted, and twisted into the demons they were now. They were as large as two average-sized men. Each had a head, two arms, and two legs, but that is where the similarities ended. Both were naked, but there were no organs to suggest if they were male or female.

Their bodies were shrivelled and their limbs elongated. Their flesh held the green and grey tinge of something that had gone to rot underwater. Where their eyes should have been were instead two concave fleshy pits. Their noses had been whittled down to two large holes that flared as they sampled the air around them. Their mouths were wide and framed by swollen dark green lips that held back mouthfuls of decaying and broken teeth. Tendrils of cloudy saliva hung from their lips and dripped on the bottom of the cage.

Cadence backed away from the creatures but could not take his eyes off them. Gilead's words echoed through his head as clear as a scream: *They parade as priests, men who worship the gods, but they are in fact dark sorcerers. They experiment on slaves with black magic. Sometimes they even turn people into monsters.*

The man in purple laid his hand on the latch that would open the door of the cage. "I wonder if my instincts are right about you," he said before releasing the latch.

Both creatures immediately bounded from the cage, leaving the door clattering behind them, and rushed at Cadence. Their movements were unsteady and clumsy but fast. Cadence closed his eyes, threw his hands over his face, and braced for impact. But it never came.

When he lowered his arms and opened his eyes, both creatures stood before him like dogs waiting to be fed. All they needed was the command from their master.

"Fascinating creatures, aren't they," said the man as he approached. "I made them myself."

Cadence did not give a response. His heart battered around in his chest like a butterfly trapped in a jar, and his muscles had petrified in place.

"Let's see what you are made of," said the man before giving a sharp snap of his fingers.

The monsters leapt up against Cadence, their green, fleshy nostrils flaring and their teeth bared. He could feel them pulling more than just his scent in through the gaping, twitching holes in the middle of their faces. They took several quick and shallow breaths followed by long and deep ones.

When they were done, they slinked back to their master and kneeled before him. The man laid the palms of his plump hands to their heads and closed his eyes.

"I see ..." he spoke as if he was savouring something delicious and rich. "How interesting ... how peculiar."

He opened his eyes and approached Cadence, gripping hold of his chin and leaning in closer. The sleeve of his robes fell back, revealing a sausage-shaped grey arm covered in dark blotches.

The grey man's black eyes squinted in curiosity as he gazed upon Cadence.

"What are you?" he asked, his nasal voice full of curiosity and something else Cadence couldn't place. Something dangerous. Something that made the hair on the back of his neck stand on end.

"My name is Cadence, son of Canaan," he finally said, shocked once more by how much he sounded like he'd swallowed broken glass covered in sand. "I am a citizen of the Empire. I don't belong here. Please let me go so I may return to my home in Naphtali."

The man turned away and rested his index finger on his triple chin, giving himself a pensive look. "That explains why you don't look like the other barbarian slaves," he said. "If you are who you say you are, then you definitely do not belong here. It's quite the mess indeed. After all, the Empire does not enslave her own people. That would be totally illegal, unethical, and completely reprehensible."

Cadence's heart fluttered hard in his chest, but this time from hope instead of fear. Perhaps this man could help him. Petra had called him Father, which meant he was a priest. He was supposed to be a man of the gods; he was supposed to be a *good* man. Perhaps if he would just listen then he could help Cadence get back home.

Home, the word rattled around in his mind like a single loose marble. Home, where he was considered cursed. Home, where he struck fear in to the hearts of everyone who crossed his path and was shunned. Home, where he was hated by his father and given away as a slave by his brothers. Home, where the Vassago sang to him and the fields and orchards were both his sanctuary and his freedom. Home, where his mother was mourning his death. It was at that moment that Cadence decided the bad things didn't matter. If he could go back to Naphtali, even if it was just to say goodbye to his mother, then that is what he would do.

"Unfortunately," the man continued while stroking the head of one of the monsters, "my pets and I have deemed you far too valuable to set free."

Cadence's heart plummeted into his stomach. "No, please …" Tears were welling up in his eyes. "Let me go!"

"Be still, beautiful boy," said the grey man. "This situation is quite easily rectified. You are going to be the solution to all my problems." He reached into the pocket of his robe and fished for something. "Fret not, you won't feel or remember a thing."

A flash of bright blue light seared over Cadence's vision before giving way to pitch black.

8
PROTEUS

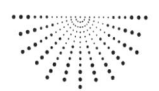

The youth dreamt of golden wheat fields that stretched as far as the eye could see under a bright, blue, cloudless sky. There was the smell, taste, and feeling of biting into a ripe tangerine and the tingling sensation it left on his lips as the juices trickled down his chin. He dreamt of a woman's face. She was warm and kind, but her features were blurred and he could not make them out. There was also a dark shadow that loomed over him, casting a fear that ran right through his body.

"Wake up!" a voice commanded, followed by the hard nudge of a foot to his calf. "We are almost there."

When the youth opened his eyes, he found himself inside an ornate palanquin attached to the roof of a scuttle. The mechanical beast crept over the flat desert terrain with its centipede legs. The palanquin had no walls and instead was open. The sheer lilac fabric draped from the four posters allowed him to see a towering wall and gigantic golden gates.

"Where am I?" he asked, trying to remember his own name, trying to remember anything.

Lounging on the other side of the palanquin was a fat,

bald man with grey skin dressed in flowing, dark purple robes.

"We have just arrived at the city gates," said the man. "My name is Father Gemini."

"I–I don't understand," the youth replied, confused. His head hurt and his mouth was dry.

"Poor boy," the man said with a pout. "The slavers who sold you to me said you would have trouble remembering. But all will be well soon; you are incredibly lucky I found you before anyone else."

"Slavers?" he asked. "I'm a slave?"

"Indeed," said Father Gemini as he picked at something stuck between his crooked, yellowing teeth with the end of his fingernail. "From a barbarian tribe on the border of The Scorched-Over Lands."

"But why can't I remember?" the youth asked, confusion giving way to a rising panic.

"The slave traders said imperial soldiers found you after a battle," Gemini said. He found what he had been looking for in his teeth and sucked it off his finger. "You were unconscious, badly beaten and ... disfigured."

Gemini picked up a golden hand mirror from the throw pillow beside him and held it out.

The youth accepted it and gazed upon the face of a monster. The left side of his face looked like it had been chewed up and spat back out. The twisted and rippled flesh looked like hardened wax drippings that ran from the top of his forehead, down the left side of his face, and down his neck onto his shoulder, arm, and even his hand. The ugly scars pulled tightly on the left corner of his lips, making his mouth look lopsided.

"I am a monster," he said to the green-eyed reflection staring back at him.

"You are touched by the gods," said Gemini, taking the

mirror away and laying it back down on the pillow. "You are a blessing for the Empire, and I shall make sure you are treated as such." He leaned forward, and his grey hand made its way towards the youth's bare thigh and crept uncomfortably high up the bottom of his tunic. The man's touch sent a wave of revulsion over the youth's body and he quickly pulled away.

"I don't understand," he said through a shaky breath and a lump in his throat. "I don't even know my own name."

"Hush, child," sighed Gemini, laying back. "All you need to know will be revealed in time. Your name is Proteus."

A trumpet sounded through the air from the front of the scuttle, and the massive golden city gates roared open like the mouth of a monster ready to swallow Proteus whole.

❦

THE SHEER FABRIC of the palanquin fluttered in the breeze, and through it the city unfolded before Proteus' eyes. On either side of the wide cobblestone road, towering ivory obelisks and gigantic alabaster pyramids erupted from the ground. The majestic structures were made of a glistening white material that was more than stone but not quite metal either. Veins of glowing golden ore ran through the buildings like rivers and radiated with a bedazzling pulse. The city felt like it was something alive and breathing.

Grand, golden airships sailed gracefully across the topaz sky and hovered far above the pyramids and obelisks. Between the airships, smaller airboats darted and zoomed over the city, rippling the air with heat and leaving a trail of glittering ichor in their wake.

Smaller but no less impressive rectangular buildings filled the spaces in between the pyramids and obelisks. The rooftops of these smaller buildings were crowned with gardens so dense the greenery spilled from the ledges. The windows of the buildings also overflowed with all manner of plants and flowers perfuming the air with sweet fragrances.

Both sides of the road teemed with the activity of thousands of people dressed in elegant, flowing robes. They passed the pedestrians in a blur of luxurious, brightly coloured fabrics. There was the crisp white of freshly fallen snow, reds as deep and rich as blood, and warm, earthy beige. The people bustled under the cool shade of giant date palm trees that lined the streets and courtyards.

Some of the people were clearly on their way somewhere and walked with a determined pace, while others stood still and spoke to one another in courtyards under the shade of the lush palms. Their skin was healthy, glowing, and sun kissed.

"Where are we?" Proteus asked, his mouth agape and his eyes wide.

"We are in the Jewel of the Empire," Gemini said, "Luciferian, the glittering city of light."

As the scuttle made its way down the main road, more and more of the city revealed itself to Proteus. The deeper into the city they ventured, the more there was to see. They passed grand temples of statuesque columns and embellished roofs dedicated to an assortment of gods, goddesses, and even minor deities. Thin pillars of dark smoke rose from the temples as burnt offerings ascended to the gods. Guardian statues had been scattered across the city like fallen seeds. Some of the gods Proteus recognised, their unmistakable likeness committed to stone in perfect detail, while others were a mystery to him.

Men and women gathered outside the temples on their way to and from worship. Bathhouses were also planted throughout the city; the sweet and sticky aroma of essential oils mixed with fine soaps and burning incense escaped their open doors and wafted through the air.

The scuttle followed the twists and turns of the road, passing gladiatorial arenas, amphitheatres, libraries, and an expansive agora.

As they continued their journey, they passed a market place that burst with stalls selling freshly baked bread, fruits, vegetables, grain, and glittering trinkets. Stall owners haggled with their customers while small children played games at their mothers' feet. The noise coming from the marketplace caused the inside of Proteus' ears to vibrate as his eyes grew wide with wonder.

At one point, Proteus found himself leaning so far over the edge of the palanquin he almost fell out. Gemini grabbed him by the neck of his tunic and pulled him back to his seat.

"Relax, child," huffed Gemini, out of breath and his bald head glistening with sweat. He wiped his head down with a cloth before producing a folding fan from the sleeve of his robe. He opened it with a *thwack* to reveal an intricate pattern of gold and purple silk before it became a blur with which he cooled himself. "I am sure you will have the opportunity to enjoy the city and all the wonders it has to offer in time," Gemini continued.

His excitement now contained, Proteus sat still inside the plush and luxurious inside of the palanquin.

"Where does all the food in the market come from?" he asked.

Gemini was still for a moment; the dot and circle on his forehead wrinkled and warped as he raised his eyebrows.

"From all over the Empire of course," he finally said. "Why would you ask such a silly question?"

Proteus opened his mouth to answer but then immediately closed it. He thought about the tangerines and figs and plums sitting in their boxes all ripe and juicy. He thought about the barrels of wheat that could easily be mistaken for gold. Out of everything else going on in the market, they seemed to call out to him most strongly. Something inside him was oddly familiar with them, the curves of their form and the textures of their flesh. When he closed his eyes, he could feel the grains of wheat running through his fingers. It was more than a thought but less than a memory. When he focused on it too hard, his mind hit a thick black void.

"No reason," he eventually said and turned his gaze down to the wooden floor of the palanquin.

While he chose not to keep looking at the city to avoid further embarrassment, there was nothing he could do to stop hearing it. The cacophony of people's voices and footsteps rang out around him as the wheels of wagons and chariots whirred past them, drawn by the clopping of horse hooves and the swish of reigns.

How could so much possibly be happening all at the same time and in the same place? he wondered to himself, choosing not to ask Gemini any more questions.

Every so often throughout their journey, Gemini would reach for the silver vial that hung from the thin chain around his neck. He would screw the cap off then raise the vial to his nose and inhale deeply from it. An expression of brief euphoria would wash over the priest's chalky face. His body would relax as if his bones had evaporated inside of him, and he would be reduced to a blob of gelatinous flesh that wobbled with the movement of the scuttle.

Just sitting across from the man caused unease to rise in Proteus' throat like bile. On the odd occasion during the ride when Proteus did look up, he found the fat man staring at him the way a hungry pig stared at the feed it was about to devour. His dark, charcoal-smudged eyes were filled with something Proteus didn't recognise but knew immediately to be afraid of.

His fear was broken by the scuttle coming to a sudden halt, and Proteus looked up. To the side of the scuttle was a high wall made of the same glittering stone as the pyramids and obelisks that littered the city. Inside the wall was a set of crimson doors ornately carved with blossoming lotus flowers and vines that weaved around each other in a complex pattern. Two guards clad in heavy golden armour stood outside the doors.

"Let's go, child," said Gemini, lifting his heft from his seat with a strained groan and causing the palanquin to tilt a little to the side. "We don't have all day."

Attendants dressed in the same plain, grey tunics as Proteus emerged from inside the scuttle and waited.

Gemini pushed a button on one of the posters of the palanquin and a small staircase ejected itself. The base of the staircase hit the road with a metallic *twang*.

The attendants rushed up the staircase and helped Gemini out of the palanquin and down the stairs. Proteus followed in silence. The guards moved in perfect unison and opened the crimson gates. On the other side stood a flourishing garden divided by a winding, white marble pathway. More guardian statues had been erected all over the garden outside sparkling conservatories and stone pavilions. Black swans glided gracefully over the mirror surface of a lake. White ibis pecked at the manicured emerald grass in search of food before squawking and taking flight only to perch in the branches of nearby weeping willows.

The pathway meandered all the way up to a grand stone staircase at the top of the hill. From the top of the staircase, the palace towered over the royal garden and the city below.

The outer layer of the palace was surrounded by tall, elaborately carved alabaster columns supporting the first floor. Twisting and delicate vines of grape and ivy had been carved into the columns and topped with heads of blooming lotus blossoms. The humongous building then reached up four more floors, ending in fields of terracotta tiles that made up sweeping roofs.

The roof of the palace was crowned with a giant golden statue of the city's patron god. Lucifer stood, muscular and tall, cast in shining gold with his sword held aloft and his robes bellowing. Proteus could make out each feather that made up the enormous double sets of owl wings that sprouted from the god's back. The fully extended wings made the god look as if he was taking flight. Set inside the wings were multiple sets of grey eyes that all watched over the entire city below. There was so much to look at Proteus thought he could have as many eyes as Lucifer and still not see everything.

"The imperial palace," said Gemini. "Breathtaking, isn't it?"

"It looks like it goes on forever," Proteus replied, feeling as small as a speck of dust among the seemingly endless splendour and opulence. "It looks like a city within a city."

"I have been a royal advisor and high ichor alchemist here for decades and even *I* have not seen every room," Gemini said as he made his way up the marble pathway. "The north side of the palace faces the river Rhiannon. The view is truly beautiful to behold."

Proteus followed as he continued to gaze around in wonder at the palace and the surrounding grounds. The staircase gave way to grand hallways with room after room on either side. The inside of the palace was a quiet place. The only sounds were the echoes of their footsteps on the cold marble floor. Guards that Proteus had at first mistaken for statues were stationed every few meters. Torches and lamps burned on pillars, providing light in the places the sunlight could not reach. Proteus continued to follow closely behind Gemini and his bellowing purple robes.

"If I lose my way here, I am sure to be lost forever," Proteus said, his small, scratchy voice echoing back at him.

"You will learn your way around the palace soon enough," Gemini replied. "You are to be my apprentice, but first we must see the Emperor."

Proteus' head began to swim. *Slave? Apprentice? Which am I? Can I be both at the same time?*

"An apprentice to what?" he asked.

"All in good time, child," said Gemini before stopping in front of two golden doors adorned with more lotus blossoms and vines.

The guards on either side of the doors stepped forward and opened them to reveal a large open room. This one was decorated differently than the rest of the palace. The columns on either side were brilliant crimson red instead of white. Red banners embroidered with golden lotus blossoms hung from the ceiling beams. At the end of the room was a golden throne, and in it sat a man dressed in white and silver.

Atop his dark curls rested a crown of golden leaves. Proteus could tell the Emperor was tall even while he was seated. Every part of the man was angular and strong, from his high cheekbones all the way to his calves. He was broad too. His shoulders looked like they could carry the world upon them, and the expression on his face suggested that they were.

Attendants, palace officials, and members of the royal court fluttered around the throne like butterflies, bringing the Emperor parchments to look at and cups to drink from. Platters of fruit and cheese had also been placed on tables within the Emperor's reach.

Gemini approached the throne with Proteus closely in tow. When he was a few meters away from where the Emperor sat, he gave a deep bow. Proteus mimicked the gesture and almost lost his balance.

"Your Imperial Majesty," said Gemini coming up from his bow, "I bring a great asset to the crown from the slave markets of Abishag."

"A true asset?" asked a female voice from the shadowy columns to the right of the throne.

The voice was soon followed by its owner. Her skin was the colour of fertile earth wet from the first rain of summer. She was draped in a dark green dress that moved around her like a current. Serpents of gold decorated her wrists and jingled as she approached the throne. A golden diadem set with sparkling green stones held back her wild onyx curls that flowed all the way down her graceful back.

She looked upon Gemini, her amber eyes glimmering with a flame-like intensity. She was fire—dazzling, warm, and full of life but dangerous and wild.

"Or is this another pet for you to do with as you please?" she continued, as she sat on the arm rest of the throne to the right of the Emperor. Her presence was strong and commanding, and it electrified the air.

Gemini's pale, grey skin flushed with colour for the first time as he gave a second low bow. Proteus watched as his mouth contorted itself into an ugly, frustrated scowl.

"A true asset, Your Majesty," he said through clenched yellow teeth. A throbbing vein had appeared on his neck. "I assure you. The child shows great promise for precognition and prophecy. The magic of the gods flows in his veins."

"This one cannot be older than fifteen summers," said the Empress, not waiting for the Emperor to respond. "Does your repugnant nature know no bounds?"

"He has the power of prophecy," Gemini insisted. "My sniffers confirmed it! There is ichor in his blood!"

"And there are cobwebs in your brain," the Empress replied, standing up from her perch on the arm of the throne and raising herself to her full height. "Those abominations of yours couldn't sniff out horse manure in a filthy stable. You were supposed to be assisting with bliss production, but instead you were slithering through slave markets looking for playthings."

"Enough," said the Emperor, speaking for the first time. His voice was deep, and it echoed through the throne room like a gong. "Touched by the gods or not, the Empress is right. You go too far this time. This one is too young. He does not look like the other slaves. Where did he come from?"

"He is of the barbarian hoards from the borders of The Scorched-Over Lands, Your Majesty," Gemini said. "He has the power of prophecy, perhaps even more! Please, allow him to be my apprentice."

The Emperor looked at Proteus directly for the first time. Proteus could not bring himself to meet his gaze, and his eyes darted to his own feet.

"No," declared the Emperor.

"Your Majesty, I must object," said Gemini. "This boy would blossom under my mentorship and prove to be a valuable asset to the Empire."

"Perhaps when he is older," said the Emperor. "If what you say is true, then you may train him in the arts of prophecy in his free time."

More colour rose in Gemini's ashen complexion, and the throbbing vein in his neck became engorged. Proteus moved half a step back in fear as he thought the man's head would explode. Instead he bowed once more.

"And what," Gemini said with a growl in his voice, "is he to do with the rest of his time?"

"I think," said the Emperor, "he would be much better suited as a companion for the prince. Perhaps it will lift the dark clouds he has been under these past few weeks."

"As Your Majesty wishes," said Gemini, bowing for the last time before moving backwards towards the crimson doors. His stare was fixed on Proteus; a deep rage filled his eyes but underneath it the danger Proteus could not place still remained.

"Guards," said the Empress looking at Proteus, "have the prince informed he shall be receiving a companion."

9
THE PRINCE AND THE PRISONER

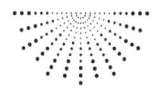

*P*roteus was escorted out of the throne room by one of the guards in gold. The guard was silent as they walked, and Proteus dared not ask any questions.

Is this what is to become of me? he thought to himself. *Am I nothing but an object to be passed back and forth between people more powerful than me?*

He followed the guard deeper into the palace through twisting hallways and past courtyards boasting fountains and pools of water that glittered in the sunlight.

No, he thought as something pulled at his insides like a voice crying out to him, but it was too far away to be heard. He thought of the fruit and grain at the market and the dream he'd had before he woke up in the palanquin. *This cannot be my life. This life belongs to someone else.*

The guard turned onto a narrow winding staircase and Proteus followed. The staircase ended at a dark wooden door studded with iron bolts. The guard grabbed hold of the iron knocker and thumped three times.

"Enter," said a voice from the other side of the door.

The guard opened the door to a large circular chamber.

Proteus looked around the room to find a large bed dressed with soft linens and thick blankets. Dozens of items scattered across the room told Proteus stories about the person who occupied it. There was a bow and arrows, wooden training swords, a shield, and three spears with bronze tips that glowed in the light. On the other side of the room, a lyre lay on a desk overflowing with maps and scrolls. Finely crafted toy horses and chariots lay strewn between miniature terracotta soldiers in a great battle that had been staged on the stone floor. Brightly coloured tapestries hung from the walls and columns, and near the desk was a table topped with a jar of water, goblets, and a handsome spread of bread, grapes, figs, and cheese.

At the window, a boy with golden hair stood with his back towards Proteus and the guard. He was taller than Proteus and covered in lean cords of muscle. He stood with a confident grace that could only belong to a prince. He was dressed in a simple white tunic adorned with a golden pattern and leather belt that drew the eye to his trim but firm waistline.

"Your Royal Highness," said the guard in a gruff voice void of emotion. "The Emperor and Empress have sent this slave boy to serve as your companion."

"I do not want a slave," said the prince without turning away from the window. "Take him back. Tell the Emperor that if he wants to lighten my mood, he should listen to me better in the future."

"I am merely following orders, Your Highness," the guard replied and stood as still as one of the guardian statues in the palace grounds.

"Leave us then," the prince said. His voice was commanding for that of a youth but warm and, to Proteus' ears, perhaps even a little sad.

The guard did as instructed immediately and the door

closed behind him with a heavy wooden thud. The prince did not turn to look at Proteus but instead bowed his head towards something he was holding in his hands.

Out of the silence between them, a voice began to whisper to Proteus as if it had come in on the breeze through the window. He was suddenly dizzy. He feared if he moved that he would lose his balance and fall. The voice grew louder before it was joined by a second and a third and then more. The cacophony broke over him in a wave of words that filled his mind with information. He became even dizzier as the room started to spin. He closed his eyes as his stomach began to churn, and then there was silence. The voices vanished as suddenly as they had appeared. Proteus then parted his mouth to speak before he could stop himself.

"I know what you are," he whispered, trembling.

"And what is that?" asked the prince, still facing out the window.

"You are the son of a goddess and an Emperor," said Proteus, still unable to stop himself.

It was as if the voices that had entered his body were now speaking on his behalf. He spoke from somewhere beyond thought, beyond knowing. All the information was there, laid out in his head as clear as an open scroll before his eyes. "A prince and a warrior," he continued. "You are destined to lead a great army into a war unlike any the world has ever seen. A war that could tear the world apart. A war so immense even the gods themselves will cower from it."

The prince turned from the window but only far enough for Proteus to make out the silhouette of his face against the bright light of the sagging sun coming through the window. There was a slightly amused smile on his face.

"I know what you are too," he said, as the smile faded. "A barbarian slave boy taken from the borders of The Scorched-Over Lands with the gifts of prophecy and premonition."

Proteus was still shaken by the voices he'd heard and what they had shared with him. Knowing the prince knew just as much about him shook him further. "How do you—" he started, but the prince interrupted.

"Do you think my father just lets anyone into his palace?" he asked, turning away again. "The Empire is constantly at war for more land and more power. Spies and traitors abound. He knew who you were the second you set foot in Luciferian. But don't feel flattered. My father does not see people. He only sees tools to serve his own devices, and he will make a tool of you yet."

"I am only a barbarian oracle," Proteus replied. "If my fate is to be a tool for the Emperor, then I am powerless to stop it."

"And what do you see in me, soothsayer?" the prince asked, his words sending a frost through the air. "Do you see a warrior prince with the fate of the world on his shoulders?"

Proteus took a moment to consider the prince's question. He did not need the knowledge the voices had given him to answer. The prince's presence seemed to reach across the room and envelop him like a wave of warm water.

"I see a boy," Proteus finally said, "who will become a man that makes his own destiny."

The prince did not respond but instead turned towards Proteus for the first time. It was like gazing upon the face of a god made flesh. The angles of his cheekbones, nose, and jaw were sharp and perfect. His eyes were the colour of river water at dawn, and his skin was flawless, smooth, and radiant. His wide mouth was crowned by a pair of full lips the colour of nectarine blossoms and twice as soft. Proteus flinched as if he'd been struck, worried about how the prince would react to his scarred and mutilated body, but he said nothing and only came closer with something cupped gently in his hands.

"What's that?" Proteus asked.

The prince opened his hands to reveal a baby bird. The tiny creature was covered in soft, grey down and sat looking up from the prince's palm. Its tiny, pointed beak opened to a wide and hungry mouth as it let out a demanding peep.

"I found it this morning in the palace grounds," said the prince. "It must have fallen from the nest."

"You need to feed it," said Proteus.

"I don't know what baby birds eat," the prince shrugged.

Proteus looked around the room, remembering the spread of food. He walked over to the table, pulled a piece of bread from the loaf, and placed it in a shallow bowl. He then picked up the jug of water and wet the piece of bread. He mashed the wet bread into a sticky paste between his thumb and index finger before bringing it to the bird's beak.

"I need you to gently hold his mouth open," said Proteus. "He won't want it at first, but if we get him to try he will take it."

The prince carefully and slowly forced the bird's mouth open, allowing Proteus to pop some of the bread paste into its mouth. The bird was reluctant at first but then started to willingly hold its mouth open for more.

"You did it!" the prince yelled as a brilliant smile bloomed on his face. "You are amazing!"

Seeing the smile break over the prince's face was like watching a sunrise—an initial thin crack of light followed by a dazzling burst that split the horizon wide open.

Proteus blushed at the compliment. The prince was striking and had a radiant beauty about him that was nothing short of divine. Proteus was an ugly and mutilated thing who was not worthy of being in the demigod's presence, let alone enjoying it. Proteus then smiled for the first time since his arrival in the city. As he smiled the scars on the left side of his face tightened. The reminder of his deformity caused the smile to vanish immediately.

"You were badly hurt." the prince said, looking up from the baby bird.

"I don't remember what happened," said Proteus. Tears welled up in his eyes but he fought back at them. "I can't remember anything."

The bird peeped loudly and impatiently from the prince's palm, and Proteus fed him more of the paste.

"This will be alright for him for now," said Proteus, his attention drawn away from himself and all he did not know about his past. "But we will eventually need to catch worms for him so he can practice hunting for food by himself."

"It would seem that you can remember some things," said the prince. His eyes then wandered over Proteus. His golden eyebrows drew closer together and his lips fell into a curious pout. "I feel like I've met you before."

"I think you would remember a face like mine," said Proteus as he turned away to make more bread paste for the ravenous baby bird.

"Your face isn't familiar," said the prince as his face faded into a deep frown. "But the rest of you is. You *feel* so familiar."

"Something troubles you," said Proteus.

"You just remind me of someone," said the prince, his face and broad shoulders crestfallen. "A boy I met a few weeks ago."

Proteus hesitated, not wanting to pry, but then asked anyway, "Why does that make you sad?"

"He was special to me," said the prince before swallowing down hard. A shadow fell over his face, darkening the blue of his eyes. "I asked for him to be brought to the palace. I also promised him something important. But when I enquired after him, I was told he was killed by a pack of dragon jackals."

A sombre silence fell between the two boys as the prince continued to hold the baby bird while Proteus continued to feed it.

"Do you have a name, barbarian oracle?" the prince asked in a playful tone in an attempt to change the mood of the room. "What shall I call you?"

"I have no name I can recall," Proteus replied. "Father Gemini told me it is Proteus. What of you, warrior prince? What shall I call you?"

"Arlo," the prince replied. "How do you know the bird is male?" he asked after a moment.

"It's a kinglet," said Proteus as he pointed at the top of the bird's head where faint red down could be seen under the olive grey. "You can tell by the ruby feathers coming in at the top of its head. Only the males bear such markings."

A gloom came over Proteus in a trickle then a storm. How could he remember all of that but not a single detail about his life before arriving in the city? He said nothing and instead let out a bitter sigh.

"I don't want a slave," said Arlo bluntly.

"Good," Proteus replied. "I don't want to be one."

"What about a friend?" Arlo asked.

Proteus didn't answer, but the question pulled him from his sadness and he could not help but smile.

"He will need a name," Proteus said as he fed the kinglet more of the bread paste.

"What about Damascus?" Arlo suggested.

"After the hero who built himself a set of wings to rescue his lover Isolde from the monster Caecilian?" Proteus asked.

"The one and the same," replied Arlo, smiling again.

"But it's a sad story," said Proteus. "Damascus was slain by Caecilian."

"The best stories are the sad ones," said Arlo. "They make you feel the most. And don't forget that Damascus did succeed in saving Isolde, even if it cost him his own life. It's romantic."

"Damascus it is then," said Proteus as he stroked the kinglet hatchling gently with his ring finger. "And yes," he continued, looking up into the prince's eyes, "I would like to be your friend."

"Good," said Arlo as his smile widened.

The prince's happiness radiated from him like a fire, and Proteus could not help but warm himself beside it.

10

GILDED CAGES AND WOODEN SWORDS

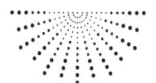

*L*ife in the palace was not what Proteus had expected it to be. For a start, he did not have to stay in the quarters where the rest of the slaves were housed.

"I want you to stay in the sleeping chamber across from mine," Arlo had said. "Then you can be near enough to help me feed Damascus."

Upon Arlo's command, a bed and clothing chest had been brought up to the empty sleeping chamber. It was smaller than Arlo's chamber but housed everything Proteus needed. He was glad to have a quiet space he could retreat to. He was also grateful for the privacy his new chamber provided. He did not enjoy bathing or undressing in front of others for fear of them gawking at the extent and severity of his scars.

Privacy was a luxury, but nights in the palace were difficult. Proteus would fall asleep and into terrible nightmares like pits of tar he could not pull himself from. The world around him would burn and the air would be filled with the screaming of men, women, and children. The faceless shrieks would roar in his ears as flames consumed him. The inferno would tear into his flesh like ravenous wolves tearing him to pieces. When he tried to focus on a single aspect of the nightmares, like the face of a person or his surroundings, his vision would become a mess of smoky smudges and blurs. They were nightmares of destruction, desolation, and a hopelessness like a great endless abyss. An unbearable sorrow would come over him, crushing his heart and causing him to cry out in misery.

When he finally mustered the ability to wrench himself back to consciousness, he would be out of breath, heart racing, covered in a cold sweat, and his eyes stung with tears. In those moments, he would lay awake in the dark, half wanting nothing more than for Arlo to be by his side and comfort him. The other half of him was grateful the prince did not see him in such a state. He would wait patiently for the first signs of dawn before leaving the bed, getting dressed, and making his way across the hallway to Arlo's room where the two would then plan their day together.

Looking after the kinglet was a meek excuse for Arlo to want Proteus closer. He had, after all, shown the prince exactly how to care for the baby bird. Yet Arlo had insisted, and it made Proteus wonder what the real reason was that the prince wanted him nearby.

TOGETHER, Arlo and Proteus nursed the kinglet from strength to strength. A cage for the bird had been brought up to Arlo's chamber but he was never locked inside. The door of the cage was always left open, allowing Damascus to come and go as he pleased.

TOGETHER WAS how Proteus and Arlo found themselves doing most things. As the weeks passed, they would spend their free time venturing into the gardens around the palace to go in search of worms for Damascus or to climb trees.

Late at night, Arlo and Proteus would often sneak into the palace kitchen and pantry. They would then steal honey, bread, olives, and cheese. After smuggling the food back into Arlo's bedchamber, they would enjoy the pilfered feast together, eating and laughing until the early hours of the morning. Arlo could easily have asked a servant to bring food up to his bedroom, but there was no thrill or excitement in that.

A comfort and familiarity had fallen between them. It had been slow at first but then came quickly and all at once.

After cooling themselves with a swim in one of the palace pools, they would lay with their wet backs in the soft grass and tell each other what shapes they could see in the clouds. The prince had been true to his word; he had indeed wanted a friend. Proteus felt lucky to be that friend. When they were not at their leisure, Proteus would accompany Arlo and the rest of the royal family on visits to the various temples across the city.

"Does nothing cease to amaze you?" Arlo chuckled at Proteus.

Proteus pulled his head back inside the palanquin they shared on their way to the temple of Solaris.

"How can you not be amazed?" Proteus responded. "There is so much to look at!"

Arlo smiled at him. His laughter had not been condescending or cruel but something of true joy. "I wish I could see the city through your eyes," he said still smiling, his face as warm and welcoming as the sun itself. "Everything seems to be a wonder to you."

"What do you see when you gaze upon the city?" Proteus asked.

The smile faded from Arlo's face. "I take great comfort," he said, "that from the moment we met my heart has been able to trust you with its truth."

"You can trust me with anything," Proteus said. His face fell into a serious expression that pulled against the boiled flesh of his scars.

"I see a cage," said Arlo, turning his head to gaze out through the sheer vale of fabric that separated the warm interior of the palanquin from the rest of the world. "I see a ball and chain of responsibility and duty I did not ask for that will be clamped around my ankle until the day I die."

"There are worse cages," said Proteus.

"I'd prefer no cage at all over a gilded one," replied Arlo.

Before Proteus could respond, the scuttle carrying the palanquin came to a shuddering halt, and a high-pitched squeal pierced the air.

"Prince Arlo!" the source of the squeal cried, obliterating the comfortable peace Proteus and the prince had become accustomed to creating between themselves.

"Speaking of balls and chains," Arlo muttered, rolling his eyes.

"Do not be so hard on her," Proteus said. "She only wants your affection and attention."

"Two things that should be mine to give freely to whom I choose," Arlo sighed as the tips of his fingers moved over Proteus'.

Excitement ran through Proteus like a thunderbolt in response to Arlo's unexpected and gentle touch, and he had no idea what to do with it. *Could this mean what I think it means?* he thought to himself. Arlo's blue eyes seemed to call out to Proteus with a siren song he could not hear but rather feel. It washed over his body like a light summer breeze breaking an unbearable heat. Proteus, unable to ignore the song, began to drift closer to the prince. Their fingers weaved over one another before Proteus was startled and pulled away.

"Priiiiince Arloooooo!" the high-pitched squeal came again, this time accompanied by a flash of red waves that bounced in and out of sight under the side of the palanquin.

"Not," Arlo continued, jerking his head towards the bobbing fiery waves of hair, "to the undeserving who make constant demands on not just my affection and attention but also my waning patience."

"Prince Arlooooooo!" the cry came again. "*Yoo-hoo*! I see you! Don't pretend I'm not here!"

Of all the things Proteus had to get used to in the palace, princess Angelica had been the most difficult to adapt to. She would visit Luciferian every few weeks from Amun-Ra and be a constant source of annoyance to Arlo from when her airship landed until it took off again. Like a weed, her presence would invade the garden Arlo and Proteus had cultivated for themselves. Angelica would consume every moment of Arlo's spare time on her visits. When she was not showing off the embroidery she'd cobbled together that week, she would jabber on for what felt like hours about idle court gossip. The worst was when she would insist upon singing for Arlo.

"That voice," Arlo complained with a shudder, "could turn a gorgon to stone."

"She is beautiful," said Proteus reassuringly. "Surely that counts for something."

Proteus could not blame the princess for her desperation. He knew first-hand the euphoric effect Arlo had on people. If Arlo treated him with the same disdain he held for Angelica, Proteus' heart would shatter inside his chest like brittle glass.

"Beauty without substance counts for nothing," Arlo replied. "Do you think," he whispered as he peeped outside the palanquin, "if I wait for the right moment to release the staircase, it could crush her?" His finger hovered playfully over the button.

"Only if you are looking to start a civil war within the Empire," Proteus said with raised eyebrows.

Arlo paused for a moment as if seriously weighing up the pros and cons before a mischievous grin played across his face. "It might be worth it," he mused.

"Stop messing about," Proteus laughed. "We are going to be late."

As soon as Arlo's feet met the ground, Angelica descended upon him like a plague of flies.

"I don't understand why we could not ride to the temple together," Angelica whined as she forced Arlo to lock arms with her. She clung to him like the seeds of weeds cling to fabric.

Proteus followed them from behind as they entered the temple, trying desperately to contain his laughter.

"Because, *princess*," Arlo replied as politely as he could but Proteus could hear the strain in his tone, "it would not be appropriate."

Arlo shot Proteus a glance over his shoulder and stuck out his tongue as if he was going to be sick. Proteus had to cup his hand over his mouth and bite into the ball of his palm to stop himself from bursting into laughter.

WHEN ARLO and Proteus were finally alone again, they would unwind from Angelica's visits. Inside the palace, Proteus would listen as Arlo played the lyre, plucking at the strings to produce beautiful melodies. There was a particular song Proteus would wait for every time Arlo played. Something about the notes felt so familiar to Proteus, as if they'd been sleeping somewhere inside him and were beginning to awaken.

"You play that song often," said Proteus. "Is it your favourite?"

"You could say that," said Arlo, setting the lyre down. "I heard it once and haven't been able to get it out of my head since."

"Are there lyrics?" Proteus asked.

"There are but I don't remember them," Arlo laughed. "I am no poet or performer."

Be that as it may, Arlo played the lyre with the skill of an expert. Proteus could sit for hours listening to the prince pluck at the delicate strings with his nimble fingers. The sweet music filled the room with a peaceful warmth Proteus would get lost in.

The only time they were apart was when Arlo attended combat training or lessons in battle strategies and politics from his tutors. With his terracotta soldiers and wooden chariots, Arlo would demonstrate what new battle tactics he'd been taught that week.

"When you bring your soldiers around like this," said Arlo, moving the small clay statues, "and focus most of your efforts on the enemy's left flank, your centre and right will be deliberately weakened until they are ready to join your left flank. This will force what's left of the enemy's army to retreat."

Proteus would hang on to Arlo's every word, genuinely intrigued by the complexities of war. When Arlo became bored with talk, he would toss Proteus a wooden sword and teach him how to spar.

When Proteus' sword clattered to the floor, for what felt

like the millionth time, bright red shame flushed over his face.

"My apologies," he said, picking up the fallen sword. "I am far from the best sparring partner."

"You are getting so much better!" Arlo encouraged as he picked the sparring sword up and handed it back to Proteus. "You are agile enough; your footwork and stance just need to improve."

Breathless, Proteus fell backwards onto Arlo's bed. He closed his eyes as he allowed his body to be absorbed by the soft embrace of pillows and blankets. He allowed the wooden sword to fall from his hand and clatter to the floor once more, this time on purpose.

Arlo followed Proteus' lead and landed next to him on the bed.

"Perhaps you are better suited for wrestling," said Arlo as he rolled over on top of Proteus.

"You are crushing me," wheezed Proteus as the air was slowly squeezed out of his lungs. But he did not struggle against Arlo or try to push the prince off.

Arlo's body was warm and firm against his. Proteus twisted his legs around Arlo's like vines over the trunks of trees and buried his face in the prince's neck. Proteus breathed him in. He smelled of sweat, musk, and orange blossoms. The tip of Arlo's nose tickled Proteus' neck and shoulder as his sweet shallow breaths rolled over him, warming his skin.

They fit together with a natural ease, but there was also an air of excitement. Proteus could feel Arlo's racing heart pound against his own.

Proteus' hands found their way to Arlo's sides before tracing their way up to his shoulders and around his neck. Arlo lowered his head, and Proteus felt the prince's lips begin to drift over the scars of his face and slowly move towards his own lips.

Arlo held his lips so close Proteus could almost feel their petal-soft touch against his own. He wanted to draw Arlo even closer, to feel all of the prince against all of himself. His hands ran down Arlo's muscle-rippled sides and came to rest on his legs just below his buttocks. His fingers slowly caressed their way over the smooth skin and up Arlo's tunic.

"What are we doing?" Proteus whispered; his words were shaky with excitement and longing.

"Only what feels right," Arlo replied before drawing closer.

Proteus' lips tingled as Arlo leaned in. He wanted to taste Arlo on his mouth, to drink everything about him in. But before their lips could touch, Proteus moved his hands and pushed Arlo away.

Arlo immediately jumped up from the bed like a startled cat and Proteus followed.

"I'm so sorry!" said the prince, his face flooding with despair and tears that quickly turned to panic. He threw his hands up and tugged at his hair in frustration, his eyes wide. "Did I hurt you? I'm so sorry if I hurt you or if you didn't want to. I just thought—I didn't know what I was thinking! Oh gods! I am so sorry! Please don't hate me! I would not be able to bear it if you were to hate me!"

Proteus stepped towards Arlo, but Arlo took a step back, still clutching his hair in his hands.

"You didn't hurt me," said Proteus, desperately trying to calm Arlo down while also fighting back tears. "And I did want it, I want it more than you could know. But we can't do this. You are the prince of the Empire. If your father discovered us—if anyone discovered us—you would be banished and I would be stoned to death. It's too dangerous. And what of Angelica? You are betrothed to her!"

"Is my entire life to belong to the Empire? Does anything that I want matter?" Arlo asked, finally lowering his hands, leaving his golden tresses in a tangled mess. "To give my love to you and receive yours in return is all I want. Why can we not be granted just that?"

Arlo fell to his knees and wept, and Proteus knelt beside him and locked him in an embrace.

"You have my love," Proteus whispered as tears fell from his face and landed on Arlo's hair. "If there is anything in this world that is yours and yours alone, it is my love for you."

Proteus held on to Arlo until both their eyes were dry and they could breathe again without choking or shuddering.

"I should go," said Proteus as they rose from the floor together. "If I stay any longer, I will not be able to leave."

"Go where?" Arlo asked, a hint of panic in his voice.

"Just to my sleeping chamber," reassured Proteus, realising that Arlo thought he meant to leave the palace or the city.

"I'm so sorry," Arlo choked.

Proteus hushed Arlo while stroking his cheeks. "No more apologies," he said. "Nothing has to change. Everything can be as it was before."

As the words left his mouth, both he and Arlo knew it was a desperate lie that poorly concealed a dangerous truth that would not be denied.

AFTER THAT NIGHT, an unspoken agreement fell between Arlo and Proteus like a heavy curtain. It was ugly and so thick it seemed to almost block out the sun.

They spent the following weeks doing the things that they had always enjoyed doing together. They spoke and laughed and swam and walked the palace grounds. But there were moments when the curtain drew back and for the briefest time they would allow themselves to enjoy the warmth of a fleeting embrace or a look of subtle longing. When the nights grew late, Proteus would force himself from Arlo's company with a heavy heart. He would go back to his own chamber where his nightmares waited patiently in the shadows to devour him once more.

11
THE SLAVE BOY IN THE SHADOWS

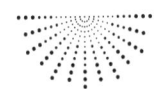

When alone, Proteus spent his time exploring the parts of the palace he'd not yet seen. While he did prefer being outside, the mysteries of the palace also interested him, and he did not like to leave the security of the palace walls without Arlo by his side.

He'd discovered grand banquet halls ready for a massive party at a moment's notice and empty rooms waiting to be used. He'd stumbled upon rooms with pools of heated water, the heavily guarded treasury, the fully stocked armoury, and several libraries with shelves upon shelves of scrolls.

Autumn had finally shattered into winter, but the cold did not stop Arlo's lessons. This left Proteus to wander the palace alone. Icy winds broke into the halls and rooms that were not being warmed by the intricate heating system that ran under the floors of the royal household. Fires and torches were not even lit in these lesser-used areas, leaving them frigid and icy.

Proteus was undeterred by the cold. Arlo had given him several fine tunics of thick wool and a fur cloak to keep the cold at bay. He'd also been presented with boots lined with lambskin. Proteus, who preferred to go barefoot or wear sandals, was reluctant to wear the boots, but eventually the icy weather gave him no choice.

On these explorations, Proteus would sometimes bump into Father Gemini. The man would appear from the shadows like something summoned from the depths of the Underworld. Proteus wondered how someone so large could move so silently.

ONE WINTER DAY, Proteus once again found himself wandering the cold, abandoned palace halls in the hope of finding something new. Father Gemini emerged, this time from the frozen shadows somewhere behind Proteus. He loomed over Proteus in his flowing purple robes and pale, grey skin like a predator stalking its prey. But this time Proteus had heard him coming. He had learned to listen for the way Father Gemini would drag his left heel ever so slightly when he walked and the rasping breath of his slime-coated throat.

"Young Proteus," he said with a wide and false yellow smile, "how goes your time with the prince?"

"Well," said Proteus, being as curt as possible.

"I have been in discussions with the Emperor," he said. The look in his eyes was there again. The starving look that suggested he could eat Proteus whole. "He would like your training with me to begin soon. Nothing too strenuous. I think an hour a week to start and then we shall see how you progress. Under my guidance, you should be able to see the future at will in no time at all."

"How did you know to find me here?" asked Proteus as the freezing breeze weaved through his hair and made his scars contract and sting. "No one comes to this side of the palace."

"I know a great many things, beautiful boy," whispered Gemini, leaning in too closely for Proteus' comfort. The priest stank like a stale, moth-eaten piece of cloth left at the bottom of a chest for too long. The clouds of breath escaping his mouth reeked with the rotting fragments of food stuck between his yellow teeth, "I can show you if you like."

Ribbons of stinking steam rose from a slimy grey tongue that slithered from between Gemini's darkened lips. The tongue came into contact with the skin on Proteus' cheek and licked him. The saliva went to frost as soon as the tongue was done passing over his face.

Images of dead bodies hanging from hooks and being drained of their blood flashed through his mind's eye like blasts of lightning. These were followed by visions of crying children huddled on cold stone floors—naked, afraid, and alone— and visions of dark rituals performed by hooded figures with foul-smelling smoke and the heads of decapitated animals.

Revulsion rippled through Proteus as he backed away from Gemini, wanting more than anything to be rid of him. "I have to go," he said quickly, unable to come up with an excuse and desperate to run.

Proteus turned sharply in the opposite direction and broke into a sprint to get away from the ichor alchemist. Using the sleeve of his tunic, he wiped the freezing spit from his face.

"You can't run forever," Gemini called after him, and the nasal voice echoed through the icy passageway. "The Emperor will have his oracle and you shall be mine!"

Proteus did not pay attention to where his feet were carrying him. He was too focused on forcing the thoughts Gemini's tongue had planted from his head. He fled the frozen, windswept passages for the warmer areas of the palace.

He was forced to stop when he was so out of breath he thought his lungs would give out and his heart would burst from his chest. He leaned with his back against a pillar and his legs gave way. He slid to the floor and buried his head in his arms. When he was able to breathe normally again, he looked up and realised that he was in a portion of the palace he did not recognise.

"You can go anywhere you like," he remembered Arlo telling him, "but stay away from the East Wing. That part of the palace belongs to my stepmother. There are things in the East Wing that could kill you with a single touch. *I* am not even granted permission to be there."

Proteus' eyes widened and his heart began to race all over again. He'd been over most of the palace by now and knew it well enough to know he was definitely in the East Wing … and he was definitely not supposed to be there.

The East Wing was not as well-lit or as well maintained as the rest of the palace. Only a handful of low, burning torches illuminated the hallway. The floor was not as polished as the sparkling marble of the throne room, and a thick layer of dust clung to the few tapestries that hung from the walls. Compared to the rest of the palace, the East Wing felt almost abandoned. Except … the clobbering of his heart in his ears calmed, and he could hear something faint in the distance.

Down the dimly lit hallway, a heated conversation was taking place, but Proteus was too far away to make out what was being said. He looked around from his spot on the floor. No guards were anywhere to be seen. It was unusual to not see at least one guard doing rounds across the hallways of the palace, but perhaps the rules were different for the East Wing.

His curiosity got the better of him and he followed the voices until they became clearer. They were coming from an open door at the very end of the hallway. Out of a habit he could not remember forming, his body automatically fell back into the shadows. His footsteps became feather light and his breathing so silent he could barely hear it.

He was now close enough to hear that the angry voices belonged to the Emperor and the Empress.

"There are rumours," said the voice of Empress Arsinoe, as commanding and regal as ever, "of leviathans being bred in The Scorched-Over Lands in preparation for a holy war. Our spies speak of weapons capable of terrible things!"

"Those barbarians are not in the business of creating life," replied the Emperor. Something in the tone of his voice sent a quiver through Proteus' body. "They are in the business of taking it. Their weapons may be great but ours are greater. We have the ichor and the full might of the Empire on our side. We have warships, ichor plasma cannons, and defences imbued with the magic of the gods themselves! No force in the known world can hold a candle to us!"

"Your lust for power will doom us all," spat the Empress. "Where does it end? When you are ruler of the entire planet? You are not just waging war with barbarians—you are waging war with their gods. How do you think that will end?"

A silence so cold came off the Emperor that Proteus shivered from his hiding place in the shadows. Arsinoe was not as easily intimidated by his ominous silence and instead doubled down.

"That's the thing about power," she continued, the ice in her voice colder than the Emperor's silence, "it is a black pit. Men spend their whole lives fighting for it, but it is never enough. And then once they have power, they waste even more time, resources, and lives trying to hold on to it. You have overreached. Your power is spread too thin. This coming war will leave us vulnerable to an attack from your other enemies. The barbarian hordes are thirsty for the blood of the Empire, and there are those who call themselves your allies who, gods forbid, would see opportunity in your weakness."

"I AM NOT WEAK!" the Emperor exploded.

A sharp slap echoed through the hallway and a nausea rose in Proteus. Something inside him rocked back and forth like a boat caught in a tempest. His muscles tensed and his jaw clenched. He wanted to run but he could not move. His body was terrified, and his mind couldn't understand why.

"Your job," Abydos then whispered so softly he was almost inaudible, "is to brew ebullience for the people of the Empire and to concoct poisons for my enemies. It is not your place to lecture me on my power. And if you want to keep that abomination of yours alive, then you would do well to remember your place!"

"As you command," said the Empress, her words as bitter as ash.

"Our forces will wait for summer," said the Emperor through gritted teeth, "and then we attack. That is the end of it."

A rush of air bellowed out from behind the Emperor as he stormed from the room and past the spot where Proteus was hiding. Proteus' body slowly came unstuck as his muscles relaxed enough for him to move them again.

He waited until he was sure the Emperor was far away before he stood up. His mind roared with questions as he made his way out of the East Wing as quickly and quietly as he possibly could.

A BITTER WINTER storm rolled over the city that night. Bone-chilling sleet fell to the earth in sheets accompanied by crescendos of thunder that rattled the walls of the palace. Gusts of wind howled through the trees outside like hungry wolves.

At the dinner table, Proteus squirmed, uncomfortable in his seat. He was eager to tell Arlo of what he'd overheard in the East Wing earlier that day but had not had an opportunity.

Meals were enough of an uncomfortable affair for Proteus without having to harbour a secret as well. He'd been taking meals with the royal family since the first night of his arrival—upon Arlo's insistence. To have a glorified slave at the dinner table with them was highly unorthodox, but nothing was ever said about it. Proteus could feel the searing glare of the servants and other slaves burning holes into his flesh as they assisted with serving food and pouring drinks.

The Emperor and Empress sat at the table as if nothing had happened between them earlier that day. Proteus tried not to stare, but when the light hit the Empress's cheek at the right angle, he could see where her skin was swollen from where her husband had struck her.

"I'm glad to see that you have found a companion you deem worthy," the Emperor said to Arlo as they'd started to dine. "I don't know what you see in Proteus that all the other boys lacked, but I am pleased your gloom has lifted."

"Yes, father," Arlo replied, not looking up from his plate but giving Proteus a soft kick under the table. They were always eager to finish their meals so they could have more time to themselves to explore the palace grounds, go swimming, or spar with the wooden swords.

The Empress gave Proteus a warm smile from her seat next to the Emperor. "If you would like," she said, "I have a healing ointment that would help soften your scars."

Proteus flushed with embarrassment. Arlo never spoke about his scars and he was not accustomed to them being brought up. "Thank you," he said, averting his eyes, "Your Majesty is too kind."

"I shall have one of my handmaidens bring it to Arlo's chamber," said the Empress before tucking back into her supper.

After the meal, Arlo and Proteus raced through the hallways to see who could make it back to Arlo's chamber first. They would often race one another, but Proteus knew he was no match for the prince's speed. Arlo was so light on his feet he almost flew. Proteus would lag behind out of breath as he watched the bulging muscles of Arlo's legs flex and relax as they propelled him forward.

Proteus was still eager to tell Arlo about what he'd heard earlier that day, but as they reached the door of the chamber, he was struggling to catch his breath.

Arlo swung the door open and collapsed on his bed. Proteus followed, closing the door behind him. He wanted to fall onto the bed beside Arlo but stopped and forced himself not to. Being around Arlo had become a carefully coordinated dance, the two of them constantly looking for each other from either side of the thick curtain. Just when they would find one another, they would pull away again. Proteus had become addicted to the prince, and if he were to let his guard down, even for a moment, the curtain would draw back, never to fall again. It was something they both wanted —Proteus felt it like the pulse of blood through his veins— but as much as they wanted it, they were also terrified.

Arlo then sat up from the bed and held in his hand a single yellow lily. He extended it up by the stem towards Proteus who admired its bright, silky petals.

"Do you like it?" Arlo asked with a wide smile on his face. "I picked it for you."

"It's beautiful," said Proteus, plucking the flower from Arlo's fingers. "Thank you ... but how? It's too cold for flowers to be blossoming this time of year. Where did you find it?"

"Arsinoe keeps a great conservatory in the East Wing of the palace," said Arlo. "She uses it to grow plants all year round with the help of her magic."

"You told me that we are not allowed in the East Wing of the palace," said Proteus, looking up from the lily with raised eyebrows.

"We aren't," said Arlo as his smile danced into his signature mischievous grin.

Talk of the East Wing reminded Proteus of what he needed to tell Arlo. He put the lily down and opened his mouth to speak when a knock came at the door. Proteus went to answer it. On the other side stood a pretty young woman.

She had dark skin that glowed with warmth under a light blue dress that accentuated her long neck. Her bloom of tight dark curls had been done up with ribbons, making her look even taller than she was. Her piercing yellow eyes moved over Proteus' scars with curiosity. In her hands she cradled a small jar.

"The Empress sent me," she said. "I am to apply this ointment to your scars."

Proteus' heart dropped. It was the second time that evening attention had been drawn to his scars. He didn't want a stranger poking and prodding at him while Arlo watched.

Arlo appeared in the doorway behind Proteus, and the young woman bowed her head.

"Good evening, Your Majesty," she said. Her head was

lifted now and she met the prince's gaze with her striking yellow eyes.

Arlo looked at Proteus and then turned back to the girl. "You can leave it with me," he said, taking the jar from her. "I will apply it."

Arlo turned and carried the jar to his desk.

"Please tell the Empress I send my gratitude," said Proteus. "And thank you for bringing the ointment."

The girl nodded. "You are welcome," she said softly before turning to leave.

"At least this smells good," said Arlo from his desk. He'd opened the jar and was sniffing at it. "Some of Arsinoe's medicines can smell and taste vile."

Proteus reached out his hand for the ointment.

"I'll do it for you," Arlo said.

The storm raged on outside, the thunder causing the glass in the window to vibrate. Proteus was unable to fight the urge and walked closer to Arlo.

Arlo dipped his index, middle, and ring fingers inside the jar and scooped out some of the oily green paste it contained. He was right, it did smell good—sweet and earthy.

"You can stop shaking," said Arlo. "I'm not going to hurt you."

"I don't like it when people look at them," said Proteus. "Especially you. At the same time, I feel like it is all people see when they look at me."

"I don't see scars when I look at you," said Arlo as he touched his fingers to Proteus' cheek. His touch was soft and gentle as the ointment sent a cool tingle over the mangled skin. "I see your kindness, your tenderness, and your warmth."

Arlo continued to caress the ointment into the scars on

Proteus' face and neck before undoing the pin that held Proteus' tunic together. Proteus let the tunic fall from his torso while Arlo scooped up more ointment and rubbed it into the scars on Proteus' arm and chest.

Arlo had seen Proteus' body before, but this was different. It was one thing to swim in a pool where he could pretend the water hid his ugliness away but another to be laid bare before another person altogether.

Proteus turned around and let Arlo apply ointment to the scar on his right shoulder blade.

"I know this symbol," said Arlo, "the Akra. It means—"

"I know what it means," interrupted Proteus, turning around and pulling his tunic back up. He didn't want Arlo to stop touching him, but he did want to stop discussing his scars. Hot tears flooded his eyes. He looked up at Arlo. The prince's face held Proteus in soft warmth like a thick blanket. "These scars make me hideous and cursed, and I cannot even remember how I got them."

"You are not hideous or cursed," said Arlo, cupping his hands over Proteus' shoulders. "You are the most beautiful person I have ever met. I don't know where you came from, but wherever it was, you did not belong there. I don't know what kind of people would do this to someone as wonderful as you, but they should hope I never meet them. I promise that I will never let any harm come to you."

Arlo then pulled Proteus forward into a strong embrace. Being so close to Arlo caused Proteus' knees to give way. He found himself wrapping his arms around the prince to stop himself from collapsing. Arlo was tall, broad, and strong. Leaning against him felt so good, Proteus never wanted to let go. The unscarred half of Proteus' face found its way to Arlo's chest as the prince's arms pulled him closer. He breathed the prince in, and the smell of sweat, leather, and orange blossoms filled his nose. He did not want the embrace to end, but then he remembered the East Wing.

"I got lost this afternoon while you were in your lessons," said Proteus, stepping out of Arlo's arms. "And I found myself in the East Wing."

The colour and warmth drained from Arlo's face and was replaced by dread. He leapt forward and grabbed Proteus' wrists. Arlo's grip was firm but did not hurt as he turned Proteus' hands over to inspect his palms. "Were you hurt?" he said with a panic in his voice Proteus had never heard before. "Please tell me you didn't touch anything. Did anything touch you?"

"I didn't enter any of the rooms. But I did stand outside a room where your father and stepmother were arguing. She was warning him not to invade The Scorched-Over Lands in the summer. He didn't want to listen. He struck her."

The dread on Arlo's face gave way to sadness. "I'm sorry you witnessed that." His voice was deep and grave. "I told you when you arrived here that the Emperor does not see people. He only sees tools he can use to help expand his empire. When a tool breaks or stops serving its purpose, he will try to repair it or he will cast it aside and find a replacement. No one is immune to this treatment. Not even me."

A shadow of sorrow cast itself over Arlo's face. Proteus did not think the prince could be more beautiful than he already was, but he was striking even in heartache.

"I'm sorry," said Proteus.

"Don't be," replied Arlo. "We all have our scars. Some on our skin and others deep beneath it."

Proteus stepped closer and took hold of Arlo's hand. It was larger than his and bore calluses from hours of handling swords, shields, and spears, but the skin around the calluses was soft and smooth as the touch of a petal.

"Your father said something that I didn't understand," said Proteus. "He said Arsinoe makes something for him. What is ebullience?"

Arlo let go of Proteus' hand and walked towards the bed. "Some say it's a poison that rots the mind and lays waste to the body. Others say it is the life force that keeps the Empire running."

"I thought the ichor was the life force of the Empire."

"Ichor has many uses. That is exactly what ebullience, or as it is more commonly called, bliss, is made of. Father Gemini, the ichor alchemist, and Arsinoe work together to create bliss from ichor. The bliss they create is then sold to the most wealthy and powerful people in the Empire who then resell it to the less wealthy and less powerful."

"I don't understand. What does it do? Why do people want it?"

"It makes them feel good," said Arlo as he began to unlace his sandals. "It makes them forget about their problems and helps them relax. Some say it makes them feel invincible, and others say it can even bring them visions of the future."

Proteus thought back to the silver vial Gemini constantly lifted to his nose and sniffed from. "Father Gemini ..." he said.

"Is a bliss fanatic," said Arlo, finishing Proteus' thought. "If he were not the most talented ichor alchemist in the Empire aside from Arsinoe, then the Emperor would have had him killed years ago. As a tool, he is still useful no matter how much bliss he inhales, so the Emperor keeps him around. It would also anger the gods. Gemini is also a high priest of Solaris. Killing him would be an affront to the god, and my father would never risk his wrath."

"Thank you," said Proteus, changing the subject as he dimmed the oil lamps and headed for the door, "for helping me with the ointment."

A roar of thunder followed by a booming crackle of lightning tore through the air, causing both Arlo and Proteus to jump.

"I despise these winter thunderstorms," said Arlo, turning to the window. "I struggle to sleep through them."

Proteus wanted to laugh, even make a joke about how the warrior prince was afraid of a little thunderstorm. But when he saw the look of vulnerability with a hint of shame on Arlo's face, the desire for playful fun vanished. Arlo was frightened and Proteus' heart broke at the sight of it.

"Let me stay with you tonight," Proteus whispered, raising his hand to Arlo's cheek and turning his face away from the window.

Arlo moved forward and their bodies pressed together.

"I'd like that," Arlo said, his lips inches away from Proteus'.

Proteus' heart wanted to leap from his throat.

"I can't—" Arlo started but was unable to finish. Tears were welling in his eyes as his lips began to tremble. "I want to be with you so badly it's tearing me apart inside." His grip on Proteus' waist tightened, pulling them closer together.

A spark ignited between them that set the invisible curtain ablaze. As it burned away, their lips drifted closer. In that moment, every worry, every doubt, and every fear Proteus harboured in his heart sank away. All that was left in the world were Arlo, himself, and the ever-shrinking distance between their lips. His heart burst with more desire than it could hold as they leaned into each other.

Arlo's lips were soft and warm and tasted of honey as they trembled over Proteus'. Their hands explored each other's bodies, first above their tunics and then underneath. Arlo's skin and muscles rippled like velvet-covered iron under Proteus' palms.

Later in the darkness, from the warmth of Arlo's bed,

Proteus watched the silhouette of Arlo's chest slowly rise and fall.

"I see you too," Proteus whispered as he ran his fingers through Arlo's hair. "You are more than just a prince or an heir or a tool for your father to use. Your kindness and gentle nature shine brighter than any other part of you."

Arlo said nothing but instead rolled to his side and pulled Proteus closer. "I wish it could be like this forever," Arlo whispered into Proteus' ear. "The two of us together just like this."

"I do too," said Proteus as his eyelids turned to heavy slabs of marble.

The comfort and warmth of Arlo's body next to his set him slowly adrift into a deep sleep. For the first night since his arrival at the palace, the nightmares were kept at bay.

12
DIVINE BLOOD AND MORTAL WATER

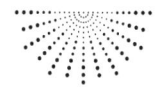

*S*now settled over Luciferian in a thick, glistening white blanket. As the weather grew colder, much to Arlo's delight, Angelica's visits to Luciferian became less frequent.

"She cannot stand the cold," Arlo said with a smile. "The winters in Amun-Ra are much less severe than here."

He and Proteus were cosied up in Arlo's chamber with two giant mugs of hot cocoa they had stolen from the kitchen. It tasted glorious—a perfect combination of sweet and creamy with just a hint of spice. He took a long sip of the hot ambrosia and gulped it down. It warmed him all the way through his bones.

"To the winter," Arlo toasted, raising his cup of hot cocoa to Proteus, "long may it last."

Proteus clinked his mug against Arlo's before taking another sip.

Winter had transformed the city, the palace, and its grounds into a wonderland full of new discoveries and activities for the youths to explore. Each morning, the ground was covered in a fresh blanket of soft, powdery snow. Icicles hung glittering from the withered branches of trees as if placed there by hand. They spent their time outside having snowball fights and sledding in the palace gardens.

When the weather became too cold to bear, they were driven inside the palace. They kept warm by the side of roaring fires and under thick blankets while the cold and ice swirled around outside. On the odd occasion, the Emperor would share war stories or Arsinoe would tell them the great tales of heroes, gods, and monsters. Some of the stories they already knew but did not mind hearing again, and others were completely new to their ears.

Proteus enjoyed the winter months inside the palace. Despite his memory loss, his scars, and the nightmares that haunted him, when he was with Arlo, his body relaxed into a comfort he felt he'd never known before. They did not need the cold to draw them close together, but the ease of the cocoon that formed around them by the fire, the blankets, and each other's warmth was made all the more luxurious by it.

When the time came to get into bed, they would wrap themselves around each other again and again like twisting vines, showering each other with kisses and caresses that steadily grew to more expansive explorations of each other's bodies and the wonders they discovered. Afterwards they would fall asleep in each other's arms. Proteus still suffered from the nightmares, but since he began sharing Arlo's bed, they had become less frequent and far less severe. He was glad to have Arlo close by when he shuddered awake in the dead of night, out of breath and terrified. His hands would reach out and find Arlo, and just touching him would put Proteus at ease.

Arlo put his mug of cocoa down and pulled a bright orange bloom of fragile, sweet-smelling flowers from a hiding spot next to him.

"For you," he said, leaning forward and brushing the flowers gently over Proteus' cheek and lips.

Arlo had made a habit of smuggling flowers from Arsinoe's magical conservatory and leaving them in special places for Proteus to find. The prince was not much of a talker when it came to his own emotions, but he would communicate with Proteus through the flowers.

"Each flower has its own secret meaning," he said, placing the stem of the flower between Proteus' fingers. "Arsinoe taught me about them."

"Who taught her?" Proteus asked, admiring the cluster of delicate orange petals.

"She is a great, great granddaughter of the spring goddess Hermia," explained Arlo. "Arsinoe knows more about plants than any other mortal in the Empire."

"You speak of Arsinoe so often, but I've never heard you speak of your mother."

"Arsinoe *is* my mother. Or at least the closest thing to a mother I've ever known."

"What about the one who birthed you?"

Arlo's voice suddenly became cold and detached. "She is the goddess Nubia."

A shiver ran down Proteus' spine. The first time he and Arlo had met, the voices of prophecy had whispered to him about Arlo's divine lineage and his destiny, but they had not told him which deity had borne him.

"The goddess of chaos and bloodshed," Proteus whispered. Stories of the goddess flashed through his mind. She revelled in the chaos of human suffering and would often be seen dancing over the dead bodies of soldiers in the aftermath of battle. Proteus thought of the depictions of her on the temple walls and in religious scrolls. Bat-like and ferocious, she was a terrifying sight.

"I've never met her," said Arlo, "and I hope I never do. She is a terrible creature. Sometimes I fear that I am just like her, bloodthirsty and without compassion."

"You are nothing like her," said Proteus. "I know you."

Arlo pulled him into a tight embrace that Proteus never wanted to leave.

"So what is the meaning of this flower?" asked Proteus, running the petals up and down Arlo's back and across his shoulders.

"Honeysuckle," Arlo replied, kissing the hollow between Proteus' neck and shoulders. "It symbolises devotion and affection. It is said that if you sleep with it under your pillow, it will bring you pleasant dreams of your true love."

This was so like the prince, to have consideration for Proteus not only in his waking hours but in his sleeping ones as well. Proteus had not told Arlo of the nightmares. He did not wish for their time together to be tarnished by the terrors of war, flames, and bloodshed.

Proteus pushed the nightmares from his mind and raised the honeysuckle to his nose. "Hmmmm," he hummed, taking in the sweet fragrance. "And who do you supposed my true love could be?"

"Well, I suppose ..." said Arlo, leaning back and resting his hands behind his head, "you will have to place the flower under your pillow tonight and see." A playful smile spread over his face like soft, golden butter.

"There *is* that stable boy who has been catching my eye lately," Proteus teased.

"Oh really?" Arlo scoffed, suddenly sitting up with eyebrows raised in mock surprise. "Well that stable boy can pry you from my cold, dead hands!"

Arlo pounced forward on top of Proteus, pinned him down against the mattress, and began to tickle him. His fingers plucked at Proteus' ribs like strings on a lyre. Arlo then brought his lips to Proteus' bare stomach and blew hard. The vibration of the prince's lips and the rough stubble on his cheeks caused Proteus to squirm beneath him.

"Stop! Stop it!" Proteus strained, trying not to shriek with laughter. "We will wake the whole palace!"

"Kiss me and I promise I will," Arlo demanded, looking up from where he'd buried his head in Proteus' torso.

Proteus cupped Arlo's head in his hands and pulled him forward. The kiss was deep as their lips ebbed and flowed over each other like a gentle tide. Proteus could taste the rich creamy sweetness of the hot cocoa that coated Arlo's lips.

"Promise to dream of only me," whispered Arlo as he pulled away, his face hovering just above Proteus'.

"Kiss me and I promise I will," Proteus whispered back.

As THE WEEKS of winter turned to months, Proteus began to learn the flowers and their meanings. Blue salvia left on Proteus' plate before a meal meant that Arlo had been thinking of him. A yellow lily left on his side of the bed meant that Arlo was grateful for him. Edelweiss stood for courage and devotion and chrysanthemum for honesty.

Arlo taught Proteus to play the lyre while Damascus watched them and sang along to the melody from the perch inside his cage. The two also continued to spar with the wooden swords.

"You are getting better," said Arlo as he placed the lyre down on his desk.

"My swordsmanship or skills on the lyre?" Proteus asked.

Arlo's mouth turned into a thoughtful frown for a moment before he said, "Both."

"Still not as good as *you* at either. I'm better with a loom."

Arlo looked puzzled. "You've never mentioned that you are able to weave."

In between the nightmares, Proteus would sometimes dream he was working at a loom. He would watch his hands weave. When he woke from these dreams, his fingers would still be moving.

"I shall have a loom brought up at once," said Arlo. "What colour wool would you like? You can have any you wish."

"Green," Proteus responded. It was Arlo's favourite.

A medium-sized loom was brought up to Arlo's chamber with a basket of green wool. Proteus sat before the loom and allowed his body to lead him. His fingers moved as if they had a memory of their own that they had, by some miracle, retained. Proteus was able to set the loom up within a few minutes. His fingers then began to move in a blur of pink flesh and green wool as he warped the loom and began to weave.

Hours passed while Proteus weaved and Arlo played his lyre. Every so often, the prince would look up with wide eyes as Proteus, row by row, produced a length of expertly woven wool.

"For you," said Proteus, carefully snipping the wool from the loom and tying the ends off. He stood up and hung the emerald scarf over Arlo's neck.

"It's beautiful," said Arlo, holding the scarf up to his cheek and smiling. "And so soft. I can't help but wonder what other surprises you are hiding."

Proteus shrugged.

"I worry about you," said Arlo as he admired the scarf in the mirror and adjusted it. The green wool brought out the colour of his eyes, turning them an even brighter shade of blue. "You talk in your sleep sometimes."

"I have nightmares," said Proteus, thinking to the visions of war and bloodshed. The nightmares made no rhyme or reason to him; there was only blood, fire, violence, and death. "I do not know if they are memories of my past or visions of things to come, but they terrify me all the same. I apologise for troubling you. I can move back to my own room."

"Please don't," said Arlo, suddenly abandoning his reflection and turning to Proteus. "I am not troubled by you; I …" he didn't finish. Instead he turned red and looked at his feet. "I've become accustomed to you," he mumbled. "If you go back, I may not be able to fall asleep."

Proteus took hold of Arlo's hand. "I will stay," he said.

Arlo looked up, his bright blue eyes meeting Proteus'. "Thank you."

THE WINTER PASSED with nights by the fire and days in front of the loom and lyre. Proteus watched as Arlo became restless. He struggled to concentrate and with every passing day battled to sit still for longer than a few minutes at a time.

"Soon it will be warm enough for me to resume outdoor training," said Arlo, leaning out the window. "I'd like you to come watch me. Maybe once it's warm enough we could even go hunting for wild boar or deer."

"I'd like that," said Proteus, looking up from the loom where he'd been working on a new tunic. He stood up and joined Arlo at the window. The chill of winter still danced on the air, but it was definitely warmer. On the ground, patches of snow had begun to melt, and small bell-shaped flowers had sprung from the ground.

By the time the long and cold winter began to properly thaw into spring, Proteus and Arlo were both desperate to spend time outside of the palace.

"I fear the winter may have left me a bit rusty," said Arlo as he and Proteus made their way to the courtyard where Arlo was to resume his combat training.

There was an excitement in his voice, and Proteus was looking forward to seeing what Arlo could do. "I am certain that you will be just fine," he said.

Spring had arrived in full force. Flowers had erupted from every corner of the courtyard which had been set up with training dummies of wood and straw. Swords, shields, and spears had also been laid out for Arlo to use.

Damascus flew around the courtyard above them, filling the air with his song along with the other songbirds that populated the gardens of the palace. Even the Empress had shown up to watch Arlo train and smiled at them from the other end of the courtyard. Proteus gave a bow and the Empress winked at him.

There was no way to predict how the blood of the gods would manifest itself in their half human offspring. There were many stories of men who could pluck trees from the ground like flowers. Others could communicate with the beasts of the forest and have them do their bidding. There were even those, provided a certain parentage, who could control the elements of nature with their minds.

It had always been clear to Proteus that Arlo was more than human. His golden skin was always radiant and perfect. And his eyes, so blue they were almost turquoise, sometimes held an ethereal glimmer behind them that was nothing short of mystical.

Yes, Proteus had always been aware of Arlo's divine heritage in one way or another, but the training grounds were where his godhead truly came to life. There was nothing rusty about him. Proteus looked on in awe as he realised just how much Arlo had been holding back when the two of them sparred with the wooden swords.

Arlo moved with the grace of a dancer and the speed of a

sprinter. As he performed his drills, he struck out with his spear like a viper. There was no hesitation, only action and precision.

Proteus watched, mesmerised by the performance. Arlo made war look like art.

As Arlo continued his drills, switching from spear to sword and back again, something inside Proteus became unsettled.

It was one thing to watch his friend battle invisible enemies with no blood being shed. But if the dummies were real soldiers, they would drop before him like shrub cuttings at a gardener's feet.

How could someone as gentle, kind, and considerate as Arlo be so ... deadly? This was the same boy Proteus had helped hand-rear an abandon kinglet hatchling. The same kind and gentle boy who presented Proteus with flowers and taught him how to play the lyre.

Proteus watched until Arlo had decimated all but one training dummy to dust and splinters and then stopped. He sheathed his sword and walked over to Proteus. The golden skin of his bare torso glistened with sweat and dust in the warm sunlight. He was not even out of breath. As he approached, he plucked a light blue flower with a wide, disc-like bloom from a vine that crept up one of the courtyard columns.

"Morning glory," Arlo said, presenting Proteus with the flower and a smile. "For affection."

Proteus smiled back at him and accepted the flower.

"I should get back to training," said Arlo, turning back to the last dummy standing.

Proteus looked down to admire the morning glory. Part of him wanted to continue watching Arlo train, but another part of him wanted to turn away. His movements started as hypnotic and graceful but in the end were violent and deadly.

Dread crept through Proteus like a shadow. Would Arlo be capable of taking a life, and if so, how would it not leave him changed forever?

He turned his attention away from Arlo's drills and focused instead on a group of bright yellow flowers that bloomed to his left.

"Beautiful, aren't they?" said the voice of the Empress from behind him.

"Indeed, Your Majesty," said Proteus, bowing.

Proteus held a healthy fear and respect for Arsinoe. She was far warmer, kinder, and friendlier than her husband, but underneath, something dark and powerful slithered around like a viper beneath a rose bush. Her beauty was incomparable to any of the other women in the palace or even the city. But even without her good looks, she would still be just as commanding and regal.

"Daffodils," she said. "Beautiful they may be, but also deadly."

"Oh," said Proteus as he backed away slightly from the yellow flowers.

"No need to be afraid," said Arsinoe as she plucked one of the blossoms. "Few are those who understand the secret shadow lives of plants and flowers. Striking and delicate they may be, but in the right hands they can be moulded into the deadliest of poisons."

"Poison is a woman's weapon," said Proteus. "Or so the Emperor says."

Arsinoe looked up at him from the bloom, her eyebrows raised, and whispered, "Poison is a *powerful* weapon. It sheds no blood like clumsy spears and swords. It is clean and subtle, sometimes leaving no trace at all. Riches and wars can be won with it if used correctly."

Proteus was hypnotised by the words of the Empress as she twirled the flower between her fingers, making the petals whirl into a yellow blur. Did he too not have a life in the shadows? he asked himself.

In that moment, Arlo delivered a decimating blow to the dummy with his sword. A crack blistered through the air as the dummy was sent into flying smithereens of splinters and dust. Proteus continued to watch Arlo as he strutted away from the decimated dummies and towards a nearby water fountain to refresh himself.

It was as if the only reason the sun rose that morning was so that it could shine on Arlo. He looked every perfect inch like the hero he was destined to be. He'd grown even taller over the winter. Hidden under thick coats for months, his muscles had grown too. His rippling form bulged and flexed proudly in the spring sunlight. His rose petal skin was dusted with fair, downy hair that thickened around his navel and at the very centre of his chest. The sun set the hair ablaze and turned it from blond to glowing gold.

By comparison, Proteus' body had not changed much at all. When he looked at himself in the mirror, aside from the scars, he saw a scrawny and clumsy creature who would probably kill himself by accident if ever given a real sword instead of a wooden one.

"I wish I had that kind of power," Proteus said to the Empress.

"There are many ways to be powerful," said Arsinoe. "Brute strength is just one. I know ways to kill a thousand men without raising a single blade."

"How? With your poisons?"

"Would you like me to show you?"

"You would teach a slave how to brew poisons he could kill you with?" asked Proteus

Arsinoe let out a laugh that echoed through the courtyard. It was not mocking or boastful but bright as if Proteus had just said something hilarious.

"Sweet boy," said the Empress. "There is no poison known to man or god that can kill me. There are very few to which I am not immune, and to those I am not I know the antidote by heart."

Who is this woman? Proteus wondered. *Where had she come from?*

From the safety of his shadows, Proteus had heard slave, servant, and courtier alike gossip about the Empress. Proteus would listen and weave the whispers together in his mind to form a story about Arsinoe. Before marrying the Emperor, she had been a princess of Aroastria, where mysterious magic was practiced and gods unknown to the Empire were worshipped in offerings of blood and flesh. Behind her back, they would murmur about the Empress being a witch who sacrificed her only child in exchange for her dark powers. The occupants of the palace would hiss to each other of how she was rewarded by the gods but also cursed with infertility for her crime and could not provide the Emperor with any more children.

Proteus could never believe such lies about someone like Arsinoe. She did not act like a witch that murdered children but rather a mother who defended and taught them. Her very presence left Proteus feeling more like a king than a slave. It was no wonder the Emperor had desired her for his wife. Around her, he must feel like a god.

Done with his drills, Arlo fell back from the fountain and on to the fresh spring grass where he spread himself out in the sunshine.

"I also know your heart," Arsinoe continued. "I see it beating within you, and it is not the heart of a slave. It is the heart of a lion that gives of itself as viciously as it defends those it loves." Her amber eyes floated over to where Arlo lay dozing on the grass.

Blood rushed to Proteus' face so quickly he could feel the

blush rise in his cheeks like flames. He dropped his head to the ground, partly not wanting the Empress to witness his embarrassment and partly not wanting her to see how his scars flushed hot pink. "Your words are kind, Your Majesty," he blurted out at his feet.

"My words are true," she said as she brought a finger just under his scar-covered chin and lifted his head to meet her eyes. "There is no companion better suited to him than you. Not in life, in friendship, in battle or ..." she paused for a moment, her bright eyes flickering from Arlo to Proteus and back again, "in love."

Her expression was not one of questioning or judgement, but of understanding. This did not stop Proteus' very soul melting inside of him and landing in a puddle at his feet. He and Arlo had taken every precaution not to show too much affection towards each other when they were not safely behind closed doors. Had someone seen them together? Had someone told the Empress? Did the Emperor also know? His thoughts and the panic they brought with them brewed like a storm inside his mind and body. Waves of anxiety began to stiffen his muscles and churn his stomach.

"Relax, child," Arsinoe said as if she had been reading his mind. "Your secret is safe with me, and I am the only other soul who knows."

"But ... how?" Proteus croaked through his tight and dry throat.

The Empress frowned, closed her eyes, and shrugged. "Nothing concrete. Perhaps it is because I am a mother or perhaps because I am a witch. Perhaps a bit of both. But more importantly, I also know that Arlo needs you. He needed you before you arrived, he needs you now in the present, and he will need you more than either of you can fathom in the future."

Proteus' mind wandered to his dreams of pending war.

They grew ever stronger. There were few nights when he was *not* woken by prophetic nightmares of clattering swords and the screams of dying men. He looked at Arlo, still basking in the sun, the smooth skin of his throat the colour of rose gold aglow. It was stretched out, firm but vulnerable, as if he were daring someone to slit it. Half god he may have been, but he was also half mortal and still very able to die.

"Can you show me how to protect him?" he asked the Empress without looking away from the rise and fall of Arlo's broad, muscular chest.

"I can show you how to dangle a man over the very edge of life and rip him back again in an instant. What you do with that power is up to you. There are even myths of a poison with the power to kill a god."

Proteus clung to the words that fell from the Empress's mouth as if she had cast a spell over him. A desire to be strong, not in the same way as Arlo was strong, but a strength of his own, began to rise within him. He wanted to be able to do more than just weave scarves and steal food from the pantry. He wanted a way to protect himself and Arlo from the nightmares that were starting to feel evermore like a real looming threat and less like mere nocturnal terrors. He thought of the prophecy that surrounded the prince. If Arlo really was to lead a great army into battle, then Proteus wanted to help in whatever way he could. He wanted some of whatever Arsinoe had that made the gossiping servants and courtiers bite their tongues and quiver when the Empress was near.

"I want to learn," declared Proteus, his words decisive, final, and a touch excited.

"Then I shall teach you," Arsinoe replied. "Meet me in the East Wing when Arlo goes for his lessons tomorrow."

13

PUPPETS OF EMPERORS AND PRISONERS OF FATE

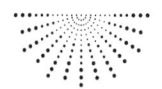

*P*roteus waited patiently at the entrance of the East Wing while fighting the excitement bubbling inside him.

"What do you think is the first thing she will teach me?" he'd asked Arlo the night before as they lay in bed. He had been too excited to sleep.

"Who knows," Arlo yawned in response, "but you won't be able to retain much if you don't get any rest." He pulled Proteus closer to him and held him tight.

"You don't have a problem with it, do you?" Proteus asked.

"On the contrary. My stepmother is one of the most dangerous women in the Empire. It will be good for you to learn a few of her tricks to defend yourself. If that is what you want."

Proteus thought back to Arsinoe's words in the courtyard earlier that day. "It is," he replied.

"Not that you will ever need to," said Arlo, suddenly sitting up in the bed, throwing his legs over Proteus and flexing his biceps. "You have me to protect you."

Arlo looked like one of the statues of the great heroes that decorated the palace gardens—every inch of him carved from flawless marble turned flesh. His muscles glowed in the low lamplight, and the sight of them caused a tingling sensation to spread through Proteus' chest. Arlo was so beautiful it almost hurt to look at him.

Proteus let out a laugh, "Oh, whatever would I do without you," he said before pushing Arlo over with his knee.

Arlo fell with a low moan and crashed into the mattress, clutching his side and pretending to be wounded.

"Oh!" he moaned. "You've killed me! There is no hope for me now! Unless …"

"Unless what?" Proteus laughed, batting Arlo with a pillow.

"You come kiss it better," said Arlo with a cheeky smile.

※

THE NEXT MORNING, Arlo had walked Proteus to the entrance of the East Wing.

"You will do great," Arlo said. "There is no need for you to be nervous."

"I'm not nervous," Proteus shot back in a sharper tone than he meant to.

Instead of getting upset and defensive, Arlo smiled at him. "Then why," he said, "have you been shaking like a leaf since before we left my chamber?"

Proteus sighed, "I'm sorry. You are right; I suppose I am a little nervous."

Proteus found comfort in Arlo's smile, and it seemed to help him shake a little less.

"I'll be thinking of you," Arlo said before producing a flower bursting with pleated petals so yellow Proteus had almost mistaken them for gold. "A marigold for good luck."

"If you steal Arsinoe's conservatory bare, she will have nothing left to teach me with," said Proteus, taking the flower from Arlo.

"I obtained that one honestly," he said with a bow. "It's fresh from the palace gardens."

Arlo then gently leaned forward and planted a single kiss on Proteus' lips. Arlo's lips were warm and soft and left Proteus holding his breath. The tingling he'd experienced the night before returned to his chest. He stood motionless as he watched the prince disappear down the hallway towards his own lessons.

He waited alone in the hallway as the sensation subsided. He brushed the tips of his fingers to his lips. He closed his eyes, trying to hold on to the sensation Arlo had left behind as long as possible.

"Nice and early." The voice of the Empress came from the top of the stone stairway that led to the entrance of the East Wing.

Proteus gazed up at her in awe. She was a divine creature whose beauty and power were worthy of being captured in paintings and stories to last for eons to come. Her wild midnight curls had been fashioned into a style that towered upwards and were held in place by a gold diadem. A silk chiton of brilliant green that reminded Proteus of deep forests dripped off her body. Her umber skin glowed under the luxurious fabric while her gold armbands, fashioned to look like serpents, wound their way down her arms. Everything about the woman seemed to be a gift from nature, as if the Earth Mother herself had created Arsinoe from clay, bark, and leaves.

"It's refreshing to see Arlo has found sources other than my conservatory for his gifts," she said, her honey-coloured eyes looking down at the marigold in Proteus' hand.

Proteus smiled back at her as he secured the flower into the pin on his tunic.

"Follow me," she said, turning away.

Proteus bounded up the stairs to catch up with her.

"You will see a great many things in this part of the palace," said Arsinoe, looking straight ahead. "It would be best if you kept them to yourself, even from Arlo."

"Arlo and I keep no secrets from each other," said Proteus, "but I promise not to tell another soul."

"Very well," said the Empress as she stopped at the end of the hallway in front of two large wooden doors. She flung them open and an explosion of colour and light flooded into the hallway.

Proteus followed her over the threshold and into a gigantic conservatory. What looked like an ancient and ruined part of the palace had been completely overgrown with flora.

Sunlight streamed in through a gaping hole in the ceiling onto a thriving jungle of greenery. Flowers burst forth from every surface, and vines crept up every wall and pillar. Even the floor was covered in thick and luscious beds of brilliant green moss. Thousands upon thousands of flowers bloomed in bright colours and dazzling shapes and sizes, from miniscule to massive. The garden radiated with the life of hummingbirds, bees, and butterflies as they fluttered, buzzed, and flew from flower to flower collecting nectar and depositing pollen. The air was thick and sticky with humidity that clung to Proteus' skin like a veil. He breathed in, and the fresh and earthy smell of living things filled his nostrils.

"It's a paradise," said Proteus as his jaw fell open.

"It's a trap," said Arsinoe. "Everything in this room possesses the power to kill."

She led him down the moss-covered walkway through

the seemingly endless forest of flowers, shrubs, vines, ferns, and towering plants as tall as trees. He followed her until the greenery cleared into a more open space with a cobblestone floor and a large wooden table. The table overflowed with glass instruments and scrolls. Behind the desk was a tall shelf lined with glass and ceramic jars, small iron pots, mortars and pestles, and a host of other strange things Proteus could not identify. To the side, a firepit crackled.

"This," she said, "is the apothecary, and it is where we will do our work."

Proteus looked around the jungle of the conservatory that had been hidden away from the rest of the palace. "How is any of this possible?"

"It is part of the magic of Luciferian." She beckoned Proteus closer as she opened the lid of a large clay jar that rested on her desk. "And with a little help from the gods."

She lifted the lid off the jar and dipped her hand inside. When it came out again, she held a palm full of glittering black earth that looked like the night sky.

"Celestium," said Arsinoe. "The soil of the gods, gifted to the city by my great, great grandmother."

"Hermia," Proteus whispered. "The goddess of spring and flowers."

Arsinoe nodded. "Celestium has the ability to grow plants at a rapid rate, bring plants back from the very brink of death, and keep them thriving no matter the season or how little water they receive. It is soil from Anthurium, the realm of eternal spring."

"So the stories are true?" Proteus knew the tale of the god who fell from heaven even though he could not remember who had told it to him. It was deeper than memory. It was something that lived inside of him, something tucked away and out of reach until he needed it. He looked around the magnificent conservatory, and his nervousness was quickly replaced with an excitement to learn.

Arsinoe taught him everything. The two spent hours together in the conservatory picking flowers or in the apothecary making not just poisons but also medicines and antidotes. She showed him how to dry, mix, and distil. To grind, pluck, and chop. To measure, dose, and store.

Proteus learned that Arsinoe was not just immune to most poisons but that she also knew how to detect them in everything.

"Trust your senses," she said. "They'll tell you all you need to know. You must sharpen them to smell the slightest hint of wine just sweeter than it should be, or the look of a cheese half a shade darker than it normally appears. These are the signs that will warn you of the presence of a poison."

"What about those that give off no smell or colour?" Proteus asked.

"They will give off a feeling," she said. "Something that you will be able to reach out and sense with your mind."

"Can you show me how?" he asked.

"You are touched by the gods," she replied. "It should come naturally to you, but I will show you where to begin."

She picked up a vial of Widow's Breath they had brewed together earlier that week. Proteus already knew that it had no taste or smell. It was also colourless. Unlike the regal purple of Tears of Nightshade or the glowing ember red of Vipercaine, this one was clear as water.

She loosened the cork on the vial and poured the poison into a small bowl.

"Close your eyes," she said, and Proteus obeyed. "Now, reach inside yourself. You will feel a warmth, less than a wave but more than a tingle. Don't forget to breathe or you will pass out."

Proteus wandered the halls of his mind looking for the feeling Arsinoe described. He remembered to breathe but nothing came to him. As he was about to give up, he found it. It was fleeting but he followed it, first walking but then sprinting until he caught up. It was a sensation he was not unfamiliar with. It was the same tingling feeling that would come over him before he would have a premonition or be given information by the whispering voices only he could hear.

"I feel it," he said. His discomfort was outweighed by his curiosity.

"Good," said Arsinoe. "Now hold onto it with your mind and push it outside your body. Inflate it like the bladder of an airship."

Proteus did as he was told, and the tingling sensation became more than just a feeling. It became an extension of his being. He could see with it colours he had never witnessed before and was unable to describe. He could feel the temperature and movement of the air around him far better than he could with his flesh.

"By the gods …" he gasped.

"Do you see the bowl of Widow's Breath?" Arsinoe asked. Her words came fast and excited.

"I do," said Proteus. The bowl was before him, but now instead of clear liquid, he saw a bowl of brilliant green. The poison was glowing as if illuminated from within. "It's beautiful."

"It's deadly," the Empress reminded him. "Now reach out for it with your mind."

Proteus inhaled and the new sense expanded around him like a bubble. The bubble was now as much a part of him as his arms or legs. He expanded it further and used it to reach out and touch the poison. Instead of feeling wet like liquid should, the poison felt grainy and soft, like …

Suddenly the widow's breath whipped out and struck him across the face.

Nausea crashed over him like a wave in a tempest. His breath was knocked from his lungs, his eyes flew open, and he stumbled backwards. Arsinoe moved to catch him but she was too late. He fell to the floor and threw up.

The Empress fell to her knees by his side and reached out for him. He squirmed away from her. She should not have to touch him, especially when he was in a state like that. The knot in his stomach sent a fresh jet of sick from his lips.

"Let me help you," said the Empress. Her normally regal and calm face twisted into a portrait of concern.

"I'm fine," said Proteus as he wiped his mouth with the back of his hand and sat up. Blood rushed to his head and he swallowed against his raging stomach. "I'm so sorry. I'll clean all this up in a moment."

The nausea subsided but was immediately replaced by searing embarrassment. He could not stand up but he could also not bring himself to look at the Empress, so he just stared into his lap.

"I am the one who is sorry," Arsinoe said, placing her palm on his hand. It was cool against his skin. Comforting. "I should have warned you. I expected you to get far on your first attempt but not to go all the way then fall off the other end."

Whatever he had fallen off of, he had landed hard. His stomach was still churning, and he could not focus his thoughts. Like a dropped glass vial, his mind had shattered against the floor when he fell.

"You will recover in a moment," Arsinoe said. "Poison is poison no matter how it is perceived. It can kill the body as well as the mind."

"I won't forget that anytime soon," said Proteus, starting to feel better.

"Don't forget it *ever*," she warned.

Proteus looked up at her. She was still kneeling beside him with her other hand now on his back. The worry had vanished from her face. Now she just looked relieved and warm.

"My, my," said a nasal and unwelcome voice as Gemini entered the apothecary. He was dressed in his signature purple robes that floated around his fat body like eels devouring a whale carcass. "The boy is a very quick study indeed."

"I still have a lot to learn," said Proteus, lifting himself to his feet. Proteus had not seen the priest since the winter afternoon when he had licked Proteus' face. Sometimes, when all was quiet, Proteus could still hear the screams the vile man had planted in his head.

"Indeed," said Gemini, licking his ashen lips before directing his attention to the Empress. "I come at the Emperor's request. He has heard about your little lessons and asked me to fetch the boy. If he has time to learn cheap female parlour tricks from you, then he is ready to learn real magic from me."

"They are not parlour tricks!" Proteus said before Arsinoe raised her hand to stop him.

"If that is what the Emperor wishes," said Arsinoe, "then I am sure Proteus can find the time in his schedule to learn from both of us."

Proteus opened his mouth to protest, but the Empress gave him a sharp look that told him to hold his tongue.

The wind had vanished from Gemini's sails. Proteus wondered if Gemini had wished to be met with more resistance so he could lord the orders of the Emperor over them in some gross display of dominance.

"Very well," Gemini pouted, looking more put out with every passing moment.

"Proteus was with me today," said the Empress, "so I think tomorrow can be his first lesson with you. Then we can alternate days."

"The Emperor wishes to go hunting tomorrow," said Gemini, rolling his eyes. "The prince insists on attending and bringing his little friend with him. We shall begin the day after tomorrow and *then* alternate."

"Will you be joining the hunt?" Arsinoe asked as a cheeky smirk played across her lips.

"I don't partake in the sport," said Gemini, stroking the silver vial around his neck. "Far too barbaric for my tastes."

"Better to let the real men handle it anyway," Arsinoe said as the smirk bloomed into a full smile. "We wouldn't want you to hurt yourself."

Gemini ignored Arsinoe's barb and turned to Proteus. "The day after tomorrow, boy. Meet me in my chambers after breakfast. Do you know where they are?"

"I am sure I will find my way," said Proteus as the nausea made a sudden return, this time unrelated to the Widow's Breath.

Without another word, Gemini turned his back to them and stormed off. Proteus watched as he reached for the silver vial and lowered his head to inhale a nose-full of bliss.

"You need to be careful of that one," Arsinoe cautioned as soon as Gemini was out of earshot. "He is a parasite of a man."

"And yet you so easily send me into his nest," said Proteus.

He found himself angry with the Empress. Over the past weeks she had tricked him into trusting her with her warmth and her kindness. It was all false.

"Have you learnt nothing in your time here?" Arsinoe said. "The only reason you have not been disposed of is because the Emperor finds you useful. Up until now you have been a companion for Arlo, but he needs you for another purpose."

"And what is that?" Proteus asked as his anger gave way to shame at judging Arsinoe so harshly in his mind.

"His oracle. If you truly possess the gift of prophecy then you could prove yourself indispensable to the Empire. You could help him win every war he wages in his quest for ultimate power."

"That isn't how it works. I can't just see things at will; they come and go as they please. Most of the time what I see and hear is just a useless, jumbled mess."

"Gemini will teach you how to control it. His talents for foresight are limited, but his knowledge is extensive."

"And what if I can't do it? Or what if I can and I refuse to help the Emperor?"

"Then you will die." Her words were sharp and drove themselves through Proteus' chest.

"Arlo would never allow—" Proteus said, but she interrupted him.

"Arlo has his own destiny to concern himself with. And you are a fool if you think anyone inside this monstrosity of a building has an ounce of power other than the man who sits on the throne. We are merely puppets in his grand performance."

Proteus was silent. Tears were welling up inside Arsinoe's amber eyes, making them glow.

"The best any of us can do," she continued, "is stay alive as long as we can so that we may still find joy in the things that keep us going."

"And what is it that keeps you going?"

"It used to be hope ... that things would get better and Abydos would one day have had his fill of power or would tire of punishing me. I hoped that he would send me away, but he cannot. He needs me too much. I have not yet outlived my usefulness or paid in full for my mistakes. I was a fool and I will never be free."

Proteus thought on Arsinoe's words as questions flashed through his mind like small explosions. He wondered about what kind of mistakes she had made and how long she had lived under punishment for them. In the end, only one thought made it from his mind and out of his mouth.

"You are the Empress of the Luciferian Empire," said Proteus. "If *you* are not free, then no one is."

"No one is free," said Arsinoe, wiping tears from her eyes and regaining her regal composure. "We are all the prisoners of fate."

14

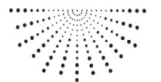

THE HUNT

*P*roteus woke to soft kisses being planted on his face.

"Wake up," Arlo whispered, running his hand over Proteus' hip.

Proteus forced his eyes open slowly. It was still dark outside, the only light in the room coming from a single low-burning lamp. It was quiet, but the air was abuzz with Arlo's excitement. Proteus sat up and rubbed the sleep from his eyes to find the prince fully dressed.

"It's so early," Proteus grumbled, still half asleep as he sat up.

"The first hunt of the season is always the best!" said Arlo, pulling the covers off Proteus' body.

Proteus pulled his legs up and shivered as the fresh, cool air washed over his skin. He rose slowly from the bed and looked around for his tunic. His eyes fell to a chair on the far end of the room near the fireplace. The last smouldering embers of the dying fire set a glow on unfamiliar clothes Arlo had laid out.

"Those are for you," said Arlo with a jovial smile. "You are going to need something a little more protective than just a tunic if we are going hunting. I had them made especially for you."

Proteus walked towards the clothes hung neatly over the chair near the fading warmth of the dying fire. A new tunic the colour of cypress leaves was waiting for him along with a leather breastplate, new sandals, and leather greaves. Proteus took a deep breath and the rich smell of freshly oiled leather filled his nose. A thin stem that bloomed into delicate light purple flowers rested on top of the breastplate.

"Thank you, Arlo," said Proteus as he picked the flower up by the stem and raised the tiny petals to his nose. They smelled of wood, moss, and earth.

"Can't have you getting injured," said Arlo. "The flower is heather for luck and also protection."

Proteus slid the green tunic over his head and the high-quality linen fell softly over his skin.

"Let me help you," said Arlo, picking up the breastplate.

Proteus allowed Arlo's hands to move over him with a quick and firm expertise. Sliding the leather armour on was second nature to the prince. Once the breastplate and greaves were secured, Arlo stepped back.

"How does it feel?" he asked.

"Surprisingly comfortable," said Proteus, tucking the heather into his leather headband. "I think I'm ready to go."

"Not just yet," said Arlo, turning away and opening the chest at the foot of his bed. He turned back and held a dagger tucked into a leather sheath. The silver handle glittered in the lamplight. "This is also for you."

Arlo held the dagger out and Proteus took it. He wrapped his hand around the handle and pulled the blade from its sheath. The metal of the handle had been moulded into braided silver vines. A single blooming lily cast in silver rested just before the handle met the hilt. The blade itself had been polished to shine so bright Proteus could make out the lines and ripples of his scars in the reflection.

"It's beautiful," said Proteus. "All of this is beautiful. Thank you so much."

"You are very welcome," said Arlo as he locked Proteus in a hug.

Proteus buried his face in the space between where Arlo's shoulder ended and his neck began. He turned his head and kissed Arlo's neck. The prince's steady pulse thrummed over his lips.

Arlo tightened his embrace and he drew a long breath in through his nose. "If we don't leave now," he said, "firstly we will be late, and secondly I will not be held accountable for the things that I will do to you. You look good enough to eat in that hunting gear."

Proteus laughed as he pushed Arlo away. Arlo then helped Proteus fasten his new dagger and its sheath onto his belt. The two gathered Arlo's hunting spears and swords and left the safety and warmth of the room for the hunt.

※

ARLO LED them to the courtyard in the palace garden where an airboat would be landing to collect them. The sun had just begun to kiss the horizon and filled the air with a bright blue wash that enveloped everything around them. Proteus followed, eager for what the day may hold. As they reached the courtyard, a head of fiery red hair accompanied by a screeching voice was there to greet them.

"Prince Arlo!" Angelica squealed.

"When did she get here?" Proteus whispered to Arlo as they stopped dead in their tracks.

Angelica bounded towards them with all the energy of a rabbit and twice the stupidity.

"Late last night," Arlo sighed. "Her first visit of the spring. I was so excited about the hunt that I forgot to tell you."

"Please be safe!" Angelica shrieked in her high-pitched voice as she threw her arms over Arlo.

Proteus watched as Arlo's face crumpled into a grimace. Arlo pulled the princess off of him as if he was wrestling an octopus.

"You should wish Proteus a safe hunt too," Arlo said as he gently freed himself from Angelica's clutches.

"What do I care for the safety of a slave?" she said as an ugly scowl clawed its way across her pretty face.

Angelica had only one of two emotions towards Proteus at any given time—animosity or complete indifference. Proteus had become accustomed to her during her visits and tried his best not to provoke her.

"Proteus is not a slave," said Arlo. His voice was deep, reprimanding, and dripping with disdain for the princess. "He is my companion and you will treat him with respect."

Proteus blushed at Arlo's words, but there was a small part of him that took pleasure in Angelica being put in her place.

The scowl vanished from her face as it drained of colour and morphed before their eyes into a pitiful expression. Proteus watched as the hot anger behind her pale eyes boiled into a third new emotion for him—seething hatred.

"My apologies, Your Highness," she squeaked as she bowed her head. "It is my hope that you *both* have a safe and successful hunt."

The princess turned to leave but not before she shot a disgusted look at Proteus that would have killed him if it had been an arrow.

As the princess left, a shadow loomed over the ground,

causing Proteus to look up. Hovering above them was one of the golden airboats Proteus had seen the very first day he'd arrived in Luciferian. Up close, he could see the veins of ichor glitter through the hull of the boat like the roots of a golden tree. The sides of the ship had been decorated with intricate carved mouldings that featured the faces of gods, twisting serpents, and blooming lotus blossoms. The ichor weaved through the carvings, making the eyes of the gods, the scales of the serpents, and the lotus petals come to life with a golden glow. The airboat touched down next to them, and several servants jumped off to assist Arlo and Proteus with their hunting gear.

"Have you ever flown before?" Arlo asked as he extended his hand to Proteus.

Proteus took Arlo's hand and was hoisted on to the boat.

"If I have, I wouldn't remember," Proteus replied as he looked around at the deck. The airboat was large enough to transport them, their hunting gear, and the group of servants comfortably. The white oak wood of the deck and hull had been polished to a shine and hummed with thin tendrils of glittering ichor.

"Well then," said Arlo as he walked towards the helm and took hold of the wheel, "it is my responsibility as the prince and your friend to show you a time that you will never forget."

Arlo began to push buttons and flip switches on the helm and the airboat began to hum with the glow of the ichor. The golden threads spread across the helm and deck in strands of shining gossamer.

"You may want to hold on to something," he said. "I was told by my flying tutor that I am ... what were the words he used again?" Arlo turned to one of the servants with a stone-cold expression on his face.

"I believe, 'reckless to the point of being a threat to the

lives of others as well as your own', Your Highness," the servant replied. "He resigned shortly after your third lesson."

"My piloting skills have improved since then," said Arlo as he gave Proteus a wink and flipped a final switch on the helm.

The airboat shot up into the air before bolting away from the skyline of Luciferian. Proteus barely had time to grab hold of the side of the boat before he was thrown to the deck. Cool air tore through Proteus' hair as the vessel darted across the clear spring sky. Behind them, the city and the palace grew smaller as they headed in the direction of a wide river, the banks of which burst with a dense cover of trees and plants. From the airboat, the river was a great meandering mirror that cut through the land and reflected the bright light blue of the morning sky.

"The river Rhiannon," shouted Arlo over the wind. After a long winter of being cooped up inside the palace, the prince finally looked at peace behind the helm. With the wind in his hair and the sunlight kissing his perfect skin, he was in his element. Proteus couldn't stop himself from smiling at Arlo.

"Beautiful," said Proteus, but he was not talking about the Rhiannon.

A SHORT WHILE LATER, Arlo landed the airboat in a clearing near the bank of the river where the Emperor and the rest of the hunting party were already waiting for them.

While the servants attended to the weapons and equipment, Arlo and Proteus went to greet the Emperor.

"Ready?" Abydos asked Arlo without acknowledging Proteus.

"Yes, father," Arlo replied in a serious tone to match the Emperor's.

"Good. The hunting of lupercalia is a task not to be taken lightly."

Proteus froze on the spot and his eyes widened so far he feared they would shoot out of their sockets. He had spent so much time being excited about the hunt that he forgot to ask what they were hunting.

"Are you sure your companion is prepared?" Abydos asked as he shot a look of disgust without a drop of concern at Proteus. "He looks like he is going to puke."

"Proteus will be fine, father," said Arlo as he slapped Proteus on the back and sent him stumbling.

Proteus was thankful he had not completely lost his balance in front of the Emperor but was embarrassed nonetheless. "Proteus will most certainly *not* be fine," he hissed at Arlo. "I thought we would be hunting wild boar or deer. Not god spawn wolves with teeth of bronze and fur of steel. Did you know even their dung is poisonous, Arlo? Their *dung*. Arsinoe keeps a jar of it in her apothecary, and it has to be a glass jar because lupercalia dung corrodes everything other than glass. And don't even get me started on what their venom can do!"

Plants were not the only poisons Arsinoe had been teaching Proteus about. He'd read at length about packs of lupercalia that called the forests on the northern banks of the Rhiannon River home. Proteus had good reason to be nervous.

"They weren't always monsters, you know," Proteus said. "The goddess Carpathia created them as a gift for her mortal lover. When he was killed out of jealousy by the god Cirrus, Carpathia's grief was so strong it twisted the lupercalia from friendly, obedient, and powerful hunting companions into the abominations they are today."

"I know the story," said Arlo. "It's one of Arsinoe's favourites. We hunt them to keep their numbers down. If not, they attack the villages this side of the river. It helps keep the people safe and helps Arsinoe refill her stockpiles."

"They are dangerous," said Proteus.

"You worry too much," Arlo said as he picked up one of the hunting spears. "We are more than prepared for the beasts." He gave the staff a squeeze and golden lightning crackled over the head of the spear. "They are no match for weapons imbued with ichor."

"A pack of lupercalia were spotted not too far from here yesterday," said Abydos. "Let's move out."

"A pack," Proteus hissed under his breath at Arlo as he took the spear the prince handed to him. "We are going after an entire *pack*? Is this normal? Have you done this before?"

"Well not me personally," said Arlo, "but all the men in the hunting party, including my father, have done it many times."

This fact provided little comfort for Proteus as he and Arlo followed the rest of the hunting party into the dense forest. The dappled light filtered through the fresh spring leaves of the trees as the songs of birds and the buzzing of insects filled the air.

Proteus followed closely behind Arlo and the rest of the party. His muscles were tense with anxiety as his eyes darted from tree to tree and bush to bush at the slightest sign of movement.

Arlo turned his head to look back at Proteus. "Stop worrying," he whispered. "I would never let anything bad happen to you." He smiled and gave Proteus' upper arm a gentle squeeze.

The singing of the birds and the buzzing of the insects died away as an icy chill filled the air. Faint whispers began to hiss in Proteus' ears like escaping steam. There was a rustling of leaves to Arlo's right before a lupercalia burst from the bushes with a roar.

The giant metallic wolf was more terrifying in real life

than Proteus could ever have imagined. He watched as the monster soared through the air and the coarse, grey steel of its fur glinted in the sunlight. Yellow fire burned behind its eyes like an inferno of hunger and rage. Its drooling jaws opened to reveal two rows of bronze razor fangs dripping with venom. Its front claws punctured Arlo's chest before Proteus had time to scream.

The prince fell to the forest floor and was pinned in place by the immense weight of the beast. Arlo was strong, but the lupercalia was stronger, and it had taken advantage of the element of surprise. Abydos and the rest of the men in the hunting party turned just in time to see the lupercalia gnash its fangs into Arlo's neck and rip. With a single twitch of the monster's neck, Arlo's flesh came away with a terrible wet crunch followed by a gush of blood that splattered itself across Proteus' face and chest. Arlo stopped struggling against the beast. Proteus watched in horror as the life and colour drained from the prince's body and he fell limp against the ground.

Proteus let out a scream but no sound came out of his mouth. The world around him spun and blurred in and out of focus.

"Proteus," Arlo hissed. He was shaking him by the shoulders and was still very much alive. "What's the matter? You are so pale."

"Get down!" Proteus screamed before jumping forward in an attempt to tackle Arlo to the ground.

While he did not manage to get Arlo to the ground, he pushed the prince far enough away before the lupercalia sprung from the bushes with a thundering roar. The beast skidded across the forest floor with the sudden stop of its own momentum, sending leaves, plants, and dirt flying through the air. It then turned to the hunting party, raised its sharp steel hackles, and let out a livid roar.

The men of the hunting party immediately attacked the beast. The Emperor threw the first ichor spear, sending it hurling towards the lupercalia. It flew through the air with a hum and crackle of lightning before impaling the creature in the neck. This, however, did not slow it down but only seemed to make it angrier. The lupercalia snarled at the hunting party before charging towards them. The men let loose their spears in a shower of golden firebolts that impaled the creature and sent waves of lightning through its body. It slowed before collapsing to the ground. As the lupercalia gave a final dying shudder, the men of the hunting party simultaneously broke out in a victory cry.

"You saved my life," said Arlo, his blue eyes darting over Proteus in wonder as his mouth broke into a smile. "How did you do that?"

"I–I don't know," Proteus stammered, still in shock. "I just saw what was going to happen before it happened."

Proteus' shaking hands wanted nothing more than to reach out for Arlo, to touch him and make sure that he really was still alive.

"Thank you," said the prince as he lifted his hand to Proteus' shoulder and pulled him into a hug. "I'll thank you properly later," he whispered.

The embrace stopped Proteus from shaking and he wanted to hold on to Arlo just a little longer.

"Father Gemini will be thrilled," said Abydos, his deep voice breaking whatever spell had been cast around Arlo and Proteus as they stepped away from each other.

The Emperor was looking directly at Proteus when he spoke, something he'd never done in the past. His dark eyes fell over Proteus like a shadow ready to consume all in its path. "I will let him know that your gift came in very handy today, young oracle. With some help from the priest, I am sure your talents will prove themselves incredibly useful."

A sudden dread crept through Proteus like strangling vines. A lump formed in his throat and the uncontrollable tremble returned to his body. It was the feeling he'd somehow unintentionally set something terrible in motion that he did not yet fully comprehend.

15

USEFUL MONSTERS

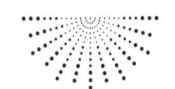

Proteus could smell Gemini from the outside of the door. It was the sweet odour of something rotting poorly masked by strong perfume and incense. He had not even begun his lessons with the priest and he already wanted to puke.

"If you don't want to learn from him, then I shall tell my father you don't have to," Arlo had said after Proteus told him the news of his lessons with Gemini.

"It's not about what I want. Your father wants me as his oracle."

"My father knows Gemini is a pestilence. I wouldn't want him as a teacher either and ..." Arlo stopped himself.

"And what?" Proteus asked.

"I don't like the way he looks at you. Sometimes I think he has mistaken you for a meal."

So he sees it too, Proteus thought to himself before his mind wandered back to Arsinoe's warning. If he did not comply with the Emperor's wishes, then it would not be long before he was disposed of.

"If I want to stay in the palace, I must remain useful to the

Emperor," said Proteus. "If I want to stay by your side, then I must do this."

Arlo sighed and stepped closer to Proteus, taking his hands. "If he touches you again, if he makes you feel the way he made you feel the last time you were alone with him, will you tell me?"

There was a seriousness in Arlo's voice that Proteus did not recognise. He thought back to the training dummies in the courtyard, reduced to splinters by Arlo's sword. The thought sent a quiver through Proteus.

"If he does," said Proteus, his voice shaking, "what will you do?"

"I will kill him with my bare hands." Arlo's words had a finality to them that frightened Proteus, but he did not press the matter any further.

When Proteus woke the following morning, Arlo's side of the bed was empty. In his place there was a single pale blue sweet pea blossom, for spiritual and physical strength. Once dressed, Proteus tucked the flower into his belt and reminded himself once again why he was going through with the lessons.

PROTEUS FORCED himself to knock on the door of Gemini's chamber. The door creaked open and the pale fat man's bald, grey head emerged from the darkness behind it.

"Welcome, young oracle," he said. The priest's tongue reminded Proteus of the slimy worms that writhed in the wet dirt of the palace gardens after a heavy rainfall.

The door opened wider, and Proteus stepped over the threshold hesitantly. The room was dimly lit. The windows and shutters had been closed tight, trapping the tepid and stale, sweet stench inside and fermenting it. Candles and lamps burned low across the chamber while incense smoke hung in the air like a dense fog. Proteus choked on his first breath inside the room while Gemini closed and bolted the door behind them.

Proteus' stomach dropped with the metallic grind of the bolt sliding into place.

"Don't want any disturbances now, do we?" Gemini said, flashing a smile of yellow teeth that made Proteus more nauseated. The sleeves of the priest's robes fell back, exposing his chubby grey arms mottled with dark purple bruises. He quickly adjusted the sleeves back into place.

A violent rattle of chains followed by snarls ripped Proteus' attention to the dark corner of the room. Two creatures that could only be described as monsters fought against heavy chains around their necks. The other end of the chains had been bolted to the wall, the only thing keeping them from bounding forward and attacking.

A flash of light burst over Proteus' vision and he stumbled backwards. A primal knowing rose up from somewhere deep inside his mind. Without a doubt, he knew these wretched creatures even if he had no memory of them whatsoever.

He recognised their twisted forms, blistered and rotting skin, eyeless faces, and flaring nostrils.

"Don't mind my pets," said Gemini. "They are harmless … until they are ordered to act otherwise."

Proteus steadied himself and tried to ignore the snarling creatures in the corner as they gnashed their fangs at him.

"Please have a seat," said Gemini as he gestured towards the other side of the chamber where two chairs waited for them.

As Proteus walked towards the chair, his eyes darted over the chamber. The walls were lined with shelves that held a variety of jars containing dead things suspended in thick, foggy liquid. Clusters of blue crystals were scattered between the jars along with an assortment of instruments that looked like they were meant for tearing things apart and putting them back together again.

Proteus lowered himself into the chair and watched as Gemini's gelatinous form slowly descended into the seat across from him. They were so close Proteus could feel Gemini's sour breath flow over him like a poisonous gas.

"There are many forms of magic," Gemini said, "but vaticination is among the most difficult to master. Those of us who are not as lucky to have been touched by the gods spend our entire lives dedicated to the study and practice of gazing into the future. Precognition, the ability you displayed on the hunt yesterday, is just one of the many ways I can help you master your oracular abilities."

Proteus did not respond to the priest. He did not even want to make eye contact with the horrible man. Everything in the foggy chamber was twisted and ugly as if designed to make anyone inside feel uneasy. Proteus chose instead to focus on his feet.

"The first thing we need to do," Gemini continued, "is unblock your third eye." He reached for the silver vial of bliss around his neck, unscrewed the top, and raised the vial to his nose. He closed his eyes and inhaled deeply. A shiver passed through his body as he screwed the cap of the vial back on. The priest raised his hand and placed his thumb on the centre of Proteus' forehead. His touch was cold and sticky.

At first Proteus felt nothing, but then a steady ripple of warm energy turned into a hot wave of vibration that crashed over his body. His eyes shook in his head, blurring his vision as his breath abandoned his lungs.

He closed his eyes, but instead of seeing nothing, he saw the city of Luciferian. It was on fire. Pillars of smoke rose from every pyramid, obelisk, and building, carrying the smell of smouldering flesh into the air. The towering palm trees and lush gardens of the city had been transformed into blistering infernos. Thick ash rained down from the sky like grey, foul-smelling snow. Rotting corpses covered in blankets of squirming maggots and skittering flies littered the streets. Screams rang through his ears as people fled through the streets away from dark shadows that pursued them. The shadows moved so quickly it was impossible to make out what they were until one stood still.

One of the shadows stopped in front of a terrified man who had fallen to the ground. The creature was little more than a corpse wrapped in filthy bandages and damaged black armour that covered festering wounds. The wounds wriggled with clusters of pus-glistened maggots. The corpse monster pulled a sword from the sheath at its side to reveal a blade that had been forged of a greasy black metal. The creature held the sword aloft before, in one agile swing, cutting the man's head loose from his body.

Proteus' vision shifted, and for a moment the burning obelisks and pyramids of Luciferian melted into blazing fields, orchards, farm houses, and barns. Proteus had no memory of these farmlands, but at the same time his heart ached with familiarity. He knew this place, but he did not know how or why. Trying to remember it was like struggling to play a complicated chord on a lyre that he couldn't get quite right. Proteus felt the overwhelming despair of hundreds of thousands of souls all screaming out at once. The farmlands faded away, and Proteus opened his eyes. He was on his back looking up at the ceiling of Gemini's chamber. His heart was beating like a war drum that pulsed in his aching head. A cold sweat dripped from his head down his neck and soaked his tunic.

Gemini's face came into focus as he loomed over Proteus with a wide yellow grin.

"My, my," said Gemini. "This is going to be much easier than I thought. You are truly gifted!"

He leaned in closer, but Proteus moved away, scrambling out of the chair and to his feet. As soon as he stood up, his head exploded with pain. His limbs felt three times their usual weight, and moving felt like navigating through thick, sticky mud.

"No," he said, stumbling towards the door. "The suffering. The pain. I can't do this. It's too much." He struggled with the bolt on the door before getting it unlatched. As soon as he opened the door, he gulped at the fresh air, free of Gemini's stench. He took a few breaths before his legs gave way from under him and the world melted into darkness.

HIS DREAMS WERE A SCRAMBLED MESS. There was a woman in the distance who sat by a loom weaving a yellow garment. She was beautiful, with dark hair that she wore up with ribbons. She called to him with a warm expression on her face that made him feel welcome and safe. He could not make out the name she was using for him, but he knew with everything inside of him that he was the one she was calling out to.

He walked towards her, but the more he walked, the further away she seemed to get. He broke into a run, desperate just to be by her side and bask in her warmth. The faster he ran, the more she faded into the distance until she'd completely vanished from view. He was left standing alone in a field of wheat. The ripe golden grain shimmered like gemstones in the sunlight as the breeze whisked through the stems.

The heads of wheat began to smoulder and then burst into flame until the entire field was engulfed in an inferno.

He covered his hands to protect his already scarred and mutilated face from the flames, but when he felt no heat, he lowered his arms and opened his eyes.

A tall, dark figure stood hidden by shadows. He wore a grey cape of thick, shiny material with the hood pulled up, covering his face. The figure turned to look at him, and inside the hood burned two gleaming green eyes. The eyes burned so bright they blinded Proteus, and when his vision returned, he was in a garden overrun with flowers and lush grass. At the far end of the garden stood a small cottage near a stream. The air was alive with birdsong and the fragrance of wildflowers. He turned his head to look around and found Arlo by his side. Arlo turned to him and smiled. A feeling of happiness, peace, and warmth accompanied the smile, and Proteus smiled at Arlo in return. A flash of lightning broke overhead, and in the same instant Arlo was transformed. The prince stood before him, mangled and bloody. There were deep cuts in the palms of his hands that oozed a greasy black pus. Dark veins of angry violet had slithered across Arlo's skin, and his once bright blue eyes were glazed over and dead. Proteus let out a muted scream and was pulled out of the dream and back to consciousness.

When he opened his eyes, he found Arlo looking down at him.

"You're awake," Arlo said as the concerned expression on his face gave way to relief. "Finally. It's been almost two days."

Proteus sat up, his heart clobbering in his chest, and looked around. He was in the bed in Arlo's chamber. Arlo didn't look like himself. The golden lustre that normally graced his skin had dimmed, and dark puffy circles framed his brilliant blue but bloodshot eyes. His wheat-coloured hair hung in dull, greasy strands in desperate need of a wash.

Proteus sat up in the bed and noticed that Arsinoe was

also in the room. She stood at the other side of the bed with a relieved smile on her regal face. "Arlo refused to leave your side," she said to Proteus. "How are you feeling?"

His head was swimming and his heart had slowed but was still beating at a rapid pace. The vision of Arlo's dead body had been burned in to his memory like a brand. He took a few deep breaths in an attempt to calm himself down. "Like I've just woken up from a good night's sleep," he lied, not wanting to worry the Empress or Arlo. "What happened to me?"

"Gemini's lesson proved a little overwhelming for you," said the Empress. "But obviously it wasn't anything you couldn't recover from. I've asked the Emperor to tell Gemini not to push you so hard."

"I'm so glad you are alright," said Arlo, taking Proteus' hand and squeezing it.

"Arlo," said Arsinoe, "go find a servant to fetch some fresh water for Proteus. I am sure he is desperate for something to drink."

Arlo nodded sharply at his stepmother before darting away from the bed and out of the room.

"I don't want to have another lesson with Father Gemini," Proteus said, sounding more anxious than he meant to. "I don't like the things I see when I am with him. And he has these monsters in his chamber. They are the most terrifying creatures I have ever seen."

The Empress nodded slowly and made her lips thin before parting them again to speak. "His Sniffers," she said. "They are abominations, mutated by dark magic from bliss addicts on the brink of death. Gemini searches for them in the slums on the border of the city or outside of bliss dens begging for any scraps and cast-offs. When the ebullience takes hold of a person, they lose themselves to it completely. Once they can no longer afford true bliss, they settle for a second- or even third-rate product called gritz. It's brewed by people in the city with little to no experience in ichor alchemy. It's unstable, illegal, and deadly."

"I don't understand why he keeps them," said Proteus. "They are awful."

"Even monsters have their uses," said the Empress. "Bliss is made from ichor, the very blood of the gods. It is the single most powerful magical substance in the world. Because of their bliss addiction in their human lives, the sniffers can detect even the smallest hint of ichor in any living thing."

"So they can smell magic?" Proteus asked.

Arsinoe nodded. "Magic that can be wielded as a weapon by the Emperor. That is why he allows Gemini to create and keep his sniffers. They also make fantastic attack dogs. I would steer clear of them if I were you."

Proteus didn't need to be told to do so. He would be avoiding Gemini and his monsters at all costs.

"I shall speak with the Emperor," she continued. "It would be best if your lessons with Father Gemini are put on hold for now. You aren't ready."

"But my lessons with you can continue, I hope," said Proteus.

"I shall see to it," said Arsinoe.

Proteus and the Empress sat quietly for a moment before Proteus chose to speak again.

"I don't understand it. Why would anyone take bliss if it was so addictive and bad for them?"

"There is much you don't understand," said Arsinoe. "Soothsayers and witches use it to enhance their magical and oracular abilities. Ichor alchemists take it to amplify their magic. For those looking for an escape from reality, it provides a euphoric feeling. It generates massive amounts of income for the Empire that funds the imperial army. Gemini is the most talented ichor alchemist in the Empire, and, therefore, he is incredibly valuable to the Emperor. Bliss is also just one type of ebullience. There is another much more potent variant of ebullience called blitz that Gemini also helps produce. Blitz can take a nearly dead soldier and transform him into a berserker for a short period of time."

"It sounds like ebullience does more harm than good," said Proteus. "How can the Emperor allow all of this?"

"Why does the Emperor do anything?" Arsinoe responded. "To hold onto the power he already has and to grab more of it."

"And you help make ebullience too," said Proteus, sounding more judgemental than he meant to.

A shadow fell over Arsinoe's face, and her expression hardened. In that moment, her amber eyes held a story too long and full of strife for Proteus to ever comprehend. For a brief second, her face crumpled with hurt before smoothing out again as she regained her composure.

Proteus' heart filled with regret and shame for speaking words he had not fully thought through. Since his arrival, the Empress had been nothing but warm and welcoming to him. She had offered him council, comfort, security, and purpose, and he'd just returned all her favours with judgment. Where would he be if it had not been for her?

"I apologise," he said. "I should not speak of things I don't fully understand."

"The world is an imperfect and broken place," Arsinoe said. "We do what we must to survive."

"If my survival means working with Father Gemini, then I am as good as dead," said Proteus. "In the past he made me uncomfortable, but after what happened in his chambers I fear another lesson with him will kill me."

Arsinoe took his hand in hers and looked into his eyes. Her expression was a strange combination of cold seriousness and warm concern. "You are stronger than you know.

The magic of the gods flows through you. You have more power than a mountain of bliss could give Gemini, and you don't need his lessons to access it. Be brave and trust your instincts, the rest will follow."

A lump formed in his throat and tears found their way into his eyes. She was saying all these fantastic things about him, but that is all they were—fantasies. She had called him powerful, but he could not remember feeling anything but powerless. How was he supposed to be brave when he was trapped?

"I am a mutilated slave with no memory of who I am or where I came from," said Proteus.

"If that is who you choose to believe you are," said Arsinoe, letting go of his hand, "then that is all you will ever be. If you cannot find strength within yourself, then choose to draw it from somewhere else or find someone to be strong for."

In that moment, the door opened and Arlo stepped back inside, carrying a jug of water.

"Sorry I took so long," he said, smiling as he poured a goblet for Proteus and handed it to him. "I thought I would fetch the water myself. I wanted it as cool as possible and I added some lemon and honey. It will help you regain your strength."

Arsinoe rose from her seat on the bed and gave Proteus a knowing look before making her way out of Arlo's chamber.

16

A GIVEN HEART

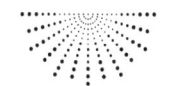

*P*roteus awoke to the feeling of something tickling his face. When he opened his eyes, he saw it was Arlo running the petals of a daisy across his cheeks.

"Do you feel like an adventure?" Arlo asked, beaming and already fully dressed. "I have a surprise for you."

Proteus' eyes darted to the window where the faint blue light of dawn had just begun to creep through. Damascus was still fast asleep on his perch in a puff of expanding and shrinking feathers.

"Gods," Proteus mumbled groggily. "Solaris has not even woken the sun yet."

"It's the best time to sneak out," said Arlo, tossing the daisy aside and pulling the blankets from Proteus' body. "The guards will be rotating their shift soon. Let's go!"

"Sneak out?" asked Proteus as he pulled a fresh tunic over his head and fastened his sandals. "As in out of the palace? By ourselves?"

"I'll explain later," said Arlo, already at the door. "Let's just go!"

Proteus stepped forward and Arlo grabbed his hand,

leading him out the door and down the staircase. When they reached the bottom landing, Arlo pulled Proteus forward, leading him quietly through the halls of the palace.

"Angelica is visiting," Proteus whispered. "She will be expecting to see you today."

"Shhh," Arlo hushed as he checked around a corner for guards. There were none.

It was eerie to see the palace so quiet. There was not a servant in sight, and Arlo had been right about the changing of the guard, as all the usual posts were empty.

The two boys crept quickly through the hallways, Proteus following Arlo's lead. Proteus' stomach was overcome with a fluttering sensation and his heart was racing. He tightened his grip on Arlo's hand, worried that if he let go he would float away. Arlo's hand was warm, and Proteus felt his grip all the way into his whirlwind heart.

"What about your battle training? What about my lesson with Arsinoe?"

"I am sure my teachers and Arsinoe can find something else to occupy their time with," Arlo whispered as he led Proteus deeper and deeper into a part of the palace he'd never been before. "They *do* have other jobs besides teaching us things. Let's give them the day off. Let's give *ourselves* the day off."

Arlo stopped and used his free hand to pull a torch from the hallway wall before turning right and leading Proteus to a worn-out tapestry. Proteus looked around at the dark and unfamiliar part of the palace. It seemed all but abandoned. No torches had been lit, and they had left footprints in the thick layer of dust that coated the floor.

Arlo let go of Proteus' hand and moved the tapestry to reveal an open doorway.

"Watch your step," said Arlo. "The stairs are steep and there is nothing to hold onto."

Arlo stepped through the doorway and Proteus followed. The torchlight illuminated a staircase that plunged down into darkness. The tapestry fell back into place and the shadows swallowed them whole.

Arlo took hold of Proteus' hand once again, and the two slowly made their way down the stone staircase. Arlo held the torch up to guide their way down the stairs.

Proteus' heart was still racing. He could hear it thumping away in the quiet darkness broken only by the crackling of the low-burning torch.

The steps ended at the floor of a large cavern of grey stone. The mouth of the cavern opened up to the sky and let pale blue light pour in, hailing the coming dawn. On the floor of the cavern, a long structure rested, covered by a grey tarp.

Arlo let go of Proteus' hand and handed him the torch.

Proteus watched as Arlo walked forward and flung the tarp off the structure it was hiding. His jaw fell open.

"You stole an imperial airboat," Proteus said.

The airboat glittered in the light of the torch as Proteus inspected it from bow to stern. It was a much smaller but much faster-looking version of the airboat that had collected them for the hunt. It too was made of white oak and featured the same beautiful carved mouldings of gods' faces, serpents, and lotus blossoms. There was just enough space for a pilot in the front and a single passenger at the back.

"Am I not the son of the Emperor and heir to the throne?" asked Arlo, not waiting for an answer. "I don't think it's possible to steal from yourself." He then jumped inside, behind the helm and controls.

"Where are we going to go?" asked Proteus.

"Get in and you'll find out," said Arlo, reaching his hand out for Proteus to take.

Proteus took his hand and Arlo helped him inside the

airboat. He sat down and watched over Arlo's shoulder as he pressed buttons on the helm. With the flip of a switch, the airboat hummed to life. Veins of ichor glittered through the deck and hull of the airboat, illuminating the cavern like a tiny sun. Proteus' stomach lurched as the airboat lifted from the floor of the cavern.

"Hold on," said Arlo over the hum as he took hold of the helm with one hand and pushed a large lever.

The airboat shot forward, launching itself out of the mouth of the cavern and into the dawn. Fresh, cool air whipped around them as the airboat sped away from the palace. Proteus turned back to see the cavern they'd emerged from was on the side of the palace that faced the river Rhiannon. He searched for the mouth of the cavern, but the airboat was already too far away and too high up for him to spot it. It was hidden behind the great green forest that spread across the bank of the river all the way up the side of the palace.

Arlo steered the airboat to follow the Rhiannon downstream and sped up. Proteus watched as the obelisks and pyramids of the glittering city began to shrink out of sight until they were swallowed by the horizon.

Proteus turned his head forward as Arlo lowered the airboat until it skimmed the river, sending a mist flying into the air. It danced over Proteus' skin and formed a rainbow over the airboat.

"Woohoo!" Arlo cheered as the airboat ascended away from the water.

They followed the Rhiannon all the way to where its mouth opened to the Cyprian Sea. Arlo brought the airboat down slowly until it came to rest on the white beach sand. The hum of the engine died down and the shimmering veins of ichor dimmed before going out completely.

Arlo jumped out of the pilot's seat before offering his hand to Proteus and helping him out of the airboat. Proteus looked out at the calm waters of the Cyprian as it glittered in the yellow morning sunlight. The massive expanse of water seemed to go on all the way to the end of the world.

"Looking at it makes me wonder what's on the other side," Proteus said.

"The only thing I am interested in right now is what is on this beach," said Arlo, and he reached into a compartment of the airboat and pulled out a blanket and basket.

"What's all this?" asked Proteus, looking at the basket. It looked heavy, but he could not make its contents out as they were covered by a cloth.

"This," said Arlo as he spread the blanket out on the sand, "is a well-deserved getaway for both of us." He pulled the cloth from the basket to reveal a cornucopia of bread, cakes, jams, honey, cured meats, fruit, water, and wine.

Proteus' eyes widened as Arlo unpacked the feast onto the blanket.

"Does the cook know you pillaged her pantry like this?" Proteus asked.

"Are you going to keep asking me questions you already know the answers to?" asked Arlo as he took as seat on the blanket. "Or are you going to come sit next to me and enjoy yourself?"

"Sometimes," said Proteus, sitting down next to Arlo. "I think you would make a better thief than a prince."

"Two things can be true at the same time," Arlo smiled as he beckoned Proteus to sit with him. The sunlight bounced off his skin, causing it to glow even brighter than normal. Proteus had spent hours studying the lines of the prince's body, but every day he found something new to be in awe of.

"Between all the food you steal from the kitchen," said Proteus, "the flowers you steal from Arsinoe's conservatory, and now an imperial airboat, you are going to land yourself on the top of Luciferian's most wanted list."

"And yet it never seems to be enough," said Arlo as he reached back into the basket. "Because there is one thing that I can't seem to steal no matter how hard I try. Something I want more than anything else."

"And what is that, thief prince?" Proteus asked, smiling at Arlo.

"Your heart," Arlo said as he pulled a bouquet of fresh purple blooms out of the basket and handed them to Proteus.

"You don't need to steal what already belongs to you," said Proteus, his heart racing as he took the bouquet and looked from the petals to Arlo's face and back again. The fluttering feeling in his stomach had made a welcome return.

"What kind of flower is this?" asked Proteus, picking up the bright purple bushel.

"Lilac," said Arlo. His cheeks flushed with red and he lowered his gaze to his feet.

"I don't remember who I am or where I came from," said Proteus, "but when I'm with you, none of it seems to matter. Because when I'm with you, I know exactly who I am and where I belong. You've never given me lilacs before. I don't know what they mean."

Arlo rested his hand on Proteus' thigh and looked into his eyes. Arlo's blue eyes shone brighter than the sea in the morning sunlight. His golden hair sparkled as the light sea breeze passed through it.

"Before you came to the palace," he said, "I don't think I'd ever felt more lost or lonely. I only ever remember feeling as happy as I am with you for one other brief moment. I'd met a boy and he made me feel like everything was going to be alright. I wanted to see if something could have been between us but he was killed before we ever got a chance. I mourned the loss of what could have been, but what you and I have together is better than anything I could ever have imagined. I don't know what the future holds, but I am so grateful to have the present with you. And if you want to try figure out where you came from, I promise to help you. We can do it together."

A flash broke over Proteus' vision and he was pulled away from the beach. Blurred images flashed through his mind's eye. Fields of golden wheat rapidly replaced by two boys talking by a river surrounded by thousands of glowing emberflies. One of the boys was unmistakeably Arlo. The other boy was hidden from Proteus' vision. His face was blurred and concealed by dark shadows. The boys were quickly replaced by a woman, the same one from Proteus' dreams. Once again, she sat by a loom outside a farm house. She called out to Proteus but he could not hear what she was saying. He tried to make out the word her mouth was forming, but before he could catch it a shadow passed over her, and the scars on Proteus' face and shoulder began to burn.

"Proteus," said Arlo, calling him back to the beach.

"What?" asked Proteus, the burning of his scars fading to a tingle.

"I was telling you what lilacs mean," said Arlo, "but you drifted off somewhere else."

"I'm sorry," said Proteus. Not wanting his visions to distract him from Arlo, he pulled his focus away from the shifting images in his mind and instead looked directly at the prince. He looked shy, almost embarrassed.

Arlo leaned in closer to Proteus and took his hand. "Love," he said. "They symbolise love."

Proteus was suddenly once again aware of his racing heart. Arlo's touch caused a giddy warmth to run through his fingers and arm all the way to his clobbering chest. Their faces moved towards each other as if pulled by a force neither of them could control nor wanted to.

Arlo's lips met Proteus' in a touch as soft as the inside of a rose. Excitement rushed through Proteus like a gale as the palms of his hands made their way over Arlo's cheeks. In return, Arlo's hands moved over Proteus' shoulders, holding onto him tightly. Proteus could have stayed lost in this moment for eternity. Everything around them could fall to chaos and none of it would matter as long as his lips stayed gently crushed between Arlo's. They could disappear in each other's embrace and be forgotten by the world. Instead, Proteus broke away and with a heavy heart ended a moment he could have spent the rest of his life lost in.

"We can't keep doing this," he said, out of breath as the kiss had distracted him from filling his lungs.

Arlo turned away looking hurt, but Proteus reached out to him and pulled him back. "I want to," Proteus said as tears welled up in his eyes. "I want to with everything that I am, but we will bring ruin upon ourselves. You are the prince of the Empire—no one would accept us or what we are to each other. An empire without an heir is a sword without a blade. And what about the princess Angelica? She is betrothed to you. And the Emperor? He would surely have me put to death."

Proteus took a breath so that he could carry on speaking, but Arlo used it as an opportunity to dive forward and kiss him again. This time Proteus did not pull away. The tears streaming down his cheeks spread to Arlo's face. Being kissed by Arlo felt like being plunged into cold water on a sweltering day, at first a breath-taking shock and then sweet relief across his entire body. Proteus allowed himself to be pulled in by the riptide of Arlo's kiss before the prince pulled away.

"My only fear was that you did not feel the same way I do about you," said Arlo, wiping away what was left of Proteus' tears from his face. "I would never allow any harm to come to you, you know that. I'd sooner die."

"I just don't see how this would work."

"So look into our future and find out."

"You know I can't see into the future when and how I wish. Even if I could, I don't think I could even trust my visions, for they are so mottled and messy. I can hardly tell the past from the present or the present from the future. I can't trust myself."

"Then trust me instead," said Arlo, taking both of Proteus' hands in his own. "There are others like us. If they could find a way to survive and be together, then so can we."

"And Angelica?" asked Proteus. "She isn't just going to go away, Arlo. Her father is a king and will want to see his daughter married to the future Emperor."

"Angelica and I will never marry. If my father does not see to it, then the Fates will."

"What do you mean the Fates will see to it? What does fate have to do with you and Angelica?"

"The same thing it has to do with all of us," said Arlo before falling silent and turning his head away from Proteus and looking towards the ocean. "I wish we could run away together. It could just be the two of us like this all the time."

"And what would we do if we ran away together?" Proteus asked. "What would our purpose be?"

"What need have we for purpose?" Arlo replied. "Could our purpose not simply be for us to be happy? We won't want for much—all we need is each other. We could make a small home for ourselves somewhere far away from here."

A powerful temptation crept through Proteus at the prince's words as he continued to speak.

"We could grow our own crops and keep our own animals. You could have a garden and plant as many flowers as you can imagine. You could make medicines and we could trade them for anything we need."

"I love you, Arlo," Proteus said. "And I will love you no matter where we are. But we cannot abandon the Empire. It would be an unforgivable act of treason. The Emperor would scour every corner of the world until he found us. I don't even need my oracular abilities to see that future. We would never be able to stop running."

There was also the question of Arlo's destiny. How was he to be a war hero if he was not there to fight in the war?

"I will find a way for us to have everything we want," Arlo said. "By the gods, I swear it. We deserve to be happy."

"I am happy," said Proteus.

"But we are not free," Arlo replied. "How can we be happy if we are not free to do the things we want to do and be who we want to be?"

Proteus thought back to Arsinoe's words. Her voice had started to take up more and more space in his head. *No one is free*, she had said. *We are all prisoners of fate.* For the first time, he got the feeling that Arlo was not telling him everything. What had he meant by saying the Fates would see to him never marrying Angelica? He'd spoken as if he knew something Proteus didn't.

The gentle waves continued to lap at the shore as Arlo stared off into the horizon. The sun was making its way steadily across the clear sky.

"I don't want to waste the day worrying about the future," Proteus said, taking Arlo's hand. "We will find a way together. I don't care what my future looks like as long as you are in it. For now let's enjoy the present."

"It's so hot," said Arlo as he gave Proteus a mischievous smile. "I think we could use a swim."

Before Proteus could protest, Arlo jumped to his feet and scooped him off the blanket. Proteus laughed as Arlo ran towards the ocean. The cool, clear waves lapped at their bodies as Arlo went deeper until they were both in up to their necks. Proteus wrapped his arms around Arlo's broad and muscular frame. Arlo rested his forehead against

Proteus' and their lips found each other. Together they allowed the water to envelop them and wash away any thoughts of what the future would hold. They were as free as they would ever be.

THE EMPEROR WAS unimpressed with Arlo and Proteus' disappearance. Proteus listened from behind a column in the throne room as Abydos scolded Arlo in a cold tone that sent icy chills down Proteus' spine.

Angelica had also not been amused and had cornered Arlo and Proteus on their way out of the throne room.

"I don't understand why you have been avoiding me," Angelica whined at Arlo. "Time and time again I come all the way from Amun-Ra and you treat me as if I do not exist!"

Proteus had stopped but Arlo had kept walking, ignoring the princess.

"Look at me!" Angelica shrieked, as her pale cheeks flushed as crimson as her hair.

Arlo froze with his back to Proteus and the princess before turning around slowly and walking towards them.

"You are right," said Arlo, his voice calm and sincere. "I have been unfair towards you. But the truth is that you are wasting your time here in Luciferian with me. I will never be able to give you what you want."

Angelica's lips fell into a pouty quiver, "B–But we are to be married one day."

Proteus watched on in nervous silence as Arlo's jaw tightened with frustration.

"You and I both know that our betrothal is a farce," Arlo said. "It is merely a way of keeping peace between Luciferian and Amun-Ra. Allow me to show you kindness in my honesty, princess. I feel nothing for you, and despite the fantasies your father has filled your head with, we shall never be married."

Proteus watched Angelica's dainty face crumble as she swallowed back hard at her tears. For the first time, he saw her for what she truly was—a frightened young girl who was doing her best to carry out her father's wishes.

"Then what am I to do?" she asked, regaining some resolve.

"Go home," said Arlo. "And take your pick of the suitors who I am sure are lining up outside your father's palace for even a chance at a betrothal to you."

"You are right," said Angelica. Her voice had grown suddenly cold with hatred as her face hardened into an ugly scowl. "I shall return to Amun-Ra and tell my father that a half-wit prince who buggers his slave boys is not worthy of my hand."

Arlo's eyes widened with rage as his palms clenched into shaking fists. "If that is what you feel you must do," Arlo growled, "then do so. You and your father do not frighten me. Be gone from my sight."

Arlo and Proteus watched the princess storm away in a huff. When the soft pounding of her angry footsteps disappeared, Proteus felt it was safe to speak.

"She will expose us."

"Let her throw her tantrums," said Arlo. "She can prove nothing. Her father needs an alliance with the Emperor more than the Emperor needs one with him. Nothing will come of this."

Proteus was silent and prayed that Arlo was right.

※

ARLO AND PROTEUS continued to slip out of the palace as often as they could in the airboat. On the days they could get away, they would leave at the first signs of dawn and not return until the cover of darkness cloaked them.

As spring slowly turned to summer, they would travel back to the beach and eat honeyed figs under the sweltering sun and cool off in the waves of the Cyprian Sea. They would venture to the foothills of the Titanian mountain range where Proteus would feed apples to the wild horses while Arlo played on his lyre. They would fish and swim in the crystal waters of the Rhiannon. Arlo would teach him the names and meanings of the local flowers that blossomed in abundance as the heat of summer grew more intense.

As they explored the Luciferian countryside, they also explored each other. Proteus' eyes had always known every line, corner, and muscle of Arlo's body. Looking at Arlo was one thing; being in his embrace was an entirely different delight altogether.

Proteus regarded Arlo as they lay under the shade of a weeping willow near the bank of the Rhiannon. He watched Arlo's muscles bulge and flex with the slightest movement under his rose gold skin. Arlo was so beautiful to look at it made Proteus ache—not just with yearning and desire but also a wonder to know what it would be like to be as mesmerising.

While not as tall as Arlo, all the sparring, swimming, and running with the prince had allowed him to put on muscle of his own. He had formed a somewhat athletic build, though Proteus felt he would always be a struggling and gangly weed. The shape of his face had also changed—it appeared longer and his cheekbones were now more prominent. All the time under the summer sun turned his skin a darker shade of olive, making his green eyes appear to glow.

Proteus allowed his fingers to wander over the velvet-made flesh of Arlo's skin and muscles. His skin was soft as cream, but the ropes of muscle underneath were steel. Arlo responded by kissing his way from Proteus' lips down his scarred neck to his chest. The prince's fingers stroked their way up to the pins of Proteus' tunic where they were quickly undone. Arlo pulled the tunic away from Proteus' body and continued plotting a map across Proteus' chest with his lips. When he reached Proteus' nipples, Arlo gently ran his tongue over them, causing Proteus to arch his back in pleasure.

Their hands caressed ceaselessly over each other. Proteus unpinned Arlo's tunic and felt the full warmth of Arlo's body against his. The soft grass tickled Proteus' bare back as Arlo continued to fill his mouth with sweet warmth. It was heaven brought down to earth for them to experience. Proteus ran the tips of his fingers over the mountains and hills that made up Arlo's back. The prince began to rock like a tide on top of him. With each thrust, Proteus' desire burned brighter and hotter, like flames being stoked by the wind.

The heat of the day and their entwined bodies caused them to become slippery against one another.

Proteus buried his lips in Arlo's neck as his hands ventured between the prince's legs where Arlo swelled and throbbed at his touch. Proteus guided Arlo to the epicentre of his yearning where he opened. Arlo stopped moving and brought himself up to look Proteus in the eye.

"Are you sure?" he asked, his expression the picture of concern and his hair stuck to his face with sweat. "We've never ..."

Proteus pulled Arlo closer with his legs, forcing him back into position.

"I have never wanted anything more in my life," Proteus whispered, and his fingernails glided down Arlo's back. His palms came to rest on Arlo's backside where he squeezed hard. Arlo groaned and pushed forward into Proteus.

Proteus let out a cry of pain followed by a pleasure that infused him like having the sun itself shine from within him.

Arlo's mouth fell open and his eyes closed as he began to thrust again. He was tender at first but steadily became more rapid, entering deeper each time.

Their bodies fit into each other as if they had been made for one another by the hands of a skilled craftsman.

Sweet pleasure rippled through them in waves that suddenly turned into a flood of euphoria as a sharp gasp escaped from Proteus' mouth. He ran his fingers through Arlo's hair as the building sensation of rhapsody pulled their bodies even closer together. Arlo began to ram into Proteus with such rapid force that Proteus thought he would be ripped apart with ecstasy.

They shuddered; Arlo cried out and Proteus felt the prince's rapture. The shuddering slowed to a tremble as Arlo's body relaxed. He fell next to Proteus, held him close, and kissed him.

Breathless and satisfied, they lay on the soft grassy banks of the river. Proteus traced lines with his fingers over Arlo's arms and chest.

Arlo let out a deep, sleepy sigh and smiled his brilliant smile, "I don't know why we didn't try that sooner."

Proteus gave no reply and instead just returned the smile.

He had learned the prince anew not only by sight but also by touch, smell, and taste. Arlo would hold Proteus close and shower him with soft kisses like summer rain, starting at his neck flowing all the way down his chest and abdomen. Proteus would breathe Arlo in, filling his lungs with the prince's sweet scent of almonds, salt, and rain.

They would lay by the river and Proteus would watch Arlo as he closed his eyes, cocked his head back, and turned his face towards the sun. Fine golden stubble on his high cheekbones and strong chin would catch the sunlight and bask in it.

When they returned to the palace from their adventures,

after making sure the airboat was well hidden, they would collapse into each other on the bed in Arlo's chamber and fall asleep, exhausted by the day, in each other's arms.

Nothing had been said to Proteus about continuing his lessons with Father Gemini, and he was grateful for it. His stomach churned at the thought of the musty chamber and the sniffer monsters. Proteus assumed that the Empress had done as she had promised him and somehow convinced the Emperor to put the lessons with Gemini on hold. For how long, he had no idea.

TOGETHER, Proteus and Arlo watched the dark green leaves of the trees slowly begin to change to yellow as autumn crept in.

Proteus laid under the shade of their favourite oak tree with his eyes closed while Arlo gently ran his index finger down Proteus' forehead, the bridge of his nose, and over his lips.

Proteus smiled. "That tickles," he said without opening his eyes.

"I am always at my happiest when I'm with you," Arlo whispered into Proteus' ear as he pulled him close. "I wish it could be like this forever."

Proteus did not reply. An ancient voice from somewhere deep inside of him began to whisper. His heart dropped as the voice hissed, *Nothing lasts forever. Something is coming that will change everything.*

17
THE BLIGHT

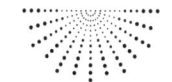

Throughout the summer months and into autumn, much to his delight, Proteus' lessons in botany and poisons with Arsinoe continued. Outside her magical conservatory, the world had given way to explosions of yellow, amber, and orange as autumn tightened its grip on the plant life. The air grew colder, and a frigid wind from the Titanian mountains began to whip through the city and its surroundings. The wind plucked the dead leaves from the trees, exposing the twisted and gnarled branches underneath.

Thanks to the celestium and other magic performed by Arsinoe, the inside of the conservatory was in a state of eternal spring. Flowers blossomed everywhere, and the ferns, monstera, creepers, and trees grew lush and thick in a thousand different shades of green all the way up to the glass ceiling.

She taught him that black hellebore root soaked in water would create a poison that could kill a man in hours. "If enough of the root is collected," she said, "it can be used to poison wells, making it a powerful tool for warfare."

Giant hogweed was handled with gloves as coming into

direct contact with its juices would cause agonising blisters, burns, and even blindness. "It strips skin of its ability to protect itself from sunlight," she said. "It's not enough to kill but good enough if you want to send a strong message to your target. It can also be combined with other ingredients to make something much more deadly."

To cause a death that required a time delay, Proteus learnt that death cap mushrooms were an excellent tool. Just one cap would be enough to kill a man. Symptoms would only start to show up a full day after ingestion, at which point the victim would be beyond help.

"Death cap mushrooms," said Arsinoe, "are perfect for political assassinations. One could slip it into the target's food at a banquet or a feast and they would only perish much later, eliminating any suspected foul play on the host's part."

Proteus absorbed as much information as possible, listening to the Empress for hours on end and assisting her inside the conservatory.

"You need to know how to use every part of the plant," she said. "Everything is useful and nothing should go to waste. While some parts of a plant are deadly and good for making poisons, other parts can be used to make medicine. Being able to harm is a powerful weapon, but knowing how to heal is just as important."

She taught him how to create everything from healing salves to perfumes, poisons, sweet oils, and even a few edible treats. As time passed, Proteus found that working with the plants and herbs calmed his mind and somehow grounded him. His thoughts became clearer with every passing day, and what was once a tempest of chaotic emotions slowly calmed to a flat and serene ocean. It was as if all the turmoil that had been stirring inside his head and heart had been poured into his work with Arsinoe and the time he spent with Arlo. With this new found sense of calm, his more mystical abilities grew stronger.

When he closed his eyes, he could sense the poisons around him, each with their own unique colour, smell, and texture. Belladonna was a deep, glowing purple, as smooth as a river rock, and smelled of burning sugar. Dog's Mercury was a sick, dull green and prickly. To the ordinary sense, it gave off the foul stench of rot, but when Proteus focused with his extra senses, it gave off the smell of cinnamon.

His visions of the future had also slowly begun to clear. They were no longer the tangled, frightening mess they once were, but brief, accurate, and simple. He would know if someone was coming to the conservatory moments before they arrived. Once he even stopped Arsinoe from knocking over a vial of acid they had distilled together from cherry laurel. Had he not caught it in time, the gas produced by the acid would have killed them both.

Arsinoe's face was calm and collected as she looked at the vial clutched tightly in Proteus' hand.

"That was a close one," she said with a raised eyebrow. "For a moment I didn't think you would catch it."

Proteus' jaw fell open as he carefully placed the vial back in its place on the shelf before turning to Arsinoe. "You did that on purpose?!" he shouted, gobsmacked that Arsinoe could be so reckless. "What if I had not foreseen it? You could have killed us both! Are you mad?"

"Yes," she said plainly as a wide smile played across her face, "but I am also incredibly impressed and proud."

Proteus took a deep breath, trying to calm his racing heart before giving the Empress a quick smile.

When he was not learning how to pull poison from petals or practicing calling on a prophecy, Proteus was with Arlo. As the days grew shorter, the nights longer, and the weather increasingly more unfavourable, the two ventured out in the airboat less and less.

Instead, they spent their time together inside the palace and its grounds. Nights were spent by the fireside with Arlo at his lyre and Proteus at his loom. Proteus' hands danced over the wool and shuttle while Arlo's twirled over the lyre strings, and the world around them seemed to grow smaller. Arlo's hands would often abandon his lyre and make their way to Proteus' shoulders to massage him. Proteus would moan at the sensation of having the tightness in his muscles kneaded at like bread dough. Next would come the kisses on his shoulders, neck, and mouth while Arlo's hands slipped down the front of Proteus' tunic. The two would become tangled in the blankets and sheets of their bed as they found each other again and again in passion.

Proteus was unbothered by the stillness of the coming winter; in fact, he was looking forward to it. It meant more time with Arlo as he could not train. Arlo on the other hand was becoming more and more restless as the days passed.

"It doesn't look too windy today," Arlo said one morning as he looked outside the window, having taken a break from his frustrated pacing across the chamber. "Perhaps we should go out."

Proteus looked up from his loom. He'd been working on a new tunic for Arlo and was experimenting with a more complicated pattern than he was used to. "A walk through the grounds might be refreshing," he said.

"I want to go further than the grounds," said Arlo, his eyes still staring out the window. "Let's go into the city."

Proteus' eyes widened as he stood up from the loom and

walked towards Arlo. "But we've never been into the city alone."

There had been the few occasions over the summer where a holiday feast had been held in the city or a ceremony at temples honouring the gods. The royal family had attended and Proteus had tagged along, but the events were few and far between. Arlo and Proteus had never been left to their own devices to explore Luciferian.

"All the more reason to go!" said Arlo, more animated than Proteus had seen him in weeks. His blue eyes glimmered with excitement and his lips parted into a beaming white smile. "It will be an adventure! We could go to the market and perhaps even see a performance by a traveling theatre group!"

"And how will we get into the city undetected?" asked Proteus. "If the Emperor catches us, he will give birth to a hydra."

"The same way we always do," said Arlo. "It's too late for today, but if we leave early enough tomorrow morning, we can take the airboat out to the city and leave it on one of the rooftop gardens until we are ready to return."

Proteus' stomach began to churn and clench with anxiety.

He looked into Arlo's eyes as they darted over his face for a sign of approval. His features were alive with desperate excitement. There was nothing for Arlo to do in the palace. Proteus at least still had his lessons with Arsinoe to keep him occupied during the day, but Arlo was not as lucky. The prince had only old tutors and dusty scrolls for company when he and Proteus were apart from each other. Proteus also knew how much Arlo hated being stuck indoors for long periods of time.

"Please," begged Arlo, taking Proteus' hands. "I don't want to do it without you."

Proteus' anxiety was overcome by his love for Arlo. He

released the breath he had been holding and sighed, "Alright, let's do it."

Just before the first signs of dawn broke over the horizon, Arlo and Proteus made their way through the palace to the secret cavern where the airboat was hidden. They had taken care to dress in the warmest of their clothes. Arlo wore the green scarf Proteus had made for him the previous winter wrapped tightly around his neck. They had dressed warmly but as plainly as possible with the idea to blend into the crowd of market goers and merchants. The last thing they wanted was for Arlo to be recognised and either mauled by admirers or, worse, for word to be sent to the palace and guards dispatched to drag them back. They would also have to be careful to avoid the imperial guards posted at different points across the market as keepers of the peace and enforcers of the law.

"Are you sure the wind won't be too strong today?" Proteus asked as Arlo helped him into the airboat.

"I checked the wind before we left our room," said Arlo, his breath turning to cloud as soon as it left his lips. "We should be fine."

Proteus watched, as he did every time they snuck away, while Arlo flipped the toggles and pressed the buttons on the control panel of the airboat. The familiar hum and glittering ichor vibrated through the airboat as it rose from the ground. Proteus' body had come to associate these sounds and sensations with the excitement his and Arlo's adventures brought him. The exhilarating beating of his heart sent a euphoric feeling through his entire body.

The airboat shot out of the opening of the cavern and was immediately battered by the icy wind. The vessel shook with a violent turbulence Proteus was not accustomed to. He watched as Arlo struggled with the helm. The frigid wind whipped around them and roared in their ears. Proteus threw his hands over his ears to stop them from freezing and immediately regretted not bringing a pair of gloves. The airboat continued to rattle and shake underneath them as they approached the city. As they descended, the shaking began to subside until it eventually stopped. Proteus looked down to see the gardens of the city rooftops had withered and shrunk back, leaving the roofs dead and eerily bare.

"At least we won't have a problem finding somewhere to land," Arlo said, not taking his eyes away from the direction they were flying in.

A few moments later, Arlo was lowering the airboat onto the roof of a building just far enough away from the market square that they would go unnoticed.

"That was a little bumpier than I thought it was going to be," said Arlo as he climbed out of the airboat.

"I thought you handled it well," replied Proteus, allowing Arlo to help him to the ground.

Dawn had just started to break, and the air was much warmer on the ground than it had been in the sky. They made their way down the side of the building using the stone steps that led directly from the rooftop all the way down to the street.

"What would you like to do first?" asked Arlo, looking around with an excitement in his eyes that Proteus loved so much to see.

"Shall we try the market?" Proteus suggested.

Arlo took hold of Proteus' hand and led the way through the winding cobblestone streets of the city. They took so many turns that Proteus eventually lost count. From the ground, the city looked like a maze, and Proteus worried they may not be able to find their way back to the airboat.

Before he could become too anxious over getting lost, the buildings gave way to a main road, on the other side of which stood the market square. Proteus recognised the market from when he'd first arrived in the city. It was much quieter than the first time he'd seen it, but the day had not yet started and there were signs of activity starting to warm up.

Merchants had started to slowly set up their stalls for the day. All down the square, the merchants scuttled around unpacking crates, jars, and amphora, setting up wooden tables and chairs, rolling out fabrics, and laying out their wares.

As Arlo and Proteus stepped forward, a sweet, warm, and welcoming smell filled the air. Proteus' stomach gave a demanding rumble in response to the beautiful scent.

"Do you smell that?" Arlo asked.

"It's coming from the bakery," said Proteus, pointing towards a shopfront at the edge of the market square. Bright orange light spilled from the open door and windows where the intoxicating smell of freshly baked goods called out to them like a siren's song.

Arlo immediately pulled Proteus forward. When they reached the front of the bakery, they looked through the window with salivating mouths at the treasures held inside. Cakes, pies, bread, and pastries fresh out of the oven festooned the countertops inside under the warm glow coming from the oven. They made their way inside the paradise of pastry with roaring stomachs as the heavenly smell emanating from the baked goods grew even stronger.

"What shall we have?" asked Arlo, looking around at the plethora of delicious options laid out before them.

Flaky and crisp phyllo pastry cones glistening with honey, stuffed with custard and cream, and topped with ground walnuts beckoned them closer. Honey cakes drenched in syrup and dusted with crushed pistachio made their eyes widen and their mouths water. They watched the cinnamon- and lemon-scented steam rise from the golden and creamy custard parcels. They took in deep breaths of the air thick with the scent of cloves, cinnamon, nutmeg, roasted almonds, rosewater, melting butter, and honey.

"It's so hard to choose," Proteus replied. "I want one of everything!"

As tempting as the idea of ordering one of everything was, they eventually settled on the honey cakes, each the size of Arlo's fist, and a bag of almond butter biscuits to share. The cake melted in his mouth and tasted so good that for a moment Proteus thought it was not just feeding his body but his very soul. The sweetness and cloud-soft texture of the honey cakes left Proteus awash with feelings or warmth, love, and fondness. The feelings were bright as sunlight, but he found no memories for the light to shine upon. Swallowing the last bite, Proteus knew without a doubt that someone had loved him once. This person had loved him enough to bake honey cakes for him, and eating them made him feel like he was home.

BY THE TIME they left the bakery, the market square had started to properly spring to life. The stalls that had been set up earlier had customers. Undeterred by the chilly autumn air, people in the market were wrapped up in warm wools and furs as they haggled with the merchants, going back and forth in a buzz of amounts, weights, and prices.

The market was a cornucopia of more than Proteus could ever have imagined. Fruits, vegetables, cheeses, eggs, trinkets, jewellery, pottery, fabrics, herbs, and spices stretched out as far as the eye could see. Just as Proteus found one thing he wanted to investigate, another object of colourful fascination caught his eye.

They lost themselves to the hustle and bustle of the market.

Street performers had shown up in droves. They watched as jugglers, acrobats, and flame dancers performed impressive physical feats. A puppet show featuring caricatures of the Emperor and his army told stories and made jokes that had Proteus and Arlo clutching their sides with laughter.

"They do my father's voice perfectly!" howled Arlo as he wiped tears of laughter from his eyes.

They spent the day exploring the market and enjoying all the wonders it had to offer. They took care not to draw too much attention to themselves out of fear of Arlo being recognised. As an extra precaution, when the time came to pay for something or to order drinks and food, Proteus took the lead. He kept the hood of his cape pulled up high to hide his facial scars. He'd become accustomed to people staring at them, especially at times when he ventured out of the palace with the royal family, but he didn't want the scars to give him away to anyone who may have recognised them.

As the day passed, the market grew busier and the air grew warmer until the sun began to set. The crowds of people dwindled and the merchants began to pack up. As it got darker, a cold chill settled into the air.

"Shall we head back?" asked Arlo as he finished a cup of a warm drink made from cocoa nibs, chilli peppers, and milk —a new luxury from the deep, dark jungles of Hadrian, or so the merchant who'd sold them the drink had claimed.

"I think now would be a good time," Proteus replied before following Arlo away from the fast-emptying market square and back to the main road.

Everything looked different to Proteus in the dark. The streets and buildings had undergone some kind of transformation in the moonlight that made them unrecognisable. They made their way at a steady pace through the tangled maze of streets and walls. Music that was at first muffled in the distance grew louder as they got closer to the rooftop where they'd left the airboat.

The building they had landed the airboat on top of was the source of the music. When they had been there that morning, the building had been still. Now it pulsed with life and sounds of people having a good time to the rhythmic beat of drums, the strum of lyres, and the sharp whistle of an aulos and pan pipes. The music vibrated through the cobblestones all the way up through the soles of Proteus' feet.

"Is it some kind of bath house?" Proteus asked, looking at the building with a curiosity about what was going on inside.

"It's a bliss den," said Arlo. "Let's go. Nothing good ever happens outside a bliss—"

Arlo was cut off by a low moan that came from the shadows at the bottom of the building. A thin, grey arm covered in dark purple, bruise-like sores emerged from the shadows and was followed by an emaciated, hunched-over body of a man. The rest of his skin was also grey and dappled with more of the dark sores Proteus had recognised immediately. They were the same sores that covered Father Gemini's forearms. The sores he tried to keep so carefully hidden under the flowing fabric of his long-sleeved robes.

The man's cheeks were caved in like cakes that had not quite risen fully in the oven. His greying beard was greasy, as was his wild bush of hair that had not seen a comb in much too long. He was dressed in a grubby tunic that may have, at one point, been white or cream, but it was now so stained and filthy that it had turned an ugly grey.

The man stumbled forward with his arms outstretched and opened his mouth to let out another low moan. Proteus counted three rotting teeth in his mouth—the rest had all abandoned the man's swollen and bleeding gums. Moving with the instinct and speed of a lion, Arlo was in front of Proteus in the blink of an eye, putting himself between Proteus and the strange man.

Proteus could then smell him. The miasma coming off the man's skin, clothing, hair, and breath was an assault. He reeked of milk long gone sour and meat left in the sun to rot. The whites of his sunken eyes had turned a sick yellow. He opened his mouth again to let out another moan, but before anything could escape his lips, he collapsed in a pile of stinking paper-thin skin, soiled fabric, and sharp bones.

"We have to help him," said Arlo, falling to his knees at the man's side. He moved the man's matted hair away from his face. "He is still breathing."

"Is he a bliss addict?" Proteus asked, concerned.

"No," said Arlo. "He suffers from a different kind of disease."

As Arlo positioned himself to pick the man up, a shriek pierced the shadows followed by a woman rushing towards them. She was of middle age and well dressed. In her one arm, she held a basket full of fruits and vegetables. Her free arm was extended as her fingers moved into the sign to ward off evil—her thumb, index, and pinkie fingers extended and her middle and ring fingers folded.

"Don't touch him," said the woman, her voice shrill with panic.

"Why not?" asked Arlo. "He needs help."

"Are you boys blind?!" the woman shouted. "Can't you see he is rife with the blight?"

Proteus looked down at the man in the gutter. Once again, his eyes fell upon the shimmering bruises the colour of rotting plums that covered his emaciated body in patchy splatters.

"What is the blight?" Proteus asked, looking up at the

woman. He'd never heard the term used before, inside or outside of the palace.

"A curse!" spat the woman, pointing at the man. "A punishment from the gods on men like him. It rots them from the inside out." She looked down at the man, her face curled up in an ugly clump of disgust. "Best you two get out of here before you catch it too." She then spat on the ground three times to show just how serious she was about warding off evil.

Arlo leaned forward towards the frail man and helped him to his feet. Proteus watched on. The man's withered and lanky limbs looked even more wasted away in contrast to Arlo's powerful muscles and glowing skin.

"You bring ruin upon yourself, young man!" said the woman.

"True ruin is brought upon those who refuse to aid people in need. And you will address me as His Royal Highness."

Arlo pulled the hood of his cape down, revealing his honey-coloured hair that weaved and curled around his head like a golden crown.

The realisation of who Arlo was left the woman looking as if she'd just been slapped. Proteus did not get the chance to look at her expression for very long before her knees hit the ground and she began to grovel.

"My apologies, Your Royal Highness. I had no idea it was you! Please forgive me!"

Arlo ignored the woman and turned his back to her, the frail man leaning on him for support.

Proteus followed.

"What are we going to do with him?" he asked.

"We are going to take him to the healing temple on the palace grounds. The priestesses won't be able to cure him, but they will make him as comfortable as possible."

A million questions flew through Proteus' mind as he followed Arlo and the sick man up the steps on the outside of the bliss den. He could feel the music coming from inside vibrating right through the wall as they ascended. His questions would have to wait.

When they reached the airboat on the roof, Proteus helped Arlo load the man into the passenger seat. The man smelled bad enough to wake the dead. Proteus swallowed back at whatever was coming up his throat in response to the man's stench. He took a moment to be grateful they were traveling by air and not in a closed and cramped scuttle.

"You will have to squeeze in next to him," said Arlo. "He is so frail there should be enough space."

"How are we supposed to get him through the palace unseen?" asked Proteus as he wriggled into the seat next to the man.

"I don't know," said Arlo as he flipped switches with an efficient urgency. "But we have to try. We can't just leave him in the street to die."

Within the next few seconds, the airboat was speeding through the air faster than Arlo had ever flown it before. Proteus had to brace himself in his seat against the force pushing down on him. As the airboat climbed, so did Proteus' anxiety, and he said a silent prayer to Augur, the god of air, that the wind was calmer than it had been that morning. The god must have been listening because while the ride was still a bumpy one, it was far smoother than earlier that day.

Arlo slowed the airboat as they approached the entrance of the cavern before guiding it in with the ease of an experienced pilot. The airboat sank to the ground with a harder thud than normal.

"Do you think anyone saw us? Arlo asked as Proteus helped him get the man out of the airboat.

"I don't know," said Proteus. "You were going so fast I'd be surprised if anyone had."

Proteus held his breath as the man put his arm around his shoulders for support. The man tried to do the same with his other arm and Arlo's shoulders, but because Arlo was so much taller than both the man and Proteus, it was awkward and clumsy. Instead, Arlo just picked the man up as a parent would do with a small child and cradled him.

Proteus followed behind them as they climbed up the staircase back into the abandoned hall in the palace. They made their way down the hall as silently as they could. That was when Proteus noticed the man's wheezing. The rasp in the man's throat turned into a roar as it bounced off of and was amplified by the empty stone walls and floor. Proteus' shoulders knotted themselves into tangles as the possibility of being caught became more of a reality with every step they took.

If the guards don't see us, they will definitely smell him, Proteus thought. He looked back at the man and saw how out of place he looked in the palace—a filthy and grimy thing surrounded by glittering opulence. Proteus' heart sank with pity at the sight as the man feebly clutched onto Arlo with his bruise-covered, claw-like hands.

Instead of taking their usual route back to Arlo's chambers, they took the quickest way to get to the healing temple. Proteus would pop his head around corners and then signal Arlo to follow if the coast was clear.

"What in the name of the gods are you two doing?" a voice rang out from behind them. Both Arlo and Proteus spun around as the blood in their veins stopped flowing.

Arsinoe's brilliant amber eyes shone with suspicion and anger as they darted from Arlo, to Proteus, to the sick man, and then back again.

Arlo and Proteus waited silently on a bench outside the healing temple while Arsinoe spoke with the priestesses and healers inside. She had helped them sneak the ill man through the palace to the healing temple, but she had not been happy about it. Proteus had watched the veins in her forehead and temples swell larger with each step they had taken. On the surface she'd been calm, but in her eyes Proteus saw a tempest brewing and felt the hot lightning of anger crackling in the air around her.

"You spoke of the blight like you were familiar with it," said Proteus, breaking the silence between them as they sat waiting on the bench. "Is it truly a curse from the gods?"

Arlo's brow furrowed into a serious expression. Seeing Arlo this way caused a deep pit to form in Proteus' stomach.

"It's not a curse or a punishment," he said. "It is a disease, an incurable one, and it is not from the gods."

"And what did that woman mean when she said, 'men like him?'" Proteus asked.

"She meant people like you and I. Men who lay with other men."

A sudden dread came over Proteus that caused his insides to tremble. He thought of how the man had looked—wasted away and only half alive. His empty eyes were still haunting Proteus, as were the dark purple sores all over his body.

"Is that going to happen to us?" he asked, still trembling.

"We are loyal to each other; we have nothing to fear," said Arlo. "The blight only affects those with more licentious tastes than you and I."

"Luciferian is a paradise of the licentious," said Proteus. "How many suffer from the blight?"

"More and more each day," said Arsinoe's voice as she

emerged from the doors of the temple. "I have been assisting the healers to find a cure, but it eludes us."

"Where did the blight come from?" Proteus asked.

"No one knows," said Arsinoe. "It appeared one day several years ago and has been ravaging the people of the city ever since. It won't be long before it spreads further than the walls of Luciferian. We have, however, seen a strong connection between bliss users and those that suffer from the blight."

Arlo and Proteus stood up from the bench to meet the Empress's eyes.

"The Emperor could order the bliss dens to close," Proteus suggested to Arsinoe. "Or stop the supply of bliss completely if it's part of the problem. You've said it yourself—people lose themselves to it."

"Don't waste your breath," said Arlo. "My father loves his riches and power more than he loves his people."

"Firstly, bliss dens are no place for members of the royal house to be seen," said Arsinoe, shooting a look of warning in Arlo's direction. "Secondly, those are both impossible suggestions."

"Why?" asked Proteus. "All it would take is a single command from the Emperor."

"The Empire runs on three things," said Arsinoe, "food, ichor, and ebullience. Removing just one would collapse everything. The supply can never be disrupted."

"I thought the duty of the Empire was to protect its people," said Arlo. Proteus wondered if his words tasted as bitter as they sounded.

"If the Empire collapses, then there will be no people left to protect," said Arsinoe. "Your father's enemies gather around him like a great storm looking for the slightest crack to seep through. Ebullience pays for the armies and weapons that defend the Empire."

"So you would rather do nothing?" Arlo spat.

"I am doing everything!" Arsinoe screamed, her face smouldered with anger.

Proteus took a step back; he had never heard the Empress raise her voice above her normal calming hum. The anger in her face gave way to something else, something between sorrow and despair. Tears glazed over her eyes.

"I am doing everything I can," she continued, her voice suddenly calm but shaky. "We have all lost loved ones to the blight. Everything that can be done is being done."

"If you say so," muttered Arlo, not meeting her eye.

"I *do* say so, and I don't want to hear another word about it."

"As you wish," Arlo said, his voice a tundra.

Arsinoe glared at Arlo and then at Proteus. "I don't know how the two of you manage to keep sneaking in and out of the palace," she said, "and I don't want to know. But don't be foolish enough to think your absence goes unnoticed. You are playing a dangerous game. Had the Emperor found you tonight instead of me, the consequences would have been incredibly unpleasant for everyone."

Arlo turned his head away from her.

She raised her hand, touched his cheek, and gently pushed his head to meet her eyes. "I care for both of you. I don't want to see either of you on the receiving end of the Emperor's wrath. Stay out of his way; he has been in a foul mood the past few weeks."

"For what reason?" Proteus asked.

"Imperial troops were sent to invade the Scorched-Over Lands in the beginning of the summer," she said. "No word has been sent from them since just before they crossed the border. I fear the worst, and the Emperor is furious. It would be wise to avoid his attention and keep out of trouble."

Arlo nodded to let her know that he understood but stayed silent.

Arsinoe turned to leave, her robes bellowing behind her in gold and white clouds. "You both need to be more cautious," she said without turning back. "And stay away from the bliss dens."

18

THE PRINCE AND THE PROPHECY

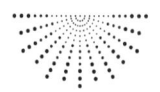

The next morning, Proteus woke early despite not getting much sleep. He left Arlo in the bed with a kiss on his forehead, dressed, and went looking for Arsinoe. He found her tending to the plants inside her conservatory.

It was hotter and more humid inside the glass temple than normal, while outside, the icy autumn wind continued to herald the coming winter. The sun grew further away, but its beams were still being amplified by the glass panels of the conservatory. Proteus removed the cloak he had donned before he left Arlo's chamber and hung it on a nearby chair.

Arsinoe had her back turned to him as she tended to a bush of hemlock.

"Your Majesty," he said announcing himself to her.

She did not look up from the deadly plant.

"I thought," she said, "that after all this time, you would know how much I detest formality among those closest to me."

"Why did you never teach Arlo how to make poisons?" he asked.

"Arlo," scoffed Arsinoe, "Arlo would grow up to be dangerous enough as it was. I wanted to teach him something of softness and subtlety. Of kindness and beauty."

"So you taught him the language of flowers instead?"

"It is not easy being a descendant of the gods." Her voice had gone cold and her eyes held a look that suggested they were somewhere far away. "I wanted to teach him that there is value in things other than war, power, and glory."

"It worked," said Proteus. "He is the most gentle creature I know."

"Then you do not know him at all," said the Empress. "He is a weapon born and bred from his mother's power and his father's hubris and lust for dominance. He is powerful and capable of great violence."

"Is that not how you would know the difference?" Proteus asked. "If you were not capable of great violence, how would you know when you were at peace?"

"You make a good point," said Arsinoe. "Keep that kind of thinking up and you could make a great philosopher one day. But be warned, the greatest weapons in the world are the ones that don't look like weapons at all."

"Like your poisonous flowers?"

Arsinoe did not give a spoken answer. She simply nodded.

"It would be wise of you to focus less on Arlo and more on yourself," she eventually said as she removed the gloves she was wearing to handle the hemlock.

"Why is that?" asked Proteus.

"Don't forget that my husband does not see people, only tools and weapons. If he does not see you as either of those things, you are as good as dead. You are here to be trained as a weapon, and that is what you will become if you want to survive."

"You and the Emperor are so different," said Proteus. "Why did you marry him?"

Arsinoe sighed. "He was not always as he is now. Power is a dangerous thing. It can corrupt even the purest of hearts and blind people to what is truly important. I should have heeded all the warning signs before I married Abydos. I thought that I could stop his lust for power before it twisted him into what he has become. I was wrong and foolish, and I also made some terrible mistakes. He already had an heir. I should have seen that I would not be a wife or his queen but just another weapon for him to wield."

"What happened?" Proteus asked. "Before Arlo was born? How does a mortal convince a goddess to bare his child?"

"When the time came for Abydos to sire an heir," she replied, "no mere mortal was good enough. He struck a deal with the goddess of chaos, Nubia, bedded her, and she conceived Arlo. After Nubia gave birth to Arlo, she abandoned him to his father's care. She left him in the throne room, swaddled in a crimson military cloak inside a shield for a crib. All while the Emperor had been courting me and then quickly took me for a bride."

"Why do you have no children with the Emperor?" Proteus asked, choosing his words carefully.

"We had a child once," Arsinoe said, her voice bitter and cold. "But I made sure that I would never again allow Abydos to sire any child of mine. He has enough playthings at his disposal."

Proteus looked to the ground and found himself wanting to steer away from the subject of Arsinoe's relationship with the Emperor. When she spoke of it, she sounded exhausted, raw, and filled with resentment and regret. He remembered the awful rumours and gossip he had overheard about her. There was no possible way they could be true. But he had not come to probe the Empress, who with every passing day seemed more like a prisoner, with questions. He had come to apologise.

"I'm sorry for the trouble I caused last night between you and Arlo," he said. "I should have held my tongue."

"The trouble was there long before you arrived," she said. "And it always finds a way of rearing its rancorous head one way or another. There was no fault on your part. Arlo has experienced great personal loss to the blight, so I cannot blame him for being so passionate."

"Who did he lose?" asked Proteus, stunned that Arlo had not told him.

"A weapons master who taught Arlo from a very young age. His name was Adrastus and he was as a father to Arlo. He died from the blight a year or so before you came to the palace. Arlo hasn't really been the same since. That is, of course, until your arrival." Arsinoe gave a small smile. "I can't tell you the difference you have made in him and how much it means. But Arlo's loss and the blight itself are of little concern to the Emperor."

"Maybe one day when Arlo is Emperor he will be able to change things for the better," said Proteus.

Arsinoe closed her eyes and sighed. "Arlo will never be Emperor," she said through the same serious frown.

"What are you talking about?" asked Proteus. "Of course he will."

Arsinoe pulled her lips into her mouth as if she was physically trying to stop herself from telling Proteus something difficult but important.

"You deserve to know," she said. "Come sit with me."

She led him to a daybed where they took a seat beside one another.

"Before Arlo was born, a prophecy was made about him.

It's part of how Abydos was able to convince Nubia to have a child with him."

"I know of it already," said Proteus, trying to sound confident, but the look on Arsinoe's face caused anxiety to creep over him like invasive vines. "It says that Arlo will lead a great army into battle and in doing so will bring peace everlasting to the Empire."

"This is true," said Arsinoe, "but there is more to it. Something you don't know."

The vines grew tight around Proteus' chest, making it hard for him to breathe.

"He will bring peace everlasting," she continued. "But he will die doing it."

A sick feeling began to bubble its way up from Proteus' stomach. His head began to spin and he wanted to puke. He thought back to the first time Arlo had taken him out in the airboat. He remembered what Arlo had said about Angelica and never marrying her. He recalled Arlo talking of the Fates before changing the subject, and it all began to make sense.

"Is he aware of this prophecy?" Proteus managed through his tightening throat.

"He is," said Arsinoe. "It is the only reason he exists. The prophecy was given to Abydos when he himself was still a boy. He conceived Arlo with Nubia with the sole purpose of fulfilling the prophecy."

Peace everlasting to the Empire? More like power everlasting to the Emperor. Proteus thought to himself.

"This can't be true," said Proteus. "Arlo would have told me. He shares everything with me."

"I'm sure he was just trying to protect you," said Arsinoe.

"The last time I checked, lying was not a form of protection."

His heart clobbered in his chest and his muscles tensed as burning tears made their way to his eyes. His mind raced and a pain broke over his chest like fractures over a jar dropped to the floor by careless hands. Arlo had been careless with him, and if he sat any longer, he was going to be sick. He bolted from the daybed and ran from the conservatory. He could hear Arsinoe calling out for him to come back, but he ignored her.

HE DIDN'T KNOW where to go as his emotions threatened to split him in two. He wanted to run away from Arlo and curse him as much as he wanted to run towards him and hold him close. He ran without knowing where he was going as tears blurred his vision. He burst through the first exit he found and into the silver autumn sunlight. He should have felt the chill of the wind, but his body ran too hot with the fires of betrayal.

How much time do we have left? He wondered as he ran through the palace grounds, past dried up water fountains, barren trees, and the guardian statues. He ran all the way to the tall boundary wall that separated the palace from the city and slammed into it. Unable to go any further, Proteus balled his hands into fists and began to punch the wall. He struck out again and again until his fists were raw and the wall was smeared with blood. All the while in his mind he cursed the Emperor and the Fates and the gods themselves. He even cursed Arlo for keeping something so important from him. *What will become of us?*

When he grew too tired and his hands too sore, he abandoned the wall. He walked through the far end of the palace grounds until he came to a stone bench under a pavilion near a pond. As he sat in front of the still water and dying plants, he longed for the beauty and comfort of Arsinoe's conservatory.

His thoughts and feelings haunted him. The longer he sat

alone under the pavilion, the more he felt like he was going to fall apart from the inside out. He wanted to scream at Arlo for not telling him the truth while at the same time hold him close because there was no telling how much time they had left together. The feeling of something coming grew stronger every day and beat away inside Proteus like a war drum.

He closed his eyes, pushed everything he was feeling away from himself, and focused on the beating. He allowed his mind to be carried away by it. Slowly, pictures began to form in his mind's eye. It was the farmlands again, and they were burning. He saw desolation and death at the hands of a dark army. He recognised them from the visions and dreams he'd had in the past. And then it hit him like a wave—the suffering. Hundreds of thousands crying out for help and then sudden silence.

He tried to hold on to the visions, but they were like oil slipping through his fingers. For the first time, he wasn't afraid. For the first time, he *wanted* to see what was going to happen. If he could get good enough at seeing the future, then maybe there was a way he could protect Arlo from his fate.

He didn't know how long he'd been sitting under the pavilion trying to glimpse more of the future when he heard Arlo's voice call out to him. He wanted to call back, but something stopped him. It was part genuinely wanting to be alone, part childishness, and part not knowing what he would say.

He emerged from the depths of his meditation at the sound of Arlo's voice. All the emotions he'd been ignoring came flooding back along with a terrible ache in both his bloodied hands. Arlo's calls grew nearer until he spotted Proteus under the pavilion and came running towards him.

"I've been looking everywhere for you," he said with a

mixture of relief and concern on his face. "Why didn't you call back to me?"

"Why didn't you tell me about the prophecy?" Proteus asked, his words direct and calm.

Proteus watched as the colour drained from Arlo's face and his lips melted into a deep frown.

"Arsinoe told me what happened," Arlo said. "She came to find me to tell me that you'd run off. I want to explain."

"Explain what?" Proteus shot back, now a little less calm. "That I only know half a truth and that you've been keeping the other half from me?"

Arlo stepped closer and put his hand on Proteus' arm. "Your skin is like ice!" he said, immediately taking his cloak off and throwing it over Proteus. "And what happened to your hands? Did someone hurt you?"

Proteus didn't answer. Instead, he just took a deep breath. The cloak was warm and smelled of Arlo—almonds and earth and orange blossoms. A fracture formed in his heart. *How long before his scent and his warmth and everything else I love about him is destroyed?* Proteus thought. *How long before he is gone forever?*

"Why didn't you tell me that part of your destiny is to die in the very same war that will bring you glory?" Proteus asked. That was the only thing he wanted to talk about.

Arlo opened his mouth to answer, but no words came out. His brows pulled towards each other and his lips fell into an even deeper frown. He swallowed as Proteus watched tears flood his eyes, turning them a darker shade of blue. He sat down beside Proteus on the stone bench and looked ahead at the still and lifeless pond.

"I'm sorry I didn't tell you," he croaked. "I was afraid. I am still afraid."

"Afraid of dying?" Proteus asked.

"No," said Arlo as he wiped his tears away with the back

of his hand. "I was afraid you could not love something that is doomed. I was so selfish. I tried not to care for you, but it was impossible. I tried to convince myself that I didn't love you, but it wasn't true. I didn't want to pull you into misery, but I did it anyway. I'm so sorry."

Proteus allowed the cloak to slip off his shoulder as he moved to take Arlo's hand. Arlo looked up at him in response, his cornflower eyes bloodshot with tears and dimmed by sorrow and regret.

"I just wish you had told me," said Proteus. "If I had known, I would have worked harder on trying to see the future. It's not too late. I can look for a way around this. I can find a path to take that ends in your survival."

Arlo sighed. "You should know that the future and fate are two different things. No matter the path we take, it will end in the same destination."

"That doesn't mean that we shouldn't at least try," said Proteus. "I won't let you give up like this. Not without a fight."

"I don't want to waste time looking for answers that will not help," Arlo said. "That is also part of the reason why I didn't tell you. I'd rather make the most of the time that we have."

"I don't want you to die," Proteus said, his voice cracking as his throat tightened and tears filled his eyes.

"I fear no fate," replied Arlo. "Not as long as I have you by my side."

And what of my fate? Proteus thought. Arsinoe's words from earlier that day came back to him, *It would be wise of you to focus less on Arlo and more on yourself.* But he could not bring himself to heed them. His love for Arlo outweighed his fear of the unknown.

"Then that is where you will find me," Proteus vowed as he swallowed his tears. "By your side, always."

Proteus meant what he'd said, but he was not going to let Arlo die. Arlo pulled him closer and locked him in an embrace. They sat in silence as the distant sun drowned the pavilion in afternoon light that held no warmth. *I will find a way*, Proteus thought to himself. *And if I cannot bend the webs of fate, then I will find a way to break them.*

19

CONSTELLATIONS OF TRAGEDY

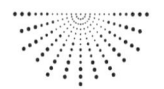

Ugly, pale crabs skittered across the wet sand in the full moonlight, making Proteus think of living bones. They did, after all, belong to the goddess Nerissa who guides the souls of those who die at sea to the Underworld.

"Swim with me," said Arlo, pulling his tunic off and casting it to the sand. It fell without a sound.

"Have the gods struck you with madness?" asked Proteus. "It's freezing! It's bad enough I let you drag me out here in the first place."

"Don't be a coward," Arlo teased. "It will be refreshing."

"I am not a demigod with the power to stave off hypothermia and fight sharks," said Proteus from his seat on the dune. "I'll take my chances here with the crabs. The fight with them would be fairer."

"Very well, suit yourself," said Arlo before darting towards the surf.

The light of the full moon illuminated Arlo's skin with a soft, blue glow. Proteus watched his muscles ripple and flex as he bounded into the water.

After the incident outside the bliss den, they had decided

to put their airboat adventures on hold. That was until that evening when the sun began to set and Arlo became restless.

"Let's go to the beach tonight," he'd pleaded. "Soon winter will be upon us and we will be trapped in the palace for months."

Proteus had opened his mouth to protest but stopped himself. Ever since learning about the prophecy, Proteus gave in to Arlo's wants and needs with far less resistance. After all, he had no way of knowing how much time Arlo had left. There was a strange part of Proteus that was honoured Arlo wanted to spend every second of his free time with him. *How many more summers will Arlo see?* Proteus asked himself. *How many more trips to the beach will we have together?*

"Arsinoe has had us watched like a lupercalia stalks its prey," said Proteus.

"We will take extra care not to be seen," said Arlo. "I want to get out one last time before the first snow comes."

A stealthy trip through the palace at the change of the guard and an airboat ride later, they were on the beach watching the calm Cyprian Sea glitter in the silver moonlight.

Proteus closed his eyes and calmed his mind. He'd been using every free moment he had to try and catch a glimpse of the future, what it may hold, and if there was any way he could prevent Arlo's death. No matter how hard he concentrated, nothing of importance came to him. As frustrating as it was, he did not stop. He tried to see the start of the war, the middle, or even the end, but all that came to him were blurred and jumbled images of burning crops and screaming people running from shadows.

"So this is where you've been running off to," a voice said from behind him.

His eyes flung themselves open, and his blood went as

cold as the water Arlo was swimming in. He spun around in the sand and got to his feet to face the Empress.

She looked calm to the point of serenity. She was wrapped up in a white, fur-lined cloak that fell all the way down her long, slender body and kissed the sand. Wild onyx hair floated gently down her back in the chilly breeze. Her high cheekbones cast shadows over her face where they blocked the moonlight, while the rest of her was illuminated by it. Her lips were full, painted a deep red and closed in a slight pout. Arsinoe was easily the most beautiful woman in the Empire.

Proteus started to get up from his seat in the sand, but before he could, she sat down next to him.

"Were you not brave enough to join him?" she asked, motioning towards Arlo. He was in waist deep and dived into the frigid water with all the grace of a dolphin.

"More like not mad enough." Just watching Arlo caused a shiver to run up Proteus' spine. He pulled his cloak up around his neck.

"I'd ask what is troubling you," said Arsinoe, "but I already know the answer."

"I don't understand why I was given these powers if I can't use them properly," said Proteus as he picked up a driftwood twig and began to draw lines in the sand. "If I could see what starts the war, then I could try stop it and not just save Arlo but countless others. But all I see is the suffering. I just wish I wasn't so useless!" He hurled the stick forward and it landed on one of the crabs.

"Do you know what the purpose of an oracle is?" asked Arsinoe.

It was a strange question, but after some thought, Proteus tried to answer it anyway. "To predict the future?"

"No," said Arsinoe, shaking her head. "Once the Fates have decided something will be, there is no force that can stop it. They preside over the endless march of time and all life and death. They are inflexible. If they have weaved an event into the Great Web, not even the gods have the power to prevent its passing."

"Then what *is* the purpose of oracles?"

"An oracle's job is not to change the future but to help guide it. Oracles are the children of Astaroth, god of prophecy, and the servants of fate, not disruptors of it."

"Well I don't think I could guide fate out of a burlap sack at this point. I focus so hard, but just when I think I can see something of use, it's ripped away from me and shrouded in black."

"Then it is obviously something you are not meant to see yet. Trying to change what has been set in motion by the Fates is a painful exercise in futility. Take it from someone who has tried and failed." Arsinoe's eyes were shadowed by a great sadness as she spoke.

"The Emperor?" asked Proteus.

Arsinoe nodded. "As I said, he was not always what he is today. I knew of the prophecy made about Abydos before I married him—that he would be the most powerful ruler the Empire would ever see but also that his power would corrupt him beyond recognition. I too told myself that I could change his fate, and now I am nothing more than a prisoner draped in fine fabrics. I knew a boy who was kind and gentle, but like so many before him and so many who will come after him, he was corrupted by power and glory. It is in the nature of all men to choose what destroys them and sometimes the people closest to them as well."

Her words rang ominously in Proteus' ears and felt more like a warning than a story.

"Arlo wouldn't do that to me," said Proteus.

"He will, my child," Arsinoe replied. "And you will let him with a smile on your face and all the love your heart can muster until it is left so broken that some days you will think it has stopped beating entirely."

Proteus fell silent. He did not agree with the Empress, but he was not in the mood to argue with her either. He got the feeling that she was speaking more about her own situation with the Emperor and less about his relationship with Arlo.

"There are many tales of mortal men taken as lovers by male gods," said Arsinoe, breaking the brief silence. "But like so many of our stories, none of them end well."

"If I was told any of those stories," said Proteus, "I cannot recall them, just like the rest of my past."

"Some choose not to repeat them," said Arsinoe. "Not for the tragic endings but rather not to encourage the behaviour."

"What happens to the people at the end of those stories?" asked Proteus.

"They all die in one way or another," Arsinoe answered. "In many cases, their immortal lovers took pity on them and in return for their suffering turned them into some of our brightest constellations."

She looked up to the heavens, so abundant with glittering stars Proteus couldn't fathom how it was even possible for anyone to tell one from the other.

"The Cup Bearer," said Arsinoe, pointing the collection of white lights out to Proteus, "The Lark, and The Charioteer to name a few."

Proteus looked up to regard the night sky and all the stars pinned against it. He followed Arsinoe's finger with his eyes as she guided him. The constellations she pointed out were indeed the brightest, but to Proteus they were distant and lonely.

"It must be so cold up there and so far away from everything," he said. "It seems almost a punishment. Like they were exiled and doomed to look down on the happiness of others for all eternity."

"The gods can be selfish creatures," said Arsinoe. "If they desire something, then no one else may have it, not even in death. Their dead mortal lovers cannot remain with the living but are also unable to join the gods in the heavens, so the gods place them directly between the two."

Proteus pondered this for a moment. "I don't think I would like to be a constellation."

"Then it is a good thing you are not the lover of a god," replied Arsinoe.

Proteus turned his attention back to Arlo diving through the waves in the moonlight. The gentle water lapped at his glistening skin. A mere mortal would have long since frozen to death. Arlo was not a god, but his mother was. It was a fact Proteus had always overlooked but up until recently had been unable to ignore.

"Are the stories of Nubia true?" he asked. "Is she as terrible as the poets say?"

"Oh no," said Arsinoe. "She is far worse."

"Should I fear her?"

"You would be a fool not to," said Arsinoe, taking in a deep breath of the cold and salty night time air. "But if she wanted you dead, then you already would be."

"So what's keeping me alive then? She must hate me for trying to protect Arlo from the whole reason he was born."

"She hates everything, so don't feel special. But she also understands the immovable will of the Fates and maybe even how she fits into the Great Web. My heart does sometimes ache for Arlo, who has never even met her and who she only sees for the destruction and glory he can bring as an extension of herself. A muscle to be flexed at her will."

"How can a goddess be so evil?" Proteus asked.

"The gods are neither good nor evil," said Arsinoe. "They

just are. In many ways, they are a reflection of us mortals. Some can be petty, prideful, cruel, and downright spiteful. But they also have a capacity for acts of great kindness, mercy, generosity, and love."

"They hide their virtues well then, for I don't see them."

"If it weren't for Nubia, we would not have Arlo. And I for one think the world is a better place for having him in it. Don't you?"

Proteus didn't answer. Instead, he turned her words over in his mind. Of course the world was a better place for having Arlo in it—he was dazzling. His laughter was contagious. When he entered a room, the air buzzed with an electric hum that made the people around him comfortable, content, and happy. Sometimes Proteus felt Arlo was the last good thing in the world ... for the time being anyway. But what would become of Arlo and the world if his mother decided to flex her muscle?

"You told me once you had a child with the Emperor," Proteus said.

"Have," the Empress corrected him. "We *have* a child."

"What happened to him?"

"Her," she corrected once again as she gazed out on to the water. "We have a daughter called Nimue. I do not like to speak of what happened to her. It causes me too much sadness."

"Do you ever wish things had turned out differently for Nimue?"

"With my every waking breath," Arsinoe said, not looking away from the waves. "But her fate was not mine to change. Nor is Arlo's yours."

THAT NIGHT, Proteus fell asleep quickly against Arlo's warm body, and he began to dream.

It was as it had always been in his visions but this time clearer and more real. He found himself looking over fields and farmhouses as the last rays of sunlight burned a dull orange glow into the horizon.

As the sun set, the fields and houses began to burn. People ran screaming from the rotting, maggot-infested soldiers cloaked in broken black armour. Proteus stood and watched on as fields and homes burned and people ran from the demon soldiers.

The people of the farms were barely armed, and the decaying soldiers did not discriminate when it came to killing. Screaming babies were torn from their mothers' arms and flung to the ground. Fleeing women and children were caught, stabbed, sliced, and left to bleed out in the dirt. Proteus tried to move; he tried to scream for help, but he found his voice inaudible even to his own ears and his muscles immovable as a statue.

As the fires grew, the screaming died down until everything burned in a bright, hot silence that twisted at Proteus' insides. He commanded his muscles to move but they ignored him. He forced his eyes shut but could somehow still see. He screamed until his throat was raw, but no sound escaped his mouth.

Embers danced in the blistering air that carried upon it the stench of burning flesh. The smell caught in the back of Proteus' throat, making him want to heave until he had turned himself inside out.

The world around him shifted and melted. When it settled again, he found himself standing over one of the slain women. Her eyes were waxy with death and turned up to the smoke-choked sky. Proteus had never met this woman, but somehow he knew her. Her throat had been slit, and her expertly made light blue dress was almost completely soaked in wet, sticky crimson. Her dark hair lay tangled, matted, and coated in dust. Despite her graphic death, it was clear she'd been beautiful in life. A force began to pull at Proteus' heart harder and harder until the pull became an ache.

I know this woman, he thought. The longer he looked at her, the more he felt it. His connection to her was something more than could be contained in memory. The loss of her tore through his entire body. He knew her.

She weaved beautiful garments for her large family. She was kind and enjoyed singing while she worked. Her touch was soft, warm, and comforting. She was caring. She was gentle. She was gone.

The ache shredded his heart open and a flood of pain poured out of him. Tears streamed from his eyes as silent screams ripped at his throat. He wanted to go to the dead woman, to cradle her in his arms and weep over her.

"Proteus!" Arlo's voice called out.

Proteus awoke to Arlo gently shaking him.

"You were having another nightmare," said Arlo. "You were crying."

"It wasn't a nightmare," said Proteus. He sat up in the bed and wiped his wet cheeks with the back of his hand. "Something terrible has happened."

"Was it one of your visions?" Arlo asked.

The light in the chamber was dim, but Proteus could see the concern in Arlo's eyes. He looked over to the window where the first light of dawn was breaking through the gaps in the shutters.

"It didn't feel like a vision of the future," he said. "It was something that was already happening and I was trapped inside of it. Someone was lost to me last night. It was someone important. Someone I will never get back again."

A lump grew in Proteus' throat and he found himself biting back tears.

"Who were they?" Arlo asked and tried to lean closer to embrace Proteus. But Proteus didn't want comfort. He wanted answers.

"I don't know!" Proteus shouted as he hurled himself out of the bed and away from Arlo. "I don't know anything! I don't know who I am or how I came to be here or why I am here. I've been seeing fragments of what was going to happen for months. Now it's finally come to pass and I did nothing to stop it. People are dead because of me. Someone I don't remember but I know I love is dead because of me!"

"What could you have done?" Arlo asked. His voice was calm, but there was a crack of hurt underneath the calm that did not go unnoticed by Proteus. "There was so much you didn't know. There is *still* so much you don't know. You've said it yourself—at a point, your visions are so scrambled you cannot even tell what is real and what isn't."

"It was getting better!" Proteus shouted, ignoring the hurt in Arlo's voice. "I should have tried harder. I could have warned them. I could have warned the Emperor. I need to figure out where I came from. I need to see a map of the Empire."

Arlo stood up from the bed and gently placed his hands upon Proteus' bare shoulders. This time Proteus didn't push away from him. His touch was soothing as Proteus looked into his eyes.

"I can help you," said Arlo. "Get dressed and come with me."

THE DOORS of the palace library swung open in front of them to reveal shelves upon shelves of scrolls. It was not a place

Proteus had spent much of his time during his stay at the palace, and his heart ached with regret as he stepped forward.

The air inside the library was thick and heavy with the smell of old paper, glue, ink, and dust.

"The maps are kept over here," said Arlo as he turned left into the maze of shelves the room contained.

Arlo returned a few moments later with an armful of rolled up scrolls under his arm. "These are the most up-to-date maps of the Empire that we have," he said.

It didn't surprise Proteus that Arlo knew exactly where to look for the maps. The library was where he took all his lessons that didn't involve a shield and sword.

He cursed himself for not asking Arlo sooner as Arsinoe's words plagued him. He *should* have been more focused on himself. Had he not been so distracted by Arsinoe's lessons and airboat trips all over the countryside with Arlo, then he would have thought to ask for this information sooner.

"What are you looking for?" Arlo asked as he rolled the maps out on an open table.

"Farmlands," said Proteus as his eyes darted over the maps. "That's what I saw in my vision, fields of wheat and corn and fruit orchards and farm houses."

Proteus gazed over the map with hungry eyes ready to devour any detail that could help him. The first place on the map he was drawn to was the capital city itself in the northern hemisphere. All the cities of legend and glory were on the map, places of wonder he'd never seen but were spoken of among the people of the palace and the city in their songs and stories. To the west of Luciferian across the Hercynian Sea was the city of Amun-Ra, and to the south of Amun-Ra lay the cities of Hadrian and Aroastria. Directly south of Luciferian, he saw the penal colony island of Dis.

A lump formed in his throat brought on by despair. What

if he was wrong about the farmlands? The Empire was vast and the unknown world that extended beyond the map vaster still. He could have come from anywhere. For all he knew, he was the son of a Tarwater whore. He swallowed back at the lump and cooled the hopelessness that was boiling in his chest.

"There's only one region in the Empire that grows such a diverse range of crops," said Arlo, pulling one of the maps closer and weighing the corners down. "It also happens to be the most important one."

He pointed to a large region far south of Luciferian.

"Naphtali," said Proteus.

"My father calls it the cornucopia of the Empire," said Arlo. "They are responsible for eighty five percent of the food production."

Proteus stared at the area. He knew it was just ink on paper, but something inside of him was drawn to it.

"It has to be here," said Proteus, running his hand over the lower half of the map. "This must be where I came from."

"It's not possible," said Arlo. "The Empire doesn't enslave its own citizens. Every man, woman, and child knows that."

Proteus ran his fingertips over the letters on the map that spelled out N-a-p-h-t-a-l-i. The scars on his face and body began to tingle. His power of premonition was trying to tell him something, but it was just out of his reach.

"Something happened to me," Proteus said, looking up at Arlo.

Arlo's eyebrows drew together. He stepped closer and placed his hand around the back of Proteus' neck. Proteus looked up to the kind, bright blue eyes he knew so well.

"We *will* get to the bottom of this," said Arlo. "I promise."

"It's a little early to be doing such heavy reading," Arsinoe's voice echoed through the library.

Both Proteus and Arlo looked up away from each other

and turned to the entrance where Arsinoe was standing. Proteus walked in her direction, glad to see her. He hadn't realised until then just how much he depended on the Empress for comfort and security. He felt like an injured child running to his mother to make him feel better. She would know what to do.

"I need to talk to you," he said. "Something terrible happened in Naphtali last night. I saw it in a dream."

Arsinoe looked at him and her slender neck stiffened.

"What did you see?" she asked with an intense stare of her honey-coloured eyes.

"There was an attack," said Proteus. "Undead soldiers—demons dressed in black—set fire to the crops and buildings and killed all the people."

Arsinoe looked away for a moment but said nothing before addressing Arlo.

"Your father is troubled," she said. "At the start of the summer, imperial troops were sent into the Scorched-Over Lands. Their orders were to conquer and send word by the beginning of autumn. When no word arrived, a second troop was dispatched to investigate. Winter is now upon us and no word from either troop has been sent. Something is very wrong."

Proteus remembered the conversation he'd overheard between the Emperor and Arsinoe the day he'd wandered into the East Wing for the first time.

His eyes darted back to the map. Naphtali shared a large border with The Scorched-Over Lands. The area was named on the map but was not completely chartered. The troops would have no idea what they were marching into. A sudden tingle broke over his body, and his mind slipped away from the library. A force overtook him and he was no longer himself. Like one of the puppets he and Arlo had watched in the market, some*thing* or some*one* else began to move his lips for him.

"Food will stop arriving to the markets soon." The voice coming from his lips was not his own. It belonged to a creature much older than him, possibly even older than time itself. "War is about to break out, and fear will spread through the Empire. Its citizens will flee to the walls of Luciferian for safety. Famine and plague are inevitable."

The force abandoned Proteus as quickly as it had arrived. It left him lightheaded and dizzy. He stumbled and Arlo caught him.

"Gods help us," said Arsinoe with wide eyes.

Proteus steadied himself. "I'm so sorry," he said. He didn't know why he felt the need to apologise. His muscles had stiffened at a sudden fear that had risen in him. It felt as if he was about to be punished or beaten for what had just happened. His heart was racing and a sweat had broken out over his forehead. His chest had grown tight as if pulled on by invisible strings, and he struggled to breathe. It was a strange fear, one born out of an instinctual reaction inside his body instead of his mind or heart.

Arlo immediately noticed the change in him and pulled up a chair that Proteus all but fell into.

"I'll get you some water," said Arlo before returning with a jug and goblet from one of the nearby tables.

Proteus took the goblet and drank in gulps as he tried to will his body into calming down.

"He looks like he is about to die," Arlo said. He had a quiver in his voice Proteus had never heard before. He was afraid. He looked at Arsinoe, his eyes pleading for her help. "All the colour has left his skin."

"Proteus," said Arsinoe, squatting down beside him. "You are safe here with us. No one is going to hurt you." She brought her hand to Proteus' sweat-drenched cheek. Her touch brought on a warm comfort that began to purge the fear from Proteus' body.

Slowly, his chest loosened and he found it easier to breathe. With each steady breath, his muscles unclenched themselves and he started to feel better.

"Am I going mad?" he asked, his voice trembling.

"No," said Arsinoe. "I've seen this before in soldiers who have returned from war. Something happens that causes them to relive battles from the past and their bodies react as if they are in danger."

"The past," Proteus said with a sudden flash of anger. "How can I be haunted by a past I don't even *remember*!"

"The flesh remembers things differently from the mind," said Arsinoe. "You need to be patient with yourself. I have a potion that can help you, but we have more pressing matters at hand. We must tell the Emperor what has happened and what is about to happen at once."

She stood up from her position at Proteus' side and turned to leave the library.

"Can you walk?" asked Arlo.

"I will be fine," said Proteus, standing up from the chair. His legs were still shaky, but he commanded them to straighten themselves and followed Arsinoe.

20
THE DARK EMISSARY

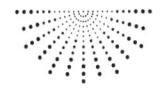

They made their way to the throne room in silence. As their footsteps echoed through the empty stone halls, Arlo took Proteus' hand in his and squeezed it gently. Proteus knew this was his subtle way of letting him know that everything was going to be alright. Proteus squeezed his hand back in return, but the gesture offered little comfort. Something had awoken within him and there was no way to put it back to sleep.

Dread was rising in him like a tide as the events he'd feared were coming had been set into motion. He tried to calm his mind and clear his heart of the chaotic emotion rushing through him. He tried to push it all down so that he could see clearly and gain insight into the future. It was too late to help the people of Naphtali, but he could still help the Empire. That was when the thought dawned on him.

This whole time, he pondered, *perhaps the Emperor has been right. He may only see me as a tool, but tools are useful to help Abydos protect the people of the Empire.*

Guards opened the throne room doors as they

approached. The Emperor was standing next to the golden throne with the last person Proteus wanted to see by his side.

Father Gemini stood in council with the Emperor. Proteus had not seen or heard from the priest since the incident in his chamber, but that did not mean the man was ever far from Proteus' thoughts. The priest looked more sickly than usual. In the months since Proteus had last seen him, Gemini had grown even greyer in appearance. He had also been forced to make more effort to hide the toll the blight was taking on his body. The flowing purple sleeves of his robes were longer than ever, covering his hands completely and brushing the floor. Proteus also noticed that he was not filling his robes out as much as he had before. The vial of bliss Gemini constantly sniffed from swung from his neck, but next to it Proteus noticed a pale blue crystal. The crystal and the vial both looked like they were becoming too heavy for Gemini's neck to support as he stood almost hunched over.

"What is the meaning of this interruption?" Gemini sneered. The chalky powder and cream he applied to his face cracked and flaked with the movements of his thin lips.

"The Oracle of Luciferian brings news of Naphtali," said Arsinoe.

Proteus' mouth fell open and he took a step back. When had he become the Oracle of Luciferian? Could Arsinoe just dish out titles as she saw fit? Or had he been the Oracle of Luciferian all along without knowing it?

The Emperor turned his head slowly towards Proteus. His dark eyes looked upon him with such intensity that for a moment Proteus thought he would burst into flame. He was dressed head to toe in full royal regalia, dripping with gold and jewels that glittered in the sunlight pouring through the tall throne room windows. Proteus had always made a habit of avoiding the Emperor at all costs; now he was being forced to not just meet his eye but actually speak to him.

"Well," said the Emperor. His deep and commanding voice bounced off the walls of the throne room and echoed in Proteus' ears like a battle cry. "Speak, oracle."

Proteus fought against his racing heart and opened his lips to reply when the tingling sensation returned to him. It started as a prickle in his scars before spreading through the rest of his body like a wildfire. His stomach sank, and once again he was taken over and spoke with the voice of another.

"Someone is coming," said Proteus. "And he brings a message with him."

As soon as the words left Proteus' mouth, there was a booming knock on the throne room doors. The tingling sensation immediately subsided.

"Come," barked the Emperor, and the doors were flung open by a gale. The wind tore through the room, blowing out all the torches and forcing all the guards present to their knees. In the doorway stood a solitary figure draped in tattered black robes. The two guards who were standing watch outside the doors just moments before lay dead at the figure's muddy bare feet.

Arlo moved with the speed and ferocity of an apex predator, ripping a sword from the sheath of the nearest guard. He sprinted in front of Proteus, Arsinoe, and the Emperor before raising the sword and rooting himself into a battle stance.

"Lower your sword, young prince," the figure hissed from under the shadows of its black and decayed cowl. Its voice was the sound of molten metal being quenched in water. "I come only to deliver a message."

"How did you get into the palace?" demanded the Emperor, his voice commanding as ever and without even a hint of fear.

The figure tilted its head upwards and the cowl fell back. Underneath was the head of a corpse. Its eyes had all but turned to gelatinous, yellowing pus inside their sockets. The grey-green flesh around its face hung loose and waxy. Proteus stared closer and immediately wished he hadn't. The creature's flesh was covered in deep lesions filled with squirming maggots. Proteus' stomach churned as he watched a clump of the tiny bone-coloured larvae fall from a gash in the creature's neck and break apart against the marble floor.

As he watched the clump of maggots wriggle at the creature's filthy feet, flashes burst through Proteus' mind. This was one of the creatures from his visions. This was one of the monsters that had attacked Naphtali. Proteus then looked closer. Underneath the tattered black fabric was the broken, dented, and tarnished armour of a Luciferian soldier.

"The Cult of Saklas works in mysterious ways," said the figure through its rotting black lips. At first glance the creature's teeth appeared broken, but when Proteus looked closer, he saw they were all sharpened to a point. A light breeze passed through the throne room, delivering the creature's stench of sweet decay to Proteus' nostrils. He had not been the only one to notice the foul smell as both Arsinoe and Gemini covered their noses and mouths.

"Speak and be done with it then," said Abydos.

Arlo stood his ground and kept his sword raised as the corpse soldier spoke.

"I come on behalf of the one true God, Saklas," the undead demonic creature said. "He is offended by your hubris in thinking you could invade his realm, the place you call The Scorched-Over Lands."

"It is no fault of mine," replied the Emperor, "if your god is too weak to protect those who worship him."

"This is where you make great fault, dear Emperor," spat the creature. "Saklas is more powerful than you can fathom, and you have doomed your precious Empire. Your invasion was reason enough for Saklas to raze Luciferian to the ground, but to add insult to injury, your troops pillaged and desecrated his temples. For your blasphemy, Saklas has vowed to erase your Empire and every man, woman, and child in it from the face of the world. Your legacy will be reduced to ashes."

Abydos smirked at this. "I would like to see this Saklas try."

"It has already begun," said the living corpse. "Why do you think you have not heard from either of the legions you sent to the borders of our land? And then of course there is Naphtali ... or shall I say, *was*."

"You lie, you foul creature," the Emperor spat.

"Ask your oracle," said the dark emissary as it raised its arm and pointed a broken, putrid finger at Proteus. "He may not know himself, but he has seen everything. There is nothing left of your beloved cornucopia but cinders and beautiful decay."

Proteus' breath caught in his throat as every eye in the throne room but Arlo's turned to him.

"Is this true?" the Emperor demanded.

Proteus did not even try to speak and instead just nodded.

"Saklas will speak with you directly now," said the corpse. Its jaw fell open so wide that the flesh that held its face together stretched down until it dangled at the centre of the monster's chest. Inside the rancid black hole of a mouth, Proteus saw an assembly of maggots and flesh-eating worms and beetles. He watched them scurry away from the light that had been so suddenly allowed to shine upon them.

"Here is my warning," a god's voice boomed through the corpse. It bellowed so loudly the very ground beneath Proteus' feet trembled and small cracks webbed through the marble. The voice was mighty and terrible as it roared through the throne room. It was a voice of thunder and lightning. A voice of hurricanes and raging winds.

"You and your people have become corrupted by the ichor that sustains your Empire," the god continued to speak through his undead emissary. "You hoard power in your capital while your citizens live in squalor and become addicted to the poison you supply them with." The corpse's pus-coloured eyes shot to the vial of bliss around Gemini's withering neck. "The poison you manufacture through the corruption of the blood of lesser gods is an abomination! You are an abomination! The Empire of Luciferian is an abomination! The Great Decay is coming for you all. I will see this world cleansed through death and rot!"

With that, all the air in the room rushed towards the corpse and began to fill it like the bladder of an airship. Proteus watched in helpless horror. The rotting flesh stretched wider and wider until in an instant the throne room and everyone in it was showered in an explosion of festering black organs and tissue.

"I can still smell it on me," said Arlo while drying off from his third bath.

"Me too," said Proteus as he looked at the amphorae of sweet oils on the shelves inside the palace baths. "You don't think we are really cursed now, do you?"

The explosion of the corpse man had left everyone present splattered with rotting remains and crawling insects.

Gemini had been the only one to scream.

"We've been cursed!" he shrieked while wiping black goo from his eyes. "Send for the priests and priestesses at once! We must be cleansed!"

Everyone else present had been much calmer.

"It's not impossible," said Arlo. "But mostly I think it was just gross. Are you alright?"

Proteus didn't know how to answer the question. When he didn't reply, Arlo stepped forward and embraced him. They stood for a moment holding on to each other, and Proteus found himself wishing he had the power to freeze the present instead of see into the future.

THEY CAME to the city in a drizzle and then a flood. Fear of the Cult of Saklas had spread across the Empire in a swarm. Wanting to avoid the same fate as Naphtali, farmers, peasants, and tradesmen from all corners of the Empire abandoned their homes and flocked to the safety of the capital city. The streets of Luciferian began to burst with the excess of bodies. As Proteus had predicted, the supply of food began to run dry. Not long after that, the plague broke out. Assisted by the cold winter, the plague spread from household to household and business to business until even the palace felt its morbid impact. Everyone from guards and soldiers to courtiers and priests had dropped dead inside the walls of the palace.

People were dying faster than their bodies could be cremated. As a solution, mass funerals were held throughout the day in which piles of the dead were burned at the same time. The pillars of stinking smoke shrouded the once glittering city in a heavy and dark smog that choked everyone—from the poorest beggar in the gutter to the Emperor himself high up in his reception chamber.

"How ..." said Abydos, closing the window he'd been looking out of to block out the stench of burning bodies, "*How* is it possible that despite having the best minds in the

Empire at our disposal, we still know nothing about this Cult of Saklas?"

"There is no record of them in our histories, sire," said Gemini from behind his purple veil. He'd told the Emperor the accessory was to protect him from the miasma of the plague, but Proteus knew better.

The blight has spread out of his control, Proteus thought, and he was glad of it. Despite the veil, he could still feel the priest's licentious gaze burning his flesh. Since his sudden and unwanted promotion to Oracle of Luciferian, Proteus had been forced into more contact with Gemini and the Emperor. When the priest drew too near, Proteus could hear his breath quicken under the veil, and it made Proteus' skin crawl.

"Our historians and scholars have found no evidence of them," Gemini continued. "There are no records of The Scorched-Over Lands, the people who dwell there, or the gods they worship."

"And they have not yet attacked any other regions of the Empire," said Abydos, his brow even heavier than usual.

"No word has been sent from any of the troops," said Rayden, the Captain of the Guard, who was also present in the reception chamber.

"What are they waiting for?" the Emperor pondered out loud before turning to Proteus. "What have you seen, boy?"

Proteus was ready with an answer, but it was not one the Emperor would be happy to hear. Since the visit from the undead man, and thanks to the potion Arsinoe had been giving him, Proteus' visions had become clearer, but they were still not precise. He had been practicing paying more attention to details in his visions that would give him clues about when and how things would happen. He would try to notice the time of day, the season, and the position of the constellations. No matter how hard he searched, no answers to Arlo's fate would reveal themselves to him.

"I have seen them, Your Majesty," Proteus said. "They will arrive at the city walls in legions at the beginning of summer."

"We need more specific information than that," the Emperor growled. "Is the Empress not feeding you her potion?"

"She is, sire," Proteus said in a whimper despite trying his best to sound direct.

The truth was the Emperor terrified him, and he had no reason for being so afraid. Abydos had never struck him, and yet Proteus would flinch away from him. The Emperor had not so much as raised his voice to Proteus, but for some reason he was terrified the man would scream at him. The potion Arsinoe had been giving Proteus had been helping him with the debilitating fear brought on by his visions, but it did not help make the visions any clearer.

The Emperor waved them away, and Proteus was overwhelmed by a sense of disappointment in himself.

THAT NIGHT WHILE ARLO SLEPT, Proteus lay awake, tortured by his inability to remember the past or predict the future with the kind of accuracy the Emperor needed. The only sound in the room was the gentle cooing of Damascus, fast asleep on his perch.

When he couldn't stand it anymore, he slipped out from under Arlo's arm and got out of the bed. He retrieved an oil lamp from the corner of the room and made his way to the library.

He found the maps of the Empire and sprawled them out on a table. As they unfurled, the smell of ancient paper and ink filled the air. Resting the lamp on the table and pulling up a chair, Proteus stared at the maps hoping they would provide him with any kind of answer. This was not the first time he had come to the library to gaze at the silent maps. He thought that if he stared at them long enough, the broken parts of his mind would by some miracle heal themselves and his memory would be whole again.

"Your thoughts look heavy, beloved," said Arlo from behind Proteus. "Care to share the burden?"

Arlo looked sleepy but still beautiful, his skin aglow in the dim light of the lamp. Proteus was not startled by Arlo's sudden appearance; he had predicted Arlo's arrival in the library before he'd even risen from the bed.

"I came from Naphtali. I know it," said Proteus, running his fingers over the region on the map. "Not that it means anything now. It's all gone. It sounds like madness. How can I mourn something that I can't even remember? Why am I afraid of things that I cannot recall?"

"Perhaps it does not do well to dwell on the past," said Arlo, pulling Proteus into a gentle embrace. "You have your place here in the present."

How could Proteus explain what he was feeling? He wanted to express why it was so important to him to find out where he had come from. The past pulled on him like a fisherman's hook, but he could never break the surface of the water. The future dragged him down into the darkness with only brief flashes to guide his way.

Being enclosed in Arlo's arms was the safest place in the world. Proteus breathed him in as he fought back tears before he realised it didn't matter. He didn't want to make Arlo understand; he just wanted a moment to allow himself to feel everything he'd been feeling. What better place to do that than where he felt safest? He stopped fighting back the tears and instead let them flow. Everything Proteus had been holding inside poured out of him in a stream of tears and shudders. All the confusion. All the fear. All the pressure to perform for the Emperor. All the sense of overwhelming loss.

Arlo held him closer and stroked the back of his head. "It's alright, dearest," he said. "I'm here for you."

Proteus could not remember being more grateful for Arlo, but his gratitude was soon overshadowed by a terrible thought. *Arlo is here for me, but for how much longer before the Fates will take him away?*

21

THINGS STOLEN AND RETURNED

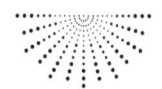

Proteus watched the sun set from the window in Arlo's chamber as he waited for him to return. The last rays of sunlight set the shroud of smog that hung over the city into a dirty, orange glow. The Emperor had summoned Arlo almost an hour before, and the longer Proteus waited, the hotter the anxiety inside of him burned. He didn't need to be able to see the future to know that something was wrong.

Proteus spun away from the window at the sound of the door creaking open. Arlo passed the threshold with slumped shoulders and a morbid expression.

Proteus had to stop himself from charging towards Arlo and instead just asked in a shaky voice, "What's happened?"

"The Emperor is sending me away," said Arlo, looking at the floor.

Proteus' heart began to race so fast that he grew light-headed. "What?" he said. "Where? How?"

"To a gladiator training academy in Amun-Ra. He seems to think that my combat skills need improving before the war begins."

"That is ridiculous! I've seen you fight a thousand times. You are better than any warrior in the Empire!"

"Of course that isn't the real reason," said Arlo, still not meeting Proteus' gaze. "He is unhappy with the way I treated Angelica. This is his way of punishing me for upsetting his political alliances. He wants me to mend things with her."

"Then I will come with you," said Proteus, stepping closer. "When do we leave?"

"*We* don't," said Arlo, his voice breaking a little. "His orders are for me to go and for you to stay here."

"But why?" Panic flashed through Proteus like a lightning storm.

"He wants you here to assist with your oracular abilities and ..." Arlo couldn't finish his sentence.

"And what?" asked Proteus. He wanted to shake Arlo until the answer fell from his mouth.

"He sees you as a distraction." Arlo said. "He told me that you make me weak, and I am to be hardened for battle. I told him that I refused to go if you could not join me. He told me that if I refused to go alone, he would have you executed."

Proteus stepped back until he felt the edge of the bed on his calves and sat down. The weight of the news pushed down on him so hard he struggled to breathe.

"My mother appeared to him," Arlo continued. "It was her idea. She said she had been watching us, and if I am to be glorious in battle, I could not have my head and heart filled with childish thoughts of you."

Proteus swallowed hard against the stone that had formed in his throat. Is this how it was to be? Were they to be at the mercy and control of gods, emperors, and mystical forces until their brief lives were totally spent? He looked up at Arlo; he was grey with sadness, his usual healthy glow snuffed out.

"How long?" Proteus asked, his voice icy with defeat.

"I am to be summoned back when the war begins," said Arlo, finally looking up at Proteus for the first time.

Sadness spread over his face and twisted through his features, and yet, even in despair, he was still the most beautiful creature Proteus had ever laid eyes on.

"When do you leave?" Proteus asked.

"An airship is being prepared as we speak," said Arlo. "I am to leave at dawn."

The sorrow inside Proteus began to transform in to anger.

"I don't know how to be here without you," Proteus finally said. "Why would the Fates throw us together only to tear us apart again?"

Arlo sat down next to Proteus on the bed and put an arm around him. Proteus moved closer.

"We will see each other again," said Arlo. "I swear it."

That night, they lay in the bed holding on tightly to each other. Proteus convinced himself that by some spell, if he could hold on tight enough and not let go, not even for a moment, that the Fates would not see them separated. He prayed to and bargained with every god he knew the name of and then all the ones he didn't.

At one point in the night, Arlo pulled Proteus closer.

"You don't make me weak," he whispered in Proteus' ear. "You make me strong. I promise that everything I do while I am away, I will do with the sole purpose of returning to you."

Proteus was still as Arlo planted kisses on his neck and shoulder, leaving his skin damp with tears.

Dawn came like a death sentence.

Arlo rose from the bed, and Proteus began to feel his presence withdrawing like a wave being pulled back into the ocean. Proteus sat up and watched Arlo pack like a mourner building a funeral pyre. When he was done, Arlo retrieved the scarf Proteus had made for him the winter before and wrapped it around his neck. He pulled the wool close to his face and rubbed his cheek against it.

"I can't come to see you off," said Proteus as he stood from the bed. "I don't want to make you seem weak in front of the Emperor."

"I understand," said Arlo, his voice flat and distant. "That would be for the best."

Proteus stepped into his embrace and Arlo's arms locked tightly around him. Their lips met, but the kiss was stiff with grief.

Arlo pulled away and looked into Proteus' eyes.

"I don't think I'm strong enough to say goodbye," he said through clenched teeth.

"Then don't," replied Proteus, stroking Arlo's cheeks with his thumbs. "It's not goodbye. The war is closer than we think. You will be called back before the start of summer."

They embraced each other again when a faint knock came from the door.

"Enter," Arlo croaked as he pulled away from Proteus.

The door opened, and on the other side stood a servant.

"They are ready for you, Your Highness," he said. "I was sent to assist with your luggage."

"I require no assistance," said Arlo. "Tell them I'm on my way."

The servant bowed before leaving.

Arlo turned to Proteus once more. "I love you," he said. "No matter how difficult things get while I am away, no matter how lonely you feel, always remember that I love you."

"I love you too," said Proteus. "Go show those gladiators what you are made of."

They kissed one last time before Arlo turned to leave. Proteus watched him walk through the door and disappear.

Damascus sang from his perch in the corner of the room before fluttering to the window's ledge where he began to peck impatiently at the glass. Proteus walked towards the window and opened it. The kinglet darted out immediately and took to the open air over the palace grounds.

He stood alone in the chamber until he could not bear it anymore. Everywhere he looked held a memory of Arlo.

Proteus abandoned the room which was so empty and yet too full of memories. He didn't know where he was going; he only knew where he didn't want to be. He thought about going to find Arsinoe and asking her what was to become of him in Arlo's absence. Instead, he chose to wander the palace halls looking for a hiding spot where he could weep or scream or curse the gods and the Fates.

THE WINTER CHILL once more pulled through the palace. Proteus found himself regretting not putting on an extra cloak before fleeing the room. He wandered on, passing the more populated halls and rooms of the palace—protected by guards and filled with courtiers—into the more abandoned spaces. The air was tight with cold. He walked through a draught that brushed the back of his neck and slipped down his back. He shivered and pulled the thin cloak he had on closer.

The more he thought of Arlo, the more his stomach churned with uncertainty, sadness, and anger. He would continue his lessons with Arsinoe while honing his oracular abilities, but without Arlo around, Proteus wasn't sure he wanted to do anything. He shook the feeling from his body and reminded himself to be strong for Arlo. He would continue working on finding a way through the future and around the prince's doomed fate. He would not allow Nubia and the Emperor or anyone else to break him. They could keep Arlo and Proteus apart and they could threaten them with execution, but they could not stop them from loving one another. As long as Arlo drew breath, Proteus would not stop looking for a way to save his life. With his new found determination, Proteus turned around to go find Arsinoe when suddenly the world around him went dark.

A bag was pulled over his head and he was pushed to the ground. He struggled against strong hands that held him down while his legs and arms were bound with rope. He tried to scream, but the bag was lifted past his mouth and he was gagged. Fear rose through his muscles, immobilising them. His body became rigid as his heart sprang around inside his chest like a trapped animal. A cold sweat broke over his skin as he was lifted from the ground and thrown over one of his captors' shoulders.

Fear turned to pure terror, and Proteus thought he was going to be sick. He fought back at the nausea knowing that if he was sick, thanks to the gag in his mouth, he would choke to death on his own vomit. Every muscle in his body was screaming at him that this had happened to him before and it had not ended well. The ropes cut into his flesh as he tried to push the gag out of his mouth with his tongue to no avail.

He'd not spent very long over his captor's shoulder before he was thrown down onto a soft surface. He recognised the luxurious softness of a palace mattress; he was on a bed. Proteus' mind raced to try and place where he was. He had definitely not left the palace—that much he was certain of. That was when the smell registered in his mind. The sickly, sweet stench of incense smoke mingled with a menagerie of sweet oils and perfumes attacked his nose from the other side of the sack. He knew that smell. There was only one place in the palace he could be.

Hands reached out for him, unbinding his hands and feet only to have them bound again in a different position. He'd been tied face up to the posts of the bed. The hands reached out once more, tearing his coat and tunic from his body and removing his boots. Naked and terrified, Proteus shivered as he tugged against the restraints.

"You can go now," said a voice muffled by the burlap bag. "I can handle it from here."

Proteus heard heavy shuffling footsteps leave the room and the door close behind them. The door was then bolted from the inside before the sack was pulled from Proteus' head.

Father Gemini's face looked down on him with a sick, yellow smile that caused Proteus' stomach to drop. He looked even worse than the previous time Proteus had seen him. Stripped of his dramatic robes and veil, wearing only a sheer tunic, Proteus could see how the blight was withering him away. His gelatinous belly had been weathered down into a low hanging distention of flesh that wobbled between his knobbed knees. The flesh that had been stretched to its limits by his immense weight now sagged and hung from his bones like a grey sheet covered in the plumb-coloured splotches. Even the skin on his face no longer fit properly and sagged, making the priest's eyes look larger. Inside his eyes, Proteus saw desperation and lust. The dark sores of the blight had smattered themselves across his face and the top of his bald head in patches of decaying flesh. The vial of bliss and the blue crystal that hung from his neck rested between his drooping pale breasts that hung from him like rotting fruit.

Proteus' nose had not lied to him; he'd been brought to Gemini's chamber. The air in the chamber was dense with incense smoke. The sniffers lay unchained in the corner of the room. For the time being they seemed relaxed, but Proteus knew they would be ready to attack anything with a snap of their master's waxy and frail fingers.

Unable to do much else, Proteus glared at Gemini.

"I knew when I found you that day in the slave market you would be able to solve all my problems," said Gemini, gesturing at his haggard body. His voice still had the nasal whine to it but it had become more guttural, as if worn down by a kind of erosion. "Thanks to your oracular abilities, getting you into the palace was easy enough. What I did not count on was that pampered palace brat interfering with my plans and making it impossible to get you alone."

Proteus wanted to scream a thousand venomous obscenities at the priest. He wanted to hurl curses at him and pray to the gods to carry them out. The gag still firm in his mouth stopped him.

"Were it not for Nubia forcing the Emperor's hand last night, I am not sure what I would have done," Gemini continued as he loosened the belt around his tunic and stripped naked. "Now you will finally be able to cure me of this accursed affliction!"

Proteus struggled and bucked against the restraints, but the ropes he'd been bound with would not budge. He watched in a helpless panic as Gemini got onto the bed and crawled towards him, his folds of clammy flesh swinging back and forth. When he reached Proteus, he began to lick and kiss his legs and torso, making his way up to Proteus' neck and face. The stench of sweet perfume failing to cover an undercurrent of rot wafted over Proteus, and he did his best not to puke. The priest's tongue writhed over Proteus' flesh like an eel, leaving streaks of stinking slime in its wake.

Proteus screamed behind the gag, but nothing more than a muffle could be heard. He tried to push Gemini away by bucking his torso back and forth, but the priest was not deterred. Gemini's body came to rest on top of Proteus and he began to heave.

"Let's get rid of that thing," said Gemini as he raised his hand and loosened the gag. "You can scream as loud as you want to. No one is going to hear you."

As soon as the gag was out of Proteus' mouth, Gemini lunged forward and stuck his tongue down Proteus' throat. Proteus then bit down as hard as he could, splitting the priest's tongue clean in half. Warm blood rushed from Gemini's mouth as he fell back and screeched in agony. Proteus leaned forward as far as he could and spat the severed tongue across the room. He then continued to spit in an attempt to get as much of the priest's blood out of his mouth as possible. Proteus' naked body and the bed around him were covered in sticky, warm blood.

Gemini clutched at his jaw as the blood poured from his mouth. A soft blue glow broke through his fingertips as he healed himself by magic. When he was done with his spell, his hands fell away from his mouth and he looked down at Proteus with a fiery rage in his eyes.

He pounced at Proteus and began to punch him hard. Gemini's blows landed across Proteus' face, leaving his cheeks and jaw burning with pain. Gemini hit him over and over again. Hot blood spilled from Proteus' nose over his face and into his mouth.

"Do anything like that again and I will feed you to the sniffers when I'm done with you," said Gemini, his newly healed tongue still clumsy in his mouth. He then positioned himself between Proteus' legs and forced them open. "Let's be done with this," he continued before making a disgusting noise with the back of his throat and spitting into his hand. He then lowered his mucus and blood coated hand to his groin and began to pleasure himself.

Proteus' eyes had begun to swell with stinging pain, but he could still see every horrible detail. He wanted to look away but he found himself unable to move.

When Gemini was done arousing his shrivelled, grey manhood, his wet hand moved towards Proteus. Proteus clenched as tightly as he could and began to cry.

As Gemini's hand made contact, the door of the chamber was blown off its hinges with a loud bang. Gemini's head flung towards the doorway and Proteus' followed.

There, in full armour, stood Arlo. Proteus breathed a sigh of relief and began to weep. Arlo's blue eyes gazed over the scene. Proteus watched as Arlo's face began to transform. His beautiful, soft face hardened with ugly rage, and creases of anger ran over his cheeks and brow. His breathing quickened until he began to pant. His muscles swelled and bulged under his armour, growing three times their usual size. He flexed and Proteus heard his chest plate groan and then crack under the pressure. Finally, his eyes began to glow white as they filled with a lightning that crackled and fizzled over his face.

"GEMINI!" he boomed in a voice that Proteus felt rumble through his body like thunder.

Gemini fell from the bed with shock. Before he hit the ground, Arlo was by his side and caught him by the neck. Proteus watched from the bed as Arlo squeezed Gemini's throat so hard the priest's face began to turn red and swell up. The two sniffers in the room snarled at Arlo. As they jumped towards him, Arlo batted them away using Gemini's body before letting it drop to the ground. The sniffers jumped at Arlo a second time. Arlo kicked the first one away and into the wall. He caught the second one by its jaws and forced them open wider and wider until the flesh at the corners of its mouth began to rip open. Arlo continued to force the jaws open until the creature's face was torn in two before the top half of its head came away with a slimy pop.

The sniffer fell lifeless to the floor as the second one charged at Arlo a third time. Arlo caught it by the neck with his right hand and the monster died with the sound of a sharp snap.

Arlo's lightning-filled eyes then fell to the spot on the floor where Gemini was trying to stand up. Arlo picked the priest up by the shoulders and hurled him against the wall on the other side of the room. Gemini's naked, grey body crumpled into a pile on the floor where Arlo picked him up again and began to punch him in the face over and over. With each blow, Gemini's face lost more and more of its form until it was reduced to a gurgling, bloody pulp. Proteus watched the priest's blood-coated yellow pebble teeth fly across the room and hit the floor. He listened to each and every terrible snap and crack as Arlo broke his bones.

"Arlo!" Proteus cried from the bed. "Stop! You are going to kill him!"

Arlo continued to beat Gemini, and Proteus cried louder for him to stop, but the prince was in a frenzy. Arlo was either ignoring Proteus or was so deep in his rage that no force in the heavens or on the earth could reach him. Arlo let go of Gemini and let him fall to the floor in a bloody mess. That was when Arlo began to kick. With each blow of Arlo's foot, the priest groaned and his bones continued to break.

"ARLO, STOP!" Proteus screamed as loud as his voice would allow him. "For the love of the gods, STOP!"

The priest's whimpers grew softer until his broken and battered body stopped moving. Arlo delivered one final kick that sent Gemini's corpse flying to the other side of the room. Arlo's foot made contact with the vial of bliss and the blue crystal Gemini kept around his neck, shattering them both. The crystal gave off a ghostly glow before turning to ash, and Proteus began to convulse on the bed.

A million memories rushed into his mind at the same time, leaving his head spinning. The world around him began to melt away and re-form before melting again. His body continued to twitch and jump as the memories surged through him one after the other.

The farmlands of Naphtali, his father Canaan, his brothers, and his mother Rebekah. He then realised they were all dead. His heart broke with grief as his brain pounded away at the inside of his skull like a prisoner demanding to be set free.

Arlo was panting as the lightning in his eyes began to dim before flickering out. His bulging muscles shrank down to their normal size. He ran to Proteus' side, pulled a knife from his belt, and cut the ropes that held Proteus to the bed.

"Proteus," Arlo said in a panic. "Proteus, can you hear me?"

"My name …" he struggled through his foggy mind, aching body, and jumbled thoughts, "… is Cadence."

Arlo's face leaning over him was the last thing Cadence saw before he fell into the void of his returned memories.

22

THE SECOND-SIGHTED ONE

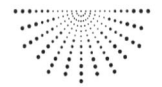

It happened in flashes and blurs. Cadence remembered Arlo lifting him from the bed. He'd been too dizzy, weak, and in pain to stand. He remembered being carried down palace hallways as the light and heat from torches and braziers passed over him.

He remembered Arlo lowering him into the airboat, and then he remembered everything else. His life in Naphtali. The cruelty of his father and what his brothers had done to him. His mother and how she would do her best to protect him. Then he remembered they were all dead. The scars on his face pulled tight as his muscles twitched under his skin. He wanted to scream but he could not find the energy.

His head fell back as the airboat shot from the mouth of the cavern, and he passed into a dark, bottomless place. He thought he was blacking out, but he was still somehow conscious and falling. His soul had come untethered from his body. He no longer felt the aches and pains from Gemini's beating, and his mind was clear.

He passed through the void—or rather the void through him—until, in the distance, he stopped and saw two small, glowing green lights. The lights shone brighter and revealed themselves not to be lights at all but the luminescent eyes of a man in black silk robes. He stood on the bank of a river that gurgled and splattered as it gently rushed by.

Cadence drew close enough to make out the man's features. He was dark and brooding but handsome. His alabaster skin held the iridescent shine of abalone shells. Dark hair sprouted from the top of his head in thick, black tufts. He had a wide face with a strong jaw that looked like it had been cut from stone. He stood like a column, taller than any man Cadence had ever seen, and was covered in muscles of glimmering marble. For a man of his size, he moved with a gentle grace and ease that was alien to Cadence.

The glowing green light inside the man's eyes dimmed and immediately Cadence recognised them, for they were the eyes that had looked back at him his whole life when he looked upon his reflection. They were the same eyes that his father had raged over and complained about.

"I know you," said Cadence; the words left his mouth and echoed through the endless void surrounding them.

"I would hope so," said the man. His voice was deep and calm, as if he had already seen and done everything in the world that could be seen and done and held no anxieties or excitements for the future. "I am part of you."

"Who are you?" Cadence asked.

"Who do you think I am?"

"I'm not sure. So much has happened. But I remember seeing you here by the river before. In my dreams and visions."

"They call me many things," the man said, turning his emerald eyes to the flowing waters of the river. "The Second-Sighted One, Son of the Weavers, Fruit of the Fates, and Prince of Spiders."

Cadence took a step back and had to stop his mouth from

falling open. This was no man at all. He was a god. Astaroth, son of the Fates and prophecy incarnate.

"Do I frighten you, child?" he said.

"I am not frightened, but I have learned to be weary of the gods. What do you want with me?"

"You are bold. There are few mortals that would dare to speak to a god like that. Then again, you are no mere mortal."

"What am I then?"

"That is what I have come to show you," said the god as he stepped forward, raised his hand, and touched Cadence's forehead.

A flash of green light exploded over his eyes and he was thrown into a vision not of the future, but of the past.

He saw his mother in the hut of a witch. Tears filled his eyes at the sight of Rebekah. For a moment, his mind tricked him into thinking she was alive and well, but then he remembered he was merely witnessing what once was.

He wanted to run towards her, to fall to his knees at her side and fold her inside of his arms. He wanted to bury his face in the waves of her dark hair and breathe her in just one final time. He wanted a chance to say goodbye. But he could not move. He could not speak. He could only watch and listen as grief ruptured his heart and tears streaked down his face.

The witch's words flowed through his mind in dizzying echoes that bounced around the inside of his skull.

A child conceived by magic will forever be touched by it.

The thirteenth son of the House of Canaan shall be a child of Astaroth.

Your son will not be of the blood of the gods, but he will be touched by them. He will be imbued with their magic.

A PROPHECY OF FLOWERS AND LIGHTNING

The soul with two bodies will make itself whole again.
The son of prophecy and the son of flowers will be tangled
 like the roots of an ancient tree.
A legendary love will bloom, only to be brought to ruin.
Their fate is tied to the fate of everything the sun touches.
The blood of the crown will commit a fault so great the gods
 themselves will cower.
The forgotten god will return, and his lightning will tear the
 skies.
His ravenous darkness will lay waste to the land.
Their love will be their victory and their demise.

THE VISION of the witch's hut melted away around Cadence until he was once again standing in the void with Astaroth. He moved quickly to wipe the tears from his eyes with shaking hands, but more flowed to take their place. He choked as he felt his shoulders slump with the weight of unbearable grief.

"You should know," said Astaroth, his voice void of emotion, "she always loved you. Even after you went missing. Even after she thought you were dead. She never stopped loving you. I would hear it in her prayers to me."

Anger began to fester deep inside of Cadence and spread a blistering fever through his body. "You knew her suffering and you did nothing to comfort her," he growled. "You knew she would die and you did nothing to protect her. Why?"

"I cannot interfere with the Great Web of the Fates," the god replied in his calm tone that, to Cadence, sounded bored and uninterested.

"That's not a good enough reason!" Cadence screamed, his words hot with rage. "You should have protected her! You should have protected *me*! My whole life I have been persecuted because of what *YOU* have made me! Where were you when rocks were thrown at me when I was a small boy? Where were you when Canaan would beat me within an inch of my life because of the so-called gift *you* cursed me with? Where were you when I was sold into slavery by my own brothers? Where were you when they did this to me?!" Cadence gestured towards the scars all over his face and body.

The god opened his mouth to speak but Cadence would not let him.

"Where were you today when—," he roared but then his voice broke into a whimper, "when that awful man put his hands on me?" Cadence wiped furiously at the tears still sprawling down his face, but the more he wiped the more tears came.

Astaroth moved towards him with his arms open.

"NO!" screamed Cadence, almost jumping away from the god. "It's too late now. I want *nothing* to do with you or any of your kind." His pulse quickened in his veins and he felt his face redden with rage.

The god closed his eyes, and his face became taught with sorrow. "I am deeply sorry that you had to endure such suffering," he said. "It was unavoidable. I had to allow you to become the man you are destined to be."

"And what kind of man is that?" Cadence spat. "A deformed slave with a useless oracular ability who freezes whenever he feels fear?"

"That is not who you are," said the god.

"Then what am I to you? A plaything? A puppet?"

"You are strong. You heard the prophecy. You will help guide the plan of the Fates to save humanity. You and the Luciferian prince have a vital role to play in the war to come."

As Astaroth spoke, a knowing washed over Cadence. It pulled at his mind, at his heart, and at his soul. It was the pull of an undeniable truth. If he and Arlo did not fight in the war, the world of gods and men would fall into eternal darkness. He also knew that if they did fight, Arlo would die. He could not see how or why or by whose hand the prince would fall, but he knew that the war would be over and won the moment Arlo drew his final breath. Anger and resentment burned through Cadence as strong as the acid that caused his scars. He tore his mind's eye from the vision and it faded away until he was facing Astaroth once again.

"The Fates and humanity can all go fuck themselves," Cadence snarled. "How much more do the gods want to take from me without offering anything in return? You expect me to defend humanity yet deny me even the smallest bit of protection when I need it most? Everyone I knew is dead. My family is dead. My mother—" Cadence's voice cracked with heartache at the thought of Rebekah as his throat tightened around itself. "My mother is dead, and now according to that prophecy Arlo has to die too."

Astaroth opened his mouth to speak, but once again Cadence would not allow him. He forced the words through his constricted throat.

"No!" he shouted, throwing his hands in the air and fighting back tears. "I don't want to hear another word from you. The gods and the Fates will take nothing more from me. Send me back to the airboat with Arlo right now."

"As you wish," said the god with a nod of his head.

Nothing Cadence had said or done had made the slightest difference to the god's mood or tone. That in itself made Cadence even angrier. Did he make no difference to Astaroth whatsoever? Everything inside of him wanted to push the god of prophecy to his limits. He *wanted* to anger the god, to see his wrath. But Astaroth would not give in. It took everything in Cadence not to pounce on him and try to tear him limb from pearly limb.

"But remember, my son, there is no escaping the Great Web of the Fates," he said as his eyes began to glow green once more. "I shall see you again soon."

"I'm not your son," Cadence spat before he was sent reeling through the void again.

HE FELT himself return to his body and the pain set in immediately. His face was swollen and stung from Gemini's beating. He opened his eyes to find himself in his seat in the airboat with Arlo at the helm.

Cadence's muscles ached from the strain he'd put them through while tied to the bed. His mind raced through what had happened as he looked at the bright pink rings around his wrists where the restraints had rubbed the flesh raw. The inside of his throat burned from all the screaming. He began to shake and felt his split lip prickle as it trembled. He swallowed his anger and commanded the tears to stop their flow. It was over now. What was done was done. Both he and Arlo were alive, and he instead decided to focus on being grateful for that.

Arlo turned his face away from the helm to look at Cadence. Cadence read a mixture of relief and sorrow on Arlo's face, but the prince said nothing.

The distant sun was beating down on the golden airboat as it sped through the air. The frigid winter wind whipped through Cadence's hair as he turned to look behind them.

"I think we got away in time," said Arlo. "No one is following us."

Cadence turned back to Arlo and leaned forward. "Was there no way we could have stayed?"

It was a stupid question, but part of Cadence had wondered if laws applied differently to royalty.

"I killed a priest of Solaris," said Arlo. "And worse yet, an ichor alchemist. My father would not have me put to death but instead would have found a way to blame you."

"Where are we going to go?" asked Cadence. They had no money and no food. He saw that Arlo was still dressed in full armour and covered in spatters and smears of Gemini's blood. He looked fresh from a battlefield and weary.

When he looked down at himself, Cadence saw he was still naked. His whole body was covered in smears of dried blood, some his own and some Gemini's. Arlo had wrapped him in the blood-stained sheet that stank so strongly of iron Cadence could taste it in his mouth.

"I don't care where we go," Arlo replied. "As long as we go together."

A sensation Cadence hadn't felt in a long time flowed through his body as Astaroth began to whisper to him. It was soft at first and Cadence did his best to ignore it, still angry and reeling from all he had learned. But the voice of the god grew louder inside his mind. Cadence had no choice but to listen as Astaroth gave him a set of instructions and directions. He did not want help from Astaroth, but they needed somewhere safe to recover. It was either the place Astaroth was sending them or the wilderness. When his mind went quiet again, Cadence ran over the words, trying to commit them to memory.

"Let me take the helm," said Cadence, getting to his feet and wrapping the sheet around his body to shield him from the icy wind. "I know a place where we will be safe."

23
ANTHURIUM

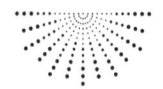

They flew until just before the sun kissed the horizon. Arlo had given Cadence control over the helm and instructed him on how to steer and control the speed. Once Cadence was comfortable, Arlo sat back and stopped instructing him. At one point, Cadence had turned back to find Arlo asleep in his seat. Cadence watched Arlo breathe as his chest rose and fell under his blood-spattered breastplate.

Astaroth's instructions and directions rang through Cadence's mind like the toll of a bell, making it impossible to think of anything else. Cadence was finally pulled away from the echoes of the god's voice when Arlo's fingers touched his shoulder.

"Where are we going?" Arlo asked, his voice groggy and dry with thirst.

"We are here," replied Cadence as he switched places with Arlo so he could lower the airboat and bring it in for landing.

The airboat touched down in a clearing in the middle of the dense forest they'd been flying over for the past hour. The late afternoon sun shone through the leaves of the trees, making them glow like freshly cast bronze. In the centre of the clearing stood a great sycamore tree. The ancient trunk of the sycamore stretched high towards the sky where its branches and leaves exploded out in every direction and dappled the orange sunlight.

"Looks like nothing but wilderness to me," said Arlo as he got out of the airboat and stretched his arms and legs.

"Astaroth spoke to me," said Cadence as he climbed out of the airboat. He tried to keep the sheet around his body by draping it over himself like a makeshift mantle. "He told me to come here."

"The god?"

"Yes. He is the reason I have my abilities. We seem to be connected."

"How so?"

"He claims to be my spiritual father. His magic made it possible for my mother to conceive me. He showed me while I was passed out. There is so much I need to tell you, but now is not the time. We need to find sanctuary first."

"I think we will be safe out here," said Arlo, looking around. "There is something about this place. It seems sacred."

Cadence felt it too. A vibration rang through the air that rattled his insides, leaving him warm and lightheaded but in a pleasant way.

"No," said Cadence as he walked towards the great sycamore tree. "There is somewhere safer. Somewhere we are supposed to be. Astaroth didn't say where. He just told me to come here and ..."

Cadence trailed off as he raised his palm and pressed it gently against the wide trunk of the tree. The wind picked up out of nowhere and whipped through the clearing. Cracks of light like the web of a spider opened in the bark of the tree.

The cracks grew wider and the light brighter until both Cadence and Arlo were enveloped in it.

WHEN THE LIGHT FADED, they found themselves no longer in the clearing but in a paradise. They were surrounded by rolling hills of emerald grass flush with hedges, trees, and massive blooms of flowers as far as the eye could see. Under a clear blue sky, a cool breeze sweet with the scent of all the flowers wafted over them.

Sprinkled between the abundance of flora were statues and fountains of white marble and gold. They depicted frolicking youths frozen in a moment of utter joy, gods, dancing nymphs, and men feasting on pomegranates, apples, and pears. The water flowing from the fountains glittered in the sunlight, and birds sang as they flittered through the air.

A goddess stood before them, warm and bright. She was tall, voluptuous, and regal, with glowing skin as dark and smooth as molasses. Her charcoal hair was an intricate design of thick locks and braids that flowed all the way down her back, almost touching the ground. The braids were decorated with pink lilies, sunflowers, and morning glories. A sheer gown dripped from her graceful frame, accentuating her meandering curves and ample bosom and making her look like a night sky filled with twinkling stars.

The goddess seemed warmly familiar to Cadence. Her cheekbones, nose, and golden eyes all bore a striking resemblance to Arsinoe. In that moment, Cadence realized exactly which goddess they were in the presence of. Every inch of Hermia, earth goddess and mother of spring and flowers, vibrated with health and abundance. She had, after all, sown all the plants of the earth with her bare hands and watered them with her breastmilk.

Both Cadence and Arlo dropped to their knees in front of her and looked to the ground.

"Cadence, son of Canaan, and Arlo, son of Abydos," said the goddess with a warm and welcoming smile. "Welcome to Anthurium, the realm of eternal spring. The Second-Sighted One told me to expect you."

"Astaroth told you we were coming?" asked Cadence without looking up from the ground. He ran through the long list of gods in his mind. They were a family, but there were so many of them that keeping track of how they were all related could prove a challenging task even when one was clear of mind. Cadence's head still ached from Gemini's beating, and the family lines of the gods were nothing but a blurred mess.

"Indeed," said the goddess. Her voice was filled with the sounds of nature—the wind rustling through leaves, the rush of a waterfall, and songs of birds—all combined into one. "He told me you needed protection. He said you'd killed a priest of Solaris; is this true?"

Cadence and Arlo finally looked up for the first time and Arlo spoke.

"It is true, goddess," he said. "It was I who killed him. I am aware that the murder of a priest is a crime punishable by death."

"That would depend," said Hermia, her face as serene as a lake on a windless day. "What was your reason? Did you kill him out of impiety?"

"No, goddess," said Arlo.

"The priest was trying to rape me," said Cadence, quickly coming to Arlo's defence. The words turned sour in his mouth as he spoke them and his cheeks began to burn with shame. "He had already beaten me, and I am sure if Arlo had not stopped him I would be dead."

"Why would a priest try to rape a youth?" asked Hermia, her dark brows furrowing with concern.

"He was an evil man, goddess," said Cadence. The words caught in his throat as he remembered what happened. His body began to shake. He fought back at the tears pounding to be released from his eyes so he could finish stating his case. "He would put awful visions in my head and look upon me with a lustful gaze that made me feel unclean. He was ill too, with the blight. He thought defiling me would somehow cure him."

"Blasphemy!" Hermia bellowed as her face crumpled with disgust. "Some who suffer from the blight believe that raping those who are touched by the magic of the gods will cure them. It is a vile fallacy. The blight rots the mind as badly as it decays the body. There is no force able to undo the magic of a god once it is done."

Cadence's gaze shot up to Hermia's face and his mouth fell open. "So it's true then," he said. "The blight is a curse from the gods."

"Not *the* gods," Hermia corrected, "*a* god, and not one among those worshipped by the people of the Empire. The blight is the work of a deity unknown to us. But you will be safe here. I shall offer you sanctuary. No creature, god, or mortal can enter or leave Anthurium without my permission. Rise, and my nymphs will see that you are both tended to."

Arlo and Cadence got to their feet before the goddess walked closer. Where her feet left the ground, the grass blossomed with delicate white flowers that bloomed wide open to greet the sky. She placed a hand on Cadence's shoulder and a warm euphoria spread across his body like butter melting into fresh bread. The pain in his head, across his face, and in his muscles abandoned him.

"Thank you," Cadence sighed.

"I must know," said Hermia. "Was the priest at all successful in his attempt?"

The euphoric feeling diminished and gave way to a powerful wave of shame that caused Cadence's stomach to clench. He did not look away no matter how badly he wanted to. The goddess was so close to him that he could see directly into her eyes. They were swirling pools of glowing gold that held a universe all their own inside of them.

"No," Cadence responded as quickly as he could. Then he remembered, and his balled-up stomach dropped to his knees and his body went cold. "S–s—" he tried to force the words out, but they refused. "Some of his—some of his blood got into my mouth."

Cadence wanted to look at Arlo but could not bear what he might see on his lover's face. Instead, he was surprised by a sudden and hard embrace that was Arlo locking his arms around him. Arlo held onto Cadence so tightly it almost hurt, and his hot tears struck the back of Arlo's neck.

"I spat as much of it out as I could," Cadence wailed. "But I don't know."

"I should never have left," Arlo cried through gritted teeth. "If I hadn't left then none of this would have happened. We should have just run away together."

"The curse of the blight is a mysterious one," said Hermia. "Even the gods are unsure of its workings. I have healed you to the best of my powers. If you are indeed infected by the blight, signs will reveal themselves in time. Until then, you both need to rest."

Arlo waited for a brief moment before releasing his grip, and Cadence dried his tears on the bloody sheet still wrapped around his body.

Nymphs appeared, summoned forth from the flowers and trees they inhabited. They were beautiful creatures, dressed in garlands of delicate flowers and soft fabrics that flowed over them like wisps of cloud. Their features were fine and sharp with skin the colour of tree bark and eyes that shone in every shade from brilliantly bright amber to deep green moss.

The nymphs led Cadence and Arlo down through the grassy hills, bushes, and blooms to a gravel pathway. The pathway meandered through beds of flowers that grew wild and vast, climbing the trunks of trees and spreading themselves across the ground like a sweet-smelling sheet.

Arlo walked next to Cadence, holding on tightly to his hand as they followed the nymphs down the path. Their steps were slow and heavy as they lumbered forward, exhausted.

THEY CAME to the edge of a stream upon which a thatched roof cottage had been built. The outside walls were overrun with thick vines of dark green ivy and surrounded by a garden exploding with wildflowers in bright oranges, soft yellows, and deep purples.

A nymph with large amber eyes and mushroom brown hair led them to the doorway of the cottage.

"I am Gossamer," she said as she opened the door of the cottage for them. "We are not accustomed to human guests. If my mistress has not met any of your needs, please call my name and I will tend to you."

"Thank you," said Arlo.

Gossamer nodded before turning to leave with the rest of the nymphs. They slowly faded away into the surrounding forest as gracefully as they had appeared.

The inside of the cottage was spacious and welcoming. Large open windows of rippled glass played with the sunlight shining through them, catching it in one colour before allowing it to burst forth in rainbows that shone on the light wood floor. Couches covered in cloud-like pillows filled a reception room, while off to the right a robust wooden table stood overflowing with silver platters of fruits, cheeses, and freshly baked breads.

Bouquets bursting with wildflowers had been scattered throughout the cottage, adding to the bright and serene atmosphere. The sweet scent in the air relaxed the muscles in Cadence's body and seemed to make it easier for him to breathe.

He'd never seen a place so close to perfect, and he felt unworthy to stand in it. On the outside he was still dirty, caked in the smears of dried blood and sticky sweat. But it was his insides that concerned him. Something in him had been disrupted and tainted, and if Gemini had given him the blight, Cadence feared that he would never feel well again. His body was no longer in pain thanks to Hermia, but her healing powers had not been able to fix the ache of his heart, the throbbing of his mind, or the fracture he felt had opened in his soul.

"I'm so sorry," said Cadence as soon as Arlo closed the door of the cottage. Tears began to fall from his eyes. "I should have been more careful after you left. I shouldn't have gone wandering through the palace. I should have gone straight to Arsinoe. She would have been able to protect me, and now I've doomed myself to the blight."

"You have nothing to apologise for," said Arlo. His voice was gruff with anger and his face heavy with the burden of remorse. "I was so foolish. I should never have left, and I should have known from the moment you were first brought to my chamber who you really were. If you do have the blight, it is I who have doomed you. I was so blinded by my mourning that I couldn't see the one I was mourning was right in front of me. I always felt something was so familiar about you but you looked and sounded so different. What happened to you?"

They sat in the cottage and Cadence took Arlo through his newfound memories. As he did so, he could not help but relive them in his mind. He remembered the burn of the acid on his skin. Arlo was silent as Cadence spoke, but his face gave away what he was feeling. With each detail Cadence added, Arlo's beautiful face became more twisted with anger and disgust before relaxing into pity. When Cadence finished, Arlo pulled him closer.

"I'm sorry you had to suffer so much," he said. "And I am sorry that I failed to protect you even when I made you a promise that no harm would come to you."

"It's not your fault," said Cadence, his throat dry from speaking. "But how did you know where to find me?"

"It was the strangest feeling," said Arlo. "I was about to board my airship when I felt like something was wrong. Somehow I just knew. I ran immediately and it was like I was being pulled towards you."

Arlo leaned in closer, but Cadence pushed him away before jumping up from the couch. "No," he said, his voice trembling. "You can't touch me, not until we know for sure if I have the blight or not."

Arlo got to his feet, and Cadence saw the prince fighting to keep the hurt out of his face.

"Don't push me away," said Arlo. "I don't care if you have the blight; I want to comfort you."

Arlo took a step forward and Cadence quickly took two back.

"We can't," said Cadence. "We can't risk for you to catch it. You are too important."

"Too important to comfort the man I love?" asked Arlo as the hurt slowly began to seep into his expression.

"Too important to the Empire," said Cadence.

Arlo stepped back as if wounded, and his jaw fell open.

"When I was with Astaroth," continued Cadence, "I had a vision. It was complete this time, not fragmented or blurry like the others. Having my memories stolen from me broke me somehow, but getting them back fixed me. I can see the future now and even some of the past as clearly as I see you standing before me. Astaroth also helped fix me somehow. I saw a prophecy that was made about us. You have to fight or the world will fall into darkness. I don't know how and I don't know why, but if you don't fight then the world is doomed."

"I will not fight and die in a war my father has created," said Arlo. "I refuse to be his puppet any longer."

As angry as he was at the gods, his visions had provided Cadence with perspective, and with it an understanding. A war was coming, and if Arlo did not fight, countless lives would be lost. The issue at hand was so much bigger than him and Arlo, the Emperor, and the gods.

"It's not only about you and your father," said Cadence. "It's about the fate of this world and everyone in it." Cadence remembered how he'd screamed at Astaroth. How he'd refused to help. But the truth weighed on his heart like an anchor, and he could not ignore it no matter how much he wanted to.

"*You* are my world," said Arlo.

"My home was destroyed by Saklas and his demons," said Cadence. "My entire family wiped off the face of the earth. Would you have the rest of the world see the same fate?"

"A family that sold you like an animal for slaughter."

"Saklas murdered my mother. She was not like the rest of my family. And this isn't about me either. There are other mothers, other families that will be slaughtered and turned into those mindless creatures inhabited by a god they do not worship."

"Everything has been taken from us," said Arlo through clenched teeth. "All we have left is each other. That is enough for me. That is the only thing I want to protect. Why does it have to be me? Why can't some other demigod save the world?"

"It is the will of the Fates," said Cadence. The truth was supposed to be a pure and freeing thing, but as soon as the words passed his lips he felt sick and trapped by its inescapable clutches. He sounded like Astaroth and Arsinoe. Worse still, he felt like the Emperor, pushing Arlo down a path he did not want to be on.

"Fuck the Fates!" Arlo yelled, and for a moment as brief as a blink Cadence saw the white lightning crackle beneath Arlo's brilliant blue eyes.

"I felt the same way," said Cadence. "I told Astaroth as much, but there is no escaping this. I know that now."

"No," said Arlo. "There is. No mortal or god can enter this realm without permission from Hermia. We also cannot be forced to leave against our own free will. This place is separate from our world. We could live out our days here in comfort and happiness."

"That's your plan?" asked Cadence. "To hide from the end of the world like a coward instead of fighting against it like the warrior I know you are?"

"Why are you acting this way?" Arlo cried. "Why don't you want us to be happy? Why don't you want us to be at peace?"

"I want that!" Cadence screamed. "I want that more than anything I have ever wanted or will ever want again! But the price of our happiness is too high. I would rather die at your side than watch the world burn from inside your embrace."

"It's not fair," said Arlo. The anger in his voice had burned away at itself, leaving behind only wisps of faint, defeated smoke.

"We can find a way to survive this," said Cadence. "The will of the Fates cannot be broken, but it may be bent."

"And if I say yes? Will you let me touch you?" replied Arlo.

Cadence looked down at his bare arms and hands. His heart raced as his eyes desperately searched for even the slightest hint of dark splotches the blight created. He turned his mind towards his body. Physically he felt fine, but he had no idea how long it would take for the disease to grab hold of him, if at all.

He looked up at Arlo. His ocean blue eyes pleaded to come closer.

"I don't want to waste any of the time we have," said Arlo. "Blight or no blight, death in battle or life afterwards. There is too much uncertainty even for your second sight to see."

Cadence felt his shoulders sag as he stepped forward into Arlo's arms. They stood holding each other for a moment before Arlo's lips found their way to Cadence's. He stripped the blood-soaked sheet from Cadence's body while Cadence's fingers fumbled over the straps and clips of Arlo's armour. Once they were both bare, Arlo led Cadence out of the cottage and into the warm sunlight. Hand in hand, they made their way to the stream where fresh clothes, towels, soaps, and scented oils had been laid out for them.

THE WATER of the stream was surprisingly warm against Cadence's skin as he stepped into the gently moving current. Once waist deep, Arlo lathered soap laced with the fresh fragrance of lemongrass and mint in his palms and began to wash the blood off Cadence's skin. Cadence did the same for Arlo, allowing his hands to slide over the muscles of his broad shoulders and chest.

They bathed, rinsed, and swam for a while, allowing the water to pass over and between them. Arlo's golden hair when wet took on the colour of rich honey. Cadence watched as water droplets danced across Arlo's skin before re-joining the water.

Arlo pulled Cadence closer and rested his forehead against his.

"Is it so much to ask that we could stay this way forever?" Arlo whispered.

Cadence clung to Arlo a little tighter. Arlo had said that he would go back to Luciferian to fight, that they would try find a way to survive. But there was a small part of Cadence that did not believe him.

Cadence didn't want to question. He didn't want to argue. It felt too good to just be with Arlo. It was safe. It was comfortable. It was love. And Cadence didn't want to spoil it by trying to force Arlo to do something he didn't want to do. Had Arlo not suffered enough? The very reason for his existence was reduced to being a weapon of a war he had no desire to fight in. Cadence didn't want to be another manipulator in Arlo's life.

"I was wrong," said Cadence. "I'm sorry."

"About what?" asked Arlo, backing away to look at Cadence.

"You shouldn't have to go back to Luciferian if you don't want to. It was wrong of me to try to force you. It should be *your* choice if you want to fight, no one else's."

"But your vision ..."

"The past is frozen, but I refuse to believe the future can't change. Who's to say there isn't some other demigod out there who can fight in this war? All that's really certain is the present, and I want as much of that with you as possible."

"Even if it means you have to watch the world burn?"

"What have humanity or the gods ever done for us?" Cadence responded. The words tasted like poison in his mouth, but the decision had to be Arlo's to make and his alone.

"Then I want to stay," said Arlo as relief broke over his face. He swam forward and locked Cadence in an embrace.

It felt good to come clean, but on the inside Cadence still felt filthy, and no amount of scented soap would ever help. Yes, the price of their happiness was too high to pay, but perhaps the burden of the world was too heavy for them to bear.

24

THE GODDESS INFERNAL

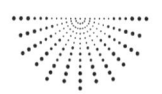

*A*nthurium was a true paradise. Arlo and Cadence spent the first few days lounging in the cottage eating the food that, by Hermia's magic, would instantly replenish itself and never go bad. The grapes were the sweetest Cadence had ever tasted. When he closed his eyes and crushed one between his teeth, it was as if pure sunlight flooded his mouth. Everything was better in Anthurium. The sun shone brighter, the birds sang more sweetly, and the air was always thick with the perfume of flowers.

As ideal as their newfound paradise was, Cadence's internal peace was regularly broken by a fervent panic. When he remembered that he might have contracted the blight, his throat would tighten with dread. In those moments, he would leave Arlo, and once on his own he would tear the tunic from his body and frantically check for any signs of the disease. His eyes would move over his body in a frenzy trying to find the slightest hint of a plum-coloured blemish. Once satisfied that he could not find anything, his throat would loosen and he could breathe easily once more. The relief didn't last long before he found himself alone, naked, and full of fear once again.

Hermia had arranged for the nymphs to bring a lyre to the cottage for Arlo and a loom and wool for Cadence. In the evenings, they sat together as they had done in the palace at Luciferian; Arlo would strum hypnotic tunes while the blur of Cadence's hands weaved tapestries, tunics, and throws. The weaving took his mind off the blight and to other places. He thought back to when he could not remember how he'd learned to weave, and an ache broke through his heart. How could he have forgotten his own mother but remembered the things she had passed down to him? He tried not to dwell on the regret and decided to rather take full comfort in the work, and there were times when he sat weaving when he could almost feel her looking over his shoulder to check it. When he weaved, he felt closer to her. Honouring her memory brought comfort from the bitter grief.

"That is *The Song of Marlow and Odette*," said Cadence, looking up at Arlo as he played a tune on the lyre one evening.

"So that's what it's called." Arlo said, smiling.

"You used to play that in the palace all the time. It always felt so familiar to me."

"You sang it the first night we met. I've never been able to get it out of my head. Sing it while I play."

Cadence took in a breath with excitement before letting out a grated and shrill note and then quickly closed his lips in a mortified grimace.

"What's the matter?" asked Arlo, his fingers abandoning the strings of the lyre, killing the music.

"My voice is not what it once was," said Cadence. "That night with my brothers. The pain was unbearable. I screamed and … I don't sing anymore. Please carry on playing. I enjoy it so much."

Arlo didn't ask any questions. He nodded and went back to strumming the lyre. Cadence watched Arlo's face for a moment. There was a brief flash of anger and lightning in his eyes before it fell back beneath the surface of his calm expression.

It did not take long before Arlo grew restless in the cottage and its surrounding garden. He began to insist he and Cadence explore the land of Anthurium more widely. The realm of eternal spring was vast with meadows, hills, rivers, streams, and forests. Together they wandered and swam. Arlo would point out flowers that grew in Anthurium that did not grow in Luciferian and some that he did not even know the names of. It had not escaped Cadence's attention that a plethora of poisonous flowers and plants also thrived in Hermia's realm. When he recognised them, he could not help his longing for Arsinoe's company and the inside of her conservatory.

"Do you think they are looking for us?" Cadence asked one evening as he sat at his loom. Arlo was busy stringing a bow he'd made for himself, to what end Cadence did not know. There was no need for them to hunt. There were no enemies in Anthurium or monsters they had to defend themselves against.

"If they are," said Arlo as he tested the tension of the bow, "they won't find us here."

"What about Arsinoe? She is probably worried sick about us."

"Arsinoe knows that we can take care of ourselves." Arlo's tone was distant and distracted. "And besides, she probably has her hands full producing bliss now that Gemini is dead."

The back of Cadence's throat pained with guilt at the

thought of the Empress. "We left her in a bit of a mess," he said.

Arlo did not turn his attention away from the bow. "We didn't have that much of a choice. And just like us, Arsinoe is more than capable of taking care of herself."

Cadence nodded in agreement, but the guilt did not wane.

***

GETTING his memories back had somehow flipped a switch in Cadence's mind. Suddenly he could see clearly into the future and sometimes even the past. He did not know how much of it had to do with the return of his stolen memories and how much Astaroth was responsible for. Either way, pieces of the future and the past were presented to him in clear flashes during his waking hours. When he laid his head down to sleep, the dreams would come.

That night, he found himself in the throne room of the palace. Sunlight streamed in through the high stained glass windows in bright reds and brilliant golds. The Emperor stood facing away from the throne and looking through one of the open windows to the palace grounds below. He stood alone as if waiting for something to happen. Then it did.

A sharp rattle pierced the air, and an ashen, alabaster creature slithered out from the shadows. The light in the throne room bounced off of her milky skin, making her glow.

Cadence needed no introduction. He was looking at Nubia, goddess of chaos, the strife of war, and Arlo's mother. Her form was more serpent-like than feminine, and Cadence could not believe something so hideous and terrifying gave birth to someone as beautiful as Arlo.

Cadence had seen her chilling likeness mosaicked and

painted on the temple walls. He had walked past her form carved from granite into guardian statues scattered throughout the city hundreds of times, but nothing could have prepared him for the real thing.

She was a terrifying sight as her serpentine features glistened in the sunlight. A set of pale, grey, leathery wings erupted from her back, casting a dark shadow on the throne room floor. She had four muscular arms that ended in long, talon-like hands. Set in the palm of each hand were unblinking red reptilian eyes. Nubia's slender frame was wrapped in ropes of muscle that flexed and twitched under her milky skin. Her head was as bare and smooth as river rock. She had a face forged of mangled, razor-sharp angles and ridges that could slice open flesh at the slightest touch. Her mouth was little more than a gash in her face that parted to reveal silvery fangs. The two eyes on her snake-like face were large almonds of the most all-consuming black Cadence had ever seen. He turned away, fearing that if he gazed too long they would pull him in and drown him like the sirens of the Hercynian Sea.

The Emperor paid Nubia's appearance no mind. As far as he was acting, the goddess was no more interesting than a servant girl. He didn't even turn to meet her many eyes.

"To what," the Emperor grumbled, "do I owe the honour of this visit?"

"The boy," Nubia hissed slowly. Her voice was the sound of blood-soaked gravel being trod upon by the feet of the battle weary and defeated.

Abydos raised an eyebrow. "You have never concerned yourself with him before," he said. "I doubt you even know what he looks like."

"You forget," she said, raising her massive hands and unfolding her palms to show off the burning eyes, "I see all."

"What about him then?" the Emperor asked.

"He is growing soft. He must be separated from the slave boy if his true power is ever to reveal itself."

The Emperor pondered on this for a moment, still facing away from her. When he was ready to speak, he finally turned to face her for the first time. "You may *see* all, but you do not *know* all."

"I know enough, impudent mortal," Nubia hissed through her fangs. "War is coming to your precious Empire. If Arlo does not reach his full potential, then all will be ash. His godhead must be unleashed."

"And you think that separating him from his favourite plaything is going to do that?" the Emperor asked, sneering.

"You are a fool. The scarred boy you call Proteus is far more than he seems."

"He is a glorified, mutilated slave boy who couldn't predict the direction of the wind if he had a weather vane embedded in his skull. He has lived in this palace for over a year. Do you not think if he was more than he seemed I would know by now?"

"His mind and his abilities have been tampered with, but he is the key to unlocking Arlo's godhead. He and Arlo are twin flames. Bound together by destiny and the Great Web of the Fates. Grief may be the gust of wind they both need to fan the embers of their abilities into an inferno."

"I could have the boy killed," said the Emperor. "Would that not accomplish the same thing?"

"No!" shouted the goddess. "They must both remain alive if you are to have any hope of winning this war. There is a delicate balance to this matter. Too much grief will break Arlo and he will rage out of control. The slave boy also has his role to play, and he must do so until the Fates' design unravels itself to us."

"Very well," said the Emperor. "But I can't help but wonder why you felt the need to tell me this in person. I understand my own motivations behind wanting to win this war, but yours are a mystery to me. What do you care if a few humans live or die?"

"I don't care if a few hundred thousand humans die," said Nubia. "I care if they *all* do. And that is exactly what will happen if you don't let Arlo win this war for you."

"*All* humans?" the Emperor asked, looking surprised—an expression Cadence had never seen on his face before.

"You know not who you fight against, Abydos," said Nubia. "Do as I say or you will doom heaven as well as the realm of men."

"What do you mean?" asked the Emperor as he stepped closer to the goddess.

"Without worship," said Nubia, "a god will go mad before turning to dark and desperate measures. Saklas is one such god."

"You know of him?" asked the Emperor, his interest suddenly highly piqued.

"Not nearly enough," replied Nubia. "I have consulted with some of the other gods, and even the eldest among us have no recollection of him. Our reach has never stretched as far as The Scorched-Over Lands. You should never have allowed your forces to invade outside the realm of the Pantheon's protection."

The Emperor's cold face twisted into ugly disgust. "You mean outside the realm of your power," he spat.

"Be careful, Abydos," Nubia warned. "You have already created a war you can't handle. Your boundless hubris shall be your undoing. You may be descended from a great god, but you are by no means immortal, and even legacies can die."

A silence thick with contempt fell between the goddess and the Emperor until Abydos spoke again.

"What dark and desperate measures do you speak of?"

"Forced worship, necromancy, and the possession of dead human flesh," said Nubia. "I am one of the darker gods, and even I would never entertain such unholy depravity."

"I'm not sure what you mean," said Abydos.

"From what we can tell," Nubia explained, "Saklas revives the flesh of the dead by inhabiting corpses with his own essence. He then has the living corpses perform rites and make sacrifices to him. In the case of the living, he does the same and takes away the one thing all gods are forbidden to take from any human—free will. He lives inside all his so-called worshippers and takes over their minds, and as a result their bodies begin to die and rot away. They are nothing but puppets of flesh. They become multiple forms for his one mind to inhabit."

"Why would a god do such a thing?"

"To avoid the loss of human worship and remembrance. When a god loses their worshippers, they go mad, and after the madness runs its course, the god withers and fades completely out of existence. As long as a god exists in the consciousness of humanity, no matter the form that consciousness takes, the god can live forever."

"Why have I never heard this about the gods?"

"It's not something the gods like humans to know. It gives them too much power. And we all know what happens when humans are given too much power." All Nubia's eyes then looked Abydos up and down, accusing him.

The breath was stolen from Cadence's lungs. *It's possible for a god to die*, he thought before remembering something Arsinoe had once told him.

"When a god does what Saklas has done," Nubia continued, "it absolutely and irreversibly corrupts them. If Saklas was prepared to do that to himself, then there is no telling what else he is capable of."

Abydos remained silent and looked away from Nubia.

"Heed my warning," said the dark goddess. "See those boys separated or I will separate them for you and then see your head separated from your neck."

The goddess gave a flap of her leathery wings, blowing out all the braziers and torches in the throne room before disappearing like rising smoke.

Cadence woke gently to birdsong and morning sunlight streaming through the blinds of the bedroom in the cottage. He rolled over to find Arlo awake and looking at him—his sapphire eyes alert and observant.

"Good morning," he said with a smile as bright as the dawn.

"I had another dream last night," said Cadence.

"Of the future?" Arlo asked, the smile fading like a ghost.

"No … this time it was of the past. The recent past. I saw the meeting your father had with Nubia before he tried to send you away. I think I understand the reason he wanted us separated. We need to speak with Hermia. I need answers."

25

THE SOUL WITH TWO BODIES

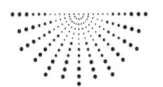

*I*t was dusk when Gossamer arrived to escort Arlo and Cadence to their audience with Hermia. The fading sunlight bathed all of Anthurium in a golden light that made the plants and flowers glow with vibrant life.

They followed the nymph through the winding pathways and past the columns, fountains, and statues that greeted them with stony smiles as they passed. Gossamer led them deep into a forest they had somehow, in all their wandering, never found before. Cadence's ears began to twitch at the distant sound of music and laughter muffled by towering trees. Just as the last of the sunlight began to fade and give way to the bright blue glow of the full moon, they came to a clearing.

On a throne of stone, overrun with vines and gigantic luminescent blooms, Hermia sat waiting for them. Before her, a large party of nymphs and satyrs danced as a band off to the side played a rhythmic tune that sounded almost hypnotic. Emberflies floated gracefully in the air like tiny stars that had come loose from the heavens to cast light over the festivities. Cadence's eyes widened at the sight of the satyrs.

From the waist up, the satyrs were normal men aside from the short horns sprouting from the tops of their heads. From the waist down, they were all shiny brown fur with legs that ended in cloven hoofs. Cadence watched, mesmerised, as the goat-men danced with the beautiful nymphs, drank from bladders of wine, and ate from the abundant spread of food set out on a long table close to the band. Their faces were slim and pinched into mischievous grins that, to Cadence, teetered dangerously between the border of fun-loving and trouble-making. His memory took him back to the stories his mother had told him of the satyrs who lived in the deep forests and woods of the world. She had spoken of their love of wine and their service to the nature deities. The satyrs, like the nymphs, were the children of Hermia and Borros, god of the forests and lord of animals. The smell of sweet pollens and nectars perfumed the warm breeze and beckoned Cadence closer.

There was a fever of festivity in the air that was impossible to ignore. Despite all he had been through and all he'd seen, Cadence found himself fighting the urge to take Arlo by the hand and dance. In the end he didn't have to fight because Arlo grabbed his hand first.

"Let's dance," said Arlo as he smiled at Cadence and pulled him forward.

Before he knew it, he and Arlo were in the eye of the jovial hurricane. A blur of dancing and laughing nymphs and satyrs swirled around them while the two boys twisted, ebbed, and flowed around each other.

Cadence grinned at Arlo. "I just realised," he said, "we've never danced together before."

"Then why does it feel like we've been doing it together our whole lives?" Arlo asked playfully.

As soon as the question left Arlo's lips, the world around them froze and went silent. The nymphs and satyrs were locked in place, as still as statues. The band had also fallen silent, leaving only the sound of the breeze weaving gently through the leaves of the trees.

"I may be able to answer that question," said Hermia as she rose from her throne, "as well as some others I believe you have for me."

Cadence and Arlo both immediately lowered their gaze out of respect. The gesture did not last long as Cadence couldn't help but admire the radiant beauty of the goddess. His eyes panned up from her bare feet and over the curves of her body. Her ebony skin glowed in the flickering light of the emberflies.

"I had a vision," said Cadence, "more like a dream, but it was not of the future. It was of the past."

Hermia raised a charcoal eyebrow as a golden light danced behind her eyes. "Has this happened before?" she asked.

"Only once," said Cadence. "When I met with Astaroth. He gave me a vision of my mother before she conceived me."

"So it seems your powers are growing," said Hermia.

"My second vision was of Nubia," said Cadence.

As he spoke the goddess's name, Hermia all but recoiled. Her soft and smooth features suddenly hardened. "Dreaming of a goddess so dark can only spell ill fortune."

"She called Arlo and I twin flames," continued Cadence. "I don't know what that means."

"Oh, but I think you do," replied Hermia.

Cadence said nothing. He looked from Hermia to Arlo and back again before simply shaking his head.

"The moon is so bright tonight," said the goddess. "Walk with me under her light and I will tell you a story."

She led them away from the nymphs and satyrs, frozen in

their festivities, and further into the clearing. Moonlight bathed the tall grass and blooms of foxglove in silver-blue light. The breeze picked up a little and danced through the clearing, turning it into a shimmering night-time ocean. The goddess spoke, and they listened.

When Spirit Became One with Life

WHEN THE WORLD WAS NEW, Spirit was whole. It was a beautiful and vast being that encompassed everything in existence. It was as much a force of nature as fire, water, earth, and air.

This additional element was the shared child of the earth, the sun, and the moon. The sun provided his seed, the moon her egg, and the earth bore and nourished Spirit.

It resided around everything from the smallest insect to the greatest of trees, but not inside. It was a force that existed on the outside of life but yearned to be a part of it. It could witness but never experience.

Over time, Spirit's longing to become one with life grew so strong that it began to fracture until it was shattered and scattered to all four corners of the universe. Splinters of Spirit fell to the earth and began to inhabit every living thing. The one Spirit had been transformed into many souls, and life was changed forever.

"TWIN FLAMES ARE mirrors of each other," continued Hermia. "You and Arlo are two slivers from the same fragment of fractured spirit."

"That is a beautiful story," said Arlo.

"But it doesn't explain what Nubia meant when she called us twin flames," said Cadence.

"Were you not listening?" said Hermia. "You may be able to see the past and the future, but you have trouble seeing what is right in front of you."

Cadence looked at the goddess but said nothing, still not fully comprehending what she meant.

"Being twin flames," the goddess explained, "means that you are two bodies who share the same soul. You are forever connected in destiny, in fate, and in power. The closer you are, the stronger your destiny burns and the brighter your powers shine. You feel it every time you are near one another and every time you are parted. Your split soul is constantly seeking out its other half. Your spirit is constantly seeking to make itself whole again."

"That's what the witch meant when she made her prophecy to my mother," uttered Cadence as all the fragments in his mind began to slide into place to create a full fresco as wondrous as it was terrible.

"You share the same birthmark, do you not?" asked Hermia.

The scar on Cadence's shoulder began to tingle. "We did," he said. "Mine was cut away."

"Only mortals are so foolish to think they can cut away at destiny," said Hermia. "The birthmark may not remain, but the destiny is unchanged. The two of you are connected on a cosmic level. You are destined to do great things together—like fight in and help win a great war."

"We don't want to die doing great things," said Arlo. "We want to live and be left in peace."

"You cannot run from destiny any more than you can have it cut out of you," said Hermia as she touched the scar on Cadence's shoulder.

Under the jagged, uneven, pink, and angry flesh where his

brothers had carved the Akra into his skin, his crescent moon birthmark began to glow.

Arlo pulled his tunic down and looked at his side, to the spot where his matching birthmark was also glowing. His mouth twisted into an angry scowl.

"I will not be held hostage by the Fates," he spat.

"We are all their hostages, young prince," said the goddess. "The sooner you come to terms with that the better. Listen to the other half of your soul. He knows this to be true." She raised her hand and gestured towards Cadence.

"I will not make him do anything he does not want to do," Cadence said. "That isn't right. That isn't love."

"All of heaven and earth are looking for the two of you," said Hermia. "It won't be long before gods and men alike figure out that you are here. I cannot force you to leave Anthurium, but I will not keep my kin out if I do not need to."

"Let them come," said Arlo. "There is nothing that they can say or do that will change my mind. I will not be a weapon in my father's war."

"At the cost of every human life in the world?" asked Hermia. "You need to change your perspective. You would not be fighting in your father's war; you would be protecting those who cannot protect themselves. They are your people, and you are their prince. Do your duty to the Empire."

Cadence's mind turned back to the words Nubia had spoken to the Emperor about what happens to gods when there is no one left to worship them.

"You are just trying to protect yourselves," said Arlo, his mind clearly on the same track as Cadence's. "Cadence told me what Nubia said to my father. Without worship, the gods will wither, go mad, and die."

"Be that as it may," said Hermia, "you would still stand by

and let all of existence fall into darkness at the hands of a mad god?"

"Maybe Saklas is right," replied Arlo. "I heard what he said through his emissary. Perhaps it is time humanity and the gods were brought down a notch."

"And in the end of it all," said Hermia, "when my power wanes and Anthurium begins to die, where will the two of you go? Back to Hathuldria where Saklas will make slaves of you both?"

"We will cross that threshold when and if we need to," said Arlo.

Cadence bit into his bottom lip. The more it was discussed, the worse and more selfish Arlo sounded. Cadence knew that in that moment, if he peered into the future, he would see humanity not being taken down a notch but utterly decimated.

"I've had enough of this," Arlo continued before turning sharply and storming off back to the satyrs and nymphs that had been frozen in time.

"You need to convince him that you have to fight," said Hermia to Cadence. "There is no other way and there is no one else. The Fates have tasked the two of you with this burden."

"It's not as simple as that," replied Cadence. "He feels he owes the Empire nothing. He has no reason to fight."

"Then you had better find a reason," said Hermia. "Before the gods find one for him themselves."

Her golden eyes fluttered over Cadence as the words left her lips, making sure he would not mistake them for anything other than what they were—a threat.

"The gods would use me as a hostage to get Arlo to fight in this war?" Cadence asked bitterly.

"The gods can be cruel. We are not accustomed to not getting our way. My approach is gentle. I cannot say the same for the rest of the Pantheon. There is no telling the lengths they will go to."

"This isn't fair."

"You are right, young oracle. It's not fair; it is fate. The worlds of gods and men need both of you to fight in this war or all is lost."

"Fight and die," Cadence corrected.

He bowed to the goddess before turning to follow Arlo into the shadow of the forest.

THEY TRAVELLED unaccompanied by the nymphs and in silence back to the cottage. Cadence was gasping for air by the time he'd caught up with Arlo. Even if he'd had something to say, he did not have the breath to say it. By the time his lungs settled, they were halfway back to the cottage. Cadence watched Arlo's face in the bright moonlight. It was as unforthcoming as uncut marble—cold and solid but with the potential to be hiding a complex sculpture of emotions inside. As Cadence looked away, he felt the warm touch of Arlo's hand slip into his. Arlo gripped firmly and Cadence squeezed back in return.

When they got back to the cottage, Cadence left Arlo on the front porch with his lyre while he went inside and poured them each a cup of wine. When he returned, he found Arlo sitting in the garden basking in the light of an emberfly swarm.

Cadence's mouth fell open as he stood next to Arlo in the yellow-orange glow. He could feel the heat coming from the swarm as they danced and twisted in the air high above their heads.

"I've never seen so many in the same place at once!" said Cadence. "Not even as a child in Naphtali."

"I remember them from the first night we met," said Arlo. "I'd never seen one before then, only heard of them in stories. They are truly beautiful. Why are they behaving this way? Is this how they mate?"

Cadence shrugged. "Maybe they behave differently in Anthurium."

They watched on as the spectacle of tiny flying lights gathered and dispersed and gathered again in a dance that lit up the garden like a miniature sun. As the moments passed, the emberflies grew larger in number and drew ever closer to where Arlo and Cadence were sitting.

"Should we be worried?" asked Arlo. "I've heard they can start fires."

"Only when a swarm is threatened or unhealthy," said Cadence. "It can happen but it's incredibly rare."

Suddenly, the swarm darted down towards them in a hurricane of light and heat. Arlo jumped up and tackled Cadence out of the way before the emberflies struck the ground where he'd been standing a split second before. The drove of light collected in a molten pool on the ground, scorching the grass beneath. Arlo and Cadence clambered to their feet and stepped further away as they watched the nearby flowers and shrubs catch flame and burn away to ash. Arlo's warrior instinct had taken over as he placed himself firmly in a battle stance between Cadence and the swarm of fire.

"What's happening?" said Arlo as he gave a nervous look behind him towards the cottage, measuring the distance between the flames and their new home.

"I'm not sure," said Cadence, the anxiety in his voice rising with the flames. "This isn't right. They aren't supposed to act this way, unless ..."

The flames grew smaller and the heat less intense before the fire died away completely. Cadence took a step forward and leaned in. Between the light of the full moon and the sparse emberflies still floating in the air, he could clearly see what had been left behind on the blackened grass—two full sets of glittering armour.

The larger golden breastplate had been expertly adorned with a shining sun in the centre. The sun was surrounded by twisting vines of blossoming lilies, meadow saffron, amaryllis, sweet William, eucalyptus, and honeysuckle. Cadence recognised and listed each of the flowers one by one in his head as his gaze slowly floated over the armour. Between all the time he'd spent with Arsinoe and Arlo, he could identify the different flora immediately, their meanings, and if they had any medicinal properties or if they were poisonous.

The smaller breastplate had been cast in silver and bore a full moon in the centre encircled by an intricate pattern of wheat, anemone, snowdrops, rue, and camellia.

Each set of armour had a matching shield and greaves that held the same pattern as the breastplates. A sword and spear also accompanied each suit. It was clear by the size which suit was meant for who. The golden armour was obviously made to fit Arlo's broad shoulders and wide chest, while the silver was slimmer and more trim for Cadence's frame. The golden sword with a swirl of lilies at the hilt was much larger and looked like it could shatter a man's skull with a single blow. The sword cast in silver was smaller and lighter, and the hilt was decorated with the same flowers as the matching silver breastplate.

The craftsmanship of the armour was nothing short of divine. The shining metal shimmered with an ethereal glow that sent a shiver over Cadence's body.

"Emberflies are the messengers of Amaranth," said Cadence as his eyes widened over the armour. "These are gifts from the blacksmith of the gods himself."

"He thinks he can bribe us with bedazzlement," said Arlo,

his face twisted up in disgust as he looked down at the armour. "The gods think us so base as to be bribed to send ourselves to certain death with a few shiny trinkets. They insult us."

Arlo turned his back sharply on the gifts before storming back to the cottage, slamming the door on his way in.

Cadence stood alone with the armour for a moment before deciding to gather all the pieces up. Just leaving them there would be an insult to Amaranth, and Cadence didn't want to risk incurring the wrath of a god. Despite the ground under and around the armour still emanating heat, the armour itself was cool to the touch. He carried the pieces onto the front porch of the cottage and left them to rest there. He dared not bring them inside out of fear for Arlo's reaction.

He looked back at them one last time before closing the door and joining Arlo inside. The will of the gods was clear; they wanted Arlo and Cadence to fight in the war. How were they to go against the will of men, of heaven, and of the Fates themselves? As the latch of the door clicked shut, he sighed, feeling more lost and confused than ever before.

26

THE UNWANTED GUEST

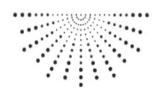

That night, Cadence watched the steady rise and fall of Arlo's chest as he slept. He didn't want them to go to war any more than Arlo did, but the difference was Arlo could not see what was at stake. The gods had to respect free will, but they would force Arlo's hand if they had to. Kidnapping Cadence and holding him ransom would be the easiest way for them to do it. The divine were infamous for whisking mortals away for their own devices. Arlo would come for him—of that Cadence was certain—but it would not guarantee that Arlo would fight in the war. He was unpredictable, and his anger at the gods would outweigh his reason.

Cadence's mind returned to the way Arlo had looked that night in Gemini's chamber—the unhinged, raw power in his body and the white lightning that flashed inside his eyes. He had transformed into something completely unfamiliar to Cadence. There had not been a trace of the soft kindness or gentle grace he knew Arlo so well for. Then there was the blood and the violence. When Cadence closed his eyes, he could see Gemini's flesh and bones being crushed into a pulp by Arlo's fists.

Something had changed in Arlo that night, and it had turned him from a kind and gentle lover into a war machine. The same hands Cadence had watched raise a kinglet hatchling had turned Gemini's body into a mangled mess of torn flesh and shattered bone.

As much as they had been at peace in Anthurium, Cadence couldn't help but notice the change in Arlo. He had not been the same since their last night in the palace. He was not as present as he had always been when they were together in Luciferian. His thoughts would wander and his fingers would freeze in place on the lyre. He seemed distracted and restless, as if he wanted to get up and do something but he didn't know exactly what. It had been similar during the winters at the palace when he would pace up and down the halls, frustrated by boredom. Since their arrival in Anthurium, Arlo's restlessness had grown steadily worse.

Cadence rolled over and stared at the ceiling when a breeze broke through the room that carried the whisper of his name. He sat bolt upright and listened carefully. Just when he was certain his mind was playing a trick on him, he heard it again. Something, or someone, was calling to him.

Unable to ignore it, he climbed slowly out of bed and tiptoed quickly out of the room. The breeze had been coming from the open front door, the same door he'd closed and latched shut before he joined Arlo in bed. His heart leapt into his throat and thumped in his ears. The voice called out to him again and pulled him towards the door. In the darkness on the porch, a tall figure stood waiting with its back towards him. As he drew closer, there was no mistaking the figure for anyone else. The scaly alabaster skin that glistened in the moonlight undoubtedly belonged to Nubia.

"Do you like the armour?" she asked without turning around. "It was my idea. I thought the flowers were a nice touch." Her icy voice sent a chill over Cadence, but despite his fear, he stepped closer.

"It's beautiful," he said, approaching her as one would a venomous animal that had somehow wandered into one's home. "It's strange to be known so well by someone who I have never met."

She was different to how she'd appeared in Cadence's vision—still terrifying but more toned down. Her posture was not as menacing. Her face was calm, free from the aggression she'd displayed towards the Emperor. Her pale, leathery wings were folded and rested almost gracefully on her back. All four of her muscular arms were at her sides and her palms inset with crimson serpent eyes faced downwards. She looked like a guardian statue come to life yet still made of stone.

"I see all," she said, and Cadence watched the two dark voids that made up the eyes on her face widen.

"Do you watch us all the time?" asked Cadence as a green nausea came over him. He thought back to the intimate moments he and Arlo shared on the banks of the Rhiannon.

Nubia scoffed as if she knew exactly what Cadence was thinking. "Do not think so little of me," she said as her gash of a mouth twisted into a scowl. "Just because I *can* see everything does not mean I always choose to look. There are more important matters for me to attend to than what you do with my son behind closed doors ... or in the open air."

Cadence ignored the jab and instead said, "Considering how busy you are, this visit must be important. What do you want?"

"You know what's coming, yet you stay here with him and play with flowers," she said, turning to look at Cadence for the first time.

"We are at peace here," said Cadence, standing his ground and trying to sound braver than he felt.

"It is not in his nature to be at peace," Nubia hissed as the lines of aggression returned to her sharp and jagged face. "You know it better than anyone. He is an instrument of war. He was born to fight."

"Is that all you see him as, a weapon?" Cadence snapped. "A pawn to be played in your war?"

"Foolish mortal, you think this war is of my making? You love to blame the gods for all the wrongs in your life because it is the perfect excuse not to look inward and see the truth. You bring all of your suffering upon yourselves."

"He doesn't want to fight. He doesn't want to die."

"He wants what *you* want!" Nubia snarled. "The only reason he refuses to fight is because of *you!*"

"I will not let him die!" Cadence shot back.

"The gods will not allow you to keep him from this war," said Nubia, her voice the crackle of burning coals. "There is much you do not know. If Arlo does not fight and win, Saklas will release a terrible weapon he does not even fully comprehend the power of. It will win him the war, but it will lay waste to everything. A great plague will run rampant through Hathuldria, devouring everything in its path. It will then spill over into the next world and the next until all life in the universe is completely snuffed out."

As Nubia spoke, a vision of this dark future came into Cadence's mind's eye—the suffering of countless beings that reached far beyond the borders of the Luciferian Empire. It was an expanse so large that trying to comprehend it would drive a man to madness. He saw the suffering of far-flung beings, their flesh being eaten away from their bones by an invisible enemy. The goddess was right. If Arlo did not fight, this would all come to pass. Arlo's face then came into Cadence's vision, ravaged by disease. He was wasted away, his flesh fetid and rotting as he clung loosely to life.

Bile rose in Cadence's throat and he willed the vision away from his mind, but the images stayed behind, burnt into his memory.

"There has to be another way," Cadence said, looking up at Nubia with pleading eyes. "There has to be a way that he can fight and live."

"You cannot bend destiny to your will," Nubia snapped. "You should know that by now. One way or another, he will perish."

"I've saved him once," said Cadence, his teeth clenched in defiance. "I can do it again."

"This is different and you know it," said Nubia. "You feel it down to your core. This is not as simple as avoiding a hunting accident; it is part of the web spun by the Fates."

"I can do it!" Cadence shouted.

"Who are you to argue with the will of gods?" the goddess spat, her black, nebulous eyes narrowing with disgust. "This war is the reason he was born, and you were born to help him. Everything you've been through so far has brought you to this point. Will you turn your back on destiny and every living creature in the universe now, knowing what you know? Running away will grant you a few years from fate, but that is all it will be before Saklas' rot claims both your lives too. Is every life in the universe the price of your love for him? In exchange for a few measly mortal years for you to live out a romance?"

Cadence had no response. The goddess was telling the truth; he knew it from his visions and there was no arguing with her. She was right, and he could no longer meet her eye. She was right about Arlo too; it was not in his nature to be at peace.

"He was born into the universe with a single purpose," Nubia continued, "to achieve greatness. You will not take it from him. He was born to fight. Born to lead. Born to die. It is the will of the Fates. If he does this, then a place will be made for him in the hall of the gods. Will you deny him that too?"

"I deny him nothing," Cadence growled as his head snapped back up to look at Nubia. "He makes his own decisions."

"If only that were true," she fired back.

Cadence could feel Nubia's hatred for him on her breath like a sweltering desert wind that whipped over his skin.

"For some reason, he hangs onto every pathetic word that falls from your mortal mouth. He would wrestle a giant if you asked him to. I know how he feels about you."

Her face curled up in revulsion like an acid viper ready to lash out. Cadence was convinced that if she could inject him with venom she wouldn't hesitate to do so.

"You are simultaneously his greatest ally and the greatest tarnish to his name," she continued, her words heavy with disgust. "He will also sire no descendants because of you, and his bloodline will vanish from existence."

He recognised the look in her dark eyes. She looked at him the same way his father always had—with the hatred and disdain one has for vermin invading one's pantry. But she was not his father, and he was no longer a small and frightened boy. He didn't care if she was a goddess. He would not allow her to bully him. He would not cower and he would not back down.

"Like you said, my presence in his life is the will of the Fates," Cadence said as a scowl formed over his face. "And who are *you* to argue with The Great Web? I will find a way to save him."

"You cannot change his destiny. He will come back to Luciferian sooner or later. Honesty is not common among my kind, but I offer you the truth; the thing about twin flames is they burn bright, but never for very long."

"And what is that supposed to mean?" Cadence asked. "I've never been much good at riddles."

"It means, simple mortal," said the goddess with a look on her face as if she were about to bite into something delicious and juicy, "that no matter what path you choose, peace and freedom or war and glory, you will both perish sooner rather than later. There is no romance to live out because there will be no life to live."

Nubia's words fell hard on Cadence's ears and clattered across his mind. His throat began to tighten all the way down into his chest and tears began to fill his eyes. He could see it in his oracular vision. Laid before him like a pathway splintering off in a million different directions—each one a chain of action and reaction that drove the present into the future. None of the pathways ended well for Arlo and himself.

"Why can he not have both?" cried Cadence, wiping hard at the tears falling down his cheeks. "Why can two things not be true? Why should he not have his glory in battle and live to grow old and die happy in his bed?"

"No warrior worth remembering ever died in their sleep," the goddess responded in her cold voice. "If he dies on the battlefield, he will be remembered as a war hero for eons to come. He may even be crowned a god. If he dies in his bed—old, decrepit, and rotting from the inside—no one will remember his name. His soul will be lost to the deepest pit of Obsidian and forgotten forever. If he does not use his godhead, then it will wither and you will be responsible. Find a way to convince him to fight."

Cadence was silent. He had nothing left to say to the goddess.

"And another thing," Nubia said. "It's not just the armies of Saklas that you have to concern yourselves with. There are whispers on the wind that say he is breeding a race of undead monsters with dark forbidden magic—leviathans. Abominations of unimaginable strength. With their help, Saklas will take the Empire in a matter of days and not long thereafter the rest of the universe if Arlo is not there to stop him. Find a way to make Arlo fight, or the gods will find a way for you."

The goddess disappeared in a plume of smoke and shadow. He stared at the armour still laid out on the porch. He looked at the blooms set into the breastplates, shields, and swords and wondered how Amaranth could make such delicate things look so strong. It was then he remembered his dream of the throne room and something Arsinoe had once said to him. A plan began to blossom in his mind.

"I may be able to find a way," he whispered to the empty air.

If he could not see a future where he and Arlo survived, then he would make one.

CADENCE DID NOT RETURN to the cottage. Instead, he ran away from it as fast as his feet would carry him. The thin blue line of dawn spun itself across the horizon as his bare feet pounded the ground. He ran through the forest Gossamer had led him and Arlo through just a few hours before. He was out of breath and heaving when he arrived in the clearing and stopped running. The back of his throat tasted of iron as he gasped for the breath to do what he needed.

The clearing in which the satyrs and nymphs had held their party had long since been abandoned. All that remained as evidence of a celebration was the wide circle of bent grass danced into submission by a hundred cloven hoofs and dainty feet. Even the emberflies were long gone as the first pale, gold strands of daylight struck the edges of the sky.

"HERMIA!" Cadence cried as soon as he'd caught his breath. His normally rasping voice transformed into a deep croak with the applied volume. His call passed into the air and faded.

He waited a moment, looking around the empty clearing before he called again.

"HERMIA! I MUST SPEAK WITH YOU!"

He was committing an act of great impiety, summoning a goddess as if he would a farmhand or a slave. But he did not have time for prayers; they took too long or too often went unanswered. He needed the attention of the goddess, and if he had to anger her to get it then so be it. He searched for the words that he knew would irritate the goddess into an appearance.

"HERMIA!" he shouted once more. "Goddess of spring time and flowers, I demand an audience. I wish to see if you are indeed as beautiful as your aunt, Lerato, the goddess of love. If you are, then reveal yourself to me! If not, then you must be as hideous as the rumours say! HERMI—"

"What do you think you are doing?" Hermia's voice shook the ground under Cadence's feet, interrupting him.

Cadence spun around to meet her eyes the colour of smouldering wood. She was angry—and with good reason. Cadence had hit the sore point he'd hoped for. The goddess had once entered a beauty contest with Lerato and lost. The result had been Hermia going into hiding for six months of that year to lick her wounds. The knee-jerk reaction of a sore loser then became the habit of a stubborn and petty niece and also made room for the other seasons. Hermia had lost face and power and had clearly not forgotten it.

Cadence had gotten what he wanted but then wasn't sure if he wanted it anymore. Hermia was a different creature entirely when she was enraged. Gone was the calm and natural beauty of serene forests and lush gardens filled with flowers. In its place stood a force of nature as powerful as a hurricane and twice as frightening. Her dark hair blew wild in the twisting wind.

"I have skewered mortals with giant thorns for less!" she said, her voice deep and rumbling with bridled rage. "What is the reason for this blasphemy?"

"Apologies, most beautiful goddess," said Cadence, falling to his knees before her. "I needed to speak with you urgently."

"Then you should have called on my nymphs for an audience," said Hermia, her eyes still flickering embers. "I am a goddess as old as the world itself, not a mongrel to be beckoned."

"There wasn't time," said Cadence. "The goddess Nubia came to me. She revealed things, terrible things. I need to convince Arlo to fight in the upcoming war, but I need your help."

"And what makes you think the demigod prince will listen to me?" Hermia said, her fury calming.

"That's not the part I need your help with," said Cadence.

"Then what?" said Hermia, the annoyance in her voice rising.

"I need you to help me kill a god."

Hermia recoiled from him as a combination of disgust and confusion wound its way across her face like invasive vines.

"That—that is not possible," she stuttered. "It cannot be done."

"Your great, great granddaughter Arsinoe, Empress of Luciferian, once told me of a poison that could kill a god,"

Cadence said. "She taught me the craft of poison. It must be true."

"It is a myth," said Hermia too quickly. Cadence could tell she was lying.

"I'm sure the ingredients for this poison are rare," said Cadence, "but if the goddess of flowers cannot provide them then no one can."

Cadence watched a flicker of interest in Hermia's eyes appear and then quickly die.

"It is blasphemy," she whispered. "We do not speak of it. For a god to act out against another god in such a way, to murder one's own kind, is against the natural order of things."

"Mortals murder each other all the time," Cadence argued. "The only time the gods condemn it is if …"

He couldn't bring himself to finish his sentence. His jaw hung open as he realised what Hermia's hesitance meant. He watched the lines of her face twist in discomfort. He saw her now glassy brown eyes try to desperately cling to the secret they had already lost grip of.

"… is if they are family," Cadence finished. "Saklas is one of you!"

"Lower your voice!" Hermia hushed as she lunged forward. "You never know who might be listening, even in my realm."

"Nubia said that the other gods didn't know anything about Saklas," said Cadence. "Was she lying?"

"Not here!" Hermia boomed before a tornado of flower petals and leaves enveloped them both.

Cadence's feet were lifted from the ground. The breath inside his lungs was pulled out by the sudden and violent wind. He panicked as he was tumbled through the air as easily as the petals that whipped past him. Leaves and small twigs struck him in the face, arms, and legs, leaving behind angry, thin scratches. He threw his arms over his head and screwed his eyes shut tightly as he gasped for pollen-filled air that was moving too quickly past his mouth. He grew dizzy, and consciousness abandoned him.

27
THE MAD GOD

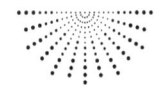

Cadence's throat made a ripping noise in the dark as his lungs filled with loamy air. He'd landed on his back against a damp surface. He slowly got to his knees as his eyes adjusted to the darkness. Hermia stood in front of him, the ethereal glow of her skin casting enough light to see by.

She had pulled them somewhere deep beneath the ground into a cavern where tree roots hung from the ceiling and dripped with water. The air in the cavern was dank, cold, and thick with the smell of wet earth.

"What's wrong with you?" Cadence coughed.

"It is safer to speak here," replied Hermia.

A nervousness came over Cadence. If Hermia did not feel safe in her own realm, where she alone had dominion, then nowhere was safe.

"Who is Saklas?" Cadence asked. "Why are the gods lying about him?"

"We are not lying. We didn't know until recently that he …"

"That he is what?" Cadence insisted.

"It's complicated. It's not about who he is. It's about who he once was."

"None of this makes sense. Tell me what is going on or take me back up to the surface."

"He is our father!" Hermia's shout echoed through the cavern before it was swallowed by the darkness.

Cadence searched the collection of stories of the gods his mother had filled his head with. There was no god called Saklas, and if there was, he was not the father of Hermia or Nubia or any other member of the Pantheon.

"There is no Saklas in the Pantheon. Your father was …" Cadence trailed off as he finally understood Hermia's words, "… your father was Mithras, the sky lord. Are you saying that Mithras and Saklas are the same god? How is that even possible?"

"Gods evolve as the belief in them evolves," said Hermia. "After my father killed Lucifer, he was shunned by gods and mortals alike. He faded from belief and therefore from the collective memory of humankind that holds the powers of the gods in place. He was forgotten. We forgot him."

"But now he is back," said Cadence, realisation hitting him. "That is why he wants to take Luciferian and destroy the Empire. That is why he wants to wipe humans from the face of the world. He wants revenge for what happened after Lucifer fell."

"He wants more than that," said Hermia. "He wants to start anew. The gods are scared. He will not make the same mistake twice, and there will be room for no other god other than himself. He wants to be the one and only god."

"Why do none of you act?" Cadence probed. "You are all putting so much pressure on Arlo and me to fix this problem when you could help."

"We cannot kill our own kin," said Hermia. "If we do, we shall suffer the same fate as my father for murdering my uncle. It is an unforgivable sin in both the world of gods and men. Do you know what it is for a god to go mad?"

"It can't be as bad as the world ending," replied Cadence.

"It's just as bad," said Hermia. "Why do you think the Scorched-Over Lands are scorched-over? As a result of his crimes against nature and lack of worship, Mithras went mad and destroyed everything."

The tingle of a vision rose up inside Cadence as Hermia spoke the words. Cadence could see the past unfold before him like a great tapestry being unveiled for the first time.

A BROKEN CREATURE wrapped in tatters hobbled along a vast wasteland. Shunned, excommunicated, and fallen from grace, the god wandered for decades that turned into centuries. Without a scrap of worship or praise to sustain him, his muscle-clad form withered away. He grew emaciated and weak of body and of mind. Eyes of the boldest blue faded to a dead grey before receding further and further back into dry and flaking sockets. His teeth began to rot and fall from his mouth before shattering into ashen flakes against the parched earth. He could call forward no storm, summon no lightning, nor conjure so much as a cloud. For ages, he wandered deliriously through a wasteland both mental and physical. The longer he wandered, the more he was forgotten and the weaker he became.

"I was once a beautiful creature," Mithras whispered to himself in a voice that sounded like wind whistling through a narrow canyon, "king of all heaven where the bright, blue, endless sky would sing my name. Feared and revered by both gods and mortals."

Finally, one day, he stumbled and fell forward into the dirt, sending a cloud of pale dust into the air. As he clung to the last threads of life before passing beyond existence, someone came to him. It was a child, a shepherd boy of eight who had come to his rescue. The boy gave the grey old man an offering of fresh water to drink and goat cheese to eat, and he brought him back to his village of tents.

Cadence did not recognise the people in the village as any of those that belonged to the Luciferian Empire. They were tall and slender with skin the colour of freshly churned butter. They wore rings of copper around their long necks, arms, and legs and dressed in rough, brown fabrics that matched their eyes. Their lips were thick and their mouths wide to make room for massive smiles of healthy, milky teeth. They wore their auburn locks in intricate braids and styles and decorated them with small copper ringlets.

The village of brightly coloured tents was a vibrant and thriving paradise in the centre of a desert. The people of the village gathered around the boy and the exiled god they were mistaking for a weary traveller who needed their hospitality.

Summoning the very last of his godhead, Mithras raised his withered arms to the sky. He motioned down with his wrists, forcing the people of the village to bow before him. From this forced worship, the fallen god drew strength, but the more he drew from them the more he needed to keep drawing. He invaded the minds and bodies of the people from the village, twisting them to his whim and contorting their souls and bodies into misshapen, ugly, and dying things.

His power descended like a plague, spreading diseases across the land. Village after village was consumed by his greed for power until everything he reached began to decay from the inside out. Nothing could escape his grasp. Animals, plants, people, and the very soil he stood upon festered with the rot of his dark magic. This is how the mighty Mithras, king of heaven and lord of the skies, became Saklas, god of decay.

"Then don't kill him," said Cadence, coming out of the vision. "Bind him, imprison him, chain him to a rock and let birds of prey feed upon him, but don't choose to do nothing."

"You have no idea who you are talking about," Hermia said, panic making her voice go higher than normal. "The sky lord was the most powerful among us. Lucifer, his twin and equal in every way, could not even defeat him in battle. What chance do lesser gods stand against him?"

"You are many. He cannot overpower you all. And he may no longer be as powerful as he once was."

Hermia gave him a concerned look. "Or he could be more powerful than ever before."

"You are frightened of him. You won't fight him directly because you are all a bunch of cowards who can't stand up to their own fath—"

Cadence stopped himself. He had made a grave error, but it was too late. He remembered how he would quiver and shake at the wrath of his own father. A wrath so powerful that even when the memories of his father had been taken away, the fear remained. He remembered the night in the palace when the Emperor had struck Arsinoe. How it had frightened him to the point where he could not stop trembling. He remembered how his father's ill temper and cruel nature burned everyone close to him. Cadence had seen how his father's malice had pitted his brothers against one another. Canaan had made everything he came in to contact with ugly and damaged. It was easy for Cadence to be brave. Canaan was dead, but the damage he'd done would live inside Cadence for the rest of his life. If mortals could inflict such carnage upon one another, then there was no telling what a family of gods was capable of.

"I'm sorry," he said. The two words could not possibly convey enough, but he did not know what else to say. He looked into Hermia's deep brown eyes that were wet with tears. She nodded at him.

"We cannot kill him," said Hermia, wiping her tears away. "We are not strong enough and we cannot break the laws by which we are bound. That is why the prophecy exists. It has to be Arlo. It has to be you."

"Then help me," Cadence pleaded. "Give me the plants and flowers I need to make the poison."

"This is a fool's errand," said Hermia. "Even if you could make the poison, you wouldn't be able to get close enough to Saklas to distribute it."

"Leave that to me," said Cadence. "I will find a way, but I need the poison first."

The goddess hesitated for a moment. Cadence watched her brow furrow as she considered his request.

"Fine," she finally agreed. "When you arrive back at the cottage, the ingredients you need will be waiting for you. Do not tell a soul that I have helped you."

"I need to know one last thing," said Cadence. "Has a demigod ever contracted the blight?"

"No demigod in our history has ever succumbed to disease," said Hermia. "They are immune to all illnesses. Their destinies are the things that kill them."

Cadence bit at his bottom lip and nodded to Hermia. "Arlo cannot know about this. If he finds out about what I am planning, he is going to stop me."

"I didn't think twin flames were able to keep secrets from one another."

"I can if it means that Arlo's life will be saved."

"The ingredients will appear in a bag under your bed," said the goddess before regarding him with a sudden and intense curiosity in her eyes. "What of your own life? Why are you trying so hard to protect Arlo? Why fight against it so hard when you know fate will always run its course? Why not just let things be?"

Cadence thought long on the answer. He was doing it because he wanted Arlo to live, so he could have the life he deserved and not just the one he was tossed by the hands of the Fates. He was doing it because out of everyone, aside from his own mother, in a cruel and chaotic world of gods and monsters, Arlo was the only one who made Cadence feel at peace, who showed him kindness, who loved him. And Cadence loved Arlo back with everything inside of him. If that wasn't worth dying over to protect, then nothing was.

"I suppose," Cadence eventually answered, "that to accept things as they are just isn't in my nature."

"Where have you been?" Arlo yelled, rushing towards Cadence as the cottage door closed behind him. "I've been worried sick about you! I thought—"

"That the gods had kidnapped me?" said Cadence. "They aren't above that. Hermia said so and your mother confirmed it. That's where I have been."

Arlo stood still and regarded Cadence for a moment. His sapphire eyes ran over Cadence from head to toe.

"Why are you so dirty?" he asked.

"Nubia called out to me. We met in the woods and I fell."

The lie tasted sour on Cadence's lips and caused his stomach to twist painfully. Reminding himself that he was lying for the greater good was little comfort, and his stomach continued to wind itself into cramping knots.

"Did she hurt you?" Arlo asked, stepping closer. He placed both his hands on Cadence's shoulders, his eyes darting over every inch of him.

"I'm fine," said Cadence, raising his hand to caress Arlo's cheek. "I promise."

He tried to sound as reassuring as possible, but Arlo could tell he was concealing something.

"What did she want?" asked Arlo, concerned.

"The only thing anyone ever wants from us," Cadence replied, "to fight in the war."

Arlo's face turned bitter with a deep frown and crunched brows. "Well, she will have no more luck than Hermia or Amaranth. We are staying here. Together. Like we said we would."

A sharp pain cracked through Cadence's chest as he took a step away from Arlo. He couldn't pull his eyes away from the demigod's. He read every tiny expression and line on his face as Arlo faded out of stubbornness and into confusion.

"We can't stay," Cadence forced the words. It was like taking a foul-tasting medicine, but instead of going into his mouth it was coming out.

"What do you mean?" demanded Arlo, the brightness in his eyes fading.

"Nubia told me things," Cadence said. "And I've seen things. Events that have been and events that are yet to come. It's not just the Empire at stake. It's the entire universe. But even if it was just the Empire, it wouldn't be right to stay here. There is no one else who can win this war. You are the only one who will be able to fight and kill Saklas, and I am the only one who will be able to help you do it. I also don't think you are being honest with me. Are you refusing to fight because *you* don't want to or because *I* don't want you to?"

Arlo looked away from Cadence to the floor and sighed.

"I don't want to lose you," he said with a crack in his heart. "I want to fight but not if it means you will die."

"If we don't fight then everyone will die. Including us. I wish things were different. I wish we had more time. I've been searching, trying to find another way, but there isn't one. We have to go back. I have to help the Emperor see what is coming, and you have to lead his army. It is the only way Saklas and his forces will be defeated. I also know that Saklas cannot take the city as long as you are alive."

"How does it end?" asked Arlo, his voice deep from holding back tears.

Cadence stepped back in shock. Arlo had never before asked him anything of the future, let alone his own.

"Tell me," Arlo pleaded. "I want to know. I need to know."

"I can't," said Cadence.

"You *can't*," asked Arlo, "or you *won't*?"

"*I can't*. The nature of our deaths is being hidden from me. I can't see it no matter how hard I try. I can see what happens before. I can see what happens if we choose not to go back to Luciferian, but that is all."

Arlo was silent for a moment as his lips disappeared into a thin line. "Perhaps," he said, "it is better that way."

Cadence nodded. He did not tell Arlo that even if he could foresee exactly how they were going to die, he would not share the information. Knowing that they were going to perish in the war was bad enough. Having the knowledge of exactly how and when they would die would drive them to madness. He thought of the story his mother had told him of the Inkanyamba—cheated by Astaroth and driven into seclusion by the cursed knowledge of their own deaths. Arlo was right. It was better that Cadence couldn't see how they would die.

"I will fight in the war," said Arlo. "But I have one condition."

"What is that?"

"Wait here for me," said Arlo before disappearing out the front door of the cottage and into the garden.

Cadence tried to see what he was up to, but Arlo was just

out of view. A few minutes later, Arlo returned with something hidden behind his back and a nervous smile on his face. He brought his hands forward to reveal a gigantic bouquet of flowers bound together with a ribbon of white lace.

Cadence's eyes widened over the grand bouquet that held gladiolus to communicate that he pierced Arlo's heart. In addition, it held bluebells for faithfulness, honeysuckle for devotion and affection, hellebore to overcome scandal and slander, bright red roses for true love, ivy for fidelity, and dahlia for commitment and eternal love.

He could identify each flower and its secret meaning in the bouquet with the exception of one. The small and delicate blossoms of crisp white with a burst of dainty stamen against emerald leaves and unripe berries were a mystery to him. Arlo had never presented him with such a flower before, and it was not one of the poisonous plants Arsinoe had taught him either.

"What's this one?" Cadence asked, running the tip of his finger over one of the white velvety petals. A nervous excitement spread across his chest as he took the bouquet from Arlo.

"Myrtle," replied Arlo with a nervous quiver in his voice as he got down on one knee in front of Cadence. "It symbolises hope and love in marriage."

"In *what*?" asked Cadence, thinking he'd misheard, and yet the excitement continued to rise, threatening to burst out through his skin.

"That is my condition," said Arlo. "If we are to fight in this war, then I want to do it with you as my spouse. I want heaven to cry every time I kiss you. I want the worlds of gods and mortals to know that no matter our fate, we belong only to each other. I'd follow you anywhere. I'd follow you straight into the deepest pits of Obsidian if it meant we could be together. Will you marry me?"

Cadence didn't know how this was supposed to work. Would the gods allow it? They could not be struck down or punished or cursed. The gods needed them, so did it matter what they would allow or condemn? There were a lot of things Cadence didn't know, but in that moment none of those things mattered. What mattered was the one thing he was absolutely sure of, and that was what he was about to say.

"Yes!" he yelled as the excitement building up inside him was finally realised. Arlo beamed as he got to his feet and locked Cadence in an embrace. Cadence leaned forward into a deep, long kiss.

That night, Cadence and Arlo laid in the bed together, their naked bodies in a tangle of silk sheets set aglow under warm candlelight. Cadence lay with his head in Arlo's lap as Arlo's nimble fingers, ever restless, wove together a crown of flowers from Cadence's betrothal bouquet. They laid satisfied in the silence while Cadence watched him weave.

Cadence broke the silence and told Arlo everything he'd learned from Nubia and his visions, conveniently leaving out the parts that involved Hermia, the things she had confessed, and the poison ingredients she'd agreed to supply. He only explained why the gods could not act directly against the god previously known as Mithras and how he'd become Saklas.

"We aren't going to die," said Arlo, not looking up from the flowers in his hands. "With you by my side, there is nothing that I cannot do. We will win the war, and then one day we will rule the Empire together."

"And how do you suppose ruling together would work?" Cadence asked, allowing himself for just a moment to live in Arlo's fantasy. It was an indulgence he was willing to entertain even if he knew it would never be. The smile on his face was real, but something was lurking behind it. He knew the ugly truth.

"However we want it to, my love," Arlo said as he placed the flower crown gently on top of Cadence's head.

Cadence's thoughts turned away from Arlo and instead to what he knew was waiting for him under the bed. He'd seen the leather pouch full of ingredients tucked subtly under the bed when he and Arlo had entered the room. He'd given it a gentle nudge with his foot, forcing it, for the time being, out of sight and out of mind. Cadence wanted to believe Arlo. He wanted the future Arlo was painting with is words so desperately instead of the one he knew was coming for them. He closed his eyes and said a silent prayer that his plan would work and Arlo would have a future, even if it meant that he would not be a part of it.

Nubia's words slashed through Cadence's mind like a dagger. *Twin flames may burn bright, but not for very long.*

28
WAR GROOMS

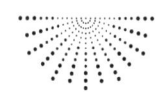

Upon hearing what Arlo and Cadence had planned, Hermia offered to assist.

"What happy news!" the goddess exclaimed with an abundant smile before she reached out to them for an embrace. "I will officiate the ceremony and give the marriage my blessing. The nymphs and satyrs will make all the necessary arrangements."

Cadence wasn't sure if her excitement was due to the fact she was relieved he and Arlo were finally joining the war, or if it was because she was genuinely happy for them. In the end it didn't matter. Between how much the gods needed them and a goddess herself officiating the ceremony, in the eyes of heaven and earth their marriage was as binding and consecrated as that of one between a woman and a man. More importantly, nothing was going to stop them. The direct blessing of a goddess was also nothing to be sneezed at. It would provide them with much needed good fortune and protection from both gods and mortals.

Gossamer had brought them each white tunics woven from silk so soft to the touch it was like wearing rose petals.

On their heads, they wore crowns of myrtle, hellebore, ivy, and roses the nymphs had made for them.

They met just before dusk under an arch festooned with flowers. A light breeze pushed the aroma of flowers, earth, and cypress through the air. A small band of satyrs and nymphs played soft music that mingled with the sounds of the songbirds singing in the trees. The first emberflies of the evening floated in the air and glittered in the fading sunlight. Gossamer and a host of nymphs looked on in eager anticipation for the ceremony to start.

Arlo looked at Cadence with a smile so warm it could make the sun itself jealous.

"You have never looked more beautiful," Arlo said.

Cadence felt his unscarred cheek flush and grow hot as the scarred side of his face pulled tight against his smile. He turned his face away from Arlo when he felt Arlo's finger on his chin, gently pulling his whole face back.

"Don't look away," said Arlo. "I want to see all of you. I want to remember you just like this, forever."

"Please join your left hands," said Hermia.

Arlo took Cadence's hand in his. The moment their palms made contact, vines of emerald ivy and blooms of myrtle and honeysuckle appeared. The vines wound over their wrists and through their fingers, binding them together.

"I, Hermia, goddess of spring and flowers, bear witness and bestow my blessing upon this union."

Two emberflies came to rest on each of their ring fingers. After their previous experience with the fiery insects, Cadence had to resist the urge to pull his hand away. But this time the tingle of their gleam was warm and friendly against his skin. The emberflies began to shine bright between the vines and flowers. When their glow faded, the emberflies were gone and in their place were bands of shimmering gold around Arlo and Cadence's fingers.

"May your love for one another thrive and bloom your whole lives long," Hermia continued. "I pronounce you, before the gods of heaven and the men of Hathuldria, married. You may—"

Arlo didn't wait for Hermia before he took Cadence by the waist and pulled him forward into a kiss. Cadence's hands found their way to Arlo's face where they stayed as Arlo crushed his lips gently over Cadence's. The embrace was all encompassing. Cadence could have lived and died inside Arlo's kiss without a regret in the world.

Hermia, the nymphs, and the satyrs broke out in a roar of applause and cheers. With the ceremony complete, the festivities could begin. Wine flowed as abundantly as the music that filled the air. Together they danced and sang and drank and ate well into the night.

Arlo swept Cadence onto the dancefloor in a movement so graceful and smooth Cadence didn't know what was happening until they were already dancing.

"I was hoping we could get to do more of this," said Arlo, spinning Cadence under his arm.

"There is still time for more dancing," said Cadence as he swayed and dipped in time with his new husband. "The war won't take place for months. It's not like we have to leave immediately. We could stay a little longer."

"I'd like nothing more," replied Arlo, spinning Cadence around once more. "In fact, I promise, for the rest of our time here, to dance with you every night and make love to you every morning."

Cadence smiled as Arlo pulled him in again. "And what about the afternoons? How shall we spend those?"

"However we please," said Arlo as he leaned in for a kiss.

Their lips met, and an electric energy passed through Cadence. For a moment, all their troubles were forgotten. All the pain of the past and the anxiety of the future faded into oblivion. Only they remained, basking in the light of one another the way flowers take in the warmth of the sun.

The beauty of this short-lived spell was then suddenly broken by a roar of thunder. Dark clouds rolled across the sky, shrouding the stars and moon. The music died as the band dropped their instruments in terror before scattering into the woods. The rest of the nymphs and satyrs in attendance followed the band in a panicked scramble.

Two dark, empty eyes set against skin the colour of ash glared at Arlo and Cadence. Nubia had made her presence known. Her sour mood was clear by her appearance. She was larger and more threatening than when Cadence had last seen her. The ridges of her face were raised, making her look venomous to the touch. Her four grey, muscled arms were resting at her sides while her wings were slightly raised. She stood tall, looming over them like a predator waiting to see if its prey would fight or fly.

"What," she said, her voice the sound of blood hitting burning coals, "do you think you are doing?"

"We've just been married," said Arlo, stepping in front of Cadence and taking a subtle defensive position as his second nature of warrior and soldier found him. "What do you think *you* are doing?"

Cadence was surprised by Arlo's bravery. He had never set eyes upon the goddess, who was terrifying at the best of times to behold, and yet he stood up to her as if she were nothing more than a drunken and disruptive guest.

"Married?" she chuckled. "What a ridiculous notion. Your betrothed will join you in Luciferian. I have made arrangements with your father. You are to be married to Angelica of Amun-Ra and ensure she carries your legitimate heir before the war. I have come to collect you."

"I will do no such thing," said Arlo.

"You will find I can be very persuasive," growled Nubia.

As the words left her mouth, a prickling broke out over Cadence's scars that quickly turned into a burn. Cadence gasped with pain as the flesh of his scars began to blister.

"Stop it!" Arlo screamed, looking at Cadence then back at Nubia. His eyes began to glow white and the skin on his face darkened.

"Agree to marry Angelica and I will," said Nubia, exposing her smile of white fangs.

"Don't listen to her, Arlo," said Cadence through clenched teeth. "She might be able to hurt me, but she can't kill me. They need both of us to win their war."

"Silence!" Nubia screeched, and the burning pain that ran over Cadence intensified. "This is all your fault! You are the one making sure the Empire will be left without an heir."

"The Emperor can have other sons," said Cadence as the pain screamed through him. "Why should Arlo fight and die and also be forced to leave behind an heir with someone he does not love? Is his life not his own to live? All you do is take from him and give nothing in return."

"Abydos will not have another son like Arlo," Nubia said. "Not another of *my* sons. Arlo is the most powerful demigod ever born. A mortal from not just one divine bloodline but two. Arlo was destined to die in this war, but his son would not only have ruled the Empire but the entire planet."

"And you would have ruled him?" said Cadence. "Was that your plan? To have the Emperor of the world as your puppet?"

"Not if you keep standing in my way!" Nubia shrieked.

A fresh wave of pain more intense than the last broke over Cadence. "I'm glad the Fates saw to that never coming to pass!" he screamed. "No one deserves to live in a world controlled by a vain, narcissistic goddess who claims to see all but only has sight for her own reflection!"

"HOW DARE YOU!" Nubia roared; her face twisted into

an ugly rage as she raised herself up. Her bones and flesh contorted, and she expanded her four massive arms and unfolded her pale bat wings. "I am a goddess born from the depths of chaos itself and you dare to speak to me with such disrespect! Impudent, puny mortal!"

Cadence fell back as Nubia towered over him and the eyes in all four of her palms began to glow a fiery red. The dark clouds billowed in the sky and were set alight by crimson flashes of lightning and thunder.

"Enough!" yelled Arlo, stepping between Nubia and Cadence. The glow behind his eyes grew brighter as his face pinched into a vicious scowl. A bolt of bright, white lightning erupted from his chest with a deafening crack and raced towards Nubia. She raised her arms and crossed them over her body. Arlo's lightning bounced off of her and was sent hurling into the clouds.

The goddess snarled past Arlo at Cadence and slowly began to shrink as she folded her wings back and lowered her arms. The black clouds receded to reveal a dark, sparkling sky, and the pain in Cadence's scars subsided and vanished.

A cruel smile curled its way over her mouth like a strangling vine. "I told your father that your power would grow," she said. "All you needed was the right … motivation." Her eyes darted to Cadence.

"If you ever do anything to harm Cadence again," Arlo threatened, the light in his eyes still bright, "I will tear all four of your arms from your body and beat you to death with them!"

"Save all that aggression for the battlefield," Nubia growled. "Gather your armour and leave for Luciferian immediately. The armies of Saklas are drawing closer and you are needed. You have generals to organise. And *you*," she turned her gaze of black flames upon Cadence, "are needed by the Emperor."

"The armies aren't due to arrive at the walls of the city for months," said Cadence. The pain had left him light headed and nauseated. "I saw their arrival in the summer."

"Did my dear sister not tell you?" An amused and satisfied looked played across Nubia's face as her pitch-black eyes darted over to Hermia then back again. "Time passes differently here. To you it has only been a few weeks, but in Hathuldria months have passed."

Cadence felt a weight drop inside his heart and panic rise in its place. "That can't be," he whispered. Tears began to flood his eyes. "We were supposed to have more time. It can't be true. Hermia, tell me she is lying!"

Hermia looked as if she had just killed something precious by accident. "Cadence, I'm so sorry," she said. "I thought you knew. Why else would the gods put so much pressure on you and Arlo to make a decision?"

Something broke inside of Cadence and his knees gave up on him. Before he hit the ground, he felt Arlo's arms catch him.

"It will be alright," said Arlo, helping Cadence to his feet before turning to Nubia. "We will leave as soon as possible. But I will not be marrying the princess Angelica. Cadence is my husband and our marriage has been blessed by Hermia. Nothing can undo it."

"If you are determined to end your bloodline, so be it," Nubia barked. "That is your father's problem. Just see to it that you make your way to Luciferian immediately." She scowled at them one last time before vanishing into her signature wisps of shadow and smoke.

A PROPHECY OF FLOWERS AND LIGHTNING

With the wedding abruptly ended, Arlo helped Cadence back to the cottage. They walked in silence with nothing but the chirps of crickets to fill the air between them. The blisters Nubia had caused on Cadence's scars had vanished, but the pain she'd brought with her visit was still raging inside him.

"We had so little time together," Cadence wailed. "They won't stop until they have taken everything from us!" His sorrow turned to anger in a flash before he flipped the table in the cottage over, sending food, dishes, and flowers crashing to the floor in a series of clattering metal and explosive bursts of breaking glass. He raised his hands to cover his eyes as he began to weep.

Arlo grabbed hold of Cadence's arm and pulled him close. His arms wrapped around Cadence's shoulders as Cadence cried into his chest. The white silk of Arlo's tunic darkened as tears saturated it.

"How did I not see this?" Cadence shuddered. "Did you know about time passing faster in Anthurium than in Hathuldria?"

"If I did," Arlo said gently as he cupped the back of Cadence's head in his hand, "do you not think I would have told you? I had no idea this would happen. I'm so sorry."

"Well, there is nothing to be done about it," said Cadence, choking on his words. He wiped his tears with the back of his hand.

Arlo pulled him back in and held him tightly.

"I'm sorry," Cadence choked. "I know this isn't easy for you either, and I know we have to go, but I–I …"

Arlo hushed Cadence as he ran his hand over his back and neck in comfort. "What is it?" he asked softly into Cadence's ear.

"I was really, really happy," Cadence managed to finish.

"I know," said Arlo, holding on tighter, "so was I."

29
POWER AND POISON

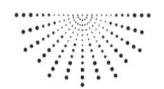

Arlo and Cadence returned to a different Luciferian than the one they'd left behind. As the city emerged on the horizon, Cadence noticed the changes from the airboat. The hustle and bustle of air traffic that once filled the skies of the great city had transformed—robust warships now replaced the sleek merchant ships and leisure boats that had once zoomed around the city. They loomed in the air as if waiting to be called to battle.

Giant white marble statues of Lucifer, Hermia, Amaranth, and Fragma had erupted from the ground around the city walls. Their features glittered with the veins of ichor that ran through them as they stood with their arms outstretched to the heavens. As they drew closer, Cadence saw an opaque, shimmering dome had formed over the city, enclosing it. Every few meters along the top of the wall, ichor plasma cannons in the shape of gargoyles with jaws opened in snarls had been installed. Groups of soldiers patrolled the top of the wall and manned lookout towers that had not been there in the past. The city wall itself even looked taller and thicker than it had been before.

"What's happened?" Cadence asked. "How were all these changes possible in just a few months?"

"The city has gone into lockdown in preparation for battle," said Arlo. "Luciferian is more than just a city; it's a living entity that is able to defend itself and protect its citizens."

Cadence thought back to the stories his mother would tell him as a child. She had said the city had been gifted with divine defences by Fragma, but the stories had not specified exactly what those defences were.

"The statues of the gods are wards," Arlo continued. "They help generate and spread the shield wall, which I see is up." He pointed to the shimmering dome.

"Will we be able to get through it?" Cadence asked as he became very aware of how close they were getting to the city and how Arlo was showing no signs of slowing down.

"The city should be able to recognise us and know we aren't a threat," Arlo said. "Also, I'm the prince. If *I* cannot get in then no one can." He smiled as he sped up.

Cadence braced himself for an impact that never came. The airboat passed through the shield wall as easily as a knife cutting through warm butter. As they passed through, the air around them glittered and left a fizzing sensation across Cadence's skin.

"Ye of little faith," Arlo chuckled, looking back at the stress that had not yet left Cadence's face.

"What would have happened if the city didn't recognise us?" Cadence asked, not really knowing if he wanted an answer.

"We would have been burnt to ashes," said Arlo as he steered the airboat towards the palace.

As they flew over the pyramids, obelisks, temples, and homes, Cadence looked over the side of the airboat. In the streets, hordes of people moved about. From the air, they looked like a colony of insects frantically busying themselves. Even from so high up, Cadence could see the number of people in Luciferian had drastically increased. Pillars of stinking smoke were still rising up from places all over the city. Cadence looked up to see the smog passing through the shield wall before dissipating into the open air. A stench rising up from the streets and buildings hit him like an unexpected slap across the face.

"The refugee problem has gotten so much worse," said Cadence, his words muffled by his hand now placed over his nose and mouth.

"And the plague that comes with them," responded Arlo, not reacting to the stench emanating from the city below.

"How are all these people being fed? No merchant ships are coming in and out, and no food is being supplied by Naphtali."

Cadence's question was answered when he saw the rooftops of the houses. The gardens that had once overflowed with lush greenery and a plethora of blooming flowers had been replaced by vegetable gardens and square patches of golden wheat.

"Celestium," said Cadence. "Arsinoe must have given them some of her supply."

"It's not a permanent solution," said Arlo. "The city cannot sustain itself on celestium alone, especially not when it is trying to feed this many people. And don't forget about the army; a soldier with an empty stomach is as useful as fire without wood to keep it burning."

Arlo brought the airship into an ascent, lifting them away from the stench. They flew around to the back of the palace and towards the cavern. Upon seeing the opening, Cadence was struck by a sudden wave of nausea and his stomach began to twist itself into knots.

"Are you alright back there?" Arlo asked, as if he knew something wasn't quite right.

"I'm fine," said Cadence as he swallowed down the bile rising in his throat. "It's just coming back here. After everything that happened. It doesn't feel …" his mind struggled to form thoughts into full sentences. "I don't feel good."

He sat back in his seat frustrated with himself. He was trying to be brave. He was trying to give in to the will of the Fates, to save the Empire and hopefully Arlo as well. But in that moment, all he wanted to do was curl up into a ball and weep. He pushed back tears and swallowed hard against the lump that pressed against the inside of his throat like a jagged pebble.

The airboat came to rest in the cavern. Cadence looked around at the grey rock formations and the green moss that grew upon them. He wanted to remember this space as it had been—a place of adventure, anticipation, and excitement for what the day would hold. A place where he would hold his breath as Arlo launched them forward into whatever adventure they were about to have together. It had been a place where he brushed the soft and warm edges of what it was like to be loved before plunging head first into it.

But it had been tainted. Now when he looked around, all he could see were spatters and smears of blood, and all he could taste were tears mixed with blood. All he could feel was the terrible ache that had been left pounding through his body. He recalled the flashes and bangs across his vision as his thoughts melted together and his stolen memories, his stolen life, came rushing back to him. It had almost driven him mad. The cavern had been a special place once. But now it was nothing more than an empty grey cave. A grave that held nothing but the echoes of loss.

"Look at me," said Arlo, climbing out of his seat and taking Cadence's hand. The golden band on his ring finger shone in a beam of light that broke through the mouth of the cavern. "No one here is going to hurt you. Gemini is dead."

Arlo said the words as if Cadence had somehow forgotten, but the reassurance was a comfort to him nonetheless. Yes, Gemini was dead, but Cadence had quickly come to learn that the world held far worse monsters than wicked priests. There were bloodthirsty goddesses willing to torture and manipulate to get their way, as well as mad, power-hungry gods who wanted to end all life across the universe.

Cadence stood up from his seat in the airboat and took Arlo's hand. "Let's just get out of here," he said.

Arlo helped him down and unloaded the bag that contained their armour, swords, and shields. Cadence patted the leather satchel at his side to check that the flowers and plants Hermia had provided were still there. He felt insane doubting himself as he had packed the satchel, but he knew he could never be completely certain. In a world of gods and monsters, things could just as easily disappear as they magically appeared, and he didn't want to take any chances. Without the poison, his plan would fall apart and with it any chance of saving Arlo.

They made their way directly to the throne room. The clattering of their armour in the bag echoed through the hallways of the palace, signalling their arrival. As they approached the throne room, the massive doors were already open.

Arsinoe was the first to see them. She'd looked up from a scroll she was reading and it fell to the floor with a sharp smack. She ran towards them with open arms and almost tackled them to the ground with an embrace. Arlo dropped the bag of armour and it clattered to the floor.

"Thank the gods you are back," she said, hugging them more tightly. "I wasn't sure if I would ever see you again."

When she released them, Cadence saw the tears in her eyes.

The Emperor did not get up from his seat on the throne. He looked as ominous as ever, but Cadence noticed the lines of fatigue in his face and the bags under his eyes. He looked tired and older.

"So glad you could join us," Abydos said, his voice heavy with sarcasm.

Arlo ignored his father and instead gave Arsinoe another hug.

She also looked tired. The past couple of months at the palace had taken a toll on her. She was thinner too. Her emerald green dress hung from her bony shoulders like a shroud. Her cheekbones, which had always been one of her most prominent features, now stuck out even more, like spines on a venomous fish.

"Your generals will be awaiting a briefing from you at dawn in the library," the Emperor said to Arlo. "You may retire, but you," his eyes turned to Cadence, "I need to see you in the reception chamber before you join Arlo."

Arlo gave Cadence a reassuring look before picking up the bag of armour and turning to leave. The Emperor rose from the throne and Cadence followed him to the reception chamber off to the side of the throne room. The chamber was a mess of maps and documents that had been sprawled out across the Emperor's desk. Cadence's eyes darted over the charts and schedules—some contained battle plans and defence strategies, while others held records of grain stores and how they were being rationed between the military and the civilians. The Emperor stood behind the desk and poured himself a goblet of wine from a crystal decanter.

"Please sit," he said as he motioned to the chair on the opposite side of the desk.

Cadence sat down slowly and suddenly realised that this was the first time he'd ever been alone with Abydos. The Emperor always had the power to make him nervous, but after arguing with gods, Cadence found the ruler of the Empire meek in comparison. He needed to remind himself that the Emperor, no matter how badly he needed Cadence's help, was still dangerous.

"Do you know what it is to hold on to power?" the Emperor asked before taking a sip of his wine.

Cadence didn't respond as he knew Abydos would answer his own question.

"It means to completely obliterate your enemy at the first opportunity," he continued. His face was tired but his voice still boomed with authority no matter how softly he spoke. "There is never room for anticipation or second chances, lest you give them time to recover, return twice as strong, and with the knowledge that you are indecisive or, worse, soft."

"I don't think anyone could ever accuse Your Majesty of being indecisive and soft," said Cadence.

"I was not referring to myself," Abydos said as he walked slowly around the desk and closer to where Cadence sat.

"I need you to look into the future for an opportunity. An opportunity to completely obliterate Saklas and his forces. I need as much information as possible. Use your powers and report back to me in the morning with what you have seen. Leave nothing out. The smallest detail could hold the greatest value. Even if it means we have to make great sacrifices."

"Yes, Your Majesty," Cadence said as Abydos drew closer. The air around Cadence began to feel thick and it became more difficult to breathe.

"Make no mistake, boy," he said. "If it weren't for your

unique ability and the difficult situation we find ourselves in, I would have had you put to death without a second thought. The supply of ebullience has been all but crippled thanks to the murder of Father Gemini. Everyone from the nobles to the peasants grows more restless and unhappy every day without their precious bliss. You have no idea what you did that night."

"*You* have no idea what *he* did!" Cadence shouted as a rage suddenly erupted out of him. "He tried to rape me! He tried to rape me to cure himself of the blight. He might have even killed me when he was done!"

"You should have just let him. One raped slave is far better than one dead ichor alchemist."

"You are every inch the monster Arlo makes you out to be."

"Don't test me," said the Emperor, his voice calm and unaffected by even the slightest hint of emotion. "Or you run the risk of finding out just how monstrous I can be."

The Emperor's large hand came down on Cadence's shoulder and gave a crushing squeeze. Pain burned through his shoulder before his mind's eye opened up to a vision.

An unknown hand drove a dagger into the Emperor's chest. It was then pulled out with a soggy pop. Red blood flecked with glimmering gold flowed from the wound, and the Emperor fell to his knees before the dagger re-entered his flesh over and over again until he fell to the ground, sticky with his own blood. The Emperor's dark eyes looked up at his murderer with a violent combination of shock and disdain.

The vision ended as Abydos's grip loosened on Cadence's shoulder. It left a throbbing ache and a fiery anger behind. Cadence remembered how his father would do the same thing to him. The hatred burning towards the Emperor and Canaan was only doused by the fact that Cadence knew his father was dead and it would not be long before Abydos was too. Cadence could report on as much of the future as Abydos wanted, but he would keep the vision of the Emperor's death to himself.

"If I see anything else pertaining to the war," Cadence said in a rigid tone that matched the Emperor's, "Your Majesty will be the first to know." He got up from the chair and turned away sharply without bowing and without being dismissed. He could not stand to look at the man a moment longer. Before the vision, Cadence would not have wanted the Emperor to see the tears of anger he'd brought to Cadence's eyes. After the vision, Cadence turned to hide the satisfied smirk that wound its way over his lips.

As Cadence departed, for the first time since he and Arlo had decided to fight in the war, a small glimmer of hope bloomed in his chest. Cadence knew the Emperor's death would take place after the war had ended. This meant they would win. For the first time, Cadence allowed himself to believe that if he did everything he was supposed to, then maybe, just maybe, Arlo was right. There was a possibility, however small, that they could rule the Empire together.

Cadence didn't allow himself to linger on this thought for too long. There was work to be done. He needed to find Arsinoe.

As HE PASSED through the doors of the conservatory, he was stopped dead in his tracks. The outside of the city had not been the only thing to go through changes since he and Arlo had left. The dense and overgrown forest of plants, flowers, ferns, and trees had been replaced by beds of grain, fruit trees, and vegetable gardens.

Arsinoe stood next to a small grove of orange trees as if she'd been waiting for him.

"The difference is striking," she said, "but unfortunately necessary."

"Was this your idea to feed the people or the Emperor's idea to feed his soldiers?" Cadence asked.

"My idea for the people with a lot of what is being produced going to the soldiers," she replied, looking a little defeated.

"Your poor conservatory."

"In times of war, sacrifices have to be made."

"And the celestium?"

"The last of it has been used up," she said, motioning to the ripening fruits and grain around them.

"Surely Hermia can just make more for you when all of this is over," Cadence said. "Then you can set everything right again."

Arsinoe gave a gentle half smile. "The gods are not what they once were. Their power is waning even if they won't admit it. Hermia wouldn't be able to produce celestium if she tried. Before the fall of Lucifer, the gods were in their golden age and capable of the most miraculous things. But after losing not just one but two leaders of the Pantheon, they slowly began to lose their way and their power."

"I wish things were different," said Cadence. "The gods lose their way and only the mortals suffer for it. It isn't right. I've seen what is going to happen. A lot of people are going to die and it's all so unnecessary."

"It is the Great Web of the Fates," Arsinoe replied as she turned her attention to a bush of azaleas, one of the few poisonous flowers still thriving in the conservatory. "Sometimes great beauty can bloom from great tragedy. Suffering shows us who we really are. It shows us what is really important. Famine, disaster, death, and war—they show us what we truly care about."

"While the gods watch on from the clouds and laugh at us."

"We were created in their image. They are more like us and we more like them than either human or god is willing to admit. They see tiny, impermanent, fleeting versions of themselves in us, and yet we are so different from them. That is why they are so fascinated by us, why they make lovers of us and have us bear their children."

"And fight their wars," Cadence interjected.

"So you know," she said. "That Saklas was once the sky lord?"

"Hermia told me," Cadence said. "How long have you known?"

"I didn't know for certain, but you've just confirmed it for me. I've had my suspicions since the day the emissary arrived," she said. "There was something so familiar about Saklas. It was an ancient and powerful energy that doesn't emanate from the other gods I have met. I couldn't quite put my finger on it until now."

Arsinoe's power of subtle deception to get what she wanted, in this case information, never failed to leave him in awe. He was reminded of the day she'd bumped the vial of poison over on purpose just to see if Cadence would catch it before it hit the floor and killed them both. Or perhaps, he then thought, feeling a little disappointed in himself, he was just an easy target to manipulate. But then he thought about how her actions had made him feel. She had been testing him; he'd passed and his confidence in his own abilities had increased. He knew he needed her, but more importantly he knew he could trust her.

"I'm going to kill Saklas," said Cadence, pulling the bag of flowers and plants from his satchel. "But I need your help to do it."

Arsinoe took the bag from Cadence, loosened the draw strings, and looked inside. Surprise was not an expression Cadence had ever seen on the Empress's face before. Her eyes widened so far Cadence thought they might pop clean out of her skull. She closed the bag quickly and hurried towards her desk in the apothecary where she locked the bag away in her desk drawer with shaking hands.

"How did you get hold of those plants and flowers?" she asked in a hushed tone. Cadence had also never seen her so close to the verge of panic.

"I asked Hermia to give them to me," he responded.

Arsinoe hung on to his every word as he described his plan to her. When he was finished, she turned to look at him, her eyes intense with fatigue and stress.

"You cannot do this, child," she said. "You are sending yourself on a suicide mission. How are you even going to get close enough to Saklas to get the poison inside of him?"

"I haven't quite figured that part out yet," said Cadence sheepishly. "But somehow I will. I've seen it. I've looked into the future, multiple futures. This is the only way to end Saklas and save Arlo."

"And what of your fate?" asked Arsinoe. "Have you considered what will become of you?"

"What becomes of me doesn't matter," said Cadence.

"How can you say that?" Arsinoe almost shouted but then stopped herself. "Of course it matters. You matter!"

"Because I am going to die anyway!"

"You don't know that! No seer or oracle has ever seen the details of their own death. There is no way you could know."

"I do!" said Cadence, his resolve suddenly leaving him. His hands shook as he lifted his tunic and turned his inner thigh towards Arsinoe.

Dread flushed her face, causing her to go pale as her eyes found the dark purple mark on Cadence's flesh.

"Oh no," she gasped. "Proteus, I am so sorry."

"My name is Cadence," he corrected her gently as he let his tunic fall over the mark.

"Cadence … you are the boy who sang the night of the Harvest Festival in Naphtali," she said.

Cadence nodded. He could feel her trying to look past his scars and piece together fragments of a face from the past.

"I remember you … but how did this happen?" she asked, her expression solemn as she took his face gently in her hands. The pity in her eyes prickled as they ran over his scars. "How did …"

Cadence pulled away from her. "My brothers," he choked. "Having an oracle in the family was not seen as a good thing."

"And the blight?" Her voice was soft and cautious, treating Cadence like something made of brittle glass.

"Gemini …" Cadence's voice croaked back at her as he forced himself to swallow his tears. "Somehow, with all the blood and—" he stopped himself as Arsinoe threw herself over him in a hug.

"That worm," she growled as she held him tighter. "I curse his name and hope his spirit is rotting in the bowels of Obsidian. I'm so sorry. I should have done more to protect you from him."

Cadence pulled away from her. "It's not your fault," he said. "But there isn't time for this. I need your help."

"Does Arlo know?" Arsinoe asked.

"No," Cadence answered. "He doesn't know anything about my plan and he doesn't know that I have the blight. Hermia assured me that demigods are immune to it. Arlo cannot know about any of this. If he finds out he will try to stop me, or worse be distracted on the battlefield. He needs to stay sharp."

"How long have you known?"

"Since just before he asked me to marry him."

"And you've been carrying this burden all this time by yourself?"

"Arsinoe, please," Cadence begged. "If I stay away much longer Arlo is going to come looking for me, or worse get suspicious. I will die from the blight if the war doesn't kill me first. I know I cannot survive but I can still save Arlo. Help me do this."

The Empress hesitated for a moment, and Cadence watched her face change as she put her emotions aside.

"Fine," she finally said. "I will help you make this poison. I've never done it before, but I know it will take a long time to brew."

"Then we need to get started as soon as possible," Cadence said.

"I have ebullience to make tonight," said Arsinoe. "Come back here in the morning while Arlo is meeting with his generals and we can begin."

"Thank you," he said as he turned to leave.

"Cadence," Arsinoe called to him.

He turned back around to face her before she said, "You must truly love him."

He looked at her for a moment with a smile, "With everything I am."

30

THE POISONED PRINCESS

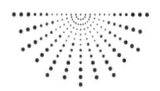

When Cadence opened the door, Arlo was on the bed with one foot hanging off the edge as he stared up at the ceiling.

Arlo's chamber had remained untouched. It looked exactly the same as the last time Cadence had seen it, with one exception. The birdcage stood open and abandoned.

"Poor Damascus," said Cadence, walking over to the cage. The small bowls used for his seed and water behind the thin wooden bars had been pecked bare. All that remained were a few brown and orange feathers scattered over the floor of the cage.

"I am sure he is fine," said Arlo, putting his hands over Cadence's shoulders. "He's a clever bird and he wasn't totally dependent on the food we would give him. He may come back."

"Maybe," said Cadence, his eyes fixed on the hinges of the open cage door. "Let's leave the cage open in case he does. I'll get some fresh water and seed too."

A PROPHECY OF FLOWERS AND LIGHTNING

That night while Arlo slept, Cadence cleared his mind and peered into the future. He stood on the walls of the city. From the south, dark, silver clouds crackling with lightning filled the horizon. Under the clouds, Saklas' army steadily marched towards the city. Their rotting grey flesh was covered in open sores that wept into the tattered black fabric of their robes and oozed from their broken armour. Cadence's heart grew heavy as he remembered that these slaves had been a thriving people before Saklas had made them into monsters. The smell coming from them was enough to make him retch.

A powerful roar bellowed through the air. The hair on the back of Cadence's neck stood at attention as he looked in the direction of what had made the terrible sound. Gigantic creatures towered over the marching army. They were unlike anything Cadence had ever seen or heard of. These creatures were no monster from any of the stories his mother had told him as a child. They were gargantuan, serpent-like beasts with green scaly skin. Four massive tusks sprung forth from mouths filled with sharp, dripping fangs. Long forked tongues whipped in and out of their mouths sampling the air, while eight beady black eyes scattered over their heads searched for something to devour. Their webbed claws pounded at the earth as they walked, causing the ground to tremble beneath them. One of the monsters reared up on its hind legs and a hood sprung up from its neck, unleashing a host of terrifying, slimy, writhing tentacles. It sent a sharp, saliva-spattered roar into the air. The earth where the saliva fell began to sizzle and smoke. These were the leviathans Nubia had spoken of.

The shield wall of the city would never hold against these abominations, Cadence thought to himself. The goddess had been right; with the help from these terrible monstrosities, Saklas would take Luciferian in a matter of days. And once

Luciferian fell, the rest of the Empire would not be far behind.

What do you seek, child?

The voice was a terrible, crackling whisper carried on the wind. Cadence could feel the weight of its ancient power. It was the voice that held the ability to sprawl lightning across the skies and command thunder.

It was then that Cadence saw it. A palanquin the size of a house being carried on the back of one of the leviathans. Inside the palanquin, between the drawn curtains, stood the god Saklas, and he was looking directly at Cadence. Pale blue eyes set into what was once a beautiful face stared at him with a curiosity that made Cadence's skin crawl. He did not look like the same withered god from Cadence's vision of the past. Bulging muscles with the strength to hurl lightning bolts had returned to his bones. He stood tall and proud but was surrounded by a terrible darkness. He did not radiate with the same glow of health and vitality as the other gods but something terrible instead. Something worse than death, like being on the brink of it without ever experiencing the sweet release of oblivion. A shock of dead white hair floated around his head like that of a corpse in water.

I know what you are, Saklas whispered to Cadence across the divide directly into his mind. His voice was an icy wind ripping through the inside of Cadence's head. *You cannot stop me, but I may be willing to strike a bargain.*

Cadence pulled himself out of the vision and with a gasp sat bolt upright in the bed. His lungs burned and his heart raced as if he had been drowning but managed to reach the surface just in time. He woke out of breath, drenched in a cold sweat, his head still ringing with the voice of the god.

"What is it?" Arlo asked as he grabbed hold of Cadence with one arm and pulled a dagger from under his pillow with another.

"Saklas," Cadence panted. "I saw him. His army is two days' march away. They are approaching from the south."

A faint light spilled in from the open window signalling the arrival of the dawn. Cadence bounded out of the bed and began to dress.

"I need to tell your father," he said as he pulled his tunic over his head and then stopped to look at Arlo. He was still in bed and the blade was still raised. "Have you always slept with a dagger under your pillow?"

"No," said Arlo, lowering the blade and suddenly looking sheepish. "It's normally two daggers but I haven't unpacked properly yet."

CADENCE HAD LEFT in such a hurry he'd neglected to fasten his sandals properly. He skidded to a halt in the middle of a hallway and tied the leather straps just well enough so he would not trip over them. Arlo had told him the Emperor would more than likely be in his reception chamber before joining him and the generals in the library.

As he raced towards the Emperor's reception chamber, his mind spun with Saklas' words. *I am willing to make a bargain.* Cadence felt a fool for letting his fear get the better of him. But how could a vision of Saklas from the future speak with him? It had never happened before, but then again, the gods' powers were mysterious.

Perhaps there is a way I can draw him out, Cadence thought to himself as he approached the passage that led to the reception chamber. Perhaps Saklas hadn't been talking to him in the vision, but instead the vision was showing him what Saklas was going to say. This idea led him to further questions that made his head spin. If the god wanted to make a deal with Cadence, what did he have that Saklas wanted? If

Cadence could figure out what Saklas wanted, how could he use that to his advantage?

Did he really think he was smart enough to outwit a god? It had worked with Hermia because Cadence understood that her weakness was her vanity and pride, but he had no idea what Saklas' weaknesses were or if he even had any at all. There were no stories about the forgotten god; if there were, then he would not have been forgotten in the first place. Either way, what Cadence had seen in the vision was all he had to go on. He needed to figure out how he could use it to his advantage. He needed to go back, try talk to Saklas again and figure out what he wanted. Only then would he be able to use it against the god.

When Cadence got to the reception chamber, the guard on duty at the door announced his arrival and allowed him inside. Cadence entered and found the Emperor behind his desk about to tuck into a large breakfast of fried eggs, roast potatoes, steaming porridge, and fresh pomegranate. The smell and look of the food sent a rumble through Cadence's stomach, and he realised that neither he nor Arlo had eaten anything since just before they'd left Anthurium. Cadence eyed the meal when a sudden discomfort came over him. It didn't seem right for the Emperor to eat so well while his people were being put on rations. Then again, it seemed like exactly the kind of thing Abydos would do.

"Well," Abydos barked, "did you come here to bring me news or to gawk at me while I eat?"

Cadence cleared his throat and, wanting to get the interaction over with, told the Emperor everything he knew as quickly as he could.

"So Nubia was right about the leviathans," Abydos said before he blew on a spoonful of the molten porridge. "Good thing all the ichor plasma cannons on the warships and walls are serviced and ready."

Cadence had never seen an ichor plasma cannon in action, but something inside of him told him they may not be enough to kill a leviathan.

"Was there anything else?" the Emperor said before spearing the spoon into his mouth.

Cadence thought about the dagger he saw entering the Emperor's chest and the crimson that had at first trickled from the wound and then gushed. He hated Abydos for so many reasons. He hated the way he used people. He hated the way he treated his subjects. He hated that Abydos was incapable of giving Arlo the love he needed and deserved. He hated the fact that Abydos had been the one to start this war. If he had never invaded the Scorched-Over Lands, then none of this would have happened in the first place. But the biggest reason Cadence hated the Emperor was because of how much he reminded Cadence of his father. If the Fates saw fit for Abydos to die, then so be it. Cadence would not warn him. He would not try prevent it. Cadence watched Abydos gorge himself on the enormous breakfast while he knew full well the people of the Empire were starving.

"No, Your Majesty," Cadence said, "but I will keep looking."

With that, he left and made his way as quickly as he could to the East Wing of the palace.

※

HE FOUND Arsinoe at her desk in the conservatory. She was hunched over with her head in her arms and wore the same green dress she had on the day before. Her dark locks flowed over her forearms and back like a bush of thick, dark vines. At first, Cadence thought she was crying. He approached slowly so as not to startle her and saw that her breathing was steady and gentle. She was not crying. She was sleeping.

Cadence leaned in closer to lay his hand upon her shoulder as gently as he could. He wanted to wake her without startling her. Just before the palm of his hand touched her bony shoulder, she spoke, her face still buried in her arms.

"Be careful," her muffled voice said. "A few men have lost their hands and some even their lives that way."

Cadence jumped back at the unexpected sound of the Empress's voice.

"My apologies," he said, wiping his now sweaty palm on his tunic. "I thought you were asleep."

"I was," said Arsinoe as she sat up, "and I wasn't."

She looked exhausted. Her eyes were swollen and overrun with tiny crimson rivers of fatigue. Her skin, normally the picture of perfect glowing health, second only to that of a god, was pale and ashen. Her beautiful lips, normally plump and filled with colour, had turned into a thin, greying frown.

"When was the last time you slept?" Cadence asked.

"I take sleep where I can find it these days," Arsinoe answered as she stood up from her chair. She wobbled on her feet at first before steadying herself. "The demand for ebullience in all its forms has increased substantially. Bliss for those who can afford it and blitz for the soldiers to use in the upcoming battles."

"Are there no other ichor alchemists in the city?"

"It is an incredibly rare skill. And those who try it without the proper instruction or training often kill themselves and cause massive explosions."

Arsinoe shrugged, causing her dress, that Cadence noticed looked two sizes too large for her, to almost slide off her shoulders. She looked haggard and on the edge of collapse.

"Why do you stay here?" Cadence asked. "You are so

powerful you could do anything you want, but you insist on remaining a prisoner of the Emperor."

"I have a duty to the people," said Arsinoe.

"This is about more than just duty. You are punishing yourself. I overheard you and the Emperor once. He threatened you. He said something about keeping an abomination alive. What did he mean by that?"

Arsinoe sighed. "You shouldn't have heard that."

"But I did. And I want to know if there is anything I can do to help you."

"My situation in this palace is beyond anyone's help."

"What did Abydos mean?" Cadence pressed.

"He was talking about our daughter," said Arsinoe.

"Nimue?" asked Cadence. "You never told me what happened to her."

"My negligence happened to her," said Arsinoe with tears welling up in her tired eyes. "I was experimenting with ichor to formulate a new kind of ebullience. Abydos wanted me to create something that would transform his soldiers into powerful war machines second only to the offspring of the gods. I agreed and was punished for my impiety."

"What do you mean?"

"She was only three years old when it happened," Arsinoe choked. "When my back was turned, she had somehow gotten into the new formula and ingested it. By the time I realised what had happened, it was too late."

"But it didn't kill her?" Cadence asked.

"Most days I wish it had," Arsinoe said, wiping her tears away with the back of her hand. "Instead, it transformed her into a monster."

"Where is she now? What became of her?"

"The same fate that befalls everything under my husband's control," Arsinoe said as the sorrow in her voice began to curdle into bitter anger. "He found a way to make use of her and to punish me at the same time. High up in the Titanian mountain range, there is a great labyrinth used as a vault to house all the conquered riches of the Empire. Abydos had our daughter locked away in that vault to serve as its guard and prisoner. If I run away, he will have her killed. If I refuse to manufacture ebullience, he will have her killed. If I refuse to obey his every whim, he will have her killed. That is the reason why I stay. Are you happy with that answer, Oracle of Luciferian?"

Arsinoe had never spoken to Cadence with such ice in her voice. He wanted to apologise for prying, to open his arms and comfort Arsinoe, but he knew the Empress did not seek comfort. She wanted solutions. She wanted justice. For how long had she lived under vicious rumours and gossip that she had eaten her child in exchange for dark powers? Cadence remembered the whispers among the servants and courtiers. He thought of the old woman who stood in the crowd in Naphtali with him as they watched Arsinoe leave the royal airship. She had called Arsinoe a she-demon.

"There has to be a way to fix it," said Cadence.

"I spend my every free moment looking for one," replied Arsinoe, gesturing around the conservatory. "It has been over fifteen years and I have not found it. Just after it happened, I created and drank a poison to kill my womb and ensure I would never bear a child again."

"I'm so sorry," Cadence said softly.

A vision then tore its way through his mind like an explosion. He saw a child of about two or three on the floor of the conservatory. Her soft, smooth skin held the same rich colour of beaten bronze as her mother's. Nimue entertained herself with a small wooden horse while Arsinoe was hunched over her desk, frantically making notes on a scroll. A pale, grey hand then emerged from the shadows, the stout fingers clutching a vial of glittering ichor. The fingers then released the vial and it rolled across the stone floor before coming to rest by bumping into Nimue's foot. Cadence watched on in horror as the toddler's chubby fingers found their way over the cork stopper of the vial. In one clumsy movement, the stopper was freed and the golden liquid spilled all over Nimue.

The vision ended there, and Cadence's mind was brought abruptly back to the present.

"There is nothing to be done about it," Arsinoe said as she adjusted her dress on her fading frame. She wiped the last of the tears from her face and summoned her regal composure. "We need to get started with your poison."

Cadence wanted to tell Arsinoe that what had happened to her daughter was not her fault. Someone had poisoned the lost princess. Someone in the palace. But he stopped himself. He needed to look deeper into the past and find out exactly who had committed such a vile act before he shared the information with Arsinoe.

Cadence remained silent and watched the Empress turn towards her desk. She waved her hand over one of the drawers and it popped out as if pushed by something living inside. Arsinoe dipped her hands into the drawer and pulled out the bag from Hermia and an ancient wooden box. The box was long and made from a dark wood that had over time become darker with years of wear. A scene had been carved into the lid and sides of the box, but Cadence could only make out a few faint details that had not been worn away by the ravages of time. There were worn-down images of leaves, flowers, and human skulls that were clear, but the rest was too faded and scratched up to make out.

"This," said Arsinoe, resting the box on the desk and opening its lid, "is the recipe for God's Bane." From inside the box, she lifted a single ancient scroll. She put the scroll on the desk and gently unrolled it.

The worn, dark yellow paper sighed as it unravelled before them. Cadence expected to see more worn-out images and writing that was barely legible. Instead, there was nothing. The scroll was empty.

"I don't under—"

"Wait," Arsinoe said, raising a finger. She leaned over the scroll and whispered something over it.

The whisper was in a language Cadence didn't understand or recognise. When Arsinoe straightened her back, the scroll began to glow. As the paper lit up, images and words began to reveal themselves as if being written by an invisible hand.

"The Pestilence of the Gods," Cadence read out loud.

"Indeed," said Arsinoe.

"Where did this come from?" Cadence asked as his eyes devoured the illustrations and instructions on the page.

"That is a story for another time," said Arsinoe. "Right now, we need to get to work."

Together they ran through the ingredients listed and illustrated inside the scroll and cross referenced them with the ones inside the bag from Hermia.

"Corpse lily," said Arsinoe as she pulled a flower from the bag with rough black petals overrun with veins of dark blue mould. She wafted the flower under Cadence's nose and he recoiled in disgust.

"That's awful!" He choked and tried not to retch.

Arsinoe let out a quiet chuckle before reaching into the bag again. "You need to be careful," she warned. "A poison powerful enough to kill a god could kill a man with a single touch. On their own, these ingredients aren't that dangerous, but once combined in the correct way they will become the most deadly poison in the universe."

Cadence nodded. "I understand."

"This one is called plague blossom," she said, pulling the

next flower from the bag. It was a small purple flower with five thin petals giving it the look of a dark star. "It grows on the graves of the gods' fallen children, mostly monsters slain by heroes."

Cadence learned that the other ingredients included in Hermia's supply consisted of glimmering aconite, strangling black hemlock, ghost orchid, festering belladonna, dragon's skull mushroom, and cadaver moss. They were all flowers he'd never seen or even heard of in his time studying and creating poisons with the Empress.

"All the main ingredients for God's Bane are here," she said, looking at the collection of flowers and plants laid out on the desk. "The rest of the ingredients should be easy enough to find in my stores and what's left of the poisonous plants in the conservatory."

Cadence's eyes fell back to the scroll. He read over the instructions, but just before the end of the text his blood ran cold.

"This says the poison takes five days to prepare. That isn't enough time. Saklas' armies will be here in less than two days."

"Then we have to hope that the imperial forces can hold them off long enough," said Arsinoe as she began to collect the mortars, pestles, flasks, and beakers they would need to start making the poison.

Cadence's throat began to tighten and he found it more difficult to get air into his lungs. "I saw them," he said. "They have these monsters with them. Huge beasts capable of massive destruction. Nubia and Abydos call them leviathans."

"I am familiar with that breed of monster," said Arsinoe as she began to grind the corpse lily and plague blossom into a dark, stinking paste. "I've never seen one for myself, but they are indeed capable of terrible things."

"We'll be dead before the poison is even halfway ready," said Cadence, defeated.

"Did you see that in one of your visions, or is that your own doubt speaking?" Arsinoe asked, looking up from her mortar and pestle.

Cadence didn't answer her.

"I thought so," she said. "Stop listening to the panicked voices in your head and help me. We are doing everything we can. Have faith that the army and Luciferian's divine defences can hold the city until we are ready."

Cadence read over the instructions on the scroll one last time before he pulled a mortar and pestle of his own closer and began to grind down on the cadaver moss and ghost orchid.

THE TWO WORKED CAREFULLY TOGETHER in silence, only speaking to ask for something to be handed to them or for the other to double-check a measurement. To Cadence, it felt like coming home. He remembered everything from the time he spent as Proteus, and while he and Arsinoe were working together it was as if nothing had changed. They moved around each other with a familiar and peaceful ease that was like slipping into your own bed after a few nights away from it. But things had changed, and the peace in Cadence's heart was short lived every time he remembered exactly what they were doing and why they were doing it.

The sun crawled across the sky, unnoticed by them until the oil lamps in the conservatory magically lit themselves. Cadence looked over to Arsinoe. The bags under her eyes were larger than they had been that morning and looked even worse in the lamplight. She looked like a ghost.

With all the ingredients prepared, Arsinoe began to add them to a beaker of crystal-clear viper venom being heated over a flame. The first batch of ingredients hit the venom in the beaker with a sharp hiss. The clear liquid took on the dark purple colour of the plague blossom.

"Once infused, that mixture needs to stand overnight before the other ingredients can be added," Arsinoe said before letting out a long yawn.

"I can finish up here while you get some rest," said Cadence.

"No," said the Empress as she closed her eyes for a brief moment before opening them again. "I will finish up here for the night. You run along, Arlo is probably looking for you. I will meet you in the dining hall for supper."

"Only if you are sure," Cadence said, giving her another opportunity to get the sleep she so desperately needed.

"I am," she said with a weary smile.

"Thank you," said Cadence as he stood up from his seat, "for everything."

"I hope this plan of yours works," she replied. "Just know that I have the utmost faith in you."

Cadence made his way to the exit of the conservatory with a shiver rattling down his spine. Thinking up the plan was one thing, but seeing it through to fruition would be an entirely different beast. He hoped it would work too, for if not they would all be doomed.

31

THE FIRST WAVE

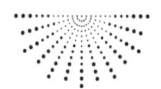

The air was filled with the cacophony of swords clattering against shields. Saklas' forces brought with them a frigid wind that carried the smell of death towards the city. Cadence emerged from the dream as if coming up from being underwater for too long.

"Another nightmare?" Arlo asked from the foot of the bed where he was dressing.

"They are getting closer," said Cadence, the echoes of clashing shields and swords crawling across his skin like a swarm of insects. "This time it was like I could feel them. They will be on the outskirts of the city walls by tomorrow morning."

"And I thought for a change you might be sleeping peacefully," Arlo replied as he finished lacing his sandals.

Cadence gave him a weak smile from his place on the bed. He had not known peaceful sleep since they had returned to the palace. Cadence pushed himself out of the bed and pulled his tunic from where he'd left it on a nearby chair.

"I need to tell your father what I have seen," he said as he pulled the tunic over his head.

"Is there anything new?"

"It seems that they will be attacking in waves. I think Saklas' plan is to try weaken the army with each wave, forcing the Emperor into separate battles over and over again until the men are exhausted, weakened, and their numbers severely cut down."

"It doesn't sound like the worst strategy in the world," said Arlo with a look that suggested he was a little impressed. "It might be what I would do if I was attacking the city."

"This isn't good. Saklas knows our weaknesses, and we are yet to learn even one of his."

"That's why my father has you." Arlo finished lacing up his sandals and sat down next to Cadence on the bed.

Cadence moved closer and wrapped his arms over Arlo. "Are you frightened?" he asked.

"Only of losing you," Arlo said, taking Cadence's hand. "No matter what happens, you need to stay away from the fighting. I cannot win the war while also trying to protect you."

"You expect me to let my shiny new armour to just be for show?" Cadence joked, but Arlo did not laugh.

"I'm being serious," he said, his voice suddenly an octave deeper. "I need you to promise me that, no matter what, you will not raise your sword in battle."

"You think I am weak," said Cadence, moving away, but Arlo pulled him back.

"I know how strong you are," he said, his face suddenly heavy with worry. "But I also know that you are not a soldier. I am the weak one because I am not strong enough to lose you. Now promise me you won't fight, no matter what happens."

Cadence hesitated for a moment, unable to look away

from the intense stare Arlo's bright blue eyes held him captive in.

"I promise," he finally said, knowing well he would not be able to keep his word for long.

When dawn broke the next morning, Cadence and Arlo helped each other into their armour. Cadence's hands had shaken as he'd tightened and fixed the straps of Arlo's greaves into place. He got to his feet and took a few steps back to examine his work. Arlo looked like a god in the new armour.

Cadence's eyes wandered over the parts of Arlo's body where sun-kissed muscle flexed against polished metal.

"How does it feel?" Cadence asked.

"Let me show you," said Arlo as he picked up Cadence's breast plate and walked closer.

Arlo lowered the silver breastplate over Cadence's head and it came to rest on his shoulders. Cadence had expected to be weighed down by it to the point where he was worried he wouldn't be able to move. He was pleasantly surprised to find that it felt almost as if the breast plate was not there at all.

"Is yours also so light?" Cadence asked, resting the palm of his hand against the embossed tangle of silver vines and flowers on his chest.

"It is," said Arlo with a smile. "It's the best armour I've ever worn."

"Do you think it's strong enough to stop a spear, arrow, or sword?" Cadence continued to run his palms over the feather-light breastplate.

Arlo chuckled as he fetched Cadence's arm guards and greaves. "They were made by Amaranth himself. If the magic of the blacksmith god cannot stop an arrow head from piercing flesh, then nothing can."

Arlo's hands were steadier and worked much faster than Cadence's had. It only took him a few minutes to have Cadence fully covered and strapped into his armour. Arlo then picked up the silver helmet and crowned Cadence with it. Cadence then picked up the shield and sword. Even with the addition of the greaves, the helmet, the shield, and the sword, he still felt light on his feet and was able to move without hindrance or discomfort. Despite the armour fitting perfectly, when he looked at Arlo, Cadence couldn't help but feel like a child playing dress up.

"You look like a true warrior," Arlo said. There was a surprise in his voice that would have hurt Cadence's feelings if it hadn't been accompanied by a look of warm pride and then excitement. "You must see yourself!"

Arlo pulled Cadence towards the full-length mirror at the end of the room and nudged him in front of it.

Cadence did not recognise himself in the shining silver armour. The helmet covered the scars on his face, leaving only the green eyes his father had hated so much staring back at him. He stood taller than normal; perhaps it was his imagination, or perhaps for the first time he felt proud to look upon his reflection.

Cadence turned to face Arlo. Tears began to fight their way to his eyes and he was not strong enough to stop them. "This is really happening, isn't it?" he said.

"All will be well, my beloved," said Arlo, pulling him close. Their breastplates pushed against each other with a light metallic scrape. He raised his hand to Cadence's face, gently brushed his tears away, and leaned in for a kiss.

The sound of trumpets then tore through the air, summoning them to the city wall and out of each other's arms.

"Are you ready?" Cadence asked, wiping tears off of his cheeks.

"I am," Arlo replied, "but you are missing one last thing."

Cadence looked down at himself confused. He was wearing all the armour that Amaranth had given him. They hadn't missed anything. When he looked up again, Arlo was holding up a stalk of small, bright purple flowers.

"Penstemon," said Arlo as Cadence took the flowers from him. "For courage."

ON TOP of the southern wall of the city, Abydos and Arsinoe were waiting beneath the shade of a crimson pavilion. Solaris had just begun to pull the sun on its journey across the sky. From a raised seat, the Emperor watched the horizon with a frustrated anxiety as he pulled at the collar of his breastplate, wet with sweat dripping from his face and neck. Arsinoe stood silently by his side and gave Cadence a reassuring wink as he and Arlo entered the pavilion.

The smoke of burnt offerings to the gods hung in the air —a miasma of charred hair, plants, and flesh. On their way to the wall, Cadence and Arlo had seen the citizens make their sacrifices at the feet of guardian statues across the city. Some of the offerings were prayers for victory in battle. Others were spells of protection for the Luciferian soldiers. Some were curses against the enemy being sent into the air for them to choke on.

On the inside of the glimmering shield wall, the city was ready for battle. Along the wall, between the ichor plasma cannons, catapults had been constructed. The buckets of the catapults had been covered with heavy black fabric concealing what lay underneath. Enormous gilded battleships glittered in the sunlight as they loomed high in the air, ready to be dispatched into battle.

Outside, the flat, arid terrain of the Luciferian desert lay in a dusty expanse of fractured beige stretching as far as the eye could see. At the base of the city wall, 10 000 soldiers stood at attention in perfectly formed groups. The men did not scuffle or twitch but instead stood like armour-clad statues armed to the teeth with swords, spears, and shields. Around each man's neck was a small silver vial similar to the one Father Gemini had kept.

Blitz, Cadence thought to himself. *For them to use at their own discretion.*

Their armour, while not as bright or new as his or Arlo's, was made of a golden metal that shimmered in the pale, yellow light of the morning sun. Cadence recognised the shimmer and stopped himself from gasping.

"Their armour is imbued with ichor," he whispered to Arlo, breaking his focus on the horizon.

Arlo nodded. "A gift from Amaranth and Fragma," he said, turning to Cadence. "I must join my men."

Cadence's stomached dropped. A cold panic tore through his body and he struggled to maintain his balance. He had not seen Arlo on the battlefield on the first day of the war in any of his visions. There had been visions of Arlo taking part and returning victoriously, but they had only taken place in later battles. As the panic froze over his body, Cadence's mind searched frantically for a clue he might have missed in his visions. Perhaps the future he'd seen had changed and a different one was about to take place. His heart began to thrum so hard he could feel it hammer through his breastplate.

"You will not fight today," said the Emperor with an uncharacteristic shake in his voice.

The breath Cadence did not know he'd been holding in

was released from his lips in a quiet *whoosh* of relief. The icy panic that had frozen his muscles began to thaw as Abydos' words registered in his mind.

"But, father," Arlo protested, "how am I to lead my men if I am not on the battlefield among them?"

"Your generals have their instructions, do they not?" Abydos snapped back at his son.

"They do," Arlo said, confused.

"Then all they need to do is follow your orders," Abydos said as he sat back in his chair, weaving his fingers together and turning his gaze back to the horizon.

"But fath—"

"Your time to fight will come!" Abydos boomed. "For now, you shall remain here while your generals do the work they need to do. I do not wish to show my full hand to my enemy on the first day of battle! We must keep them on their toes! Your power will be showcased in good time! Be patient!"

In that moment, Cadence's heart sank for Arlo. Any other father would have kept his son out of battle in order to preserve his life for as long as possible. Not Abydos. To the Emperor, Arlo was nothing more than a strategic move of power to be played at his will.

Cadence turned to Arlo just in time to watch his face sink with disappointment and shame. He reminded Cadence of a dog that had been beaten by its owner for being too excited.

"I thought you said they would be here at dawn," Abydos barked at Cadence, almost lifting himself from his seat.

Cadence closed his eyes as a whisper floated through his mind and sent a shiver over his body. The army could not yet be seen, but he could feel them drawing nearer as the whisper grew louder. *We are coming, young oracle*, it hissed in Cadence's ear, and he knew it was the voice of the forgotten god. *Speak with me. I want to offer you a bargain.*

"They are here," said Cadence as he opened his eyes and tried to shake Saklas' voice from his head.

"I don't see anything," said Arlo, his ocean eyes focused on the line of the horizon.

They were heard before they were seen. Just as Cadence had foreseen, the rhythmic clashing of sword against shield ripped through the air towards Luciferian and broke against the city wall like a great wave. A shadow—thin, dark, and dreadful—appeared on the edge of the horizon that soon turned into a storm cloud made up of soldiers in black. As the horizon darkened, Cadence thought back to his visions of how this very same army of demons had laid waste to Naphtali.

He remembered the festering, maggot-infested open wounds that oozed black pus. He recalled the gnashing fangs that had torn into flesh. He remembered how they moved with an unnatural speed and were able to conceal themselves in shadows. Cadence had shared this information with the Emperor who, at the time, had seemed unworried.

Cadence looked up at the faint glimmer of the shield wall that encapsulated Luciferian. He wondered how something that looked as delicate as a spider web could be strong enough to protect them.

Turning his gaze to the Emperor, Cadence saw he was drenched in an anxious sweat. His fingernails dug into the gilded arms of the chair he sat in as his eyes widened further and further at the sight of the army that stampeded towards the city.

Abydos raised his arm, forming an arrow with his palm. "ATTACK!" he screamed as his arm dropped like a heavy sword.

At the Emperor's command, trumpets exploded into the air. The men below gave a collective battle cry. The noise sent a vibration up the city wall and into the soles of

Cadence's sandals. Cadence scanned over the men charging forward and saw many of them reaching for the vials of blitz around their necks before inhaling deeply from them. As the blitz coursed through their system, the movements of the soldiers became faster and their muscles grew larger and bulged under their skin. The war cries grew louder until they became one booming roar. Arlo, Cadence, Abydos, and Arsinoe watched on as the Luciferian army charged forward to meet their enemy on the battlefield in a thunderous crash.

The only other time Cadence had seen ichor weapons in action was on the hunting trip. The spears used to hunt and kill the lupercalia were only a small taste of what blades charged with ichor were capable of. He was unable to tear his eyes away from the carnage. Golden lightning crackled up the blades of the swords, sending a tingle through the air Cadence could feel break over his skin. Soldiers on both sides were being torn to pieces within seconds. Flashes and explosions of molten gold erupted as the ichor swords made contact with the rotting flesh of Saklas' forces.

Unfortunate Luciferian soldiers, overwhelmed by the unnatural abilities and feral fighting style of the enemy, were torn limb from limb. The dusty earth beneath them was saturated with blood before their bodies hit the ground. If Cadence listened carefully, he could almost hear Nubia rejoice. As far as Cadence knew, she didn't want them to lose this war, but that was not going to stop her from revelling in the bloodshed. Cadence's stomach turned as he pictured the goddess's sick, fang-brimmed smile. She liked to remind everyone that she saw all, and Cadence knew without a doubt that every one of her awful eyes was focused on the battle taking place before him. She was lounging somewhere invisible and undetectable watching the swing of every blade while salivating in delight.

Cadence tore his thoughts away from Nubia and instead

focused them on Arlo and the Emperor. Their attention was consumed by the battle. Saklas' forces were making headway, pushing the Luciferian soldiers back closer to the city wall. When the soldiers were only a few meters from the base of the wall, the floor began to vibrate under Cadence's feet. His eyes shot up to look at Arlo who was looking at the giant guardian statues that had erected themselves every few meters along the wall. The arms of the statues were still elevated, powering the shield wall over the city, but the eyes of the statues had begun to glow. A crackle and buzz filled the air, growing louder as the golden light in the eyes of the statues grew brighter. The top of the wall began to vibrate so violently that Cadence's eyes shook inside his skull and his vision began to blur.

Cadence could feel the searing heat coming off of the statues against his skin. Blasts of hot golden light erupted from the eyes of the statues and tore through the air with a sharp roar. The blasts hit the dark soldiers, incinerating them where they stood. One moment they were whole and engaged in the battle, the next they were a cloud of grey ash. One after the other, the enemy soldiers were vaporised in a wave of golden light. When the blasts coming from the eyes of the statues stopped, all that was left of the soldiers was a dirty cloud of soot and ash that hung in the air like fog. The Luciferian soldiers left on the ground choked, coughed, and spluttered on the remains of their foes. Flecks of dark grey ash floated up over the city walls before raining down.

The Emperor watched on with his cold eyes. The anxious sweat he'd been drenched in all morning had finally dried up. A light breeze blew the cloud of incinerated soldier dust away from the city. As soon as they could breathe clearly again, the surviving Luciferian soldiers on the battlefield thrust their blood-covered spears and swords into the air and began to cheer.

"That defence will not be easily repeated," Arsinoe said to the Emperor as she rose from her seat next to him. "The city cannot defend itself indefinitely. Sooner or later, we will either run out of food or the city's ichor supply will need to replenish itself, and the shield wall will fall."

"That is a concern for another day," said Abydos, his eyes focused on the celebrating soldiers. "Today is for victory!"

He stood up from his seat and turned to leave the pavilion. "Come, Arlo," he called. "We must congratulate your generals and see to the victory feast."

Arlo caught Cadence's eyes as he turned to leave. The look on his face told Cadence that they would talk later.

The servants and slaves in the pavilion followed the Emperor and the prince, leaving Arsinoe and Cadence alone.

"He would feast with his soldiers while the city is on the brink of famine, and all to celebrate a meaningless victory," said Cadence. "This was just the beginning. Much worse than what we saw today is on the way." His mind was consumed by the visions of the leviathans coming to tear the city and everyone inside it to pieces.

Arsinoe walked to Cadence's side and rested her hand on his shoulder. "Abydos knows what is coming," she said. "You have been sure to keep him informed. The feast serves the purpose of bolstering the men's morale before things become more difficult. Let them have their victory."

"I can hear him," said Cadence. There was a tremble in his voice brought on by a hot and sticky dread that was simmering inside of him. "I can hear Saklas calling out to me in my head. He wants to meet with me, but I can't allow it until the poison is ready."

"It won't be ready for a few more days," said Arsinoe. "You need to stall him."

"Patience is not a virtue possessed by any of the gods," Cadence replied. "But I will do my best."

"We must join Abydos and Arlo at the feast tonight," said Arsinoe, letting her hand fall from his shoulder. "The Emperor will want the royal family presenting a united front."

Cadence scoffed. "I am no member of the royal family."

"You are married to Arlo, are you not?" The words left her mouth like daggers being thrown at a target.

"I am," said Cadence, confused.

"Then you are part of this family, and more importantly, like it or not, you are part of this war. The men need to see that the Prince Consort and Oracle of Luciferian is alive and well with the rest of the royal family. It will give them confidence. You have a duty now, a responsibility to the Empire."

Cadence cringed at the sound of the title. It was the first time he'd even considered it, let alone heard it out loud. He wanted to say that the Empress must have been joking, but her words were as serious as the expression that weighed heavily on her beautiful face.

"I will be there," he said in a tone trying to match that of Arsinoe's.

"Good," she said. "I need to add the last few ingredients and perform the next steps in the process to produce the God's Bane. I shall see you tonight at the victory feast."

Arsinoe turned to leave, but the tension she had left in the air lingered like a bad smell. Cadence thought back to earlier that morning when he had seen himself in the mirror. It dawned on him that Arsinoe was right. When he and Arlo agreed to join the war, he had expected the battles, but he had not realised that when they were married he would be bound to the royal family and the Empire itself. How was it possible that he could see the future but at the same time be so blind?

The dread inside him came to a boil. He knew the Empire needed him, but the realisation that he was at the front and centre of the war as a figurehead was a whole new burden to grapple with. His thoughts turned to the battles he had foreseen, the bloodshed of today's battle paling in comparison. How was he to celebrate knowing that the day was coming when sweet victory would curdle into bitter defeat?

32
PLAGUE FIRE AND DIVINE LIGHTNING

Soldiers poured into the courtyards and ballroom of the palace to be greeted by an immense feast. A spread of roast meats, vegetables, fish, fruits, nuts, and cheeses had been laid over the hundreds of tables scattered across the palace. Music blared as the chatter, shouts, and howling laughter of the soldiers bounced around the halls of the palace as well as the walls of Cadence's head.

He stood in the shadows, where he had always felt the safest, before making his entrance. His mouth was a sandpit despite having drunk an entire jug of water, and his armour had somehow gone from featherweight to being so heavy his breathing had become laboured. He watched and listened as the soldiers celebrated before forcing himself from the shadows.

He walked with feet of marble towards the royal family where a seat next to Arlo had been left open at the table of honour. Arsinoe gave him a nod of approval as he sat down, and Arlo immediately grabbed hold of his hand under the table. His touch was firm and urgent, like reaching out for Cadence had been something he'd wanted to do all night.

"Thank you for being here," Arlo said, turning to face Cadence. "I know this is not easy for you."

"I would do anything for you," Cadence whispered back. "But this feast is a wasteful mistake."

"My father thought it necessary," said Arlo. "He has won many wars in his time and is considered among many as an excellent strategist."

"This is different from the other wars your father has fought," Cadence said, looking away from Arlo. "This is a war with a god. And not just any god. At one point he was the king of the entire Pantheon."

"That is why my father has you at his side," Arlo said, his grip tightening on Cadence's hand and loosening again in a sign of reassurance. "You have foreseen Luciferian's victory."

"He cannot rely solely on my visions. The future is as fickle as a whore. It changes all the time depending on the actions taken in the present. My visions are helpful when they are accurate, but if I am wrong, it could be disastrous."

"My father would say that you have too little faith in your abilities."

"And I am saying that he has *too much* faith in them. Abydos thinks that we are safe. But he has turned the city into a prison. If this war lasts longer than we anticipated, the people inside the city walls, which includes all the soldiers, will starve. Saklas will win without having to lift a finger, and Luciferian will no longer be a city but a tomb instead."

"This feast is happening. I trust you, but tonight cannot be undone. Have a cup of wine. Enjoy the food and the festivities. These men," Arlo gestured across the dining hall at the tables of rowdy, drunk, and laughing soldiers, "may not live to see another celebration."

Cadence's gaze was shot forth by Arlo's arm like an arrow and landed on the faces of the men. Some were unharmed while others bore wounds that had been dressed in bandages, but all of them were having a good time. He was not the Emperor. He could not see the men just as soldiers or tools of war. Each one of them was a life connected to the lives of their families and friends, and in turn connected to the Empire itself. *That is the reason they fight*, Cadence thought, *to protect what is most precious to them*. Today they had succeeded in doing that and they needed to be celebrated. Who was he to try take that away from them?

"You are right," said Cadence, "but that doesn't make me wrong. If things do not go as planned, we may all come to regret this night."

"I will speak to my father about your concerns when we meet with the generals in the morning," Arlo said as he thrust a cup of wine into Cadence's hand and raised his own. "But for now, let us drink to both being right."

Cadence gave Arlo a small but earnest smile as they gently crashed their goblets together.

THE NEXT DAY, as Cadence predicted, the second wave of Saklas' forces arrived before the walls of Luciferian. This time the wall shook with the sound of the rotting army bashing their swords, hammers, maces, and axes against their shields. There was a breeze on the early morning air that carried the stench of festering flesh through the shield wall and into the city.

"There must be three times more of them here than yesterday," Arsinoe said as she looked upon the horde from her seat under the pavilion. "Where are they all coming from?"

"Saklas has spent centuries wandering the Scorched-Over Lands collecting them," said Cadence. His chest felt tight against his breastplate as he looked over the army, waiting for Abydos to make the first move. "And he has also made undead slaves of the defeated Luciferian soldiers."

"We too have more men in reserve," said Abydos before nodding to one of his generals.

Below them, the city gates began to grind open, letting out a flood of soldiers encased in golden armour. The men let out battle cries as they charged on Saklas' army. Cadence watched as they carried out an organised attack towards the battle. With swords raised, they were spurred on by blitz-induced fury. The drug gave them the ability to fight longer and harder, but Cadence doubted it would be enough.

They watched as the golden army was being engulfed by the darkness of shadow. It would not be long before Saklas' forces devoured them whole. Their ichor weapons were no match for the sheer number of demonic soldiers.

"We have to do something," said Arsinoe, turning to the Emperor.

"Release the plague fire," said Abydos through a jaw so tight he was almost inaudible.

"Have you taken leave of your senses?" Arsinoe said as the colour drained from her face. "It will kill everything on the ground, including our own men. Send the warships out instead."

"It's too soon to use the warships," Abydos growled at her through gritted teeth. "It would be a waste of ichor, and the plague fire is better suited for this task. The men's armour will protect them." He turned to the general on his right and gave the order. "Release the catapults!"

"No!" Arsinoe screamed, but the imperial guard did not take orders from her, and the general signalled the men stationed by the catapults with a blow of his trumpet.

"What if the wind changes direction?!" Arsinoe screamed. "You could kill us all. You promised if I created the plague fire that you would only use it as a last resort!"

Arsinoe may as well have been begging at the foot of a guardian statue for all the response she got from Abydos.

Along the length of the city wall, the black sheets covering the buckets of the catapults were pulled away. Inside the buckets were large, spherical glass bottles containing an acid-green liquid. The liquid began to bubble violently as soon as it was exposed to the sunlight.

Cadence looked from the catapults to Arsinoe's face and back again. The Empress had turned a seasick grey-green at the sight of the loaded weapons. He thought immediately of the hogweed Arsinoe had taught him about and how it could inhibit the ability of the skin to protect itself from the sun. He watched as the green liquid fizzed and bubbled, beating at the glass walls of the bottles, demanding to be let out.

"Is it hogweed?" Cadence asked Arsinoe.

"No." She shook her head as tears punched their way out of her eyes. "It is something much worse."

The ropes and gears of the catapults whirled and spun as the bottles were flung into the battle. There was a moment of pristine silence in the pavilion as everyone present watched the bottles fly through the air before coming down again. They glistened in the sunlight and exploded in distant pops and shatters before hitting the ground. Clouds of foul, dark blue gas expanded over the battlefield like a sudden impending storm. It was a mist as thick as soup that slithered over the men on both sides of the war, completely hiding them from view. Cadence watched as the blue gas expanded, danced, swirled, and folded in on itself. He might have thought it beautiful if he were not so terrified by it. For a moment, the battle cries, clashing of weapons, and screams of the dying came to a halt before being replaced by coughs, chokes, and splutters.

"Archers!" Abydos boomed.

The men on the walls drew their arrows and waited as

the tips were set alight. As soon as the heads of the arrows caught flame, the archers released them. The burning arrows flew into the gas, and all at once the air on the battlefield made a ripping sound as it was torn apart by a flash of blinding blue flames. The rip quickly became an explosion so powerful the blast flew towards the city and enveloped the shield wall. Cadence's eyes followed the blue flames as they rose overhead. If the shield wall had not been in place, they would have also been engulfed by the plague fire.

The flames then quickly receded, and when the ringing in Cadence's ears subsided, he could hear the screams and wails of the men below.

Abydos had been wrong. The ichor armour had only partially protected the Luciferian soldiers. In the places where their skin was exposed, angry red blisters had formed. Those who were still alive screeched as they peeled the armour away from their bodies. With weak and shaking arms, they desperately clawed at their breastplates, trying to lift them from their torsos. Some of the men's fingers had been reduced to twitching, smoking nibs. The arm guards and greaves slid off their limbs, taking sticky, bloody chunks of flesh with them. The flesh that was left behind had come alive with angry blisters and boils that expanded and burst only to reform into more blisters again moments later. Some of the burnt men blinded by the fire stumbled around clumsily in torment as their flesh melted inside their armour.

"What have you done?" Arsinoe gasped at the Emperor, unable to tear her eyes away from the horror as her hands flew over her mouth.

"Sacrifices had to be made," said Abydos. His words were cold and unfeeling as he avoided looking at the gruesome results of his actions.

Cadence shook as he reached out for Arlo's hand. They found one another and Arlo's palm was wet with sweat.

Their fingers locked and they held on to each other tightly as they continued to watch the carnage below. Cadence's stomach churned, and he swallowed hard to prevent himself from being sick.

The soldiers from The Scorched-Over Lands had been spared the agony of surviving the plague fire. Their smoking corpses littered the battlefield like smouldering piles of waste set alight and left to burn. Cadence was watching the smoke rising from the corpses when his jaw fell open in terror as they began to move. Slowly, the corpses of Saklas' soldiers began to rise up. Their limbs twisted and quivered from the ground like writhing worms until they were once again on their feet, swords in their hands.

Abydos flew up from his seat and leaned over the edge of the wall. His eyes bulged from his skull, and his teeth gnashed against each other. Arsinoe bolted to his side to get a closer look herself.

"How is this possible?" the Emperor suddenly barked at Cadence.

"I–I don't know," he said, stumbling over his words. "None of this was in any of my visions."

The Emperor's head whipped towards his general. "Get the reserve forces and remaining generals out there now!" he screamed before turning to Arlo. "You wanted to fight, now is your time."

Cadence's heart sank at the Emperor's words. Arlo nodded at his father and darted out of the pavilion, pulling Cadence along with him. He only let go of Cadence's hand when they had reached the staircase that led to the foot of the wall.

"There isn't time," Arlo said, "but I promise to make you proud."

"I don't want you to make me proud, you idiot," Cadence cried. "I want you to come back alive! Promise me that."

Arlo leaned in and caught Cadence around his waist, pulling him into an embrace. Just as quickly as their lips found each other they were separated again.

"I will do my best," he said as he donned his helmet and sprinted off down the stairs and into the shadows.

Cadence returned to the pavilion with shaking legs and in a cold sweat. Arsinoe waited for him with open arms. She locked him into a tight hug.

"Fear not," she whispered into his ear. "He is a being of great power and an excellent warrior. He will return to us."

"We don't know that," said Cadence, stepping away from the Empress. "He is destined to die in this war."

"He is destined to win it first," Abydos growled as he spun away from the wall and lumbered back to his seat. He beckoned one of his generals closer and began giving him instructions.

Arsinoe followed Cadence to the edge of the wall where they stood watching and waiting for Arlo and the reserve forces to emerge from the city gates directly below them.

"The God's Bane is almost ready," Arsinoe whispered. "We just need one more day."

"It might be too late if this battle is not won," said Cadence. "If Saklas' forces could survive the plague fire, there is no telling what else they could be immune to."

"Perhaps they can only be killed by ichor weapons," said Arsinoe. "The blasts from the guardian statues worked."

"He *is* waiting us out," said Cadence. "He knows his forces can only be cut down by ichor weapons, and you said yourself that eventually the city will need to replenish its ichor reserves."

"The city is not spent yet, and there are still the ichor cannons on the city walls, the warships, as well as smaller airships that have been fitted."

"The leviathans are on their way with the ability to swat warships out of the sky like flies."

"Have faith in the gods and your husband. They just need to buy us a little more time. The poison will be ready by sunrise tomorrow."

TRUMPETS SOUNDED and the gates of the city were cracked open. Cadence and Arsinoe looked down as the reserve forces emerged through the gates with Arlo in the lead. Cadence spotted the gleam of his helmet immediately as it stood higher and shone more brightly than those around it.

Arlo let out a war cry, and without hesitation the troops stormed into battle. Saklas' reformed forces met them head-on as they crashed into one another like a black tide against golden rock.

A new life was breathed into Arlo from the moment his sword connected with the first enemy soldier. Watching him train had been one thing, but seeing him in real battle was another experience entirely. He fought as if he was performing a dance, cutting his attackers down with a brutal grace. Cadence could not tear his eyes away from him.

His movements had a hypnotic effect that caused the volatile anxiety inside Cadence to dissipate. The longer Cadence watched Arlo fight, the more his muscles unclenched themselves. Arlo's sword and armour glowed with the power of the ichor with which they had been imbued. Streaks of golden lightning shot out from Arlo's armour in tendrils, causing their targets to explode on impact and sending sticky black goo flying through the air.

Golden lightning crackled up and down the length of Arlo's blade. As soon as he cut one enemy down, a new one was there to take its place.

"They are severely outnumbered," said Arsinoe, turning to Abydos. "We are going to lose this battle!"

Abydos raised his hand without looking at Arsinoe. His eyes were fixed on the battle. "You underestimate my son," he said.

Cadence turned back to the fighting. In the second he'd looked away and back again, Arlo had begun to move faster. He was carving through the undead like soft butter with his sword at a pace so rapid he was turning into a blur of gold and white light. Cadence had to rub his eyes before looking back to make sure he was not hallucinating. Arlo looked bigger and taller too. His already large muscles were now bulging under his armour as he cut down demon after demon with his sword. His skin and eyes were alive with a white glow that shone from inside him like starlight.

Bolts of lightning arced from his body, sending attackers hurling away from him and tearing them to pieces. The rest of the Luciferian soldiers were also making headway in the battle, but the more dark warriors they cut down, the more seemed to appear. The cloud of rotting, coal-clad soldiers seemed to be enveloping the ones armoured in gold.

"Charge the guardian statues again!" Arsinoe screamed at Abydos. "Send in the warships! Do something!"

"Wait!" Abydos boomed from his seat.

As the word left the Emperor's mouth, an electric thrum filled the air. Arsinoe and Cadence looked back. The humming sound was coming from the battlefield and, more specifically, from Arlo himself. A lightning storm of white and gold had formed around the prince and the thrumming grew louder with each passing second. The vibration of the energy coming off Arlo's body pulsated through the city wall, and Cadence felt it in his feet like a rapid heartbeat.

With a great sonic roar, the energy that had been building around Arlo exploded outward. The crackling concussive force tore through the armada of enemy soldiers, blasting them to pieces. Their flesh sizzled and burst as they were struck by the wave of lightning. From the top of the wall, Cadence could hear the snapping of bones and the popping of skulls as the monsters' heads erupted on their necks.

He heard the cracking of ribs as he watched the chests of the demon soldiers implode as if the air had been sucked directly out of their lungs. The light coming off Arlo grew blindingly bright, and Cadence was forced to throw his forearm over his eyes. The air crackled with a static force that sent a prickling sensation over Cadence's skin. There was a brief silence followed by a sharp ringing in Cadence's ears. He cautiously peeped over his forearm and saw the light had vanished. The blast had levelled the battlefield. Saklas' demonic, undead soldiers were nothing more than scorch marks in the dirt.

The Luciferian soldiers had been unharmed but were all cowering on the ground, slowly curling themselves out of the foetal position around a shallow crater that had been the epicentre of the explosion. Cadence's heart did a somersault into his throat, and the ringing in his ears was suddenly accompanied by the booming of his pulse. At the bottom of the crater, Arlo lay on his back. His eyes were closed and Cadence could not tell if he was breathing.

"NO!" Cadence screamed, bolting out of the pavilion and down the staircase that led to the city gate. With each step, a violent fear constricted his chest as if he'd been caught in the grip of a giant fist. The faster he tried to move, the slower the world around him became. The staircase seemed to stretch out before him in a never-ending labyrinth that reverberated his own fear back at him.

"No, no, no! No!" he cried as his feet finally reached the landing of the staircase, and he sprinted towards the closed city gates. Panic ensnared his entire being like a rabbit caught in a trap. The more he struggled, the more twisted in the trap he became. "Open the gates!" he howled at the guards as he ran.

One of the guards, his face a blur in Cadence's now tunnelled vision, stepped in front of him. "We cannot, the Emperor gave strict—"

"I am the Prince Consort and I command you to open the fucking gates!" Cadence boomed at the guard as he pushed the man backward. The man stumbled but did not fall and gave the signal for the gates to be opened.

Slowly the gears and pulleys that held the giant gates closed began to twist and whir. A crack of light appeared in the centre of the gates. As soon as it was wide enough, Cadence ran through it. He began to pick up speed as he weaved between the scattered and dazed soldiers who were slowly getting to their feet.

He found himself having to jump over bloodied corpses with snarled and melted flesh. The milky, white gaze of dead eyes rushed past him as the stench of charred flesh and hair grew thick in the smoky air. The sticky, black ooze, all that was left of Saklas' forces, stuck to the bottoms of his sandals and slowed him down. His head began to swim as the invisible fist around his chest tightened its grip.

He finally reached the edge of the crater and without slowing down jumped right into it. Heat came off the ground in waves that rippled the smoke-clogged air. Cadence fell to his knees beside Arlo.

The prince lay on his back, his eyes closed and his face spattered with dried blood and grime. He had returned to his normal size. Heat was radiating off of his armour in waves and yet was cool to the touch when Cadence placed his palm on Arlo's breastplate. Cadence leaned over him, searching desperately for any signs of life. He scoured Arlo's breastplate for the steady rise and fall of breath. His eyes frantically searched Arlo's hands and legs for the slightest twitch.

"Arlo!" Cadence shouted as he grabbed him by the shoulders and shook him gently. "Arlo, open your eyes! Speak to me!"

"Did we win?" said Arlo groggily as his eyes fluttered open, two pools of blue surrounded by angry red rivers.

"We did," Cadence choked as tears of relief began to flow down his cheeks.

Arlo slowly sat up and Cadence locked him in an embrace.

"I thought I'd lost you," he whispered as his tears fell onto Arlo's neck.

"I'm still here," said Arlo, pulling him closer.

They stayed like that for a moment before Cadence helped Arlo to his feet. Together they walked back up the battlefield past the bodies of fallen soldiers and the puddles of blood and black muck that slowly seeped into the ground. The bodies of the fallen men lay in twisted, melted heaps. Some of their mouths were still wide open in the screams they had died making, agony etched into their faces. Smoke continued to rise from the charred and melted bodies, filling the air with an acrid stink. As they reached the city gates, Cadence turned back for a moment. Somewhere beyond the smog-filled air, he could hear Nubia rejoicing in the bloodshed.

33
A SKY ON FIRE

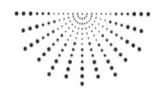

He didn't die today, Saklas' voice hissed. *But he will if he continues to fight.*

There was something in the god's voice that held the property of glass being shattered—unexpected and unpleasant. It came from every direction at the same time. Cadence flinched at the sound of it.

There had been no celebration feast that night. When Cadence and Arlo returned to the palace, they went directly to their chamber. Together they helped each other out of their armour, bathed, and laid down together in their bed. The last thing Cadence remembered was falling asleep with Arlo's arms wrapped around him.

He was somewhere deep inside his own mind now. It was a dark place, as if he had somehow fallen into a void. It was like being deep underwater—peaceful and serene, where normally nothing could disturb him, but not this time. This time Saklas' voice and presence swirled around him like a poisonous fog.

The final wave of my army marches on the walls of Luciferian as we speak, said the god. *There is no way Abydos will win this war. His army has been crippled, and the ichor that flows through the city cannot protect him forever. But there is no need for you and your love to die with everyone else. I can offer you redemption. Give me the Empire and I will reward you.*

"And how am I to do that when the Empire is not mine to give?" Cadence answered.

Convince Arlo to stop fighting, Saklas said. *If he stands down, my armies will be able to take the city and the Empire with it that much faster, and I will spare your lives.*

"He would sooner die than surrender," Cadence said.

There may be another way. If he were to be stripped of his godhead, then he will be unable to fight.

"You can do that?"

I was once king of all the gods. There is much that I am able to do.

"His godhead is part of who he is. There is no way I would ask him to give it up."

Then take it from him instead. I can show you how. Meet with me and I will give you all you need.

"I can't."

I will be waiting if you change your mind, young oracle, said the god, his voice retreating from Cadence's mind and growing further away. *But don't wait too long or you shall both perish.*

When he woke, it was still dark. The flames of the oil lamps burned low as he pulled himself from the bed and threw his tunic on. He looked back at Arlo still in a deep sleep. He watched Arlo's bare chest rise and fall with deep breaths as he had done so many times before, and his heart ached.

Saklas' offer was a tempting one. What if, after all his searching, this was the solution he'd been looking for? What if making a deal with the forgotten god was the only way to save Arlo's life? Even if it cost him his godhead, at least he would still be alive. But it would also cost the Empire, the lives of everyone in it, and then, if his visions were true, the lives of every living thing in the universe. It should have been an easy decision, but it wasn't. Cadence knew he should only want to do the right thing, but he found himself more and more wanting to do the wrong one.

"I will make this right," he whispered to Arlo before turning to leave the chamber.

WHEN HE ARRIVED in Arsinoe's conservatory, she was not there, but the God's Bane was. A glass beaker of deep blue liquid bubbled over an open flame. Cadence closed his eyes and tried to see the poison with his mind. Slowly the liquid came into focus and he could see it for what it truly was—a sticky grey mess. The sweet smell of flowers and leaves rotting deep inside the earth came off the liquid in waves. It twisted and rippled inside the beaker as sharp spines rose and fell from its surface like a writhing snake getting ready to strike out in anger. It was not just a poison but rather a venomous wild animal with a mind of its own. The God's Bane emitted a dark energy that left Cadence feeling haunted, like he was being watched by a force he did not understand and could not see.

"Marvellous, isn't it?" Arsinoe asked from behind Cadence, and his eyes flew open.

"Unlike anything I've ever seen or felt," said Cadence. "It feels …" he paused trying to choose his words carefully, "… evil."

"All poisons are," said Arsinoe as she moved forward to remove the beaker from the flame. "It's ready."

She poured the steaming blue liquid from the beaker into a vial before topping the vial with a cork. She then covered the cork in a thick layer of sealing wax and blew on it to help it dry faster.

"You are certain this is the only way?" she asked, clutching the vial with hesitation.

"Saklas wants to meet with me," said Cadence. "He wants to exchange mine and Arlo's lives for the city."

"He is lying. There is no way he can take the city while Arlo still breathes."

"Not entirely. There is no way Saklas can take the city while Arlo is still a demigod. He wants me to steal Arlo's godhead from him."

Confusion began to run a marathon over Arsinoe's face. "How is such a thing even possible?"

"It doesn't matter. I just need to get close enough to him to deliver the poison."

"Are you sure you don't want Arlo to know what you are doing?" she asked as she finally handed him the vial.

"If he finds out he will try to stop me," said Cadence, taking the vial from Arsinoe. The glass was warm to the touch. "He made it clear he wants me nowhere near the battlefield. If he found out I was going to meet Saklas in person, he would have me chained to a wall if it meant keeping me safe."

"Very well," the Empress nodded. "Coat your sword in the God's Bane but do not come into direct contact with it. It will kill anything it touches instantly."

"Thank you," said Cadence as he tucked the vial inside the pocket of his tunic. "For everything."

"Good luck," said Arsinoe. "May the gods protect you."

Cadence turned to go, but Arsinoe grabbed hold of his wrist. He looked up at her. She had been through a morbid transformation. The war, everything that came before it, and the fear of what might come after had taken a brutal toll on her. She still held herself with the graceful poise of a powerful royal woman, but she was changed forever. Under the golden silk dress that clung to her bones, more of her once toned muscular but lean body had wasted away. The glowing beauty he had met (what felt like an eternity ago) was nowhere to be seen and in its place had left the makings of a crone.

"You are as a son to me," she said. "I need you to know that."

"I do," Cadence said as he stepped closer and locked her in a hug. Her wild black curls reached up and tickled his nose and mouth. Her tears fell against his tunic with a light patter before the fabric drank them up. "And you are as a mother to me. You are as much a part of my reason for doing this as Arlo is. I've already lost one mother and I cannot bear losing another."

He took her gently by the shoulders and pushed her away slightly. He planted a single kiss on her cheek and gave her a smile.

She nodded at him, signalling him to go. She watched him disappear from the conservatory through her tear-blurred eyes.

When she was certain he was gone, she whispered to herself, "But I cannot bear losing another child."

CADENCE HURRIED BACK to Arlo's chamber. Before he was halfway there, the war trumpets sounded from the city walls. Something had been spotted on the horizon. As Cadence catapulted himself down the halls and up the stairs, his mind rang with the sound of the trumpets and thoughts of the leviathans.

"Where have you been?" asked Arlo as he struggled with his greaves.

Cadence immediately dropped to Arlo's side and helped him. "I couldn't sleep," he said as he finished fastening the left greave before moving on to the right. "I decided to take a walk and lost track of time."

They hurried as Arlo helped Cadence into his armour. When they finished, Cadence adjusted his breastplate and felt the vial of God's Bane move inside the pocket of his tunic.

"Are you alright?" Arlo asked, his blonde brows furrowing with concern.

"As alright as I can be under the circumstances," Cadence replied.

Arlo was so beautiful; his eyes were an ocean that held everything dear to Cadence in their depths. "Please be careful on the battlefield today," he finally said through a throat that had suddenly become unbearably tight.

"Do you think that today is the …" Arlo didn't finish asking his question.

"I haven't seen anything past the battle today," said Cadence.

"But you are sure we win?"

"We win. But I can't say at what cost."

"The prophecy is wrong. You yourself have said that no future is set in stone. This war will be won and then you and I will live the rest of our days in peace. Together, like we always planned."

"Together," said Cadence with a half smile. The vial of poison had suddenly become a lead weight in his pocket that held his spirit down.

With a heavy heart, Cadence followed Arlo to the city gates where what was left of the Luciferian army stood waiting for him.

"Knowing that you are watching me fight from the top of

the wall gives me courage," said Arlo. "Have faith in me and all will be well."

Is that what all his plans amount to? Cadence thought as Arlo embraced him one last time before they separated. *Faith?*

Their fates were twisted together like the roots of an ancient tree. That is what the witch had told his mother so many years ago. If Cadence were to leave their combined destinies in the hands of the gods, they would both die and all the world would burn to the ground. The gods were shallow, vapid, and spineless creatures with all the strength of the universe on their side, but they were unable to find the bravery to wield it. He did not lack faith in Arlo's abilities but had no faith in the gods themselves.

"One last thing before I forget," said Arlo before pulling a bright pink flower with frills for petals from behind his breastplate. He offered it to Cadence.

"A peony," smiled Cadence, and he took the flower, "for good luck."

"And for love," said Arlo, "don't forget love."

"Never," said Cadence as Arlo kissed him quickly on the cheek.

The feeling of his lips reminded Cadence of the very first kiss Arlo had ever given him. Not the one on the beach the first time they had snuck out of the palace together, but the time before that. It had also been the first time Arlo had ever given him a flower, just before his first lesson with Arsinoe. It had been so long ago, but the feeling was the same. The hot rush of emotion that tore through him—knowing that someone was there for him, that someone loved him, that someone could wish him well and not want anything but the very best for him after being alone and lost for so long. He tucked the peony into the pocket of his tunic next to the vial of God's Bane.

Cadence watched as Arlo mounted his horse and led the Luciferian army through the opening in the city gates. Arlo flashed him a last confident smile of shining white teeth before becoming a blur with the rest of the soldiers. As soon as the top of Arlo's helmet disappeared from sight, Cadence bolted for the staircase that led up to the pavilion on the southern wall. When he arrived, Abydos and Arsinoe were already in their seats.

Upon seeing him, Arsinoe rose from her seat and walked towards him.

"Should you not be getting ready?" she asked in a hushed tone so as not to be overheard by the Emperor.

"I don't want to go unless I am sure this is the right time. I know that if I see the leviathans that this is the correct battle. The final battle."

A monstrous shriek tore through the air and both their heads spun towards the battlefield. Inside a gigantic dust cloud billowing up from the ground like a storm, shadowy figures moved, growing larger as they stampeded towards the city. Cadence recognised the terrible creatures from their silhouettes alone. The leviathans.

"I *should* be getting ready," said Cadence as he ran from the pavilion.

HE DARTED BACK down the stairs and through the side streets of the city. The shrieks and growls coming from the approaching beasts bounced off the buildings and echoed down the roads, making Cadence feel like the leviathans were snapping at his heels. When he reached the gates of the palace, he was out of breath but had to keep going. The guard stationed at the gate let him through immediately as he raced to the entrance. He sprinted down corridors, through doorways, and past servants and slaves. He finally stopped to catch his breath at the doorway behind the tapestry that led to the cavern where the airboat had been anchored. A moment later, he bounded down the steps into the cavern and climbed inside the airboat.

Working as quickly as his shaking hands would allow him, he dipped into the pocket of his tunic and fished out the poison. Forcing his hands to become steady, he broke the wax seal on the top of the bottle. The cork came out with a soft pop followed by a waft of unpleasant sweetness. With his free hand, he reached for the hilt of his sword but stopped. Instead, he reached further down his belt and pulled out the hunting dagger Arlo had given him. He held the blade of the dagger over the side of the airboat and away from himself. He then carefully lowered the vial of poison towards the blade. The dark blue liquid hit the steel with a hiss followed by soft popping sounds as it dripped off the end of the blade and hit the ground below. Cadence gently shook the dagger before carefully sliding it back into its sheath. For good measure, he then pulled out his sword and repeated the process. When he was done, there was still poison in the vial to spare. He returned the cork to the vial and slid it back inside his pocket.

He turned his focus to the front of the airboat. The dials, switches, and buttons of the helm glared up at him like an angry animal that did not want to be touched. He closed his eyes and took a deep breath, trying to remember the order in which Arlo would start the airboat.

"You can do this, Cadence," he reassured himself. "You've watched Arlo do it a thousand times."

With trembling hands, he reached out to the helm and slowly began to flip switches and push buttons. The airboat hummed to life as the veins of glowing, golden ichor began to flow from the helm to the deck and around the sides of the boat. He then slowly brought the correct toggle up, and the vessel began to vibrate as it rose into the air. All that was left to do was gently ease the throttle forward.

The airboat blasted from the opening of the cavern with a boom. The starboard side had scraped against the rock opening of the cavern as it launched forward. Cadence was thrown backwards into the pilot seat with a force that knocked the wind from his lungs. He grabbed the throttle and pulled it back, bringing the airboat to an immediate halt. He was almost thrown over the helm and out of the vessel.

"Gods alive!" he shouted as he scrambled back into his seat. His pulse throbbed in his ears and his heart all but leapt from his throat. "How does Arlo make it look so easy?!"

After taking a moment to collect himself, he tried to accelerate again. He took a firm hold of the wheel and slowly turned it towards the battlefield. As the airboat came round, Cadence felt the warmth drain from his flustered body.

The skyline outside of the shield wall was alive with explosions, shrieks, battle cries, and blasts of light. The warships had been sent into battle and frantic chaos had broken loose in the sky. Bulging grey clouds of dust and smoke plumed up from the battlefield. The clouds were being illuminated by the explosions of white lightning being hurled from Arlo's body as the battle raged on between the two armies.

Bright, golden arcs of ichor plasma shot from the cannons on the warships and tore through the air with the sound of a thousand thunder bolts. The arcs landed on the scale-clad backs of the leviathans who writhed back and forth in agony before lashing out with their gigantic jaws and slithering tentacles. Their fangs split the bulkheads of the warships like twigs, sending a monsoon of splinters showering through the air. Other smaller warships were plucked clean out of the sky by titanic jaws. Cadence counted twelve of the beasts engaged in active battle while more appeared in shadows behind the clouds on the horizon. The battle had widened across the length of the city wall. There was no course around the carnage. If he wanted to get to Saklas, he would have to fly directly through the mayhem.

He took a deep breath before reaching out his hand once more for the throttle. The airship whipped forward and he was catapulted directly towards the frenzy of blood, teeth, and lightning. He dodged arcs of ichor plasma while at the same time avoiding the snapping jaws and thrashing tentacles of the leviathans. The rotting breath of the beasts polluted the air as they shrieked upward towards the sky. The stench of the monsters brought on waves of nausea made worse by the erratic way Cadence flew the airship in his choppy yet effective attempts at evasive manoeuvres.

"Saklas!" he called out into the pandemonium of battle that surrounded him. "I am ready to meet you!"

An arc of ichor plasma missed the airboat by inches, only singeing some of Cadence's hair. It had blasted past him with a dull electric buzz. He liberated a hand from the helm to pat down at the smouldering section of his hair and make sure the top of his head didn't go up in flames. As soon as he was confident he was no longer in danger of catching fire, he returned his hand to the helm with a firm grip.

"Saklas!" he yelled again. "It is I, the Oracle of Luciferian! Show yourself!"

The wind whirled around him, whipping through his singed hair and drowning out his cries. His arms began to ache as he struggled desperately to steer clear of the blasts from the plasma cannons. Men aboard a nearby warship called out to him and shook their fists in anger in his direction, but he could not make out what they were screaming. He spotted a clear patch of cornflower blue sky above the warship, turned the airboat towards it and pushed the throttle. If he could get just above where all the chaos was taking place then he could seek Saklas out in peace and safety.

That was when the voice echoed in his head. But it did not belong to the immortal Cadence had been calling out to.

What do you think you are doing, mortal? Nubia demanded in a snarl.

"I'm going to save your son," Cadence shouted as he sped towards the break in the clouds above.

He could not see the goddess, but her icy presence had enveloped the air around him. His chest tightened and his breathing became laboured as he tried to keep focus on not being hit by a stray arc of ichor plasma or landing up in the jaws of one of the leviathans below.

Arlo will be the one to defeat Saklas, Nubia screeched. *He will go down in history as a hero of war. He will live on in the hearts and minds of men for eons to come! I will not let you take his glory from him!*

The wind around Cadence's head tore into his ears. He had to fight every overwhelming instinct to let go of the wheel and throw his hands over them to stop the aching.

"What good will glory be to him if he is dead?" Cadence screamed back into the madness that surrounded him. "I care only for Arlo, not for his glorification!"

Then you shall die sooner rather than later! Nubia shrieked.

A powerful wind hurled the airboat directly into a blast of ichor plasma. Cadence tightened his grip on the wheel as the lightning that coursed through the helm caused every muscle in his body to contort and burn. The blast tore through the hull of the airboat with a roar of pure, unbridled energy. Cadence heard the panels of the airship groan before they burst into a million tiny splinters as the airboat was torn in two.

The half of the airboat he still occupied plummeted

towards the ground as Cadence desperately tried to regain some form of control. He flipped the scorched switches and toggles. He pushed buttons that were churning out smoke like chimneys. Veins of glowing ichor flickered and sparked over what remained of the airboat and provided a little lift before spluttering out.

The ground beneath him was approaching faster as he choked on the smoke and fumes that plumed from the helm. His eyes watered, his throat stung, and his stomach lurched. He screamed. There was a violent stop and the immediate cacophony of metal, wood, and bone being crumpled against earth as easily as parchment inside a clenched fist. Like a candle being blown out at midnight, the world went dark and cold around him.

34
THE TEMPTATION OF THE ORACLE

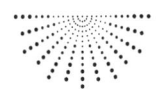

*C*adence woke to agony searing through his body. The worst of the pain burned through his left arm and spread all the way to his fingertips and shoulder. His throat burned from the dust and smoke in the air. When he forced his eyes open, his vision was blurry, but slowly the angry, grey, lightning-filled clouds above him came into focus. He'd landed on his back. His head throbbed with a repetitive ache.

Too sore and scared to make any sudden movements, he first tried to wriggle his toes. They moved as commanded, and Cadence took this as a good sign. When he tried to lift himself to his feet, pain flashed through his left arm, causing him to fall right back. He looked down; he was swollen and bleeding from his elbow to his fingers. He could see no bone shining through the bloodied flesh, but something told him without a doubt that his arm was broken. He took a painfully deep breath in and tried again. Supporting his weight under his right arm, he was able to slowly get himself back on his feet.

His balance was unsteady at first but improved as his vision began to clear. He fought against every muscle in his body screaming at him to lay back down again. The airboat had crashed just outside of where the battle was taking place. He could still hear the shrieks and roars of the leviathans, the screams of men, the clatter of weapons and the blasts of ichor cannons in the distance. He looked up and saw the necks of the terrible beasts as they whipped back and forth. Some of the leviathans clenched mouthfuls of soldiers, their flesh skewered by hundreds of fangs as long as swords. The men were still alive enough to be aware of the terrible fate that had befallen them. As the beasts flicked their massive reptilian heads back, the men fell down the monsters' throats, screaming. Other leviathans roared and snapped at the warships that hovered just out of their reach. The warships pelted the monsters with blast after blast of ichor plasma, spears, and arrows. It took multiple strikes just to weaken the beasts and even more to kill them. When one hit the ground, it would send a wave of dust into the air so large it darkened the already cloud-shrouded sun.

"Saklas!" Cadence choked into the dust and smoke that churned around him as he clutched his left arm to his body with his right.

He waited for a response as the clouds of bitter choking dust and smoke blew over him. The only thing inside of him that burned hotter than the pain was his hatred towards Nubia.

"Saklas!" he screamed, so desperate to be heard he tore his throat apart from the inside. "Forgotten God! God who fell from heaven! God of rot! Show yourself!"

Again, he was met with silence. He looked down at his feet. The armour didn't have a scratch on it, but his legs and feet were covered in blood and dust from scratches and scrapes where splintered wood and rock had bitten into his skin. His sword and the dagger had also remained in place at his side despite the crash.

A familiar whisper rang through his ears like the hiss of a venomous snake.

I am here, young oracle, Saklas called.

Cadence looked up. In the distance, under the clouds of dust and smoke, a shadow had materialised and was steadily approaching. As it drew closer, the shape and lines of the shadow grew more defined. It grew taller and darker until the forgotten god emerged from the whirling veil.

There were elements of his features that Cadence recognised from his visions.

The eyes were the same blue of ice that had been frozen for millennia and reflected a clear, endless sky. The hair was the same silvery white that shimmered in a light source that came from the god's glowing skin. That was where the similarities stopped. Saklas was muscular and tall, but in comparison to the other gods, who vibrated with an aura of life, he felt dead. It was as if the very air around him became noxious as it blew over his fog-grey lizard skin. He lacked the humanity of gods like Astaroth, Hermia, and even Nubia. There was a serpentine quality to his movements that chilled the blood in Cadence's veins.

Cadence stepped back, and his eyes fell to the god's pale, bare feet. They ended in sharp black talons where toenails should have been. In his wake, his footprints left behind bubbling puddles of rotting ooze. When he came to a stop, the earth beneath him blackened and began to smoulder. The sparse, short tufts of desert grass beside him began to wither and decay before Cadence's eyes. Saklas was not death. He was something worse. He was a festering wound on the world that would never heal. He was the source of eternal putrefaction.

"Have you come to do what I have asked?" Saklas said, his voice a sharp and terrifying wind.

"I–I ..." Cadence stuttered, trying to buy time to get within stabbing, or at least slashing, distance of the god. He was careful not to start reaching for the hilt of his sword no matter how badly his fingers itched for it. "I don't know if I can." He finished his sentence as he limped closer to Saklas.

"There is much I could reward both of you with in return," the god responded.

A gust of wind enveloped Cadence and he was lifted gently off the ground. Stunned, he shut his eyes tightly to protect them from the sand blowing into his face. As the wind wrapped itself around him, all the pain in his body began to dissipate. The stinging scratches and cuts he'd received during the crash were awash with a tingling sensation before the pain was no more. The wind gently placed his feet back on the ground before dying down. When he opened his eyes, he found his arm was no longer broken. His fingers had returned to normal; he wriggled each of them one at a time and then all together to be sure. His head no longer pounded. His joints no longer ached. He stood for a moment in a combination of stunned silence and sweet relief.

The tingling sensation then drew his eyes to his left arm. The mutilated flesh of his scars had vanished. His hands shot up to his face; the skin his fingertips found was not the texture of melted candle wax, but soft, smooth, and completely restored. Cadence let out a gasp as a lump formed in his throat. He allowed his fingers to frantically traverse his cheeks, his neck, and his shoulder. He smiled and the tight pull of his scars on the corner of his mouth was no longer there. The macabre work of his brothers had been completely undone.

"Convince your love to relinquish his godhead and give

me the Empire," said Saklas. "Or I can show you how to take it from him. I would do it myself, but it has to be done by someone the demigod truly loves."

Cadence's eyes shot away from his healed body and back up towards the god. The magic Saklas had performed had a euphoric effect. For a brief moment, Cadence had forgotten who he was and what he had come there to do.

"Or better yet," Saklas continued in his haunting voice, "convince him to join me and I will make room for the both of you in my new world. You can have everything your hearts have ever desired."

The world of dust and smoke around Cadence began to melt away. The clouds of grime and choking smog slowly vanished as if someone was painting over them with giant invisible brush strokes. Beneath his feet, from the cracked arid ground, lush grass emerged in a wave that rolled out before him. Cadence watched the miracle come to life around him as he was suddenly surrounded by a garden of wildflowers, shrubs, and towering trees.

When he looked down from the branches of the trees, a cottage near a stream had appeared a few hundred meters in the distance. It was a replica of where Arlo and Cadence had stayed during their time in the realm of eternal spring.

The thatch-roofed structure was surrounded by a vibrant garden, bursting with colourful blooms of roses, honeysuckle, lavender, daisies, poppy, and wisteria. Emerald ivy climbed the walls of the cottage in thick, twisting vines. Ribbons of smoke curled up from the chimney before being carried off by the light spring breeze. The smell of freshly baked bread and cakes wafted through the air and beckoned Cadence forward.

"I can give you all of this," said Saklas as he leaned over Cadence's shoulder. "I can give you all of this and more."

As he spoke, a boy no older than four or five emerged from the door of the cottage. There was something unnervingly familiar about the way he looked and how he carried himself. Cadence knew the golden shine of his hair when lit up by the sun. He'd run his fingers through that hair a thousand times. He watched in awe as the boy ran into the garden with an energetic excitement. Cadence knew that run; he had watched a larger version of the child's feet kick up sand as they bolted across the beaches of the Cyprian Sea. He knew every inch of the child's sun-bronzed skin. The child looked up to reveal the same bright green eyes that greeted Cadence every time he looked in a reflective surface.

Cadence had to stop himself from stumbling backward with shock. "This can never be," he said through a gasp. "This is impossible!"

"Anything is possible when you are in the favour of a powerful god," Saklas whispered into Cadence's ear. "This world of fickle gods and weak men doesn't understand you. I have looked into your heart, young oracle. You have known nothing but scorn and calumny from men and gods alike. Leave this world of consternation behind and become part of something so much better."

Saklas was finally close enough for Cadence to strike if he moved quickly. But he could not take his eyes off of the scene in front of him. A desperate longing, unlike any he'd ever known, pulsated from his aching heart as tears began to fall from his eyes. The god's words echoed through his mind as his thoughts wandered back to his childhood in Naphtali.

All the old loneliness and hurt began to strum through him like the strings of a lyre being plucked by the fingers of a skilled musician. He had belonged to a father who despised him, a community that shunned him, and a family that had maimed and deformed him. The flames of hatred inside his heart burst forth in a sudden inferno. Hatred for the abilities

Astaroth had cursed him with. Hatred for his father and Abydos. Hatred for Nubia. Hatred for the people of Naphtali who were now nothing but ash. For a moment, he thought the worlds of both gods and men deserved to burn. It would be so easy to agree. To give Saklas what he wanted. But it made no difference which path Cadence chose, as his own path only led to one place.

"It doesn't matter what you can give me," Cadence said as the tears continued to flow from his eyes at the precious illusion that surrounded him. "I have the blight. I am not long for this world."

"What I give," said Saklas as he reached his icy hand up Cadence's tunic and placed it against the spot of blight on his inner thigh, "I can take away."

Cadence felt his forehead furrow in shock as nausea began to ripple through him. When the god removed his hand, the nausea broke and Cadence lifted his tunic. The dark purple spot had vanished.

"You *are* the cause of the blight," Cadence gasped as he let the tunic fall.

"I have not been able to enter the city, as you know," Saklas smiled. "So I chose to weaken it from the inside instead, long before Abydos even considered invading The Scorched-Over Lands."

"You are a monster," Cadence whispered.

"I am a god!" Saklas boomed as a blinding, milky glow came to life over his dead blue eyes before dying down again. "And I do as I please! Now make your choice! Life in an eternal paradise with your love, or death at my hands."

The vision of the garden, the cottage, the creek, and the child were still vivid before his eyes. Never had he been more tempted. Everything he and Arlo had ever wanted and more was at his fingertips. He had no concerns about whether or not Saklas was telling the truth. A god's word was their bond, and once a bargain was struck, the god would be bound by the laws of their ancient magic and would have to deliver. He and Arlo could live in peace and somehow even have a child of their own. Cadence's chest ached with longing at being so close to a world where everything he'd ever wanted was within his reach.

His lips began to move to form the word *yes.* But then he thought of his mother. She who had loved him. She who had done her best to protect him. He thought back to the stories she had filled his head with and the skills she'd taught his once clumsy hands. He remembered her smile and her laugh. He thought of her beauty inside and out. His mother had been a beautiful thing that inhabited a cruel world, but Saklas was the one who had taken her away.

He found his hatred redirected towards the dark god. He was an abomination, a forgotten, abandoned thing that refused to die and instead had chosen an existence of eternal decay. Rebekah would not have wanted the world to burn, and so Cadence could not let it. He then thought of Arsinoe, of her strength, her kindness and her goodness. He wanted the world to carry on for her so that she, like Rebekah, could light the way for others when they fell into darkness. He wanted Arsinoe to be able to find a cure for her daughter's curse.

The scene that surrounded Cadence melted away, and he was back on the dust-suffocated outskirts of the battlefield.

Saklas, still by Cadence's side, was pointing into the distance. "Best make your decision quickly," he said. "The demigod approaches."

A rumbling vibrated through the ground as streaks of white lightning crackled towards them. Cadence didn't need to look closer to know Arlo was thundering in their direction with fury in his eyes.

All Cadence needed was one good cut. A scrape of his

sword would be enough to deliver a deadly amount of the God's Bane. In a desperate panic to strike the god before Arlo arrived, Cadence moved for his sword as quickly as he could. With a tight grip and a metallic scrape, he freed it from its sheath. He turned his body and swung the blade with as much force as he could muster to slice into Saklas' waist.

35
THE TANGLED WEB AND THE MAGNOLIA TREE

Cadence had been fast, but not fast enough. Arlo had moved faster than the time it had taken Cadence to blink. The prince slammed into Saklas with a concussive force that sent Cadence flying backwards. He lost his grip on his sword somewhere between being hit by the shockwave and landing with his back on the ground.

Winded, Cadence struggled to fill his lungs with air as he scrambled to his feet. He wanted to look for the spot where his sword had fallen, but he could not take his eyes off the violent battle between Arlo and Saklas.

The two struggled against each other in hand-to-hand combat while blasts of white and blue lightning flew from their bodies. Arlo dove towards Saklas and gripped the god under his arm and around his ankle. Arlo then hoisted Saklas into the air and flung him to the ground as if the god was no more than a child's straw doll. Saklas lay still, and Cadence broke his attention away from the battle to search for where his sword had fallen.

His eyes darted over the cracked, dusty ground until he

found the blade a few meters away. He darted towards it and plucked it up with shaking hands. When he looked up again, Saklas was writhing on the ground. The god's flesh pulsated and rippled as if a million tiny insects were squirming beneath it. With each new laboured breath Saklas took, his squirming flesh and bulging frame expanded until he was four times larger than he had been when Arlo had thrown him down. Greasy black feathers began to excrete themselves from the god's pale, dead skin until he was covered in a cloak of slippery onyx.

Arlo stood back in horror and confusion at the crunch of bones and squelch of muscles as the god's hands and feet twisted and morphed into gigantic, sharp black talons. The thick mass of pale white hair that adorned the god's head began to fall out in soggy clumps. The grotesque flesh the fallen hair revealed was mottled, pitted, and overrun with throbbing veins and oozing lumps. Teeth began to fall from Saklas' mouth; molars dangled from tendrils of thick saliva before dropping to the dirt.

The bizarre sight made Cadence's stomach lurch, yet he couldn't tear his eyes away. Once all his teeth had fallen out, the god's face began to stretch and remould itself into a sharp, blackened point. A grotesque vulture-like creature with a sharp beak and glowing white orbs for eyes had replaced Saklas' human features. The god, now a monstrous black-feathered beast of prey, rose from the ground and cast a towering shadow over Arlo. Saklas extended and beat his greasy black wings, sending a stinking smog into the air. The wretched stench hooked the back of Cadence's throat and pulled, causing him to gag. Saklas let out a shriek from his spear-sharp beak as he continued to beat his wings and rose into the air. He ascended past the rolling clouds of dust, up higher beyond the clouds and out of sight.

"Arlo!" Cadence screamed, quickly coming to his senses as he began to run towards the prince.

"Don't!" Arlo screamed back at him. "Don't come any closer! Find cover before Saklas comes back down again!"

Cadence ignored the instructions and instead kept running towards Arlo. "You have to use this," Cadence panted as he reached Arlo and offered him the sword. "It's coated with a poison that will kill Saklas."

Arlo took the sword and looked at Cadence, looked up at the sky, and then back again. His muscles bulged as his glowing eyes widened.

"You weren't supposed to be here!" he shouted as lightning sparked over his eyes. "You promised me that you would stay off of the battlefield!"

"If I had told you, you would have stopped me," said Cadence on the verge of tears. "I had to help you. If I didn't then—"

Cadence was cut off by a roar that rocked the air. Instinctually, both he and Arlo looked up at the blurry onyx dot that grew larger as it descended towards them.

"Run!" Arlo shouted.

Cadence didn't need more prompting. He bolted away as fast as he could. When he turned to see if Arlo was by his side, he saw Arlo hadn't moved. The prince was standing at the ready with the poisoned sword raised and his eyes glowing.

Saklas struck the ground with a boom that almost knocked Cadence off his feet. Through clouds of beige dust, Cadence saw the black talons and beak of the titanic monster. The giant, undead vulture swiped and pecked at Arlo as he jumped and dived to avoid being impaled or torn to pieces.

As the dust clouds began to settle, Arlo saw his opportunity. He leapt at Saklas with the sword aimed directly at the god monster's throat. One of Saklas' talons swiped at the sword but missed and struck Arlo's hand instead. Arlo lost his grip and fumbled to catch the sword. One of the god monster's oily black wings extended itself and fell over Arlo, concealing him from Cadence's view. Saklas pecked and scratched and tore at his torso in an attempt to rid himself of Arlo. The bone-white eyes of the monster glowed and crackled with lightning before sending forth several blasts of light aimed at the prince. Flecks of golden armour flew into the air and glittered for a moment in the dust-filtered sunlight before falling to the ground.

Saklas' milky eyes then widened with surprise before turning to confusion and then a cold dread. The beast let out a shriek before throwing Arlo from his chest. Arlo's body hit the ground facing away from Cadence. On the back of Arlo's breastplate Cadence saw crimson seeping through holes and gashes.

Cadence bolted forward but did not get far before Saklas began to beat his wings. The wind thrown out by the god's massive feathers blew sand into Cadence's eyes before picking him up off his feet. The gale then immediately calmed and Cadence fell to his knees. He pawed at the sand caught in his watering eyes, desperate to see, desperate to get to Arlo. Once his vision cleared enough, he saw Arlo had still not moved as Saklas stumbled back and forth.

The god's wings had fallen and were now dragging in the dirt behind him. Feathers fell from him in clumps before melting away into steaming puddles of black pus. As Saklas stumbled around trying to keep his balance, Cadence caught sight of his chest. Embedded just below the god of rot's neck was the glinting flower-adorned hilt of the silver sword. Arlo had plunged the poisoned blade deep.

Saklas began to splutter, cough, and caw as he blundered around trying to stay on his feet. More feathers abandoned his body, exposing enflamed flesh that sagged from the bone. Steam and putrid smoke began to rise from the melting flesh as the god writhed back and forth on his withering talons. The coughs and caws from his shrinking beak began to fade before they were replaced by the screams of something much more human. Unintelligible shrieks and cries of agony rang through the air. When the god finally fell, he was nothing more than a massive heap of melting, bubbling, oozing flesh.

There was a moment of serenity as Cadence watched the last signs of life leave the god's decimated body. The silence was quickly replaced by a wave of cacophony. Thousands of breastplates, shields, and swords clattered to the ground all at the same time. Then came the fall of the leviathans as the great monsters smacked into the dirt, never to rise again. This was followed by the cries and trumpets of victory.

CADENCE TREMBLED as he stood up. Terrified of what he was going to find but desperate to know, his feet carried him forward to the spot where Arlo lay. He fell to his knees at Arlo's side. His eyes were closed and his breathing was shallow, but at least he was still drawing breath. Blood leaked from the gashes in his armour where Saklas' talons had found their mark.

"Arlo," Cadence called to him, gently caressing his bloody cheek.

The prince seemed to come to life at Cadence's touch and the sound of his voice. His ocean blue irises were offset by vicious, tiny bloodshot rivers. His face strained with pain as he tried to get up, but his body refused.

"D–Don't get up," Cadence stuttered, his voice as shaky as his hands. "Here, let me try make you more comfortable."

He removed his oxblood-coloured cape from the clasps on the shoulders of his breastplate. The immaculate fabric was now tattered and stained, but once carefully bundled up it made a decent pillow. Cadence carefully lifted Arlo's head before sliding the bundled cape under it. Cadence shuddered at the touch of Arlo's skin. It was clammy. Arlo's skin was never clammy; it was always warm and as soft as lily petals. His healthy, sun-kissed glow had also started to abandon him, leaving behind a chalk dust colour. The colour of death.

"I'm so sorry," Arlo whispered.

"There is no need to be sorry," Cadence said as he moved a strand of Arlo's hair from his face. Even dirt and dried blood could not tarnish its golden lustre when the clouds cleared for a moment and the sun shone upon it. "Everything went to plan," Cadence continued. "Everything is going to be alright. We can be together now."

He was telling the lie through a failing forced smile as his lips began to quiver and his chest began to ache. Something was very wrong.

Arlo's palms opened at his sides to reveal oozing, black lacerations. Grey tendrils of poison had cast themselves out from the wounds like nets and crawled their way across Arlo's paling flesh.

Cadence gripped his head in terror. "When you lost your grip on the sword ..." he whispered as tears began to stream from his face.

"There was no other way," Arlo winced as blood began to leak from his nose and ears. "I had to stop him."

Cadence couldn't speak. When he tried, a quiet guttural croak was all that would escape his throat. This was all his fault.

"D–Did I do it?" Arlo whispered.

Cadence took a deep breath in an attempt to keep his

composure. "You did," he whispered through quivering lips. "You slayed Saklas. All will be right now."

It wasn't a lie. All would be right, just not for them.

"I want to be closer to you," said Arlo. "I'm cold."

Cadence shuffled closer to Arlo's broken body. The dust was still settling around them. Cadence gently lifted Arlo's head on to his lap. Arlo's eyes were open but unfocused.

"I can see it," Arlo said, his eyes widening.

"What can you see?" Cadence asked, his body shaking with grief and his face wet from tears.

"Our home," said Arlo, his voice growing softer. "The cottage. I see you weaving in the garden. You're waiting for me."

"You should go to me," said Cadence. Each word was like forcing a burning coal from his throat.

"I'd like that," Arlo's voice grew ever weaker. "It's so warm here with you."

The life inside Arlo's eyes dimmed, faded, and with the final rise and fall of his chest, died out. Cadence felt Arlo go limp as his soul left his body.

He let out a cry so loud all the gods turned to look upon him. He could feel them watching from their hiding places in the sky, but he didn't care. His ability to care for anything had left with Arlo's soul. He wept, hunched over Arlo's body. Arlo's corpse. His tears fell onto his dead husband's blood-stained face and ruined armour. Guilt and grief wracked through him in unrelenting waves. He was unable to move, unable to do anything but wail.

It was only when he felt the world grow cold around him that he looked up for the first time. The sun was setting and the stars had begun to make their appearance. His swollen eyes stung at the sight of the burning horizon.

A cool wind picked up around him, and at his back he felt a familiar presence.

"What do you want?" Cadence growled as he bit back long enough at his pain to speak.

"I have come," said Astaroth, putting a hand on Cadence's shoulder, "to comfort you."

Cadence recoiled from the god's touch as hard as he could without moving away from Arlo's body.

"I don't want your comfort!" Cadence snarled at the god while simultaneously trying to block Astaroth's view of Arlo's body, like a starving dog protecting a castoff bone. "I don't want anything from any of you! Get away from us!"

The god sighed, his bright green eyes glowing in the fading light. "I tried to warn you, child. There is no defying your fate. One way or another, what needs to pass will come to pass."

"You didn't come here to comfort me," Cadence's voice cracked under grief as the shaky foundations of his resolve began to take strain. "You came to gloat. Congratulations. I'm so thrilled that the Great Web unfolded in your favour. Now go away!"

"What I am trying to tell you," Astaroth said, his lullaby voice as calm as ever, "is that this was not your fault."

"Of course it's my fault!" Cadence croaked. "I should never have created that poison. I shouldn't have lied to Arlo. If I had told him the truth, if I had done things differently, then he would still be alive!"

"Nothing you could have done would have changed this outcome. Deep down inside, you know that to be true. You have done the world of gods and men a great service, and I would like to reward you."

"This is the second time today a god has offered me a reward. The one thing I want is the one thing I know even the gods are not capable of granting. You cannot bring him back."

"I cannot. Once a soul has passed into the land of the dead, it is beyond any being to return them. But there are a great many other things I am capable of."

An anger flashed through Cadence like a sudden explosion. "You have done enough," he whispered. "I want for nothing. I still have half a vial of God's Bane in my pocket. If you do not go away, I will *make* you go away."

Cadence did not have to look at Astaroth to know the god was frightened. He could feel Astaroth's fear as the air seemed to tighten around him and became a little more difficult to inhale. The god vanished and the air loosened itself around Cadence.

"Cowards, all of you," he sneered into the cool night air.

By now the sun had disappeared, and the full moon cast everything in her silvery blue light. Stars looked down from their pale and distant constellations of fallen heroes and slain monsters.

Cadence looked down at Arlo's face, still beautiful, even in death, but a pale ghost of everything he once was. All the light and life that he held inside his body was gone forever. He looked at Arlo's wide, slightly parted lips and wept. He would never again feel the warmth of them pressed against his own. He would never see Arlo smile again or hear his laugh. He would never be able to listen to the prince play the lyre again. He would never again feel the encapsulating warmth of his embrace. All at once the world felt so empty; Cadence could no longer bear it.

With trembling hands, he reached inside his breast plate and his fingers wrapped around the peony Arlo had given him earlier that day. He pulled the flower out and opened his fingers. Arlo's final gift was withered and crushed but still beautiful. Still precious. He placed the flower on Arlo's chest. He lowered his head towards Arlo's and planted a final soft kiss on the prince's forehead.

"I'm sorry I failed us," he whispered.

His hands fumbled as he unsheathed the hunting dagger from his belt. The poison was potent; he knew he would not feel anything. He would be dead before he hit the ground.

His mind raced with everything that had brought him here. He thought of how much suffering he had failed to prevent, especially for his mother. He thought of Arsinoe and her lost daughter and hoped for their freedom. His final thought was of Arlo.

"I love you," he cried before driving the poisoned dagger deep inside his chest.

Death was like letting go of a rope he'd been holding onto for too long. All that was left was the relief of oblivion. It didn't hurt as much as he thought it would. It didn't hurt at all.

The Origin of the Magnolia Tree

Hermia took pity on the young lovers, their lives cut so incredibly short. On her command, their bodies were lifted into the air by the West Wind and laid down in the realm of eternal spring. Here, Hermia transformed them. Their mortal flesh began to twist and harden until a great magnolia tree stood where they had been laid to rest.

The lush, plump leaves rustled in the cool breeze and glimmered in the sunlight. Between the leaves, large white flowers with petals of cream bloomed into existence and greeted the sun.

Here, the heroes Arlo and Cadence stood moulded together. They were now safe from the little wills of men and gods alike. Safe from the shackles of destiny, fate, and prophecy. Finally at peace. Locked in an embrace for all eternity.

EPILOGUE

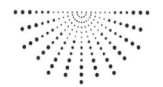

She waited until she was alone. She waited until the celebrations of victory were done and the crowd's cheering had completely faded away.

The war had been won and the world had been saved, but the cost for it felt too high. A price so great was paid, and yet an order was given to make sure history ignored it. No songs of Arlo and Cadence would be sung. No statues would be erected. No light would dare outshine Abydos and his vanity.

She let him have his glory, for it was the last thing she would ever allow him to have. She would correct history as easily as he could rewrite it. She would erase him.

The letter had been left for her to find on her desk inside her conservatory.

Dearest Arsinoe,

If you are reading this letter, the war has been won but Arlo and I have been lost.

I could not leave for the realm of Obsidian without letting you know—what happened to Nimue was not your fault. I had a vision of the past. In it, your daughter was not cursed by your negligence but by the hand of your husband. The Emperor had Father Gemini steal a vial of the experimental ichor and roll it over to Nimue while your back was turned.

I wanted to tell you sooner, but I needed time to look more clearly into the past. I wanted to provide you with as much detail as possible. I wanted you to know exactly who was responsible for your suffering. One of the men is already dead, but the other is still very much alive ... for now.

It is my hope this information brings you comfort and frees you from the bonds of guilt. Be his prisoner no longer.

Thank you for all you have been to me and all you are going to be for Nimue and for the Empire.

Find your daughter and cure her. Fix everything the Emperor has broken so badly. I know you will not let mine and Arlo's sacrifice be in vain.

All my love,
Cadence.

SHE FOUND Abydos in his reception chamber poring over plans he would never get to see to fruition. She'd not expected him to mourn the death of his son. But she was somehow still surprised when not even a single tear was shed over the loss of Arlo. Then again, this was the same man who had poisoned, cursed, and banished his own daughter.

Arsinoe missed Arlo. She missed him with such a heavy heart that if she jumped into the ocean she would sink right to the bottom. She missed him so much she would scream into her tear-soaked pillow until her throat was raw. She mourned Cadence too and the way he and Arlo were together. Knowing them had made her world a better and brighter place. Without them, she'd been cast into a bitter darkness.

So much love and potential and beauty and warmth wasted because Abydos would not know the limits of his power and greed.

Perhaps she had been driven mad by grief and anger. Or perhaps she was finally ready to accept the man she'd loved so dearly, so long ago, was lost forever, and it was time to finally meet her own destiny.

The handle of the dagger was ice against her palm, but she gripped it so tightly it began to burn.

The vial of God's Bane had vanished with Cadence's body, but Arsinoe had no need for it. Not for this. Not a trace of poison of any kind would be found because none would be used. She wanted to kill him in a way that could not be traced back to her but also in a way he would understand. Violent and brutal. There had to be blood.

She tapped Abydos lightly on the shoulder. She wanted to see his face as she drove the dagger, with all the malice she had towards him, deep into his chest. She stabbed him where his heart should have been, but knowing him so well, she worried there was no target for the blade to meet.

She pulled the dagger out of him with a wet pop and watched the crimson blood saturate his golden robes first in a trickle and then in a wave. He fell to his knees and she watched his face morph from confusion to anger and back again. Arsinoe raised the blade once more before sending it down into the Emperor's flesh a second time, then a third, and then a fourth.

She stood, out of breath, and watched until he no longer had the energy to make expressions, and the light in his eyes dimmed and then died. She threw the dagger on top of him and screamed for the guards.

She told them how an assassin sent by one of his political enemies had murdered the Emperor in cold blood. She had arrived just in time to watch a shadow escape through the window. The assassin could very possibly have been sent by King Lemus of Amun-Ra, angry over the betrothal of his daughter to Arlo being withdrawn.

No one would be brave enough not to believe her. She was Her Serene Royal Majesty, Arsinoe Titan, Viper of the Empire, Sorceress of Aroastria, and Empress of all Luciferian.

ACKNOWLEDGMENTS

To my mothers, **Laetitia** and **Annalie**,

Motherhood is a strong theme throughout this book.

Firstly, there is Rebekah whose love for Cadence is unshakable even in the face of fear and adversity. Even after losing all his memories, Cadence's connection to her is never lost. It is one of my deepest regrets that I did not give her and Cadence an opportunity to say goodbye to each other (the story just didn't allow for it), but I like to believe that their love and connection transcend time, distance, and even death.

Then there is Nubia, who is hands-down a terrible mother. The creation of her character was fuelled by endless examples and tragic stories of narcissistic parents and the unfortunate children that suffer under their abuse.

Lastly there is Arsinoe, who was my favourite character to write. For her, motherhood is a complicated thing. She feels she failed her own child but is the best possible stepmother to Arlo and also becomes a stand-in mother to Cadence/Proteus. She is not without her flaws (no mother is because, SHOCKER, mothers are also human beings), but she loves, protects, and guides her children the best way she knows how.

I could not do all of this writing about motherhood and not think of my own mothers. That is why this book is dedicated to the two of you. You have both poured so much of your time, energy, love, wisdom, patience, and habits (good and bad) into me. I would not be the person I am today if it were not for the two of you. Thank you for everything. I love you both so much.

To **Isabelle**,

I cannot thank you enough. Your insights and opinions have been more than valuable—they were priceless! Thank you for correcting my many, many grammatical errors and for all the hard work you brought to the table to make this book the best possible version of itself it could be. Thank you for your stellar work ethic, attention to detail, passion, and how invested you were in Cadence and Arlo's story.

To **Ryan**,

Thank you for reading this book when it was arguably at it's very worst. I don't know what I would do if I didn't have you. It's not easy to share a very early draft of my work, but you make it much less difficult. Thank you for making me feel safe and for all your input, opinions, and hilarious notes. Waka-Chaka.

To **Dad**,

Thank you for being NOTHING like the fathers that I wrote about in this book! Fatherhood was also a strong theme in A Prophecy of Flowers and Lightning. Canaan, Abydos, and Astaroth are all terrible fathers. That said, I wouldn't know how to write bad fathers if I didn't know what an amazing father looked like, and that is all on you. I love you, Dad.

To **Berno**,

When I told you I wanted to write another book, you looked at me like I was a crazy person. That is mainly because I am crazy, and you know I am not the easiest person to be around when I write. Thank you for all your unwavering support and love through all the ups and downs over the two years it took to get this book out. Thank you for all the fires you put out so that I could have time to write. I could not ask for a better partner.

To **Lauren**,

Thank you for letting me read you the first draft of a very badly written sex scene and for helping me work out the dynamics and words (at 1 o'clock in the morning) so that it would be a less badly written sex scene. I'm sorry to say the word "nipples" still made it into the final draft of this book, but a lot of the other words that gave you "the no feeling" didn't make it in. Thank you for being my friend, for supporting my writing, and for always listening to me when I need you.

To **Catherine**,

You have been part of my journey in publishing/self-publishing since my very first book. I don't know if you remember, but you have actually been reading and helping me with my work since we were in high school! Your guidance and honesty over the past few years helped me build so much confidence in myself, and I am so grateful for you. Thank you for always being a voice of reason when I need it but more importantly a supportive and irreplaceable friend.

ABOUT THE AUTHOR

Michael Ferguson was born and raised in Benoni.

He spends most of his free time in his purple bathrobe writing, eating chocolate, and watching dated TV shows. When he is not doing those things, he is making a fool of himself on several different social media platforms, including but not limited to Instagram, TikTok, and YouTube.

He is a chatterbox and attention whore of the highest order. Go say hello to him on one of the aforementioned social media platforms; he will like that.

He now lives in Pretoria.